Between Flames and Deceit

Book One of the Dragon's Heart Duology

M. A. Frick

Also by M.A. Frick

The Fate Unraveled Trilogy:
Forcing Fate
Following Fate
Fulfilling Fate
***

The Dragon's Heart:
Between Flames and Deceit
***

Standalones:
The Petulant Princess

For all the girls who refuse to settle.

Prologue

KALLIAS

M olten wax surged around my signet ring, binding Radaan's fate. My blood pulsed, humming through my veins as I lifted the ring, revealing the precise, crisp edges of my seal.

It was done.

Months of preparation, tedious negotiation, and decades of war—all culminated in this moment.

Beside my signature, scrawled across the scroll in jagged crimson strokes, a name forged in blood.

Nereus, Dragon King of Draconia, Lord of the Wild Shores.

Above it, sketched with the same harsh strokes, *Nienna, Dragon's Heart.*

A tremor passed through me as I scanned the oath one final time. This was the last chance to cast it into the flames and start anew. Yet as I read, there wasn't a single thing to change. Nienna, daughter of the dragon king, would be given to my son in exchange for a grain tithe and the exemption of taxes on Radaan's goods.

In return, Nienna would bring the dragons' power to Radaan—with the promise that if war called, they would ride to her aid.

I sighed, leaning back in my chair, gaze drifting to the treaty of Vellos beside the contract. After seventeen years of conflict—over three of failed negotiations, countless deaths and sacrifices—at last, we reached terms with the Velli.

And it all hinged on this contract with Draconia.

The Velli were unyielding, starving, pushed beyond their limits. No matter how hard I tried to project strength—pretending we could endure the war, that our soldiers and supplies were infinite—I knew the truth.

My people were battered, spread too thin. Women tended the fields well enough, but I lacked the men to pull the harvest. Crops rotted in the autumn rains, sowing next spring's wild growth.

Children went hungry, fatherless. Widows struggled to survive. A generation passed, knowing nothing but war.

I promised the next would know nothing but peace.

Radaan needed dragons—power to deter Vellos from invasion. Without them, another attack was inevitable.

Triumph stirred within as I studied the scrolls side by side. It had taken me a lifetime. Finally, *finally,* I would know peace.

NIENNA

Wind whipped through my hair as a black-tipped tail snaked around my knees with a quiet hiss.

"I only want to see!" I protested, bracing against the purple-hued appendage.

As I leaned over the Nest's edge, the updraft slammed into me, stealing my breath. It thrummed with power, urging me to leap, to feel wind tear at my skin, to soar like my dragons.

Behind me, the dragon queen huffed, her tail coiling tighter around me like an unyielding vise. I was her wingless hatchling, the Dragon's Heart.

Far below, the cities appeared as fragile toys, dwarfed by the height of the Spire. The Nest sat at the highest peak of Draconia's dark palace, where bones littered the floor and the biting wind stung my skin. Yet in that stark, chilling expanse, a strange calm settled over me, as though the winds themselves cradled me. There was no place in the world I felt safer.

Argos swept through the sky, his massive shadow blotting out daylight, a blur of green and blue followed close in his wake. Tsunami, irritable, snapped at his tail. My father, a mere speck on Argos' back, seemed almost swallowed by the distance. Behind them, ridden by my brother, Gyrak—small and black as night—spun through the air, spewing a jet of flame at the wild blue.

Tsunami ducked, dodging the blast before pivoting toward the Nest, earning a grumble of displeasure from the dragon queen at my back.

"They're just playing," I mused, scanning the sky.

Riderless and restless, Tsunami refused to leave our land. Instead of venturing to the Wild Shores as other wildlings did, she prowled our skies, a constant thorn in our side. Even the Dragon Riders struggled to keep her in check.

To contain a ship-sized meddling beast was a full-time job.

A flash of white streaked across my vision. I clenched the muscled scales beneath my fingertips, my heart lurching into my throat. That was not a rock gull's mottled hue, but the unmistakable gleam of a dove—a symbol of peace.

Although the sight of it eluded me at this distance, I knew a scroll was attached to its foot. It flew with purpose, soaring toward home, to the loft where the message would be read.

That parchment carried my future—a promise that I'd sail to another nation and marry a stranger to save my people. Signed in blood, a Draconis oath could only be purged by dragonfire.

Tsunami lurched, caught the updraft, and veered toward the dove.

"No!" I screamed, but the queen was already moving, already scrambling to the edge. Her massive form blocked my view as she towered over me, a deafening roar ripping from her throat.

Jaws snapped just shy of the poor bird, and it plummeted.

Gyrak shot between Tsunami and the dove, his wings a blur. Argos flew toward the Spire, and his enormous paw snatched the falling creature out of the air.

The great black dragon hovered a breath, and I locked eyes with my father across the expanse. Sorrow darkened his gaze, lips twisting into a pained smile before his beast descended, spiraling toward the earth. They pulled up at the last moment and veered for the landing, a jagged outcrop that led to the throne room.

My father had not surrendered me willingly. I saw it in the tightness of his jaw, the way his hands shook before he shoved it behind a mask of stoicism. To ask me to marry a prince in a foreign kingdom wasn't a decision he made lightly. It was a sacrifice that weighed heavy on him—on both of us. Our people were starving, their bellies hollow, their strength faltering.

Our island could only sustain so much. Any crops we managed to grow withered beneath the relentless seasonal whirlstorms. The wind tore through the fields, as though the earth itself was protesting, scattering the seeds before they could take root. And with each passing season, it became harder to coax life from the soil.

My people needed food to survive, to push into the Wild Shores and expand. They depended on me to forge alliances and secure their future.

No, it wasn't an easy thing for the Dragon King to give me away, but it was his duty to use me.

Just as it was my duty to marry the prince of Radaan.

Chapter One

Nienna

I burned with the need to kiss my betrothed.

Quite literally.

Heat bloomed within, forming beads of sweat at my temples. Scythe leaned over, her fingertips brushing my skin as she dabbed at the perspiration along my brow. A sharp breath caught in my throat, my body fighting to wrangle the internal raging blaze. It was as if Argos, my father's dragon, bathed me in his flames.

"Not much longer now," Edith murmured, the lady's maid my mother insisted I bring, her voice meant to soothe.

I pressed a hand to my ribs, struggling to swallow the dryness that clung to my throat. The weight of it all sank deep within me. I'd never been a decent Vessel. In years past, my father humored my attempts to carry magic, to bear it like our people who used the magic from the Dragon Riders. But I always failed. The dragon's power slipped through my fingers, scattering like ashes on the breeze.

My lack of control marked me as weak, a flaw we worked hard to conceal.

Gyrak crooned from above, his wings cutting through the sky. He sensed my discomfort and circled, his call soft yet insistent, as though trying to ease my pain. I forced a smile, ignoring the ache that gnawed at me, and turned my gaze out the window. My brother Ronan and his dragon Gyrak accompanied us. Their presence served as more than a royal escort, but as a deterrent against the Velli.

I studied the vibrant city as we neared. Rolling plains stretched wide, quilted with golden and emerald fields, the sunlight glinting off ripe wheat as waves rippled through the crops. Sturdy, quaint houses lined the cobblestone road, bluebirds flitting about around them. Laughter filled the air as commoners grinned, their joy as bright as the day itself. They had reason for joy—the treaty with Vellos had been sealed just a fortnight ago. The war was over, and my father's final demand regarding my marriage was met. He was no different from any other king, willing to use his daughter to secure alliances. But he drew a line when it came to my safety.

My journey began the day the dove arrived. When I spotted the bird clutching the news, a heady mix of dread and relief warred within. The uncertainty of my future faded—the guessing game of who I'd marry put to an end. However, the knot in my stomach remained, knowing I would wed a stranger.

Ronan knew Prince Tallon. He called him immature—hardly the verdict I expected from my younger brother.

But I could do worse.

The flames inside surged, desperate to break free. A gasp slipped from my lips, and I ducked my head, eyes squeezed shut against the pain. The magic clawed at me, a torrent of fire waiting to burst. I clenched my fists, focused on maintaining an iron hold.

Scythe pressed a cool cloth to my brow, her touch a fleeting relief. My gown strangled me, the fabric a silken cage. The air thickened, each breath harder than the last. I couldn't breathe—couldn't escape the stifling pressure.

Each bump and jolt brought on waves of agony. A whimper tore out as the carriage lurched over the bridge, and I clutched the padded seat to keep from combusting.

"Almost there—loosen her hair," Edith said, voice sharp. Scythe moved with haste as the older maid focused on lacing up my boots with practiced hands.

I envied Radaanian style of dress. Their garments were modest, yet far freer than ours. As a Draconis, the rules were strict—trousers for men, breeches for women. To be caught without them was to be shunned. And anyone daring to wear sandals would put a stain on their family name.

After all, every Draconis aspired to be a Dragon Rider, and riders wore sturdy coverings over their legs *and* boots—regardless if magic was melting their insides.

The fine leather squeezed my calves as Edith drew the laces tight. Scythe leaned over, yanking hairpins from my hair, letting golden waves cascade to my hips. The pressure built, suffocating and unbearable—yet I was born for this.

I forced my irritation down, drawing in a steadying breath as the carriage slowed to a halt. My fingers drummed against the seat, waiting for Ronan or one of the guards to open the door. I ached for the cool breeze, craved fresh air. Sweat slicked my palms, while heat flushed my cheeks.

When the door finally opened, a draft swept past me. It carried the faint scent of jasmine and earth, lifting tendrils of my hair and cooling my feverish skin. I forced my legs to move with purpose. No rushing, no stumbling. I would not make a fool of myself in front of my betrothed. I was a princess, and I would carry myself as one.

A Radaanian soldier bedecked in hues of gold and green lowered the carriage steps, the metal groaning with age. He extended a gloved hand, the scent of flowers faint in the air. I placed my clammy palm in his, the cool material a brief reprieve. With care, I lifted the hem of my dress and stepped out.

Gyrak clicked, his concern evident as my boots hit the uneven cobblestones with a solid thud. I smiled at the massive beast as his wings unfurled, casting a shadow across the courtyard. With soft eyes filled with quiet affection, he was more puppy than apex predator—a perfect match to his rider.

Ronan dismounted in one fluid motion, yanking his flight goggles down to his neck. The scent of wind and leather clung to him as he scanned the courtyard, his gaze sharp and calculating before he flashed me a roguish smile. He had faith in me.

With shoulders squared, I drew in another breath, bracing myself, then faced the High Court of Radaan.

The agonizing burn within blazed outward as I stood before the throng of nobles and soldiers. Their bright, extravagant garb clashed in a garish assault on my senses. As I lifted my chin, I recalled Draconia's meager count of noblemen and knew from the palace's sheer sprawl before me that this crowd was only a fraction of what they could muster.

The men's hair, shorn close, contrasted with the women's, left to flow down their backs like rivers. Tanned skin spoke of a heritage rooted in hard fieldwork. The women's gowns swept the ground, while the men's sleeves billowed in absurdly wide folds, an obscene waste of cloth—frivolous in a way that would have drawn scorn back in Draconia.

But this was to be my country now.

My gaze danced over the crowd as women whispered behind painted fans, their eyes drifting over my frame. Men openly appraised me as if I were some trophy waiting to be claimed. I shifted my focus to the palace entrance, expecting to find Tallon walking down to meet me.

Instead, a man stood tall above the crowd, his hard gaze fixed and unwavering. An aura of command clung to him, one that demanded attention. With shoulders squared and hands clasped firmly behind him, he radiated unprecedented pride. Guards perched like sentinels at his side, and despite having no crown on his brow, I needed no introduction. I knew exactly who he was.

King Kallias.

In Radaan, royalty bore a mantle in place of a crown—a reminder of their duty to their kingdom. The gilded adornment weighed heavy on his shoulders, yet he towered as if burdened by nothing more than a featherweight. It draped over layers of green and gold, the colors of his realm.

Pain clawed its way through my chest, spilling down my arms in waves as if the fire within sought freedom. My body jerked, betraying me with a flinch I struggled to restrain.

Weakness had no place here.

"Where is Tallon?" Ronan hissed, offering his arm to me.

My hand quivered as I rested it on the crook of his elbow, allowing him to lead me through the crowd. Blood roared in my veins, each pulse demanding me to release the chaos clawing within. I forced down a gulp, feeling small. Radaan had no Vessels, held no magic—they wouldn't understand my struggles. Fainting here would mark me as weak, unworthy of marriage to the prince.

"Please tell me he's here," I murmured under my breath. My sweeping gaze found no other with a mantle or yoke among the masses. If I remembered correctly, Prince Tallon would be wearing a silver yoke, signifying his station.

Bystanders stared, their scrutiny roving over my clothes, scrutinizing every detail of my appearance.

"He's not—the flaming son of a–"

"Ronan, I can't hold it." My jaw clenched as I wrestled to contain the blaze searing my core. If I didn't release it soon, it would devour me.

Gyrak let out a low snarl and took a ground-shaking step toward us. My brother shook his head at his dragon and pressed his lips together, guiding me up the stone steps. I gathered my dress, the silk clinging and useless against my fevered skin, and heard the heavy thud of Gyrak's retreat in response to Ronan's silent rebuke.

"He can't be far." His voice held a note of forced calm—an attempt to bolster me.

Surely there were only a handful of steps, yet each stare pressed in on me, and the raging magic within made each one feel like scaling a tower. Heat flared, scorching me beneath the surface, and my skin flushed crimson.

"Princess Nienna of Draconia." The voice of authority, the voice of a *king*, called out in greeting. His words sliced through the murmurs, silencing them with a tone that commanded regard.

I glanced up, meeting the cool, assessing gaze of King Kallias. Strands of silver threaded through his dark hair, swept back from his face, framing his stark features. His skin, bronzed from years under an open sky, contrasted with the slight shadow along his jaw, lending him a roguish air that hinted at something sharp, almost dangerous, beneath his nobility.

I expected the king to be clean-shaven, draped in one of those ridiculous puffed-sleeve shirts.

Instead, he met my gaze with a faint nod, his voice smooth as he spoke my title. "The Dragon's Heart," he intoned, dipping his head in a show of respect. "Welcome to Radaan."

Magic crackled, flaring sharp and raw. My eyes clamped shut, bracing against the surge of pain.

My brother stepped forward, willing to speak for me. "King Kallias Sunspear of Radaan, Lord of the Plentiful Plains, Warrior of Sun and Flame, I present my sister, Nienna Draconis—the Heart of all Dragonkind."

At the top of the dais, my nails dug into Ronan's arm.

"Where is Prince Tallon, her betrothed?" My brother's question cut through the silence, an intense demand that made me wince.

"The prince is... away. Regrettably."

My gaze shot to the king, fury igniting alongside the inferno within. His steady, unblinking eyes held mine, an eerie calm that challenged my rage.

"I will see to the princess' welcome," he continued. His tone was secure and unshaken, as if nothing could unsettle him.

It became glaringly obvious that this man did not react. Every movement deliberate, every word measured. Broad shoulders held the yoke with effortless grace. He'd worn it so long, the weight no longer seemed to register. His posture remained rigid, commanding, and the intensity of his gaze sent a chill down my spine.

"There are traditions," Ronan bit out.

A muscle twitched in Kallias' jaw, the only sign of his irritation. I wanted to silence my brother—if I stepped into the palace without releasing the magic, I'd ignite the stone beneath our feet.

There were some things more mortifying than saying a few phrases out of turn.

"Yes, and they will be addressed," the king said.

"She must surrender her pact."

"Princess Nienna may deliver her seal when Tallon returns."

"It cannot wait," I gasped, each word scraping from my throat, barely above a whisper. I held the king's stare, the world falling away until only the two of us remained. His presence was distant, implacable, while the fire inside me raged. He, as a Radaanian, was devoid of magical abilities. And much like his people, he couldn't fathom what was happening, what I endured. Even as poor a Vessel as I was, I still had more ability than his entire court.

He had a choice—let me release the magic, or turn us away. Ronan would gladly allow me to unleash it in any way that suited me. Perhaps I'd set fire to the nobles while we skipped off into the sunset. He never wanted this marriage for me to begin with. The thought of his sister being traded like property gnawed at him, regardless that I embraced my fate.

Kallias' shoulders rose with a deep breath as he stepped forward. I recoiled, horrified by his curt approach.

"Deliver your seal," he said.

Not a request, nor a demand. His voice held only the weight of inevitability as he pressed into my space. I craned my head back, and his harsh blue eyes flared with irritation at my sharp intake of breath.

"It's the Dragon's Kiss," I whispered, words trembling with a silent plea—make someone else take it.

It was one thing for my betrothed to claim the seal. We would marry—become equals. If I faltered, Tallon would accept it.

But to bestow my Dragon's Kiss to King Kallias? Unthinkable.

If something went wrong, he would be far less receptive. He'd never forgive me. He wasn't my equal, but the father of my betrothed—the one who bartered for my hand.

"Yes. And your presence, your duty, is to seal this kingdom with Draconia. I sired the blood that flows through Prince Tallon's veins. To bequeath your pact on me is the same as delivering it to my son."

Except it wasn't.

His gaze flicked over my face, then softened, as if he could read my hesitation. His tone lowered, a quiet command. "Let's not keep the masses in suspense."

Ronan growled, squeezing my hand once before stepping back. He threw out his arms, warning the guards to maintain their distance.

This couldn't be happening. I was supposed to kiss Prince Tallon. My lips had touched no one but family. I would have kissed any noble or servant present—anyone—not the king of Radaan.

But here he stood, waiting, his face open, resigned to whatever came next. He wouldn't force me. I caught something in the depths of his eyes—uncertainty? Was he wondering if I'd walk away? Abandon the blood oath?

No. Draconia was starving. We needed this.

My hand trembled as I reached out to cup his face. Every instinct screamed that this was wrong—this wasn't how it should be. I wasn't supposed to kiss him.

I *couldn't.*

His stubble scraped against my damp palms. A rush of shame crawled up my neck—he'd sense how nervous I was.

My gaze dropped to the king's lips, pressed into a tight line, and a knot of panic twisted my stomach. My heart slammed against my ribs, each beat a thud of protest.

I drew a shaky breath, and rose onto my toes, fingers trembling as they cradled his head. Gently, I tugged him lower, the heat of my touch seeping into him. My body trembled as I leaned in, eyes closing, then pressed my lips to his forehead, the embrace soft and hesitant, as if the very act might tear me apart.

Gyrak's magic exploded from me in a firestorm. Flares shot into the sky, spiraled our bodies, a twisting pillar of fire. The heat seared, blistering as real crackling flames flickered into the shapes of dragons, their ember wings brushing against my flesh.

The Dragon's Kiss was the seal of Draconia—binding—a mark of engagement, a pledge of peace. It was the promise of shared days, a lifetime entwined with another.

It was my first kiss.

And I had given it to the wrong man.

Chapter Two

NIENNA

"That flaming prick!" Ronan seethed. "When he gets here, I'm going to skewer him!"

Gyrak rumbled in agreement, a low vibration that seemed to resonate through the courtyard. His ember-bright eyes drifted shut as my fingers stroked his scaled muzzle. I'd miss the dragon—far more than my brother—though I'd never tell him as much.

"He's expected tonight, then?" I asked, pressing my temple to the dragon's heated jaw. For a beast larger than any house, he handled me with care, each touch soft as a wingtip. The dragons all treated me as if I were one of their own—a delicate hatchling, fragile yet beloved.

"Kallias only said 'soon.' Blast it! What does 'soon' mean? I know Tallon detests court, but sea beneath, you'd think he'd possess enough sense to receive his betrothed!"

He resumed his pacing, boots scuffing the courtyard's sun-warmed stone. This was the one place big enough for Gyrak, allowing me to bask in his comforting presence. The dragon's slow breath, steady as a heartbeat, grounded me in a way no words could.

"If this marriage matters so much to Kallias, he should keep a tighter rein on his son!"

"The prince is nineteen." I laughed, casting a bewildered look over my shoulder. "If Father demanded something you didn't want, would you follow his orders?"

"I'm a Dragon Rider—it's different."

The title gave my brother too much freedom. Not only would he inherit Draconia's crown, but his bond with a dragon granted him a commanding presence few dared to question.

"He's still a prince." I stepped away from Gyrak, who chuffed at the break in contact, lifting his head. "Perhaps he doesn't wish to be tied down."

My brother shoved his blond hair off his eyes, the sharp blue orbs sparking with irritation. "See? You can't compare me," he snapped. "If it were for Draconia, I would do anything!"

I scoffed, crossing my arms. "Eighteen and willing to marry yourself off?"

Ronan's temper flared, then fizzled, as always. In a debate with me, he never stood a chance. Not because of my age—two years gave me a little more wisdom—but because he wielded his dragon's strength as much as his own. With Gyrak at his side, he never had to rely on words when he could simply call on fire and fury to incinerate anyone in his way.

"For king and kingdom!" He laughed, raising a hand in a mock salute, his grin as fierce as ever.

No, I couldn't imagine my bold, headstrong brother tying himself down anytime soon.

I saw the same flash of surprise in the eyes of every ambassador who came to Draconia's shores. Ronan and I were our parents' only children, yet to most, my worth lay solely in my womb. Which kingdom would my father trade me to? Whose heir would I be expected to bring into the world? Even at the tender age of twenty, nobles made it clear they saw my childbearing years slipping away.

"You'll do well here, sister."

Ronan's sigh carried a hint of pride as he stepped forward and clapped a hand on my shoulder. I laughed, shrugging him off as my brave smile faltered, if only for a moment. These times with him would be confined to his visits from our distant island. I'd miss him. The thought left a dull ache.

"I intend to." I flashed him my brightest grin. "This is home now."

After bidding Gyrak farewell, we entered the palace, flanked by guards and led by a noblewoman named Fyrn'sol. She had been assigned as my guide and guardian, though something in her watchful hovering chafed at my spirit. King Kallias himself had escorted me into the foyer, then left me in her care, mentioning he would see me at the evening meal.

Despite all this talk of alliance and duty, a lingering sensation gnawed at me—that here in Radaan, I was little more than a piece on their board. A pawn in their game. For all the titles and courtesy, I felt less like a princess and more like a tool—to be taken out, displayed, or set aside when convenient.

"Fyrn'sol, might I ask when Prince Tallon is expected to return?" I inquired, following her through corridors flooded with light. The high ceilings seemed to banish all shadows, while rich paintings lined the walls, echoing the vibrant colors woven into the thick carpet beneath our feet. Vines crept into every corner and cranny, lending life to the grandeur.

"The prince is... indisposed." She brushed a strand of hair from her face and offered an apologetic smile, almost as if his absence troubled her, too. "But he's expected soon."

That single word was all they'd told me. Where was he? Indisposed. When would he return? Soon. How could a prince just... vanish? Couldn't the king summon him? If Ronan or I ever wandered off against Father's orders, we'd be hauled back in Argos' claws.

Kallias, with his rigid disposition, didn't seem like a man to tolerate disobedience, yet he allowed his son to flout tradition. All I knew was courtly customs, the expectations as familiar to me as the pulse in my veins. I enjoyed a measure of freedom, but I'd always known my fate—to be promised to a prince, to become queen, and to master the art of royal conduct.

But if Tallon avoided court and palace life, what would that mean for me? Would he leave me behind, appearing only to sire an heir? Or would he drag me along, expecting me to play the part of an ordinary noblewoman at his side?

"Are you well, Your Highness?"

Fyrn'sol's concerned tone snapped me from my thoughts, and I offered her a faint smile, shoving my worries aside to untangle later.

"It's been a long journey," I said, hoping it would excuse my distant mood.

"I can imagine! They say the dragon pulled the ship to speed you along—is that true?"

"Yes." I laughed, a sound softer than I intended. "Prince Ronan's dragon wore the harness."

"To think how swiftly our ships might sail if we had such beasts!"

My smile stayed in place, though my heart clenched. Gyrak had worn that harness only because of my royal blood. The idea of dragons pulling common merchant vessels struck as near sacrilege.

"Those *beasts* belong to the Wild Shores and Draconia," Ronan snapped, words clipped and curt.

I frowned at his sharp tone. He held no regard for his tongue.

"Oh, yes–of course." Fyrn'sol pressed her lips together, as if there was more she wanted to say, but my brother had crushed her confidence.

The walk to my rooms stretched into uncomfortable silence. I tracked the halls we passed and the sun's shifting angle through the windows. The faster I could navigate this palace on my own, the better. The sun sank toward the horizon, casting everything in a fierce, golden glow. Radaan was a warm land—beautiful, vibrant, and full of life.

Draconia, too, was warm—but storm-tossed. My island home endured the great whirlstorms for two seasons each year. Those same tempests brought the first dragons to our shores, yet it was these relentless tempests that forced us to seek Radaan's help.

The breeze that drifted through the windows was nothing like the violent gales that tore across our island. Those winds ravaged crops and slowed the construction of our stone houses to a crawl. With this new alliance, however, we would finally gain the food we so desperately needed to sustain our growing population, along with the materials to build homes for our people aiding our expansion.

Fyrn'sol halted and announced, "Princess Nienna of Draconia."

Before us stood an ornate door, towering and intricately carved. Fresh designs adorned the wood, and a smile tugged at my lips as I fought the impulse to reach out and trace the dragons depicted in mid-flight.

A wave of sadness washed over me. I would likely never set foot on Draconia's shores again. The only dragons I would see now would be the ones that belong to riders—or Gyrak on my brother's rare visits.

"You are the Dragon's Heart." Ronan's voice softened—he always seemed to know my thoughts. "You are part of them, and they are part of you." He gave my shoulder a reassuring pat before stepping back.

Guards stood at attention along the corridor, two at each door—including mine. Radaan still clung to the echoes of war, its people and king adjusting to the fragile peace. The soldiers wore full plate armor, painted in green and gold, their visors flipped up to reveal youthful faces. They bowed deeply, eyes respectful.

I couldn't help but wonder how many of them had missed the carefree youth Ronan had enjoyed, instead thrust into the brutal war with Vellos. The guard to my right could not have been older than my brother.

The guard to my left stepped forward, his broad shoulders bracing against the massive door, shoving it open.

Any lingering unease about my rooms vanished in an instant.

Golden sunlight bathed me in its rays, casting the space in a blinding glow. My heart unfurled like a leaf basking in the summer heat, eager to absorb the warmth.

"Scythe, the curtains."

"No." I dismissed Edith with a wave, stepping further inside, my gaze fixed on the golden light. A window, unclouded by imperfection, faced the setting sun. Its radiance was fierce and powerful, yet held a strange comfort.

Like my dragons.

"Is there anything you need, Your Highness?" Fyrn'sol's voice reached me from a distance, as though she were far off, a dragon's flight away.

"No, that will be all. Thank you." I closed my eyes, letting the warmth of the sun's rays wash over me.

"I'll fetch you for the evening meal, sister," Ronan called from the doorway, then the latch clicked shut.

"'Tis a blinding light, Your Highness." Edith's tone, though firm, held a hint of complaint—the closest she'd come to one.

"Yes, but it is beautiful." I sighed, opening my eyes against the onslaught. "Are there shades to dull it?"

Scythe pulled a thin fabric across the window's length. It softened the light, turning it from blinding to welcoming.

These rich accommodations were a temporary place during my engagement to the prince. Once the ceremony was over, we would share a wing together.

A union I already botched.

I forced the memory of kissing King Kallias from my mind. My hands twitched, recalling the roughness of his stubble beneath my palms, the warmth of his skin against my lips. The fire's heat pressing in on us, the scent of warm spices lingering in his hair.

He was the father of my betrothed.

And I kissed him.

The tips of my ears burned. I would not–

"A bath is ready for you, Your Highness."

I could always rely on Edith to pull me from my daydreams.

Heavy blue fabric brushed against my ankles as I made my way to the dining hall. I fought the urge to fidget, my hands betraying my unease. Guards flanked me, trailing behind Ronan as he navigated the corridors ahead.

These endless halls would take time to master. The Spire in Draconia, with its towering height, had been my childhood playground. I climbed its vertical expanse when I wasn't in the Nest. Radaan's palace, by contrast, sprawled outward in winding corridors, each branching in different directions, unlike the steep, unyielding stairwells of home.

"They told me Kallias sent a captain after him," Ronan said.

"How can he loathe me without even meeting me?" I muttered, the words slipping past my lips before I could stop them. The realization that my betrothed fled the palace at the news of my arrival was a cruel blow, enough to shatter some confidence.

"'Tallon doesn't like the high court."

"I *am* the high court, Ronan." I spoke through clenched teeth, forcing a smile as we passed a nobleman who bowed in respect, his gaze flicking to mine with a touch of unease.

"Aye, but he hasn't met you yet."

I shot him a glare, annoyed by his use of the common tongue. Mother would've slapped him for that 'aye.'

He chuckled, knowing full well what caused my ire. "You'll change his mind, I'd wager."

I only hoped so.

To have a betrothed who ran from me, as if I were some kind of monster...

"Chin up." My brother's tone softened, kindness beneath his jest.

I drew in a deep breath, straightening my back as though I could shake off the weight of my frustration. My shoulders were tight, and the impulse to snap at him nearly overwhelmed me, but I held it in check, lifting my chin instead.

Ronan's laughter bubbled up again, the sound light but somehow knowing. He flashed a grin at me with a mischievous wink.

The corridor opened into the dining hall, and my feet moved on instinct, driven by discipline rather than desire. War or not, Kallias had earned the title 'King of the Plentiful Plains' for good reason.

The rich scents of roasted meats, spices, and fresh-baked bread flooded my senses, more overwhelming than welcoming. Darkness may have fallen outside, but inside, the hall gleamed with lanterns and candles, their flickering light casting long shadows across the crowded room. The tables were buried under heaps of food, enough to feed an army. My people were starving, yet here, excess spilled over every surface.

Where, in such abundance, could one find a place to sit?

"Her Highness, Princess Nienna of Draconia. And Heir Apparent, Prince Ronan. The Dragon's Heart and Second Rider!"

The herald's voice echoed through the hall, and the crowd fell silent. All eyes shifted to us, sharp and heavy. My throat went dry, the ache of sandpaper scraping against bone, and I struggled to swallow past the knot that tightened with every breath.

Ronan flexed his arm under my grasp, a quiet reassurance that I could face this moment.

And here I was, the older sister—trained for this—and I faltered.

The sea of unfamiliar faces pressed in, and a tremor stirred within me. I managed a smile, but my gaze swept beyond them, searching for something to steady my nerves.

Across the room, eyes the color of a summer sky locked with mine. From a table elevated on a platform, King Kallias rose and dipped into a slow bow, his stare never wavering.

My heart pounded, as nervous as a stag sighted by a dragon. I trained for this—was *born* for this. My brother released my arm and bowed, and I sank into a low curtsy worthy of a king.

"Welcome, Princess Nienna and Ronan Draconis."

His voice sent a jolt down my spine, igniting a swirl of curses in my mind. Was it fear? Fear of him? Or of the weight in his tone?

I straightened, the murmurs of the crowd buzzing around me—whispers about the foreign princess now in their midst. One misstep tonight, and it would be my only legacy. Ronan guided me down the aisle, and I held my head high, forcing my gaze forward, ignoring the temptation to glance at my feet. There was no obstacle in my path to trip on, to slow my advance to the dais.

The vast dining hall could easily swallow my entire set of rooms. Each step toward the platform stretched into what felt like an eternity. King Kallias' gaze did nothing to calm the trembling in my hand or the frantic rhythm of my heart.

We halted before the stairs, and I fought to keep my composure as he looked down at us. A red mark marred his forehead—a faint burn from the Dragon's Kiss. Heat crept up my neck, shame curling in my stomach. I hadn't controlled the magic as I should have.

This would be where Ronan left me. Where the prince would retrieve me.

Kallias offered a tight smile, gesturing toward the seat beside him. "Princess."

Tallon was meant to sit between us. I was to remain with my betrothed during our engagement. Yet, not only had I given my seal to the king, but now I was seated at his right hand—reserved for family.

I'd be family soon.

My gaze flicked across the platform, pausing on the few nobles and ambassadors fortunate enough to dine with royalty.

I couldn't climb the stairs alone. It would be too independent, too bold. To approach the king's table without an escort was a breach of my status as a princess.

The room fell silent, tension pressing down as murmurs faded to whispers. My finger tapped against my thigh, a minor act of control amid the uncertainty. A man shifted, his gaze drifting toward the king at his side. Kallias turned, a crease forming between his brows. Confusion—or perhaps irritation?

Surely, he knew that without Prince Tallon, I dared not approach.

The nobleman spoke to him in hushed tones, and Kallias' summer-sky eyes flicked back to me, scrutinizing. A muscle pulsed in his clenched jaw—a sure sign of his annoyance. Ignoring decorum, he rose from his seat.

No. Not him. Anyone else—a noble, a servant!

But my silent pleas went unanswered as he descended the twelve stairs—I counted—each step slow and deliberate.

The golden yoke draped over his viridian overcoat caught the lantern light, mocking my unease with its quiet, polished gleam. Brown boots wrapped his muscular calves, grounding his presence in shades of earth. A flicker of excitement sparked as I noticed them—practical, sturdy things. Not the sandals worn by his people.

My gaze drifted to the broadsword at his hip, swaying in tandem with his stride. This was no ornamental blade, but the weapon of the man they called the Warrior of Sun and Flame, a title earned by skill, not ceremony.

He raised his chin and extended his hand, palms rough with calluses—shaped by labor rather than privilege. What work had he done that resulted in a commoner's hands?

With lips pressed in a firm line, I bit down against the urge to hesitate. I placed my clammy hand on his, heat rising to my cheeks as I cursed the tangible evidence of my nerves. I kept my fidgeting under control and held my expression steady, but the betraying sweat on my palm was a stark reminder of my humanity, as undeniable as it was inconvenient. Some bodily functions I had no choice but to fall victim to.

King Kallias' grip felt cool and constant—firm without crushing—as he inclined his head, guiding me up the stairs.

"Dine with me." His words, pitched just above a murmur, sent a ripple of relief through the nobles, followed by whispers of approval rustling through the hall.

Though the tension eased, a fresh wave of shame twisted in my chest as I gathered my dress to ascend the steps. I had made no mistake. No, this error belonged to Radaan's court—but I would be the one bearing the brunt of palace gossip.

The princess, shunned by her betrothed, fetched by his father.

Dinner was only the beginning of my problems.

Chapter Three

NIENNA

"Please remain still, Your Highness." Edith's voice held calm patience as she wove my long blonde tresses into an intricate braid, the sunlight casting a warm glow over us.

I closed my eyes, drawing in a slow breath to settle my racing thoughts. Last night, I managed to evade most conversation, and King Kallias, for his part, seemed all too eager to ignore me. The nobleman beside me, however, had been a fountain of knowledge, a relentless source of information, regaling me with far more than I ever imagined about the mountain goats of the northern region.

Goats.

I squashed the irritation that bubbled up at the thought of the evening's bizarre discussion. Goats were important to Claydon'sol—it was vital to remember what each noble valued. If ever the topic turned to the uses or breeding of mountain goats, I knew exactly who to call upon. He would be more than happy to lecture anyone within earshot for hours on end.

"You're certain he's here?" I asked, doubt threading my words. I had reason to question Scythe's information.

"Aye."

Edith stiffened, her head snapping toward Scythe with a sharp glare.

"Err, yes, Your Highness." Scythe offered her an apologetic smile, then turned back to me with a genuine grin. "I overheard it in the kitchens while fetching your morning tea. Prince Tallon arrived last night. Caused quite a stir, or so the staff says."

"Gossipmongers," Edith muttered under her breath.

"And you're sure he was just in his cups? Not injured?" I asked, ignoring the older maid's exasperated sigh.

"I'd say there'd be a lot more commotion if he were. As it is, Rosalie mentioned he often gets lost in his spirits. Nothing to worry over."

Yes, a drunkard for a betrothed. Nothing to worry over at all.

Teeth gritted, I studied the princess in the mirror. She sat tall and composed, her hair neat and combed. Her pale face was scrubbed clean, and sea-colored irises gleamed, sharp and watchful.

My father wouldn't saddle me with a marriage to a drunken sot. I feared a husband who overindulged in wine far more than one who might be mortally wounded. To be fair, if he were injured, perhaps I'd find it easier to forgive his absence at my receiving.

"I'm sure you are eager to see him tonight," Scythe added. She paused, her fingers stilling as she laced my boot, a distant smile tugging at her lips. "You'll finally meet the man you're promised to."

"Scythe. Boots!" Edith hissed.

The young maid snapped to attention, resuming her task. Edith's sharp gaze caught mine in the mirror as if she understood my pain.

"I hope he won't wait until tonight to see me." I forced a chuckle, the sound hollow. The notion of him missing my arrival, only to delay our meeting until the ball, felt absurd.

Surely, he'd call for me before the evening's festivities.

He did not, in fact, call for me before the ball.

I bounced between irritation and hurt. The sting of his public disregard twisted into something sharper—annoyance at the slight, but deeper still, an ache of rejection. I had accepted my role. As a princess, forming alliances was my birthright. Tallon, a prince, was bound to the same fate. His duty was clear—to forge connections with other kingdoms, securing his rule over Radaan.

The alliance between Draconia and his kingdom was vital. We needed each other. Food was scarce. Our grain supply was unreliable, and though the waters offered fish, it could not sustain us forever. And the dragons required a tithe, one that increased with each passing year.

Radaan needed the protection our dragons provided—their ability to mobilize over sea and mountain, their firestorms capable of razing entire armies. Kallias and Tallon needed respite from the endless war, a decisive move to secure their fragile peace.

And yet the prince continued to disgrace me.

Edith sat on a stool, her knitting needles clicking, her attention absorbed in the work. Scythe had made herself scarce, sensing the thickening tension. I kept my temper in check, watching the hours stretch, morning slipping into high noon, then fading to evening.

And still, he never summoned me.

I sat on the chaise, bedecked in the vibrant blues and muted greens of Draconia. A necklace of mother-of-pearl rested against my skin, a perfect match to the finery that adorned my wrists and ears. The sea-green gown, one of my finest, flowed in waves, cascading along my frame with effortless grace. Black boots laced tightly over my knees offered a nice contrast to the delicate tiara nestled in my hair—a silver band adorned with pearls, diamonds, and sapphires that caught the light with every movement, drawing attention to my face.

A knock echoed through the room, and I raised my chin, casting a sharp, deliberate glare. "Come in."

The door swung open with surprising silence, its weight a testament to its craftsmanship. Ronan entered, leaving his guards in the corridor behind him.

He wore his finest garb. Traces of silver and pearls glinted along the dark leather, sculpting his muscular chest. Unlike the rough uniform worn by most riders, his was lined with smooth silk. His black goggles sat cocked atop his head in a roguish way, as if anyone could miss that he was a rider.

"Father would be beside himself," I sighed, giving his goggles a pointed look as I stood.

"He should have come."

"You know as well as I, he would if he could."

Edith set her knitting aside and leaned in to smooth the folds of my dress, ensuring every line fell without a crease.

"Pah! Old man." Ronan scoffed, though his lopsided grin softened the jab.

Argos took a battering in his last flight—a whirlstorm hurled him into the jagged crags that surrounded Draconia. His wing, broken and scarred, marked the end of his flights across the sea.

Still a fearsome beast to behold. But, for a grounded dragon, its rider remains earthbound as well—king or not.

Edith tucked a stray lock of hair behind my ear, scrutinizing my reflection before stepping back—satisfied. Ronan extended his arm, and I steadied myself with a breath before resting my hand on the crook of his elbow.

"Tallon visit you?" he asked, tone casual as we passed the guards posted in the hall.

When the door thudded shut behind us, it echoed the hollow ache within, a weight pressing down as my heart sank. "No."

His muscles tensed beneath my grip, his steps faltering. With a clenched jaw, my fingers tightened, urging him to keep moving. His anger matched my own, but we couldn't change the situation.

The first time I'd see Tallon would be under the watchful stares of hundreds of nobles.

"That flaming son of–"

"Of King Kallias," I finished, casting a sidelong glance at the guards flanking us in the corridor. Any slip could be overlooked, but I dared not let my brother's words spark gossip that might reach the prince's ears.

"He arrived last night!" he hissed.

Barely standing, by all accounts.

"Yes, and I'm sure the journey left him... exhausted," I said, forcing a cordial tone.

The strangled sound in the back of his throat caught somewhere between a scoff and a growl. He strode beside me in silence, no doubt concocting some clever slight to avenge Tallon's absence. I'd need to steer the prince well clear of him this evening.

"Is Gyrak eager for tomorrow morning?" I asked, guiding the conversation to a safer topic. A couple bowed in tandem as we passed. I returned the gesture with a nod and polite smile, trying to orient myself with the bright halls twisting ahead.

"More than I am," he answered. "I'll be on dragonback for far too long."

"And here you are, a seasoned Dragon Rider, grumbling about your backside's saddle sores."

"You got a ship, *Princess*. Try riding dragonback for days on end with no breaks to take a–"

"Ronan!" I hissed, cutting him off. I forced a grin at the guards, who pretended not to listen, grateful no nobles lingered within earshot.

"You romanticize it, sister," he teased, stretching arms wide. "Oh yes, soaring through the skies, high above all troubles—*free* as the wind!"

His mocking theatrics drew a giggle I couldn't contain. I knew too well the grueling reality of dragon riding—the strength demanded to handle a creature's every surge and dive, the endless drills to build up endurance, and the discipline to avoid blacking out mid-flight. Young dragons could soar for days and their riders required discipline.

After all, crossing a vast sea with nowhere to land brought its own indignities—things better left undiscussed in polite company.

As we approached the private entrance to the ballroom, a lightness eased into my chest. No matter the hardships, Ronan always found a way to lift my spirits. He'd get into trouble—I'd pull him out. And I'd never regretted a moment of it.

A bittersweet smile ghosted over my lips at the thought of him leaving. With whirlstorms approaching, we wouldn't dare risk Gyrak in the skies. Once he departed, I would truly be alone—left with only my ladies' maids. Edith, my steadfast nursemaid since childhood, and Scythe, my handmaid and closest friend. But neither could replace my brother.

I straightened my spine, sealing away the ache. This was my life, my duty. I would take it as it came.

We moved through corridors unfamiliar to me—not that many weren't—and stopped before a towering set of doors. A squire worked through the line of assembled nobles, scratching notes onto a long parchment. His sleeves bore a modest puff, a mark of his position within the royal staff. Beside him stood a man with a hawkish nose and bushy white brows that cried out for a trim, his sleeves billowing in an exaggerated display of rank.

They glanced up as we neared, and the squire hurried forward, cuffing a small boy at his side, who scurried down the hall like a startled mouse.

"Your Highnesses! Welcome! Right this way, if you please!" He gestured for us to bypass the line.

I maintained an amicable grin, eyes straight ahead. Even so, the vivid pinks and purples adorning the women caught my attention. My preference leaned toward muted shades, deep tones. Yet as this kingdom's future princess, I needed to embody its elegance, to appear as though I belonged. One day, as queen, I would set the fashion standard.

A nervous thrill wound tight as Ronan guided me closer to those giant doors. White as bone, they stood engraved with delicate, gilded trees that stretched upward, reaching for the vaulted ceiling. I marveled at the workmanship—a forest inviting me to step forward, to lose myself in its gleaming depths of ivory and gold. I imagined brushing my fingers over the smooth curves and carved hollows, as though a single touch might pull me into that shimmering world.

No art within this palace would escape my prying eyes. I wanted to explore each carved panel, study every painted ceiling and century-old vase. These halls would become mine to know and cherish, and one day, I would leave my own touch in its decor, something worthy of these storied walls.

"His Highness, Prince Tallon of Radaan, will descend the opposite staircase and–"

"Take my sister, yes," Ronan interrupted with a low growl, silencing the page.

I pinched his forearm, a warning hidden in the pressure. *Manners, brother.*

"Yes, Your Highness." The page nodded, stiff and curt. "Once they reach the landing, you may descend in turn."

A mischievous smirk pulled at the corner of Ronan's lip. "Right behind you, Princess."

I resisted the urge to roll my eyes at his antics. Mother would have set propriety aside and smacked him without a second thought.

A boy, no older than seven, scurried over, breathless, as he tugged at the man's overcoat.

The squire scribbled a quick note on his parchment before signaling to the guards with a brisk wave. "Yes, yes. This way, Your Highnesses!"

I drew in a slow breath, careful to keep it hidden from watchful eyes, and steadied myself as the massive doors pulled open.

A tide of cheerful conversation rolled over me like a fog, thick and hazy, while the dense, cloying smell of perfume and flowers crowded my senses. I gripped Ronan's arm, and he flexed beneath my grasp—a silent promise. He wouldn't leave me. Not yet.

For one last evening, he stood beside me.

Light from mirrored chandeliers and wall-mounted lanterns cascaded over the stairs, the plush red carpet running down to a matching set of doors on the opposite side. My stare locked onto them as they cracked open, my heart thrumming with the anticipation of finally laying eyes on Prince Tallon.

A man stood silhouetted there, his piercing green gaze catching mine across the expanse. Nervous butterflies swarmed in my belly as his mouth curved into a crooked smirk. The crown resting in his raven-dark hair gleamed, its embedded diamonds and emeralds sparkling against the backdrop of his regal bearing. There was no mantle for the prince then.

"His Royal Highness, Prince Tallon of Radaan!"

A faint dizziness swept over me as I took in his form. Tall and lean, he carried a hint of lingering boyhood awkwardness, though at nineteen, he was on the cusp of something more formidable. He would stand just above my height. Still, even from this distance, his face seemed kind—and sober.

"Heir of King Kallias Sunspear! Son of the late Queen Eldeiade!"

Did he get those intense green eyes from his mother? Would his frame one day rise to match that of his father's imposing breadth and stature?

With a twist of his body, he swept into a bow, his gaze still locked on mine. A flicker of insolence lurked in that look, as if he were mocking us. My grin wavered, unsteady with a pulse of nerves.

This was the man destined to be by my side for a lifetime.

"Presenting His Royal Highness, Prince Ronan Draconis, rider of Gyrak the Black; and Her Royal Highness, Princess Nienna Draconis, the Dragon's Heart!"

My brother bowed, and I sank into a curtsy, rising with Prince Tallon. I kept an iron grip on my brother's arm as we moved, step by deliberate step, down the stairs, each footfall reminding me to breathe.

His boots, polished obsidian with silver buckles, gleamed under the lights as he took the opposite staircase. His attire—a black tunic and trousers paired with a deep red overcoat—clung to his frame. Rings sparkled on his fingers, but I refused to look away from his glittering gaze.

That crooked smile, a slant of mischief or perhaps defiance, seemed etched as a permanent stain on his features. I hoped it hinted at a jestful nature, like my brother, and not the hardened cruelty I'd glimpsed in the sneers of others. Surely Prince Tallon was no bully.

One wouldn't direct such harshness toward his future wife and queen.

My boots struck the landing, high above the crowd, on equal footing with my betrothed. As we closed the distance, I tipped my chin, meeting his intense gaze. His eyes roamed over my features, drifting to my neckline.

Heat crept into my cheeks under his bold, open appraisal. But he was to be my husband, after all.

I could only hope he liked what he saw.

"Prince Tallon." My voice pitched higher than I intended, but I resisted clearing my throat.

As he offered me his arm, his green stare cut to my brother.

"My *sister*, Princess Nienna Draconis," Ronan's friendly tone carried a subtle warning—a reminder, "the *Dragon's* Heart."

"Your Highness." Tallon dipped his head, and a stray lock of dark hair fell across his brow in a boyish way. A stirring instinct to tuck it back tugged at me. Instead, I eased my hand from Ronan's arm.

This was it—my presentation to the masses as the future bride of Radaan's heir.

My fingers rested on Tallon's forearm, and the light connection brought on a spark of nerves, prickling and hazy. Such a simple, innocent touch, yet it meant so much, bound me to him in more ways than one. Did he care that I'd given my pact to his father? That he missed the Dragon's Kiss? If he did, he didn't show it.

We turned to the crowd as one. My practiced smile set in place. Still, I cursed the way the corner of my lips twitched downward. Masses of nobles, ambassadors, and foreign dignitaries spread out before us, watching for any crack in my composure.

"Behold! Your future King and Queen of Radaan!"

The herald's voice rang out, and my grin faltered, tension tightening my throat. Polite applause rippled through the audience, along with cordial nods and shallow bows.

But my gaze sought the king.

He watched us, his piercing eyes narrowed beneath dark brows drawn low to match his frown. Though he stood hundreds of paces away near the dais, his displeasure reached me as clearly as if he'd spoken. A flush of heat crept over my cheeks. Had I not been under every eye in this hall, I might have folded under the weight of his scrutiny.

Who could be so foolish, careless even, to make such an announcement? To proclaim a future king or queen—not heir apparent—while the current ruler still reigned?

"Let's not keep them in suspense."

Warning bells echoed in my mind as my gaze tugged back to Tallon. Weren't those his father's words when we met? He flashed me a predatory smile and took the first step to the ballroom. I swallowed my nerves and followed, avoiding the angry glare from across the room.

As soon as our boots hit the polished floor, the nobles closed in. I kept up my amicable countenance, struggling to remember names, territories, and allegiances. While I recognized most of the names, matching faces to their titles and recalling their interests felt like an impossible task.

"Ah, my lady—you'll have to excuse me." Tallon's eyes glinted with amusement as he smirked down at me, lowering his arm—and my hand along with it. "I have business to attend to."

Without me? At a ball announcing our betrothal?

With no more than a one-armed shrug, he plunged into the crowd. I stared after him, stunned.

He left me? Alone? Among a sea of nobles and dignitaries? A cold, sharp edge flooded my veins with an icy chill. I might have been raised for this, but all I knew was Draconia's high court. Radaan was another world entirely.

A nobleman with bushy white hair tied back into a puff at the nape of his neck caught my eye. His grip on the elderly woman at his side tightened as they started my way.

No. No more goats.

I lifted onto my toes, scanning the crowd as though searching for someone. With a nod to myself, I pressed forward, people parting as they realized who I was. My steps carried me toward the only fixed point in the room—the dais.

And also, quite effectively, took me further from Claydon'sol and his tedious conversation of mountain goat breeding.

My boots halted on the carpet as realization struck—I was moving closer to King Kallias. His furious gaze flashed in my mind, and I stepped back. He had to know I had no part in the announcement, but seeing me without his son after such a claim to the throne was something I wanted nothing to do with.

"Ah, Your Highness!"

A royal did not display irritation.

"Princess Nienna! I forgot to mention goat hair!"

A princess loved all her people—and the quirks that came with them.

With yet another wide grin pasted to my cheeks, I turned to greet the Sols. It seemed fate had decided I needed to learn more about goats and their... hair.

It could have been a worse evening.

The palace could have caught fire, the ceiling collapsing to bury us all. Alas, I spent hours with Claydon'sol and Gayle'sol, listening to endless talk about Kuh'lir—goats that dwelled in their mountainous region. The debate of sheep versus goats stretched into the night.

One glass of wine was my sole companion.

Prince Tallon moved through the crowd, flanked by a group of young nobles. I caught his gaze once, and he smirked, as if he found my conversation with Claydon'sol amusing. I threw a smile right back at him, all teeth, making sure he knew I noticed him.

He disappeared after that.

Asking questions kept the Sols talking. I had to mind my words, careful not to provoke my father's temper—one of the many traits of his I inherited. It was safer to listen than trust my tongue and lips to remain polite. My brother was lost in the throng, and Tallon abandoned me. I nodded in encouragement as Gayle'sol, a short, frail woman, rambled on about a buck that they captured for breeding.

"And he is quite content!" She beamed, pausing to sip her wine.

A wild buck, penned with hundreds of does. Hardly a life to protest.

"They usually fight a bit," she drawled, "try to escape. But this one, he's–"

"Claydon'sol."

The king's interruption sent a tremor through me. I would have been content to let these two go on about their goats rather than confront King Kallias.

"Your Majesty!" The Sols bowed and curtsied as I faced him, dropping into my own curtsy.

The music that flowed over the happy din shifted, fading to a tense note, signaling the start of the main event.

"I beg your leave. Princess Nienna is needed," he said.

I lifted my stare from his polished boots, tracing the sharp lines of his snug dress clothes. His plush green velvet overcoat clung to his broad shoulders, lined with accents of gold. His mantle's glare challenged the sharpness of his gaze. He watched me with an intensity that felt as if he could peer straight through my soul, all while offering a courteous smile to the nobles.

"Of course! Come, dear," Claydon called, his voice light with excitement. "Let's find a good place to watch the dance!"

I kept my expression poised and content, ignoring the guard that trailed the king. Bystanders gave us marginal space, none daring to approach as he stepped closer.

"Where is Tallon?" His voice pitched low, lips barely moving as he offered his arm.

Dread hit me like a physical blow, but I stifled the flinch building beneath my skin. I wouldn't offer excuses for someone who abandoned me in his own court.

"I haven't the slightest, Your Majesty. Last I saw, he was making for the doors to the hall."

His hand rested over his belt, a subtle gesture that barely concealed the tension in his posture. I stole a glance at his face. The slight pinch of his brow made it clear—he was far from pleased that the prince had run off.

Perhaps he should have taught him better manners.

"Greaves." The name sent the guard shadowing him off in another direction. I tried to mask my intrigue. Kallias would send a mere bodyguard after his son?

As the king guided me toward the ballroom's center, I set my wineglass on a passing servant's tray. He was leading me to the dance floor—where I'd wait for my betrothed to join me, if he managed to return in time. With jaw clenched, I flexed my free hand, struggling to steady my nerves.

The crowd parted before us, a hush falling over them. My pulse quickened, blood roaring in my ears, drowning out the music as the dancefloor cleared.

The notes blared, almost deafening against the nobles' murmurs. They watched with eager grins and bright eyes. One misstep now, and my reputation would plunge further into the mire.

Kallias pressed forward without hesitation, heading straight for the cleared floor. My heart slammed into my throat.

"Your Majesty," I croaked, ashamed of the way my voice faltered.

He dipped his chin, but kept his gaze fixed ahead, as though he were a bull set on the task at hand, intent on charging.

"Am I to share a dance with Prince Tallon?" I whispered. Uncertainty slithered beneath my skin. I despised it—not knowing how to carry myself, or what to expect. The first dance was meant to celebrate our engagement, the highlight of the evening. Surely, he wouldn't leave me alone on the floor.

Kallias' cheek twitched—a sharp, subtle movement that revealed his mounting frustration. I sincerely hoped it was not aimed at me.

"I will escort you in his stead."

A cry of dismay rose in my throat, but I swallowed it back, keeping my expression composed. Once more, the king had to take his son's place. Was this treaty truly between me and Tallon?

No, it was between Draconia and Radaan. I was Draconis, and Kallias was Radaanian. It was the same.

Except it didn't feel that way.

"It will be my first Radaanian dance." I lifted my chin, forcing another smile to mask the ache gnawing at me. "It's regrettable that you've not shod your boots in steel," I muttered, hoping he was more forgiving than his rough exterior portrayed.

"I fear you'll not fare any better." His lips twisted into a slight grimace. "It's been years since I last danced with a woman."

The agony in my heart softened a fraction. He wasn't angry about my bluntness. He understood my discomfort, related to my pain.

I relaxed, the tension in my shoulders easing as he spun me into position. His grip firmed around my hand, holding me at arm's length. My polite expression trembled and faltered, unable to hold against his severe frown.

He wore the look of a man resigned to his torturous fate.

Poor soul. Cursed to dance with his future daughter-in-law while his bodyguard tracked down his son.

His hair, streaked with silver, framed a jaw set with quiet resolve. Short stubble, gleaming with flecks of gray, dotted his chin. Dark brows dipped over troubled cornflower blue eyes.

I gripped his hand delicately, then lowered myself into a deep curtsy—deeper than I would for Tallon. Kallias demanded more honor from his station. And deserved more respect for attempting to set me at ease.

With a gentle tug, he pulled me closer as the harmony swelled, its rhythm in sync with my thudding pulse. His warm hand rested on my waist, and I shivered at the slight pressure.

His touch felt wrong—searing through the layers of my dress. Another man's hands on me. Heat flushed my cheeks. I'd danced with other nobles, but always under my father's watchful eye. Surely, my brother lingered in the crowd somewhere, but I had no idea where. I was on display, the center of attention at high court—dancing with a man who wasn't my betrothed.

I peeked up at him and tried another shot at humor. "Have you danced with many men in recent years?" My hand settled on his shoulder, searching his gaze for some sign that he understood my good natured intent—that he wouldn't dismiss me as a foolish girl.

"Who do you think I practice with?"

His grunted response clashed with his frown, and I smothered a genuine grin. He seemed far more unnerved than I. Strange, since I'd only been taught this dance in the privacy of my home, never before in public. Perhaps it was the fact that he wasn't dancing with me by choice, but out of obligation.

Music cascaded over the room, stringed instruments singing sweet notes that mingled with the soft rustle of silken dresses and the rhythmic tap of polished shoes. The rich, melodic hum seemed to settle deep within, vibrating through the floor as if the very air were alive with the sound.

"Well, I'll be living at the palace, in case you haven't heard," I murmured. "I've been bound to my room all day. Perhaps the next time you need a partner, I can assist you."

His jaw twitched, teeth grinding as his gaze fixed on my ear. He guided me through the steps in silence, his movements sure but tense. I dropped my focus to the mantle on his overcoat, the golden chains swishing with each step. I matched their rhythm, letting the music wash over me.

Despite his evident unease and my inexperience with Radaanian dances, we flowed seamlessly. He led, and I followed, the steps becoming as effortless as breathing. A quiet reassurance settled in my chest—I was made for this. This alliance was no mistake.

My thoughts drifted, the music's crescendo stirring emotions I hadn't expected. His hand at my waist remained firm, unyielding, while the other clasped mine with steady strength. His scent, a mix of sunshine and cinnamon, clung to me, drawing me closer as if to anchor me to the moment.

I wondered what scent Tallon carried.

As if he could read my thoughts, Kallias' hand twitched at my waist. My eyes snapped to his, and I saw the shift in his expression before he slowed our movements. His glare cut through the crowd, and the music responded in kind, fading to a soft interlude, as if the very room bent to his mood. He stilled, and despite the smooth flow of the dance, my breath quickened, as if he'd stolen it from my lungs.

Without a word, he dropped my hand and pulled away from my waist, storming off the floor with a furious stride. I froze, watching him go, heart pounding.

Tallon swaggered over, a smirk twisting his features, Greaves trailing behind. My fingers twitched with the urge to slap it off his face.

Kallias stalked past a servant with a tray of wine glasses, snatching one without breaking stride. In a fluid motion, he tipped it back, draining the glass before lowering his chin to meet his son's gaze. As they passed, Tallon's smirk evaporated, his brows drawing down in a sharp, heated glare.

They exchanged no words, yet the weight of their silence rippled through the room, thick with tension. Greaves pivoted on his heel, falling in line behind King Kallias. Meanwhile, Tallon sucked in a breath large enough to puff up his chest, his forest-green eyes locking with mine. Again, he gave me a half-hearted shrug, as if offering an apology.

I reined in my irritation, forcing my expression into neutrality as he stopped before me. With a flourish, he stooped into a bow so exaggerated it almost bordered on mockery. My jaw clenched tight to keep from snapping at him, demanding where he disappeared to. Instead, I dipped into a respectable, measured curtsy. I wouldn't give him as much respect as his father received. He hadn't earned it.

His grin was boyish as he extended his hand. When I placed mine in his, his touch landed on my waist, but it felt lacking—fragile, almost as though it were an act, a thin veneer of sincerity.

I pushed the thought aside, shaking off the discomfort as the music enveloped us. The melody wrapped itself around me, coaxing my body into the rhythm, pulling me into a trance of familiarity—one I knew better than the man I was bound to marry.

Chapter Four

NIENNA

When I headed to my rooms in the early hours past midnight, exhaustion seeped into my bones. Ronan never resurfaced, and Tallon once again left me to fend for myself. When he did, noblewomen swarmed, relentless in their questions and prying glances, all questioning why I danced with both Kallias, and his son.

As if any of it was my choice.

At least I escaped more talk of those infernal goats.

With my back straight and chin high, I moved through the corridors, guards on either side. But each step pulsed through my aching heels, and my temples throbbed with a dull, unyielding rhythm. The dress strangled my ribs, squeezing what little air remained. All I wanted was my bed, to fall into it and let the world carry on without me.

The corridor stretched ahead, the light from wall-sconces catching the edges of engraved doors as I passed each one, my guards trailing close but silent. I knew where my quarters were, at least, even if exhaustion blurred the finer details.

My gaze drifted to the carvings, all grand in their own way, hinting at rooms just as large as my own. A massive boar rearing against a spear-wielding warrior caught my eye. I slowed, studying the intricate details—the warrior poised, braced, yet dwarfed by the creature's sheer size. A beast large enough to challenge a dragon, if it could ever take to the skies. Gyrak would be thrilled at the chance to battle a boar of that magnitude.

Dragons ruled above and below, dominating earth and sea alike.

Well, most of it.

Unseen monsters lurked in the ocean depths that even dragons feared.

The treaty binding Draconia and Radaan did not come without sacrifice on our side. My father didn't just send me; he demanded much of our dragons, asking them to cross the sea. Born to the Wild Shores, the beasts now kept to our island, closer to their ancient territory than Radaan. A massive whirlstorm—the largest in recorded history—once grounded the beasts to our lands. Having them soar for days over the open sea went against their nature, a strain they would never have endured by choice.

We approached my door, carved with the image of dragons soaring above an island fortress, Draconia's banner snapping at the tower's peak. My lips tugged into a faint, wistful smile. This might be the last glimpse of my homeland I'd ever have.

Two guards flanked my doorway. An uneasy chill pricked my skin. I reminded myself that men, not shadows, stood behind the armor. Yet the anonymity unsettled me—I couldn't read their faces, learn their names, or tell them apart. Draconia felt worlds apart—there, I knew the staff and their kin, shared stories, trusted them like family. Here, I had to win them over, show them I wasn't a stranger in their halls to be feared.

When I entered my room, Scythe shot to her feet, nearly knocking over the chair in her haste. Edith's stern look pinned her back into place but rose with careful dignity.

After the door clicked shut, I released a groan that would have scandalized half the court.

"Are you well, Your Highness?" Edith questioned, her tone carrying a faint rebuke.

I sifted through curses in my mind, knowing she would only invent a creative way to remind me of my decorum if I voiced them. As I moved toward the dressing room, Scythe sprang into action, loosening my laces with swift, practiced hands as I walked. My lungs expanded, savoring the first real breath I'd drawn all night.

"Hot water, Scythe." Edith's tone brooked no delay as I sank into an overstuffed chair, my head tipping back in surrender.

Scythe darted off, still buzzing with energy. "So, how was it? Was he as handsome as you dreamed?" she called over her shoulder, her excitement bright against the solemn walls. In truth, she was more suited to court life than I was.

"He wasn't hard on the eyes."

I sighed, and Edith knelt before me, working at my boots' laces. Radaan nobility insisted on heeled sandals that lifted them inches from the ground, as though height alone could command authority. King Kallias wore practical flat heeled boots like mine, which made me wonder—if Tallon ditched those ridiculous shoes, would I stand taller than him?

If I had a say, I'd do away with those heels. And the absurd puffed sleeves.

"I've heard all the maids swooning over him," Scythe piped in, pouring steaming water into the bath.

Radaan might lack dragons, but their hot-water pipes were a gift I could grow to appreciate.

I laughed, feeling a bite of chill brush my toes as Edith tugged off my second boot. "Two days, and you've already infiltrated the servant's ranks?"

The stockings followed, freeing my feet at last. I wiggled my toes and relished the freedom but also mourned it—knowing I would have to rise to disrobe.

"Oh, the things I know!" Scythe cackled, and I chuckled in response as Edith rolled her eyes. She rose, offering her hand. I groaned, letting her pull me to my aching feet and finish unlacing my dress.

"You'd be surprised what you can learn when you trade dragon secrets."

"You don't know the secrets of dragons." I retorted as the fabric pooled along the floorboards. I kicked it aside and tugged at the waistband of my skin-tight breeches.

"But I'm the handmaiden to the Dragon's Heart!" Scythe's voice was muffled as I wiggled free from my trousers, hurrying toward the bathing room.

"So you're trading *my* secrets!"

Scythe straightened, flipping her long brown braid over her shoulder. "As if you have any."

"Your murder will be my first!" I grinned as I headed for the steaming tub.

"Ladies!"

We spun to face Edith as she heaved a tired sigh, her gaze sharp and tired. She'd been awake before me and wouldn't rest until later—unless I dismissed her. I cocked an eyebrow in challenge.

"Before you send me off, let me plait your hair," she muttered.

I twisted, giving Scythe a sly wink, and she giggled, then busied herself pouring lavender oil and mint leaves into my bath. We'd talk after the old maid retired.

I stepped in with a moan of relief. The heat sank deep into each muscle—hotter than anything Draconia's waters offered. With my head rested against the tub's lip, I submerged my body, warmth enveloping me.

Edith handed Scythe my robe, then got to work weaving my hair.

"I'll be looking forward to a late morning," I breathed, eyes drifting shut. Would it be wrong of me to sleep here rather than my bed?

"Will the prince be fetching you?" Scythe asked, pulling my foot from the water, massaging oils into my tender heel.

"He better," I groaned, savoring the pressure. "He abandoned me on the floor tonight."

"No!"

"Twice."

She slapped an oiled hand over her chest, eyes wide in disbelief. Her gasp held all the horror I once felt. By now, it long since melted into irritation and annoyance.

"I had to dance with King Kallias."

"On the night of your betrothal?!"

A sharp tug on my hair indicated Edith was done with my complaints. Scythe would spread the news among the servants, but they already knew. The nobles who witnessed the ordeal, however, would be the real problem.

"See to her feet! If she has blisters, I'll hold you responsible!" Edith's reprimand was sharp, unforgiving.

I bit back a laugh at Scythe's murderous glare. She yanked my other foot, hauling me across the slippery basin. My head plunged beneath the surface, and I flailed, water rushing up my nose. Coughing and sputtering, I gripped the tub's edge and shot upward, splashing bathwater everywhere.

"You're going to drown her!" Edith snapped, yanking my hair back with force.

I choked and pulled my feet out of Scythe's reach, tucking them under me. She snickered, then began mopping up the puddles along the floorboards.

When the bath was over, my hair plaited and wrapped in silk, I dismissed Edith. She would tend to me in the morning. Scythe would see me to bed, staying in my room as usual. I yawned, watching the older woman slip through a small door hidden behind the tapestry in my receiving room.

Scythe squealed, her grip tightening around my hand as she yanked me through the rooms toward my sleeping chamber.

"I *have* to show you!"

"Tonight?" I moaned, dragging my feet. She was the sister I never had—in every way that mattered.

"You'll want to see it, I promise!"

She tugged me over to a giant chest wedged against the wall. Moonlight spilled through the window, casting pale shadows on the light wood. Vines snaked across its surface and delicate glass flowers shimmered on top.

"Help me move it!" she hissed, releasing my hand to brace herself on the opposite end.

"Are we rearranging furniture? At this hour?" I groaned, but still gripped the side, readying myself.

"It will be worth it!"

She grunted, shoving her slight weight at the wood. With a few muttered curses, we managed to move it. She let out a delighted squeal and crouched, peering behind it. I leaned over her, squinting at the wall.

Or rather, the small door embedded there.

"Old servant passages?" I raised an eyebrow as she dusted the frame. I couldn't imagine a maid crawling through such a tiny opening to sneak between rooms.

"Not at all! These don't connect to the servants' quarters." She tugged at the latch, but the aged wood resisted her pull. "Get a light!"

Sore feet be cursed. I wouldn't miss an exploration for anything.

"Well, where does it lead?" I asked, retrieving the candle from my nightstand's lantern.

"It's from the war. All the royal quarters have one." She peeked at me, eyes glittering with mischief. "*All* of them. And they all connect."

"So they can sneak from room to room?" I scoffed.

She pulled the swollen wood free of the frame and snatched the candle. "No, silly. For when assassins are afoot."

As she stuck the small flickering light into the space ahead, a spider web caught flame and flared up in a sudden burst. I gasped, scrambling back as Scythe swatted at the flash with her bare hand.

"Careful!" I hissed, shoving her shoulder as I crouched beside her.

The hall was cramped. Wide enough for a few people to crawl through, but barely taller than my waist. I would have to wriggle through the darkness, brushing past spiders, mice, and who knew what else.

And it was dark.

"I'm so excited!" Without waiting, Scythe plunged through the cobwebs as she scuttled along, oblivious to the mess she left behind.

I dropped to my hands and knees, following her with a reluctant grin. After the night I'd had, this strange detour felt like a welcome change. The passage was neglected, cobwebs hanging thick in every corner.

"It's an escape route," she whispered, her eyes flickering around the suffocating dark. "All the rooms connect so the king can summon his family."

My lips formed a line, my gaze lost to the darkness. The temptation to stumble upon Tallon's room was too great. What secrets lay behind his door? Then again, he grew up in this palace. He must've explored these passages countless times. If I were caught, the consequences wouldn't be just an embarrassment or an impropriety. It would be a shame I couldn't escape, a mark that would linger long after the moment passed.

I dared not speak louder than a whisper. "How did you find out about them?"

"Berth—a stuffy old servant," she whispered. "He was snooping around, asking about your mother."

"The queen?" I ducked under a thick strand of webbing, flinching as something skittered to my side. I squinted into the shadows. Whatever it was, it was too small to worry about.

"Aye, 'Queen of Dragons,' he called her. In exchange for a few juicy tidbits about her, he shared these old passages with me."

"Not just my secrets, but my mother's as well." I sighed, dust and grime clinging to my hands as I crawled. I couldn't fathom how I'd explain the state of my robe to Edith in the morning.

"Have faith," she reassured me. "I told him nonsense—something about you being born in the Nest."

"Common knowledge," I muttered.

She paused, and I leaned over to see what had halted her. A massive rat skeleton glinted in the flickering candlelight. "You've seen dragons swallow cows, and you're scared of a dead rat?" I chuckled, then took the candle. I moved past, shuffling down the dusty passage with a grin.

"Common in Draconia, but here it's a bit more... shocking!" she mused, the rustle of fabric assuring me she followed.

The path stretched on, swallowed by the endless darkness. We passed several side passages but kept our course straight, the most reliable route for retracing our steps. The air grew heavier, colder. Conversation dwindled, our words drowned by the creeping silence. Then, faint voices filtered through the stillness. We froze, exchanging tense glances in the dim light.

"Chicken." Her brown eyes twinkled in the candlelight, a daring smile lifting one side of her mouth.

I glared, thrusting the candle at her before inching forward. We could still turn back, slip away unnoticed, as long as whoever spoke wasn't in the tunnel.

The voices swelled, growing louder as we snuck along, each hand and knee placed with deliberate caution. We dodged rat droppings, stepped over decaying mice, and skirted low-hanging webs, the air thick with dust. My throat itched, but I fought the urge to clear it.

We stopped at a door embedded in the wall. Like the others, it was latched from the inside and coated in grime. No light bled through the cracks, a sign it had been kept hidden just as mine was.

A sudden crash jolted me, and I snapped a quick look at Scythe. Her lips tightened, but her eyes gleamed with excitement. She crept closer to the door, pressing her ear to the filthy surface.

I followed, our faces so close that our breaths mingled in the stale air.

"—knew I wouldn't be here," a muffled voice said, distorted by layers of wood, but youthful in its outrage.

"No, I *demanded* you be here." The depth of that baritone sent the fine hairs at the nape of my neck on end. It was too distant, too unclear to identify, yet I felt it in my bones.

'The king!' I mouthed, eyes widening in shock. Panic surged, urging me to flee, to dart down the passage.

Scythe dropped her jaw, blinked, then snapped it shut with a sly grin.

"In case you haven't noticed, I don't obey your whims." The younger voice bit back. Tallon—it had to be.

"You've had your youth," Kallias' tone resembled that of a growling beast rather than a regal king. "You've had your fun. Now you will step up—inherit Radaan. It's time you learned your duty."

"Radaan is mine–"

"*Will be.* Not yet, Tallon." The king's words sliced through his son's defiance.

My teeth sank into my lip, desperate to stay quiet.

"I don't need a queen to rise to the throne," the prince said. His tone dripped with taunting malice, as if goading his father.

"Radaan needs her. Not you," Kallias shouted. "Another repeat of tonight's events and you'll send her packing—if she isn't gone already."

"She was fine."

A crash. A grunt. "Treat her that way again, and I'll banish you to the valley beneath."

"Just as you threatened Mother so many times." Bitterness strangled Tallon's scoff.

My pulse quickened. This conversation was not meant for my ears—but I couldn't stop myself. Even Scythe's expression shifted, her excitement replaced by a flicker of genuine fear.

"This isn't about you—or her," Kallias snarled. "It's about your kingdom, boy. Act like an heir, or I'll treat you as the bastard you are."

I recoiled, the words stinging. Terror poured through me, freezing my veins. Scythe's face mirrored my shock as we both backed away, barely able to move without making a sound. On shaking limbs, we fled down the passage, praying they hadn't heard our frantic scramble.

My heart pounded, refusing to calm even as we crawled onto my plush carpet and shut the door. Neither of us spoke as we shoved the chest back in place, then slumped to the floor in exhaustion.

Scythe grabbed my hand, squeezing it tight, forcing me to meet her eye. "It's just a phrase," she said. "Simple name-calling."

Bastard.

Coming from King Kallias, I wasn't sure how much truth lay in her statement. Or his.

Chapter Five

NIENNA

When Edith arrived in the morning, I was already awake. Scythe had smuggled my robe and headscarf away for washing, and the older maid's skeptical gaze landed on me, though she kept her questions silent.

"Lady Fyrn'sol requested your company for tea after you bid farewell to His Highness Ronan Draconis." Edith tugged my hair free of its braid, her tone careful. "Several high ladies are expected as well."

I rolled my shoulders and straightened my spine. It was better to deal with their whispers and accusations directly than let them fester behind closed doors.

Why couldn't Tallon stand by me for just one evening? Next time, I'd cling to his arm and stick to his side like a sucker fish.

I swallowed, my thoughts flickering to the king's words from last night. *Bastard.* Surely Scythe was right; it had to be a curse hurled in anger, nothing more.

There was so much about Radaan royalty that I now questioned. Across the seas, people knew there was no love lost between Queen Eldeiade and King Kallias. She'd died nearly two years ago, a victim of the same plague that had swept the palace. Yet after last night's talk of banishment, I wondered if there'd been more to their rift than mere estrangement. No king would idly threaten to exile his queen; it would tarnish not only his family but the kingdom's honor.

Radaan thrived on principles of honor and respect. Elohios, the god they worshiped, demanded no less from the royal line. I knew the basics of Radaanian beliefs, though religion held little place in Tallon's life—or so I'd been told—and so I hadn't prioritized it myself.

Scythe had slipped away that morning, intent on finding anything she could about the late queen. If there was truth in the king's capacity for violence, I needed to know if it extended to those in his path—particularly those close to his son.

I frowned at myself in the mirror. On the dance floor, Kallias behaved with an almost surprising warmth, the hint of a friendlier man beneath the iron mask. Cold, yes, and remote, but he didn't strike me as someone who would murder a wife. Or his son's future bride.

"A little longer, and you'll have permanent lines from that frown," Edith hummed, snapping me out of my thoughts.

I drew in a deep breath and let it out slowly, loosening the tension in my brow. "I'm just... concerned about the tea," I admitted, smoothing my hands over my dress.

"Princess, you were raised among dragons. A few high ladies with too much lace and perfume are hardly worth fretting over."

I scoffed and grinned, though a pang pulsed through me at her words. The beasts held more honesty than these courtiers, I was certain. At least a dragon wouldn't hesitate to show its teeth before going for the kill.

A hollowness settled in my chest. Soon I'd be saying goodbye to Ronan, to Gyrak, to the only pieces of home I had left.

"I still can't fathom why Prince Tallon abandoned me," I muttered, eyes drifting to the emeralds Edith pinned in my hair—reminding me of the green of Kallias' coat from last night.

"Perhaps he had other matters to attend to." Her lips thinned, though she didn't seem convinced by her own words.

The exchange I'd overheard told me otherwise. He had no affairs that mattered—at least, not according to his father.

"I'm sure it was important."

I forced the lie to sound easy, then rose as Edith helped me into a gown that shimmered like liquid sunlight. Golden fabric poured in graceful cascades with a slit on one side to keep it as functional as it was formal. Beneath, gold-toned breeches and leather boots kept me grounded in practicality. Thankfully, the hem hid them from view, allowing me to blend in with Radaan's style without losing myself.

Edith clicked her tongue, fingers tugging at the snug fabric that clung to my arms. Her pursed lips spoke volumes about her disapproval of my refusal to embrace the kingdom's bulbous-sleeved fashion.

But I was Draconis. No ridiculous, puffed-up sleeves would cover my shoulders.

Once she declared me presentable, I stepped out, my frustration flaring as guards fell into place beside me.

"The courtyard," I ordered, eyeing their steel-plated bodies. No amount of ornamental sunshine and forest-green paint could soften their rigid stances. Their heavy footfalls herded me forward like livestock.

I clenched my jaw, resolved to memorize the castle's winding corridors. The faster I learned, the sooner I could navigate on my own, free of the clamor and presence of armored shadows.

As I padded down the hall, thoughts of King Kallias crept back. He didn't travel with a pack of guards—only one. Maybe I could make the same request. A single guard I could get to know in this unfamiliar place, who might feel like a friend rather than a jailor.

The hallways unfurled in quiet beauty around me, each turn revealing lush greenery that softened the marble walls and polished floors. Vines had been trained to grow across the stone, their tangled paths like threads of living art. Small-leaved ivies mingled with massive fronds that stretched almost to my waist. Green tendrils, pulsing with life, reached for the sun filtering through stained glass windows, as if the plants themselves were straining against their confines. I understood that yearning too well—seeking sunlight, the freedom of open skies.

A pang of sorrow thudded through me, knowing I would likely never feel the rush of dragonflight again. I buried that ache, pushing it down with all the others. This was my place now, my duty. Whatever Tallon did or didn't do, I was still a princess, bound by everything I'd been trained to uphold.

Relief washed over me when I recognized the paintings at the end of the corridor. The guards hauled open the towering doors to reveal the courtyard—grand enough to receive a dragon.

Gyrak's massive maw filled my vision as I stepped forward, his teeth glinting as he lowered his head. I stopped short, grinning at the guards' startled mutters.

"I missed you, too." My hand rested on his warm, smooth scales.

He gave a contented rumble, one gleaming yellow eye turning to study my face, his gaze piercing yet comforting.

Ronan's voice cut through, laced with amusement. "I'd take a few steps back," he warned. "He sneezes—you're all kindling."

I scoffed, but the guards gave us some distance, shuffling for space.

Ronan adjusted his flight goggles, ruffling his light hair with a casual swipe. "You danced with the king."

Not a question. His steady gaze found mine, his usual irritation giving way to open concern. My little brother—ever watchful, ever loyal—was worried about me.

"Tallon was indisposed," I muttered, keeping my voice low.

Ronan's mouth twisted, and a muscle in his jaw feathered as his annoyance deepened. "Seems he's always missing when it matters," he growled. "I looked for him when the dance began—he was nowhere."

No, Kallias had to send his guard to drag his son from the shadows.

I forced a bright, practiced smile. "The treaty's between Radaan and Draconia. Trust me to do my duty, Ronan."

"You deserve better," he grumbled, pulling me into a fierce hug. "If it weren't for the whirlstorms–"

"I know. You'd stick around until I grew so sick of you I'd have to banish," my tongue slipped over the word, "banish you home."

He pulled back, eyes narrowed, but I cleared my throat and turned my attention to Gyrak, burying any stray emotion in the dragon's warm gaze.

"I will do this, Ronan. Father signed the treaty. Radaan and Draconia will be joined. A tardy prince won't stop it."

"Father would have the fleets brave the whirlstorms for you. Never forget that, Nienna."

A bittersweet smile tugged at my lips as I pushed a stray lock of his sand-colored hair from his brow. Always my protective little brother. "Go on, then. You're wasting daylight."

He snorted at my attempt to get rid of him, then wrapped me in another rib-crushing hug. I wheezed, sure he'd cracked something. When he pulled away, he flashed a bright smile, one that wiped the frown that had marred his handsome features.

"It's a good day to fly," he said, throwing his hand to the skies before sauntering over to his dragon's shoulder. "A kiss for luck?"

I chuckled as Gyrak brought his fangs within a hand's breadth of my face and waited. Shaking my head, I settled my palms on his scaled lips and gave him a quick peck on the nose. "Ride the winds. Fly fast. Take him home."

He trilled, lifting with a powerful stretch. Ronan barely had time to settle before the dragon launched, propelling skyward with a force that sent a string of curses from my brother—words more suited to a sailor than a prince.

A crack split through my heart, and tears pricked my eyes. I didn't know when I'd see him again. Next season—or years from now?

Straightening, I blinked all emotions back. When I faced the guards, my smile felt bright and proper, though I caught one still staring after Gyrak—likely in awe.

"Take me to Fyrn'sol."

They led me through the winding corridors, their armor clanking in a steady rhythm. It was unseemly, perhaps, to walk without a noble's escort, but I wanted to learn these halls. Idle chatter would only slow that goal.

Around a bend, they stopped short, stiffening in salute. I hesitated, stepping forward to peer past them.

King Kallias stood before me, his head inclined in a curt nod. "Princess."

I dipped into a curtsy, rising with a practiced smile. His gaze lingered, cool and discerning. Where he walked with a single guard—Greaves—I was trailed by four.

How unfair.

"Your Majesty," I replied.

His brows knit together, lending him an air of perpetual contemplation. The sparse stubble on his jaw seemed almost subversive, as if daring the court to follow his lead and leave their chins unshaven. The golden mantle gleamed in the bright light shining through the windows, its weight pressing against the deep green of his tailored jacket. He wasn't soft like the ambassadors who had frequented Draconia. He carried the stance of a soldier—coming off the heels of a war.

"You have no escort." Not a question—a flat statement, delivered in that low voice of his.

"I just came from seeing Prince Ronan off. Now I'm on my way to join Fyrn'sol for tea," I said in explanation.

The corner of his eye twitched, and he took a deep breath before extending his arm. "I will see you to her."

My heart sank.

Why did he keep offering to help me if I was nothing more than an inconvenience to him? Why did he treat me this way?

"Begging your pardon, Your Majesty, but I wouldn't want to steal you away from whatever pressing matters you're attending to." I forced the grin to stay on my lips, the curve never faltering.

His gaze flicked over the guards flanking me. "I have time."

Time enough to be encumbered by my presence.

I tried again, softening my smile and dipping my head. Perhaps if I played coy, he would leave me be. "I wouldn't want to be a burden."

"It is my duty to see to your needs."

It was Tallon's duty—not his.

And yet, he kept stepping in.

I swallowed the lump in my throat, placing my hand on his arm. "Thank you."

As he shifted, his fingers brushed the buckle at his belt. I resisted the urge to pull away. The subtle strength of his muscles moving under my grasp was far too familiar, too unnerving.

"Dismissed."

I glanced back as the guards dispersed, retreating down the corridor we had just crossed. Only Greaves trailed behind. I offered him a smile—which he staunchly ignored.

Kallias kept a steady pace, mindful of my shorter strides. My shoulder brushed his biceps—this close, I had to tilt my head to glimpse his frown-ridden face.

"Thank you for sparing my ears," I said. "Their armor is quite loud."

The furrow in his brow eased a fraction, and he nodded in understanding. "A necessary evil. Vellos signed a treaty, but precautions must remain to uphold it."

"Do you fear they'll withdraw?"

We turned down another passage. I was already lost.

"If I did, you would not be here." His lips pressed into a thin line, gaze averted from mine. "Still, I'll be relieved when you're wed. Dragons are a better deterrent than the clang of swords and armor."

I ducked my head, my fake smile faltering. His honesty surprised me. It was blunt—a far cry from what I expected from another kingdom's high court. Yet, it underscored my role. I wasn't a person to him—I was a tool of security.

"Three seasons, and dragons will patrol the Craggs," I said, forcing brightness into my tone.

Nine months. That was all the time I had to decipher Tallon's heart before our union sealed the treaty.

And still, he ran from me at every turn.

"The days should pass quickly," he replied.

I fought to keep my face neutral, stifling the disgust that rebelled in my mind. I didn't want hollow reassurances that we'd somehow get on. If anything, I appreciated his bluntness, and preferred if he'd admit to being eager for an heir.

Which reminded me of the conversation I had overheard, his words lingering. If Tallon was a true bastard, my child—and I—would have no claim to Radaan. It would be worse than being a spinster princess in Draconia.

We halted at a door, and Greaves darted ahead to open it, obscuring the fine details of the engraved wood. I mourned at the loss to study its beauty.

"Princess Nienna," the guard announced.

King Kallias gave me a gentle nudge. I released his arm, offering a smile to the women lounging inside, their porcelain cups clinking as they rose in a collective gasp of recognition. The room stirred with their hurried movement.

"Peace, ladies. I'll be on my way," the king said, stepping back with his usual calm. He faced me, voice soft. "Good day, Princess. Enjoy your tea."

Greaves cleared his throat, drawing Kallias' attention before he stepped into the hall.

"Thank you!" I called after them.

His guard fell in step behind him, and I watched the gold mantle sway against his back, the sound of his departure growing fainter. Somehow, he was the one man in the palace who both terrified me—and seemed to care for my wellbeing.

What a conundrum of feelings.

I returned my focus to the room, drawing in a slow breath. Faces marked with barely concealed skepticism, and distrust met mine.

Fyrn'sol emerged from the group, setting her teacup on a small table, and beckoned me in. "Please, come in, Your Highness! I beg your pardon—we had no idea the *king* would be escorting you! Quite the shock!"

Her kind eyes sparkled with mischief as she extended her hand, her voice warm. Dressed in a fine blue gown, sheer fabric spilled around her feet like waves on the shore. How she managed to walk in it was beyond me. Her blonde hair was piled high on her head, clear gems woven into the curls.

She guided me inside as a servant shut the door behind us. The women swarmed me with introductions—names and titles flying fast, each one competing for my attention. I committed as many as I could to memory, though the older women's wary glances stood out against the more eager stares of the younger nobles.

"It seems you've made quite the impression on the king, Princess," May'neer said, lifting a tiny cup to her lips. Cloudy gray eyes met mine over the rim, probing for answers.

"I was returning from saying goodbye to my brother," a dreamy sigh drew my attention to a young brunette, whose name escaped me, "and was found without escort."

"I sent one to your rooms!" Fyrn'sol gasped, pressing a hand to her chest as she lounged on a deep couch.

The women draped over the furniture like blankets, while I sat stiffly in the high-backed chair reserved for me, rigid and proper.

"Do you know when Prince Ronan might return?" the brunette asked, her eyes filled with hope.

Curse my brother. What had he been up to when he disappeared last night?

"Alas, I do not," I replied, shaking my head with a sympathetic smile.

"Not only did King Kallias escort you, but he danced with you," another older woman piped up from a nearby chair. She slumped to one side, as if sitting upright was too taxing for her plump frame. Gray hair curled around her face, attempting to be tamed in some sort of style, though I couldn't place how.

"And he received you at your first dinner."

"And she kissed him!" The last comment came from a younger woman, no older than her teens.

I shot her a sharp look of disapproval. "It was the Dragon's Kiss, a symbol of the alliance between our families." I kept my tone firm. "It was not an embrace of passion, but one of familial ties."

Though it *should* have been.

The girl faltered, her shoulders sagging under my pointed rebuke.

"Truth be told," an elderly woman said, "it seems Prince Tallon has been absent from a great many duties."

I bit my cheek, watching her pour steaming tea into a gold-rimmed cup, dropping two sugar cubes into the mix with deliberate care.

"King Kallias is filling in where the heir apparent avoids his responsibilities," she continued, then brought me the drink, her eyes warm and open.

I searched her gaze, trying to detect any malice, but she wore a bright grin, her expression more critical of the prince than of me.

"His Highness has a great many responsibilities to see to." Fyrn'sol threw a heated glance at the older woman, then reached over to place a pale hand over my own—her expression empathetic. "He was indisposed."

Indisposed in his cups. I held in my sigh.

"We will have plenty of time to get to know each other," I said, offering a nod that was more for show than belief. I took a sip of the tea, savoring the heat that spread through me.

I stayed with the women for several chimes while they discussed the intricacies of high court politics, absorbing names, places, and details that flitted through their conversation. No amount of royal study could prepare one for the realities of stepping into another kingdom, expected to know the subtle nuances of every discussion and gesture.

The younger noblewomen were easier to converse with—curious, eager to learn about Draconia and Ronan. The older women, however, held their judgment close. Their eyes were sharp, testing each word I spoke. I chose my replies with caution, sidestepping the unspoken jabs aimed at both me and Tallon.

Only once did I need to assert myself when a woman suggested the prince might have objected to the alliance.

"Noblewomen are not privy to the matters of kings," I'd said, my voice steady but firm. The words held weight, even if I tempered them with a careful calm.

She blanched, then a furious crimson overtook her face before she rushed to apologize. I smiled, accepting it with grace, then shifted the conversation to the sweltering heat of summer and the vacations various nobles were planning.

After what felt like an eternity of polite discourse, I was relieved when they announced that the tea was gone.

I rose, smoothing my skirts, and offered the women a smile. "Thank you for having me, however, I must retire to prepare for the evening meal."

Fyrn'sol nodded, offering her arm, and I linked mine with hers.

"It has been wonderful having your company! I'll see you to your rooms." She gave a nod of dismissal to the others. A chorus of goodbyes followed us, and two guards fell into step at our backs.

She heaved a sigh, her shoulders slumping a fraction. I couldn't help but let out a soft laugh, then tilt my head, curious.

"I daresay, some of those women have fangs instead of teeth," she muttered, rolling her eyes.

The gesture reminded me so much of Scythe that I had to swallow another laugh. "Older nobility always struggles with the next generation."

"They could lift others up instead of judging so harshly," she said with a half-grin, patting my hand again. "Call me Fyrn."

The Sol family had been the most welcoming of all the nobles, even if her parents could talk about nothing but goats.

"I wanted to tell you," she began, her voice softening as she glanced at me. "If you'd like to spend time with Tallon..."

I raised an eyebrow, prompting her to continue.

"He attends the midday council. King Kallias has ordered that he attend for the next week."

Ordered. Not requested.

I tucked that piece of information away to ponder later. "I would love to sit in."

"Allow me to escort you tomorrow. It would at least give you time to sit beside him," she offered, her voice dropping a notch. "He can't run from you there."

I laughed, my lips curving into a wide smile. "I like your thinking. Besides, It will be a welcome opportunity to learn more about Radaan."

"It's quite boring—a bunch of old men talking about trade and boundaries," Fyrn droned. "The perfect place for a nap."

A picture hanging on the wall snagged my notice, and I slowed—the scene so vivid it seemed to come alive. A warrior clad in gold plate fought a massive... *hog* for lack of a better word. Dead men littered the ground, their bodies forming gruesome piles. The golden warrior braced a spear against the earth, staring down the beast, nearly three times his height.

"Ah, the Great Hunt," Fyrn murmured, stopping with me to admire it.

"I've never heard of it," I breathed, drawn into the vibrant colors.

The white sun behind the beast cast a halo of light off the warrior's glowing armor. Upon closer inspection, I realized that the golden sheen wasn't just a reflection—it glowed, as if alive.

"Mammoths are rare these days, but when they wander into our borders, the king is summoned to deal with them," she explained.

I couldn't help but stifle a scoff. Kallias was called upon to handle a pest? She was quick to notice my shock.

"It's a rite of his title," she explained, her tone almost teasing, "his obligation to protect his people, and all that."

I shot her a look, caught off by her informal language, and she winked.

"There's far more exciting things than slaying a mammoth during a Great Hunt." Mischief sparked in her eyes again, that familiar glint that reminded me so much of Scythe. "Come, come!" She tugged on my arm, restless to move forward.

I hurried to match her pace, eager not to be left behind. I didn't want to curb her infectious energy. She was proving to be an ally here, and I needed all the friends I could get in this strange new kingdom.

Spinning down another hall, Fyrn pushed open a door and tugged me inside, slamming it shut on the guard's faces—or rather their helms.

Glee took years off her face as she snatched my hand and pulled me deeper into the room. It was a small library—or perhaps more of a study. Shelves stretched from floor to ceiling, each one crammed with books of every size. A massive desk sat in the center, sunlight pouring in from the window behind it, dust motes floating in the air like drifting leaves in an unseen breeze.

Fyrn dragged me further into the room, then waved toward a large painting that dominated one of the walls. It took me a moment to understand what I was looking at, and when it hit me, my cheeks burned with sudden heat.

"See?" A giggle escaped her lips as she noticed my blush. "Much more exciting!"

"I daresay. Is he wearing the mantle?" I asked, doing my best to keep my voice steady despite the flush that spread across my face. I wondered how long the couple had been in that position on the canopy bed for the artist to capture such an intimate moment.

"The Great Hunt is a test of Elohios. The celebration after is blessed by Veridis. After the death, it's required that life be celebrated." Fyrn's tone dripped with mischievous delight as she took too much pleasure in my discomfort. "One day, it may fall upon you to complete this task." She spoke as if informing me of an inevitable future duty.

"The queen is to wash the blood from the king's body." She paused dramatically, and I raised an eyebrow, urging her to continue. "All of it. Everywhere."

"And the likelihood that mammoths have been eradicated?" I squeaked, the very thought of such a task making my stomach churn.

"Unlikely." Fyrn grinned wide, her teeth flashing. She took my hand, and together we gazed at the painting. "It's so romantic."

A small sound of acknowledgment was all I could muster.

The king was smeared with blood, and a cloth dangled uselessly from the queen's fingers as she lay beneath him, her back arched, caught in a moment of passion. The furs wrapped around his hips alluded to some sense of modesty.

Paltry as it was.

"The late Queen Eldeiade demanded it be removed from the halls," Fyrn said.

I could imagine why—a matter of decency.

"She never completed the rite, leaving King Kallias to perform it alone."

A faint sorrow lingered in her voice, and I caught the sadness in her eyes as they flickered across the painting.

"It's an important tradition," she continued, then pinned her eyes on me. "I won't speak ill of the dead, but it didn't endear her to the people. King Kallias never had the love of his queen. He only had Radaan. Tallon will have more with you. He will learn to love you if you just give him a chance."

How many chances did he need?

Chapter Six

Nienna

The evening meal was torture—a slow bleed of patience and pride. I'd come to terms with marriage, even a loveless one, but nothing prepared me to be so blatantly ignored.

Tallon greeted me at the stairs with a charming smile, one that promised so much but delivered nothing. He led me to sit at his right, placing himself between me and the king. After that, he proceeded to ignore me for the rest of the evening, summoning nobles from the main floor to engage in idle banter, leaving me isolated. Every polite question I ventured met either a dismissive shrug or a smirk that chipped away at my resolve.

I stabbed my fork into my untouched dessert, a delicate piece of pie dusted with sugar and brimming with warm apples. The rich scent was heavenly, but my appetite soured under the weight of my irritation. I nudged it around my plate, lifting small bites to keep up appearances.

Tallon's voice rose over the din, smooth and melodic, lacking his father's thunderous command. Though a prince nearing manhood, he sounded like the young nobles at Draconia, all jest and bravado with little substance. Only a year younger than me, he held an entire kingdom in his hands; shouldn't that burden have molded him into something more substantial?

"You can ride out tomorrow to see them!" A noble, all grins and eagerness, blurted, his brown hair unruly.

"I'd love that!" Tallon leaned back, teeth flashing in a broad smile. "Send for me at the tenth hour."

I waited, poised, yet invisible.

"Perfect! Father will be pleased!"

I waited still.

The prince laughed, his attention unwavering. "The palace could always use more hounds. You can never have too many."

"A breed of retriever from Draconia excels at hunts," I interjected, my voice steady as I met the noble's surprised stare.

Tallon twisted toward me, his polite smile fixed, but the warmth in his emerald gaze chilled into guarded stone.

I forged on. "They brave rough waters to catch rock gulls. I would love to see–"

"I'm sure you'd prefer to spend your time picking through gems or fine clothes over muddy hounds, Princess."

The rebuke struck, sharp and unyielding, but I held my expression—a practiced mask of serenity—as the sting settled into silence. Tallon watched, eyes searching, a slight twitch at his lips.

A smile. Not a sneer. It had to be.

"On the contrary, I would love to see them." My tone remained even. I would not yield.

"Kaden, when is feeding time?" His gaze pinned mine, unwavering, his challenge unspoken yet clear. Two royals locked in a battle of smiles and silence, testing boundaries in a hall full of masks.

What a finely spun farce.

"At the seventh hour Your High–"

"Make sure they're fed something live. I'll be there to watch." Tallon's sneer lifted his nose, barely concealing a snarl. "Off with you."

My smile slipped, unwilling to humor his rude dismissal of the noble any longer.

"There will be bloodshed, Princess." His voice dropped as Kaden'lon bowed and hurried down the stairs. "Best you stay here—it wouldn't do to have you faint in front of the commoners."

"I was raised among dragons, dear Prince. A bit of blood doesn't faze me," I replied, sweetness threading through each word, though the effort strained my patience. "And those of Lon descent are hardly commoners."

If he was going to take public jabs with his words, I would hand them right back. His head tilted, amusement flickering in his eyes, but I saw the edge in his smirk. Forcing a smile, I fought the ache in my cheeks as he met my defiance with a scoff, shrugging a shoulder.

"So be it." He turned to the hall, leaning over his plate. His overcoat dipped into his dessert as he beckoned to another nobleman.

My shoulders slumped a fraction, and I took a deep breath to steady myself. When I lifted my gaze, I caught King Kallias' eyes—clear blue like Draconia's skies, and just as piercing. His stare weighed on me, and warmth crept over my face, unmasking my irritation and anger toward his son. His brows remained drawn in contemplation, a muscle working in his jaw. When his attention shifted to Tallon, he released me from his scrutiny. I glanced back down, nudging a piece of apple that had slipped free from my pie, counting each passing minute until I could escape this charade.

Edith stayed in my rooms that night. When dawn broke, Scythe roused herself to help ready me in the soft gray light. She handed me a slice of fresh bread, its crust still warm, smeared with a thick spread of berry-red jam. The tang paired well with the smooth bitterness of the black tea I sipped, its faint steam curling into the cool air as Edith's hands moved in deft twists, braiding my hair with gentle, practiced tugs.

Today, I'd don a gown to retain my femininity—but not without a reminder for Tallon. If he wanted me to watch hounds rip apart prey, he'd see me as I was—a descendant from Dragon Riders.

When Edith retired, Scythe helped me dress in a pair of thin dark breeches beneath a gown crafted like a masterful painting. Deep sapphire hugged my chest and gave way to swirls of burgundy that ended in crimson spilling over my black boots.

"As if you would shy from a little blood." Scythe snickered, her words laced with a smirk as she fastened a ruby necklace around my throat.

"If only Tallon could see Argos feed," I scoffed.

My father's dragon sired a brood each year, and he raised them until they could hunt on their own. Every feeding, he brought in a mid-sized whale, tearing it apart until bloody entrails scattered the ground—a gory feast for his dragonlings. Their hunger blurred any distinction between friend and foe. I'd seen it firsthand because Dragon Queen Kalepsi named me Dragon's Heart the day I was born, a bond that marked me for life.

Scythe sighed, eyes gleaming with a dreamlike hue. "I imagine Tallon would have a change of tune if he were slapped with a bloody organ or two."

I laughed, tossing my braid over my shoulder as I spun to see my reflection. The colors, the dark strength of the outfit—it was perfect.

Without waiting to be summoned, I headed to the door. It was half past the sixth hour, and I didn't trust *His Highness* to remember to call for me. When I entered the hall, the guards snapped to attention, one turning my way.

"Take me to Prince Tallon," I said with a soft smile.

I tried to glimpse his eyes behind the narrow visor, but he was cast in darkness. With a curt nod, he pivoted, metal armor clinking, and started down the corridor. I followed in silence, pressing my lips together. I needed to talk to King Kallias about these guards—soon, they'd feel like shackles.

Early morning quietness hung in the air as I walked. Shafts of pale sunlight stretched across the halls, illuminating paintings, plants, and carved relics that I mentally mapped as we passed. Here and there, staff moved with swift determination, bowing or curtsying as we went by. The nobles, of course, still slept.

The guard led us out into the already warm air of the courtyard.

I knew it.

A gathering of horses filled the space, all flanked by guards. Among them stood a striking black steed adorned with scarlet tack, its coat gleaming in the sunlight. Birds darted overhead, their songs cutting through the thick silence. Tallon broke from his conversation with the king, his eyes snapping to me as I dismissed my guard and crossed the courtyard. I lifted my chin, skimming their faces, my smile laced with venom I refused to hide. The prince didn't mask his irritation either; his fists clenched tight, his frown a deep furrow.

Kallias, however, studied me with—was that approval in his gaze? His eyes swept over my split dress, pausing with a hint of scrutiny before rising back to my face. A slight tilt of his head showed curiosity.

"Princess Nienna," Tallon hissed. He actually hissed.

I would marry him, a man I didn't know, one who ignored me. But I'd be no man's doormat.

Kallias' brows snapped together, his glare fixed on his son. "Princess Nienna, bright morning." Sunlight glinted off his mantle, scattering the rays. "What brings you out at this hour?" The king, it seemed, had mastered the art of civility.

"Prince Tallon invited me to witness Kaden'lon's hounds at the hunt," I replied, letting my smile sharpen as I turned to the prince. "It appears he forgot to send for me."

"I also forgot to prepare a horse for you." Tallon grinned. "Perhaps next time."

"Prince Tallon." The king straightened, his frame stiff with a glare so frigid it could cut steel. "Royalty of Radaan do not lie."

The depth, the rage that darkened his father's voice sent a shiver down my spine. *Never lie to Kallias.* I tucked that truth away.

Tallon's eyes narrowed, his lashes lowering with an agonizing slowness as though resisting the urge to roll them.

"Then I'll travel with a single guard," Tallon muttered, waving a dismissive hand at the two guards waiting beside their mounts.

I glanced at the beasts, a flicker of nerves stirring within.

"After the council meeting, see to the temple," Kallias added, his voice edged with a sharp note. His fierce gaze locked with mine, and my smile softened—whether out of gratitude or unease, I couldn't tell. His jaw clenched, a muscle flickering beneath his skin, before he turned and strode toward a garden in full bloom, his guard trailing in silence.

Tallon released an exasperated breath. "Do you ride astride, *Princess?*"

I bared my teeth in a smile laced with mock sweetness. "I ride horses as well as dragons, *Prince.*"

"Always with the dragons."

"It's a good reminder," I murmured. *For both of us.* I rode with my father and brother—in parades. To be frank, I didn't have the same bond with horses as I did with the mighty beasts that took to the skies.

Tallon snorted, motioning to a horse. His guard knelt, offering me a foothold. The black stallion met my gaze, neck arched, nostrils flaring as it stamped a hoof. Shoving my nerves aside, I gathered my skirts and grabbed the reins as I stepped into the guard's waiting hands, his expression one of patient indifference. As he hoisted me up, I slid a leg over the saddle, adjusting my dress as the beast sidestepped beneath me.

With only a hum of amusement, Tallon mounted and nudged his stallion forward, leading us out of the courtyard. The remaining guard cast a brief glance my way, his gaze unreadable, darkened by the shadow of his helm, before he followed the prince into the sunlight. Teeth gritted, I pressed my heels into the horse and it surged, eager to match pace with the others.

I was no burden. Not some tool to be left behind. I was a princess.

The ride through the outer palace grounds and city streets blurred in a flurry of movement. The horse's antics kept my focus split—its neck arched, its steps jerking between a trot and the hint of a canter, as if it longed to break free. Each time I adjusted my grip, my lips pressed into a stubborn line, determined not to lose control.

The city fell away faster than expected. A few short minutes brought us from the palace courtyard, through the bustling streets, and beyond the walls. Fields rolled out, stretching wide and open, green waves that rippled under the day's first light. Dew evaporated as the sun rose higher, a faint mist lifting from the earth, drifting skyward.

Tallon let his horse break into a full gallop. Grateful for the release, I allowed mine to follow in a swift canter. Though the pace jostled me, it seemed to calm the stallion, and I caught a flicker of amusement in Tallon's gaze, his silent dare hanging between us.

Kaden'lon's family estate soon emerged, a low sprawl of stone and timber, the braying of hounds reaching us well before we turned onto the drive. Their yelps and barks filled the air, and the scent of damp earth mixed with the warm musk of animals. Servants moved about, some carrying bundles, others herding dogs toward the large house.

Like many of Radaan's buildings, the Lon residence stretched outward, long and low rather than towering. Shadowed in the early light, it wrapped around itself, concealing inner courtyards from view. Sunlight skimmed over its sturdy walls, the structure seeming to fold into the land rather than rise above it.

Kaden emerged from the house, his smile broad, exuding an almost childlike delight. Loose tan trousers and an unlaced white tunic revealed more collarbone than decorum might demand, though he seemed oblivious—or worse, indifferent—to my presence as he greeted us. A flush crept over his cheeks when his gaze met mine, his casual attire sending an unwelcome jolt of surprise through me. He knew I was coming. He couldn't bother with a proper coat?

"Good morn!" he called, blushing when he glanced my way.

"Morn!"

Tallon dismounted, tossing the reins to his guard. He strode forward, embracing Kaden with a broad smile, turning the man back toward his house, their conversation dropping to a low murmur. The young noble twisted, peeking over his shoulder, his features burning a richer shade of red.

A hot wave of humiliation crashed through me, leaving a bitter taste. My betrothed, a prince, discarded me like rubbish, abandoning me to dismount alone. The indignity cut deeper than mere neglect—it was deliberate. It was insulting.

The guard edged the horses closer, perhaps sensing my intent. I dismounted with practiced ease and landed with a crisp thud. Tallon's eyes flicked my way, and my glare followed him, a sharp reminder that I hadn't missed the slight.

My boots ate up the ground with brisk strides. I swept past them as a steward rushed to open the door, bowing as I approached.

When the men caught up with me, I allowed my tone to bleed with all the venom I could muster. "I do believe it's feeding time?"

Tallon met my stare with practiced indifference—impervious to the fire behind my eyes.

In the kennels, the prince treated me as little more than a shadow, a mere inconvenience in his domain. I stood beside him, unacknowledged, as we watched the dogs tear into live rabbits—a grim display that left the air thick with snapping jaws and a sharp, metallic scent. I glanced his way, eyebrows raised, as he shot me a look, perhaps expecting me to pale or shrink back like some highborn lady.

Kaden's mother, Jianth'lon, refused to set foot in the kennels during feedings. She had even tried to tempt me away with promises of tea, but I declined. I wanted to show Tallon that I could face his world, brutal though it was, without hesitation.

I was his betrothed, bound by duty to forge peace between our nations. Despite his apathy, I pushed forward, determined to make this alliance more than a hollow arrangement. He, however, shrugged off my every effort, leaving a slow, bitter anger simmering beneath my skin.

Hours later, as we returned to the palace, my mind lingered on the moment when I pointed out a hound that hesitated to eat its prey, saying how it might make a good hunting companion. Tallon *laughed*—an outright, genuine, mocking laugh. The memory blazed, filling my vision with a wash of red.

The horse tensed beneath me, picking up on my fraying patience and drifting focus. Then, with a sudden jolt, it bolted, tearing down the road in a frenzy of pounding hooves and flaring nostrils.

My riding lessons had been safe, confined to parades within city walls or leisurely outings with my family. I had never galloped, never felt a creature surge beneath me with this wild, reckless force.

And so, in my panic, I made the most foolish decision—I dropped the reins.

My arms locked around the horse's thick neck, my fingers digging into its rough coat. A startled curse left my lips as its head jerked up, cracking against mine with a force that sent stars bursting across my vision. Behind me, Tallon's whoop rang out, mocking and exuberant, as we careened forward.

I squinted against the wind and the sting of coarse mane whipping my face. My teeth clashed hard, snapping down on my tongue, and a metallic warmth seeped into my mouth. I spat the blood, cursing the beast beneath me as it thundered toward the distant city.

I'd ridden dragons—beasts that made this creature seem tame in comparison. My father or brother always sat behind me, their hands firm on my waist. If I could ride a creature that feasted on horses, I could surely keep my seat on one.

Blinking against the blur, I focused on staying balanced, ignoring the horse's joyful grunts as it pounded over the road. A single slip would send me hurtling toward the ground, leaving no hope of recovery against the hard-packed earth.

I reached for the leather strap snapping in the wind, fingers brushing close, desperate to catch the reins. If I could gain just enough control, I'd steer the beast in tight circles until it tired itself out.

The horse stumbled as I stretched, throwing me off-balance. My stomach lurched, and I slipped sideways, clinging to a handful of mane with one arm while I tightened my leg over its back, clinging to its side. I gritted my teeth, cursing my own stupidity as I dangled, muscles straining to keep my hold.

We barreled through the city gates, the din of startled shouts and cries swelling around us. I blocked out everything but the raw burn in my leg, clamping down with every ounce of strength I had left. The stables lay ahead, and if the beast kept running, I might just hang on that far.

My grip wavered, fingers sinking deeper into the black mane, ready to yank out a fistful with me if I fell. But then a second set of hooves drummed close beside us. My heart leapt in my chest as another rider closed in, their horse steady and sure at our side. My mount shied as they leaned in, catching the reins as it whipped past.

"Whoa," they murmured, his voice calm and coaxing.

They eased the horse's pace until we fell into a rough trot, the black beast's wild energy ebbing.

My legs gave way, and I slipped.

Something snared me by my waist, hauling me upright, crushing me to a broad chest—the rider steadied both horses into the courtyard. My legs dangled, feet brushing the side of the horse, while I clutched his arm as though it were a lifeline.

"Thank you!" The words escaped in a breathless squeak, and I ducked under his jaw as he glanced over the expanse.

"Greaves."

The single name struck like a hammer, freezing my pulse in horror.

The king's guard rode up, dark eyes blazing as he seized the runaway horse's bridle, yanking it aside with barely restrained fury. He glared at the animal, his jaw set, refusing me even a glance.

Kallias shifted beneath me, his powerful thigh flexing as he dismounted in one fluid motion that carried us both to the ground. He caught my weight as I staggered against him, savoring the last seconds I had before I forced myself to look up.

Shame burned my cheeks as my gaze met his glacial blue stare, shadowed and stern beneath a furrowed brow. His fingers brushed the corner of my mouth, a thumb grazing where blood clung to my skin, his jaw clenched in outrage.

I swallowed, stepping back to steel myself, then lifted my chin. "The horse got away from–"

"Where is Tallon?" he interrupted, the quiet command in his voice sharper than a shout.

I sucked in a sharp breath, my nerves morphing into irritation. "Your *son* was offering exclamations of excitement as my steed tore off, *Your Majesty.*" I snarled. If he wanted to cut me off, so be it. I could be just as rude.

His eye twitched, his grip tightening, reminding me he still held me close.

"Are you well?" he asked, the faintest pause before his gaze flicked down my disheveled dress.

"Well enough," I shot back, stepping away, my shoulders squared. "Perhaps next time, consider a better trainer for your war horses."

"You made it!"

Tallon's voice cut through the tension, drawing our attention. He and his guard entered the courtyard, his grin faltering as he noticed his father standing by my side.

"That beast is the fastest in the stables—no way we could've caught him." He laughed, the sound as casual as if we'd all shared some harmless joke.

"You–"

Kallias' hand clamped onto my arm before I could unleash the retort gathering on my tongue. I turned, ready to shake him off, to rage against his interference—but the fury seething in his gaze stilled me. Raw, controlled wrath blazed across his face as he released me, stalking toward his son.

"Down."

The single, frigid word left the prince white-faced, and he slid from the saddle without protest. Kallias loomed over him, one hand gripping his shoulder in a punishing grasp, his fingers digging deep until Tallon winced. The king leaned close, his voice too low for me to hear, his expression lethal.

Whatever he said, it transformed the prince's gaze, his once-sharp eyes narrowing as they found mine. I shivered beneath the venom in his stare.

Now I understood what Ronan meant when he warned me of Tallon's immaturity. But couldn't my brother have warned me of the extent of his stupidity? He was more than a spoiled brat—he was cruel, with a streak of malice that ran deep. I wanted nothing to do with him or his kind.

Kallias' grip tightened, drawing a grunt from his son before allowing him to shrug free. The prince slunk back, his defiance blunted by his father's warning, but the king didn't spare him another glance.

He turned to me instead, the golden yoke at his neck swaying with his movement. His jaw flexed as he closed the distance, his steps deliberate, carrying an unspoken command I could feel settle in the air. For the first time, I hoped he'd dismiss me—to order me to my chambers, away from Tallon and his dark moods. I longed for the safety of my rooms and the loyal presence of my handmaidens.

The king's gaze softened for a fraction, as if he sensed the exhaustion beneath my composure. He jerked his chin toward the palace in silent agreement, and I turned at his side, leaving Tallon behind. Kallias' hand rested at the small of my back, his touch steady, guiding me farther from the prince.

Away from the man I was supposed to marry.

Hours later, with my face washed and fresh clothes free of horse hair and sweat, I slipped out of my chambers. Edith protested in vain, but I ignored her, gliding past as I left. If Tallon attended council meetings, so would I. I might despise him for his cruelty, but he was the future king of Radaan, and I intended to rule beside him, not waste away as some broodmare forgotten in the shadows.

Not once had he checked on me, not a single message sent. My vague report had ignited Scythe's fury; she threatened to slip herbs into his wine, enough to keep him at the chamber pot till dawn, but I managed to restrain her—not that it wasn't tempting.

Yesterday, I maintained a quiet resolve to charm him, to unearth some common ground where friendship might root, if nothing else. That plan now felt as insubstantial as morning mist.

A guard swung open the door, and I strode through, chin lifted, eyes scanning the room. Heavy with polished wood and gilt trim, the chamber held a grand oval table, its expanse surrounded by chairs, some unoccupied and lined in neat rows nearer the doors for any nobles who cared to observe.

At the head, Kallias loomed, gesturing to a map laid open across its surface. His eyes caught mine mid-sentence, his hand pausing above the land's sprawled illustration, his gaze shifting with an unspoken question. Around him sat noblemen and a few dignitaries, their robes rich and refined. The prince, however, lounged back in a seat apart from the others, positioned with a young noble, Fyrn'sol at his side.

Fyrn spotted me and, with an inviting smile, scooted over to make space by Tallon. I took a steadying breath and approached, hiding the instinct to ask her to place herself between us.

"...and Edon's men will be needed for the harvest." Kallias' voice resumed, redirecting my attention.

His gaze hadn't left me—watchful, unyielding. I offered him a slight bow of acknowledgment before slipping into the empty seat beside Tallon, my presence ignored as he confided with the noble on his other side.

He bristled as I tucked my skirts close to be sure we weren't touching. The thought that this cruel, shallow *boy* might one day share my bed made my skin crawl.

"I'm glad you came!" Fyrn whispered, leaning in.

She smelled of roses and wore a low-cut pink gown, her hair falling in loose curls over her shoulders. Her fingers wrapped around mine, giving a gentle squeeze. I returned her smile, and, feeling Tallon's eyes on me, lifted my gaze to meet his cold stare with a grin as false as his own. The nobleman on his other side edged over a fraction, sensing the tangible animosity between us.

I leaned back with a smirk as if to say, *You'll need to try harder if you want to scare me away*, then settled into my chair with the intent of absorbing whatever I could from the council meeting.

To be fair, it was a boring ordeal. It soon became clear the gathering would be more tedious than enlightening. Tallon and his companion barely paused in their quiet but persistent chatter about an upcoming horse race, their voices filling the space around us and drowning out what little sense I could make of the council's proceedings. From the bits I managed to catch, the conversation centered on preparations for the harvest and the allocation of soldiers across Kallias' lands.

Why would the king's forces need to assist with crop collection? Did he use his army for common labor during harvest, or were there troubles brewing beneath the surface of these mundane orders? But each time my attention focused, Tallon's prattle about some magnificent steed named Fleetfoot disrupted any understanding I might glean.

"Darius, when is the ambassador from Vellos to arrive?" Kallias' firm voice cut through, pulling my focus back to him.

"He is due next week, Your Majesty." Darius, sturdy as a mountain, inclined his head in acknowledgment. He wore his years like a seasoned warrior, short white hair and beard giving him the air of an elder general, though I had yet to confirm his rank.

Kallias' eyes flicked to me before resting on his son, then back to the table. "The treaty demands we accommodate the ambassador's needs," he said, bracing himself on his hands as he studied the map, "but that doesn't mean he has free rein. I want two guards shadowing him at all times—and an additional guard posted at Princess Nienna's hall."

I straightened, unable to keep silent. "Surely the six stationed there are sufficient?" I'd counted them myself, those hulking shadows standing at every door and corridor. A seventh seemed superfluous. I already felt like a bird caged in steel.

The king's gaze pinned me in place—an impenetrable wall of glacier-blue. "Another guard will be stationed at your hall," he replied, a flat command. The tone held no give, no invitation for argument.

I sank back in my seat, holding his stare, though inside I seethed. One more set of eyes felt as pointless as the rest; what could he add to the watch they already kept?

Kallias returned to the map, his jaw tight as he dismissed the meeting. "If he arrives with an entourage, deny them entry." His gaze darkened, his lips pressed thin. "Until tomorrow."

He pushed off the table, that ever present golden mantle swaying with his movements as he left. Greaves followed. They offered no further acknowledgement of our presence.

He was the king, after all. He had places to be.

"Free at last." Tallon stretched, a gesture lacking the dignity expected of a prince. A lock of hair fell over his brow as he gave Fyrn—not me—a sly smirk.

I swallowed my pride. "Would you take me to the temple?" The words tasted bitter. He was the last person I wanted to ask for anything, but Fyrn's hopeful presence reminded me of my attempts to make this arrangement bearable.

He wrinkled his nose as though I'd suggested mucking stables. "What for? It's filled with dusty crooks who cling to the old ways. They'd sooner control the throne than serve it. I'm retiring—and you'd do well to do the same."

His insolence struck deep. This was more than mere arrogance; he was defying his father's order with a smug satisfaction, assuming I'd follow like a meek child.

I turned to Fyrn instead, keeping my voice light. "Fyrn, would you mind escorting me in his stead?"

Color bloomed over her cheeks as her gaze darted to Tallon, but she dipped her head and nodded. "It would be my pleasure."

With that, we rose, smoothing our skirts as we moved for the door, leaving the prince behind without another look.

He didn't deserve a second glance.

Chapter Seven

KALLIAS

She would meet the Velli. There was no changing that. The treaty would stand, for now. The ambassador would tread with care, mindful of the significance his actions carried, but the thought of what could happen if it all fell apart gnawed at me. If the treaty broke before Tallon and Princess Nienna's union, I couldn't predict how Draconia would react. Would they take sides—leave us to face the consequences alone?

A slow breath escaped me as I walked down the sunlit corridor, my gaze catching on a servant watering the plants that lined the eastern hall. Their bright green leaves shimmered under the streams of water, a stark contrast to the agitation curling in my chest. The more I observed Nienna, the more my unease grew.

She was fire—a wild thing easily extinguished by the wrong hands. And Tallon, with his mother's arrogance and his own reckless nature, was more than capable of snuffing out that spark. I feared what he would do to her—how he would suffocate her spirit under the strain of his pride, smother it under those ridiculous heeled boots.

The image of her clinging to the horse as they entered the city gates shot through my mind, pulling my seething rage to the surface. His immaturity nearly got her killed. His thoughtlessness and disregard for others was dangerous. It had to be curbed.

Never having seen war, he had no idea how to lead men into battle, where their lives hung by a thread. He didn't understand the weight of walking across fields soaked in blood, the earth squelching beneath boots, knowing every step might be his last. The stakes were beyond him, and it seemed he didn't care. If he truly did, he wouldn't act like a spoiled child. Radaan was too fragile to endure another war—not with him at the helm.

I stepped out of the palace, drawing in the fresh air as the sun's warmth seeped through my clothes. The world lightened—if only for a moment. I was doing what I could with the cards Eldeiade dealt me.

Nienna was headed toward a loveless marriage, much like my own. But I had learned to suffer it for the sake of my kingdom. She would too, in time.

Eldeiade had been a match chosen by my father—a high noblewoman from our western border. She was polite enough. Or perhaps I'd been naïve. Maybe she was simply skilled at feigning kindness. Regardless, after the wedding, I realized the truth of the monster I married.

It was one thing to face my people's criticism. The mocking words of councilmen, though painful, I could bear. But to have the person I trusted to stand by me become the one to drive every cruel jab deeper—it was a betrayal I hadn't prepared for.

Siring an heir became a task I wanted to wipe my hands of. After my parents died, it turned into a grim ritual. Each month, she summoned me like a stud to her stable—a call I couldn't evade.

Eyes closed, I let my steps guide me through the garden, following the path to the temple that lay between the palace and the city.

Guilt pricked at me as I remembered the relief I'd felt when Vellos launched its first attack on our border. Skirmishes flared at first, letting me time my visits to avoid her. Then the situation tightened. We sought peace, but Vellos demanded land. Emissaries came to the palace. We scrutinized them at every turn, searching for any opening to end the conflict without bloodshed.

Then Eldeiade called for me. I was within Reem's city walls, not during the appointed week, yet still close enough to be bound to answer her summons.

The next month, she announced her pregnancy with Tallon.

I never cared whose blood ran in his veins. He grew up as mine, raised to inherit Radaan's throne. Eldeiade kept him close—a lioness, pulling him into her orbit, guarding him. Until her death, he trailed her skirts like a lost pup, unaware or unwilling to venture beyond her reach.

The temple's cool shade enveloped me, its chill like the hand of Elohios easing the weight from my shoulders. Priests noticed my approach and slipped back into the alcoves, leaving the temple quiet. No doors barred entry. Elohios demanded an open house, welcoming all to his justice and truth. I paused inside, letting my gaze settle over the simplicity of the room.

Greaves began the slow work of unlatching my yoke—his presence a constant, loyal shadow. The limestone floor, bare and plain, stretched toward the altar where Elohios stood carved in stone. Sword raised in one hand, scales balanced in the other, he surveyed the barren hall, his fierce gaze a silent judge poised over the souls who entered.

Red linen hung along the walls, casting a deep warmth over the room's austerity. When Greaves lifted the mantle from my shoulders, I took one of the tight-rolled crimson mats from a woven basket near the entryway.

He set my yoke on the altar, and stepped aside, keeping a silent vigil while I approached the shrine. Before Elohios, I was no king—simply a man like any other. We stood as equals in the eyes of the god, judged by faith alone. I spread the mat and lowered myself, knees protesting as they met the unforgiving stone.

A slow breath steadied me as I bowed my head, my heart open in silent prayer.

Tallon never came.

Chapter Eight

NIENNA

We caught sight of Greaves near the temple's entrance, hand resting on the simple dagger at his hip. Twin hilts jutted from behind his shoulders, and he nodded to us as we passed.

"The king prays at midday, every day," Fyrn murmured.

To our right, the gardens sprawled in a riot of color—fragrance so thick it drenched the air. The fields outside the city shimmered green with new growth, but here? This place flourished in a wild display, each flower bursting in unique shades and shapes. I doubted I'd ever learn their names. Thousands of blossoms stretched toward the sky, bending to the care of servants who worked in steady rhythm, hands dark with soil, voices lifted in quiet, melodic hums as they planted, weeded, and coaxed life from the earth.

To our left, a pale wall rose, separating the palace grounds from the city of Reem. The temples sat embedded in its stone—not towering, gaudy structures, but understated and graceful.

A warrior statue loomed with sword raised where Greaves stood. The next temple's entrance bore the figure of a woman, seated with one hand outstretched in quiet welcome.

"Every day?" I asked as she slowed. "Quite the religious man."

"Some say he started as a reprieve," she leaned in, her voice a near-whisper, "to escape the late queen."

A dry chuckle escaped. The king needed an excuse to slip away? From a woman? More likely, he'd silence her with a glare if she spoke out of turn.

Or banish her.

I cleared my throat, eyes drifting over the smaller temples. "So, which god does Tallon worship?"

"The prince? He doesn't."

My gaze narrowed. "Yet his father prays daily?"

"He doesn't take after the king," Fyrn said, tugging me further from the warrior's temple. "He stayed close to the late queen, hardly left her side. She doted on him, raised him while King Kallias fought the war."

I glanced back over my shoulder, and Greaves caught my eye before dipping his chin. So Tallon took after his mother—a truth that explained much about his strained bond with Kallias. Would he ever mirror his father?

I could only hope.

"Men worship Elohios," Fyrn continued, steering me toward the statue depicting the woman. "If women follow religion, they seek Veridis, the Mother of All Living."

"And what of the others?" I asked, peering down the path to the temples fading into the distance.

She took my hand, guiding me closer to the temple's entryway. "Vallor, Inneki, Cersi—the rest are lesser gods who serve the Mother and Father."

When we reached the entrance, I marveled at the beauty etched into the statue's face—her eyes bright with a fierce, playful wisdom. Though chiseled from rock, her gaze brimmed with life, and her lips held a sly, inviting smile. Wind seemed to press against her, tugging at her carved gown—one thin enough to leave little to the imagination. Every fold of fabric and strand of hair so meticulous that it stirred awe in me.

"I'd like to know the artist," I said, dipping into a low bow before the statue, trying to mirror their reverence. If the Radaan worshiped these gods, I could at least be cordial.

"The one who carved Veridis?" Fyrn sank into a curtsy beside me. "I'm sure it's in the records somewhere. You favor art then?"

As we approached the main doors, the guards behind us eased their pace. For a moment, I wondered if this was the single place—besides my rooms—where I might escape them.

"I do. Paintings tell entire stories. Statues like that one hold worlds. Tomes capture emotions." I paused, catching her amused smile. "I plan to devour every piece of art Radaan offers."

She tilted her head, an eyebrow raised with interest. "Then I'll show you the best of them," she said, adding a wink before guiding me inside.

Fyrn flung the door open, and my breath caught. The interior stretched out before me, soft and welcoming. The last temple I'd seen, or glimpsed, had been cold and rigid. This one, by contrast, felt warm, inviting.

Two priestesses paused, their gazes lingering on us as I took in the room. Pink, a blush as delicate as rose petals, colored the walls, laced with gilded veins. Flowers, not cut but alive, hung from the ceiling, their vines trailing down to pots suspended along the walls, their fragrance sweet and intoxicating.

At the room's head, twin doorways, draped in sheer white tapestries, led beyond. At their center, the altar seized my focus, commanding my attention.

An undeniable pull tugged me closer. Fyrn moved ahead, eager to introduce us to the priestesses, but I stood frozen, captivated. A statue depicting a woman heavy with child, sat cross-legged, cradling a delicate seedling in her hands. Its gilded roots stretched downward, woven into the marble, which was shot through with gold veins—an artistry I'd never encountered.

Though there were many things I'd never seen before.

The woman atop the altar mirrored the same alluring, mischievous beauty of the figure beckoning at the temple's entrance. The craftsmanship was identical—every strand of her hair brushing against her face, almost concealing her soft grin.

"Would she like a fur?"

My gaze flickered between Fyrn and the older woman. Middle-aged, with smile lines around her warm brown eyes, she stood with quiet authority. The younger priestess, still a girl, peered from behind her.

I softened my expression with a small shake of my head. "In Draconia, we worship no gods. Beyond the might of the dragons, we live and breathe by the sweat of our brow."

"Veridis watches over all, even those of another faith," the older priestess replied, dipping her chin. "I am Vama. Should you require assistance, do not hesitate to ask." She stepped back, ushering the young girl away through a nearby doorway.

"The dragons are mighty in their own right," Fyrn said, her eyes scanning the room.

"If we have gods, they are the ones we listen to," I replied, stepping toward the wall to inspect a painting of a woman embracing a child in a sunlit field.

"Yes, listen to them," she giggled, her tone light, "or get eaten."

I chuckled, trailing my finger along a vibrant leaf, green streaked with pink, the blotches like splatters of paint. "True."

"They say you were raised in the Nest, among their own babies."

"I was," I said with a quiet shrug. "Though it's not nearly as exciting as it's made out to be."

I followed the vine's winding path, my fingers brushing the textured painting on the wall—a seed and a child, one tethered to the earth by roots, the other connected to its mother through the cord of life.

"It must have been dangerous."

I nodded, more to myself than to her. "The dragon queen—she rules the Nest—allowed my mother to birth me there. Other females lay only with her permission. She oversees all broods—like an aunt or grandmother. She took me under her wing, refusing to let me leave for my first year of life."

"Isn't it in a high tower? I've seen the paintings!" Fyrn shivered, and I chuckled at her discomfort.

"It's quite exposed to the elements, yes. But there was no safer place for me than tucked against her side."

"Your mother's?"

"The dragon's."

Her face twisted with shock and horror. I laughed, throwing my head back. She didn't even try to hide it.

Blinking, she snapped her mouth shut, offering me a tight smile. "And your title as the Dragon's Heart?"

"A title only. The queen welcomed me, and my father rides Argos—the largest male in Draconia. Because of that, I was accepted by all dragons. They tolerated far more than they should have when I was younger." I sighed, glancing back at the guards in their gleaming armor. My smile wavered. "One day, I'll tell you how I chased a full-grown Argos out of the Nest."

She shuddered, but stepped forward, guiding me outside. Tallon might be a fool, but Fyrn? She was proving to be a worthy companion. With her and Kallias, who'd saved me from near-death, life in Radaan might be bearable.

Radaan's court would be the end of me.

The mirrored chandeliers above burned with harsh light, sending sharp glints across the red carpet. The white dance floor shimmered, and the gold pillars, wrapped in twisting vines, did little to soften the harsh glow. Beauty surrounded me, but for all its elegance, it was a desolate place. Empty—like a gilded cage.

I escaped Claydon'sol once again—and the praises he sang about a new cord woven of goat's hair fibers—and found myself cornered by a lesser noble. He prattled on about barley prices, a subject I knew nothing of, while I forced a smile and endured his complaints. All the while, Tallon drifted through the crowd with ease—too absorbed to acknowledge my presence.

Once, his eyes met mine—an open, mocking grin flashed on his lips—before he turned and disappeared into the sea of faces.

A princess, yes. But I was still a woman. And right now, I could hardly breathe.

I needed air. Or I might scream.

Someday, I would walk through Radaan's court with confidence. I'd be the one others sought out, who knew how to navigate the awkward silences and strained smiles. I had imagined my betrothed would be there to guide me, his steady presence at my side. Instead, Tallon abandoned me at every turn, mocking my every attempt.

Rage soured the wine in my stomach. I was no footstool to be placed under his feet.

Proper. Cordial. Polite. All the perfect traits my mother drilled into me. I had been raised for this. That truth echoed in my mind, each repetition driving the point home.

"I shall pass your concerns to Prince Tallon, who I'm sure will be most eager to hear them." Hardly. The man cared for nothing beyond petty games. "However, I must excuse myself, as I am needed elsewhere."

The noble—what was his name? Raymond? Rayneer?—smiled with unearned gratitude. Curse it all. I listened to him drone on for who knows how long, and I couldn't remember his name?

He dropped into a bow, and I walked away, forcing my steps into a slow and steady pace though every muscle screamed to flee the suffocating room. I lifted my chin, scanning the crowd. My gaze landed on Tallon—there he was, tucked in a corner with a group of young nobles. Their brows furrowed, their faces serious for once. Frowns all around.

His friends were more important than his future wife. The thought burned as I reined in my fury, smothering the sharp sting of betrayal. Striding with purpose, I crossed the ballroom, refusing to allow another nobleman to approach me with empty pleasantries. The heavy air seemed to press in as I reached the doorway and stepped into the cooler hall.

A grimace twisted my lips as two guards fell in behind me, their footsteps matching mine in mechanical rhythm. I fought the urge to lift my dress and flee—away from the incessant chatter, the hollow masks, the endless parade of smiles that held no warmth. When I rounded a corner, my frustration swelled, threatening to crash over me.

I spun on my heel, my voice sharper than intended. "You are dismissed."

They froze, their postures stiffening like statues. One glanced at the other, his helmet hiding any trace of thought. How could they see anything?

"We may only be relieved by the royal family," the first responded, his voice clear and unyielding despite the barrier of metal between us.

"I am soon to be a member of it. I assure you, I can handle myself tonight." The words slipped from my lips, but the smile I forced felt as sharp as a blade. I hoped it didn't come across as threatening.

"Be that as it may–"

"I'm sure Prince Tallon would be greatly distressed to learn of your lack of respect for his future bride's wishes."

His stance faltered, as if that statement carried weight. His armor creaked with the subtle shift of movement, and they exchanged a brief, uncertain glance.

"I take my leave. Goodnight."

I spun away, my footsteps quick and deliberate as I moved down the corridor. The temptation to run clawed at me, but I resisted, keeping my pace steady. I held my breath, listening for the telltale clink of armor or a shout to stop me, but the silence remained.

A sigh of relief escaped me as I turned down another hall, the distance between us growing with every step. The thrill of escape coursed through me. At least, for now, I was free.

The corridors gleamed, their light persistent even in the stillness of night. Mirrored lanterns hung from the walls, casting sharp beams that scattered like diamonds, tracing arcs of brilliance across the ceiling and floor. The vines crept along, draping from above, softening the hard edges, lending the palace a cozy warmth.

This hall's floor was lined with wood, its smooth surface hidden beneath a long carpet woven with intricate geometric patterns. I traced the shapes with my gaze, a small smile tugging at my lips. The design was beautiful, orderly—so unlike the untamed chaos of nature, yet it somehow belonged.

Through tall windows, I glimpsed the soft pink of the setting sky. This palace stretched on, an endless expanse of courtyards, gardens, and patios. Surely, somewhere within it all, there must be a rooftop where one could entertain.

I slowed at the junction, eyeing each hall. A slight, uncomfortable tightness gripped my chest as I realized—

I was lost.

A servant emerged from a room, the door creaking as she pulled it shut. I rushed toward her, but when her wide eyes snapped to mine, I forced myself to slow, realizing I startled the poor soul.

She dropped into a deep curtsy. "Princess!"

"Good evening. Where is the entrance to the roof?"

"The roof?" she squeaked, blinking as she rose.

Had I been wrong? Was there no rooftop space to unwind? It seemed such a waste, especially in a land where the sun reigned and plants flourished. In the Nest, I could understand, but here, with its mild breezes and warm sunlight?

"Begging your pardon, you startled me is all," she stammered, offering a nervous smile. "Right this way."

Relief swept through me, and I anxiously rubbed the muscle between my thumb and palm. She swept down the halls—her steps confident and purposeful. She knew where she was going.

Unlike me.

The corridors were unnervingly quiet, the faint murmurs of the ballroom fading as we ventured deeper into the palace. The nobles and guests were all in attendance, and servants were scarce—perhaps not wanting to risk crossing paths with the higher class on their way to their rooms.

Glimpses of vibrant paintings lined the walls, their rich colors striking, but I couldn't bring myself to stop and admire them. I was beyond that now. I needed air, and this servant was my ticket.

The walk was short, but the pace she set had my heart thumping and my cheeks flushed by the time we reached a spiral staircase. I glanced up, taking in the sight of it tucked into a shadowed corner of the palace. The staircase rose toward a balcony that ran along the inside of a gathering room, overflowing with more plants. Vines curled around the railing, carefully kept away from the steps to prevent any calamities.

Unlike the stone spiral staircases in the Tower of Draconia, this one was wrought from twisted metal, its intricate ironwork both sturdy and beautiful.

"Would you like me to escort you up?" the servant asked, her voice quiet.

"Thank you, but that is all."

She smiled and hurried off, eager to return to her duties.

My fingers brushed against the cold railing, its surface fashioned into a vine. Leaves curled underneath, creating a natural cradle for hands that brushed along the metal. As I lifted my foot to begin climbing, I froze, crouching with a breathless laugh of disbelief.

The stairs, though smooth, were carved with intricate scenes. Beneath my feet, lily pads and fish swam. I paused, watching the depiction of a frog's life cycle unfold before me, from eggs at the lowest steps to a tadpole that grew and sprouted legs. Higher still, the tadpole became a tailed frog, and at the top, it shed its tail.

I grinned at the last step, where the frog seemed to smile back, its tiny form etched in the stone. As I shook my head, the weight of the night lifted from my shoulders. If frogs could grin like that, perhaps I could tolerate Tallon's behavior for a while longer.

The balcony was just ahead, a doorway framed by the twilight sky. When I stepped outside, a cool breeze rushed over, tugging at my dress. Fresh air wrapped around me—a welcomed embrace.

The sandstone wall was waist-high, its surface glowing in the last rays of the sun. My hands spread over its warm edge and I leaned into the breeze, letting it pull at my hair like a banner. I laughed, breathless, the wind cutting through me, a sensation that felt as freeing as being on dragonback.

I closed my eyes and let the fading sunlight wash over me. The cool air tugged at my skin, a fleeting comfort in the stillness. The world slowed, and I stood grounded, untouched by its relentless demands.

Just one brief moment—where I could remember who I was, not the pawn I had become.

Just a moment.

Chapter Nine

KALLIAS

She shot from the balcony door to the wall with a level of speed that caught me off guard. I twisted, settling one elbow against the sandstone, just as she spread her hands and pitched forward, braced as if to fall.

Beside me, Greaves flinched, a small movement betraying his impulse to reach out, as if he might somehow hold her back. My pulse thundered, a rush of adrenaline as I realized how far she was from my reach—I wouldn't catch her.

Thank Elohios—she drew in a breath, her eyes closing as the breeze washed over her. My shoulders softened, tension easing from my muscles. I swirled the cup in my hand, staying silent. Behind me, Greaves held his ground, my constant shadow.

Amber sunlight stretched across her golden hair, catching strands and drawing them back like ripe wheat bending under a warm wind. Her deep green dress would have the high ladies whispering with either envy or disdain, half of them plotting to replicate the style by morning.

An emerald collar hugged her neck, as did the fabric that molded to her torso, accentuating her shape before it fell to her hips and flared. The front hem cut slightly shorter than the back, revealing those ever-present leggings and boots.

A mark of her heritage. A reminder of who she was to me—a promise of peace.

"You survive a runaway horse," I called, drawing her startled gaze as she whirled toward me. "Yet you seem perilously close to throwing yourself over the edge." A faint smile pulled at my lips.

Her eyes sparked, and she dipped her head, hands clasped demurely before her. "King Kallias, I didn't mean to intrude."

Something in the formality twisted inside me, her calling me king, as though it put a wall between us. She was a free spirit, fire-lit and untamed, her sharpness softened only by the loyalty she showed with Tallon, her claws sheathed but always ready.

"Kallias," I corrected, sighing as I swirled my drink again, gaze drifting back to Radaan. "Call me Kallias."

"I'm sure there's a law somewhere that requires me to use your title," she murmured, strolling over to lean against the wall beside me.

Maybe I should have kept my guard up, worn the cold mask I reserved for everyone else. But I came here to escape the weight of politics. Eldeiade never followed—she wouldn't dare risk her hair to the breeze.

Nienna had burst through the door, unbothered by wind or decorum, a clear sign she'd tired of the pretense and its demands.

"And I'm sure there are rules about a prince letting a princess ride an untested horse," I grunted, taking a sip from my mug. Heat spilled down my throat, the spice coaxing a fire within.

"I usually keep my seat." Her tone turned indignant.

I cast her a sidelong glance, catching the furrow deepening between her brows.

"I've just never ridden in open country before," she said.

"Open country?"

She sighed and braced her forearms on the wall, peering at the gardens below. Where Tallon shied from heights, she seemed to revel in them.

"Draconia is... not small. Perhaps it is, by your standards." She let out a nervous laugh. "But we own the seas, not the plains. Horses are few, ridden only within the cities. They have no space to run free. I've always been confined when in the saddle."

"In fairness, I should've known better," I offered, trying to ease the sting of her pride. "Tallon brings younger horses when he rides out to the hounds." I paused, then added, "I'm thankful you're unharmed."

She pressed her lips together as if she wanted to say more, yet held back. I remembered the chaos—the moment I'd pulled her to me, heart pounding in my chest. One wrong move from the horse, a single misstep, and she might not have survived. And that blood streaking her face?

My jaw clenched, rage simmering beneath the surface. Tallon never went to the temple seeking forgiveness. But for this, I would make him seek mine.

"Be free with your words," I said with a rueful smirk. "I wager you're sick of the masks and pretenses as well."

"Yours or your son's?"

I choked, sputtering on my cider. She slapped a hand over her mouth, as though she could shove the comment back in.

When I caught my breath, a bitter laugh escaped me, and I shook my head.

"You may see me masked, but I always speak the truth. Tallon, however..." The words tasted heavy, a weight settling on my chest. I failed him, letting his mother mold him while I fought a war, neglecting him. He'd become a stranger, a man I no longer trusted—and she was bound to marry him.

"I see past his mask." Her voice softened, her gaze meeting mine.

The look in her eyes unsettled me. That resignation. The acceptance that she was just another pawn in the game, a piece to be bartered. I knew she was—as was I. We all were. For the sake of our kingdoms, we gave up pieces of ourselves, sometimes in the form of who we married. But the quiet spark beyond her resignation stirred anger within.

"He's still growing, still maturing." I turned to the distant fields, patchworks of green and burnished gold stretching toward the horizon, roads and paths weaving between them like scars on the land.

She sighed. "He's *nineteen.*"

A quiet pause settled between us. She shifted her weight, her gaze tracing the edge of the wall as if searching for words, yet none came right away. Her shoulders eased, though a faint tension lingered in the set of her jaw.

"I had nothing to do with the announcement at our ball," she murmured at last.

I squinted into the distance, already aware—Tallon orchestrated that. But she wanted me to know, wanted to make it clear she held no designs on the throne.

Unlike my son.

"Tallon's eager to be rid of me," I said, my tone flat. She remained silent, offering no denial. "But I suspect these old bones will keep me here a few years yet."

"You don't look a day over thirty."

I chuckled, then tossed back the last of my cider. Let her keep that lie. Perhaps it was my ego—I'd probably need to repent for indulging.

Gods, it was refreshing to have someone to be open with.

"Do you come here often?" she asked.

I straightened, casting one final, lingering gaze over my lands—lands I had fought for, shed too much blood for. "When court gets to be too much."

She turned that mischievous smile on me. "And that's fairly often?"

I scoffed, a half-grin forming. "Yes, I'd say more nights find me here than not."

"I apologize for storming into your space. I won't–"

"The palace is yours, Princess," I cut in. "You may go where you will, when you will. If you'd like to join me, or claim the roof as your own, please do." I dipped into a bow, one worthy of a princess... and perhaps a little deeper.

"Nienna—"

I straightened, cocking an eyebrow in question as she turned fully, facing me. She leaned against the wall, and the sun blinked out behind her, casting the space in ruddy shadows.

"—My name is Nienna." A sly smile curved one corner of her mouth.

"Goodnight, Nienna."

"Goodnight, Kallias."

I started for the door, Greaves following. She wasn't just a raging fire; she was a candlelight, flickering, brightening every room she entered. Her honesty, the ease with which she jested with me—it surprised me.

Perhaps the dragons had raised her with confidence, a sense of self that didn't need approval. She would play the court's game, but on her own terms.

The door clicked shut behind us.

"Kal."

I paused at Greaves' call, twisting to face him as I descended the staircase.

"Her guards," he murmured, his tone low.

Curse it all. I'd been too caught up in her antics to notice. "She lost them." I couldn't help but smile, amused.

"Ordered them off, I'd wager." He spoke in hushed tones, always so low no prying ears could hear. His brown eyes held warmth, a familiarity born from years of trying to lose each other in our youth.

"Go on then. I can manage, but I won't risk her."

He gave a short nod and spun back toward the balcony, his sword swaying with each step. Beneath his clothes, the weight of his plated leather armor shifted. She'd be safer with him by her side than with any of the castle guards.

I shook my head, descending the stairs alone. She was already smothered. When the Velli came, I'd have to tighten security even more.

Unease sifted through me at the thought of a Velli—ambassador or not—in *my* home? Meeting them on the border was one thing, but *inviting* them inside? It felt like a violation. I'd done everything to protect and preserve this palace, even when Eldeiade ruled in my stead.

With a steadying breath, my mask slid into place. Stern face, chin high, eyes cutting. The yoke pressed against me with every step, a chain of duty, one that reminded me why I was letting the Velli inside.

And why I was allowing Nienna to marry a man who wanted nothing to do with her.

Chapter Ten

NIENNA

I recited the names of Draconia's bull dragons in silence, resisting the urge to cuff the prince. He lounged beside me, head tipped back as he stared at the ceiling, his arm slung behind a nobleman who sat a bit straighter. Every time I glanced his way, Tallon offered a smirk, his gaze pompous and haughty.

General Fallione loomed over the council room's map, his finger tapping the jagged mountains that separated Vellos from Radaan. "We have enough to fortify the southern Craggs. But pull more men for the harvest, and we couldn't fend off an attack to the north. I'm telling you, you need to leave each tower stationed with three companies at least."

"Attack," Tallon mocked under his breath.

Gyrak. Argos. Lyne. Tewar.

Kallias cast his son a cold look, then bent over the table, scrutinizing the range. "Those men are needed for the harvest; they've been promised a six month reprieve." His thumb traced each watchtower on the map, a flicker of tension in his brow.

Tallon propped himself up, his smirk as cutting as a drawn blade. "We have a treaty signed by King Guntarri himself," he drawled, voice oozing confidence. "Unless the reason we are allying with Draconia is because you're nervous it won't hold."

The nobleman to his right murmured with faint interest, and I pressed my lips tight, biting back words that itched to escape. Most of the council held their tongues, unfazed, as if Tallon's interruptions were as ordinary as the council's own breath. But a handful—those younger members who would one day shoulder the kingdom beside the prince—watched him with a mix of curiosity and reluctant acceptance.

Kallias leaned forward, bracing his hands against the table, his glare pinning Tallon in place. The chains of his mantle swung just above the map, a gleaming reminder of his authority—*he* was king. A silent rebuke.

Tension thickened, coiling like a storm cloud, as father and son waged a wordless battle with locked eyes.

Enough of Tallon.

"May I speak?" I asked, not waiting for an answer as I rose to my feet, the fabric of my dress whispering as I shook it into place.

Kallias' gaze snapped to me, his brows tightening, as if weighing whether I might side with his son, challenging him in the open.

I was not so foolish.

"Please." The king's single word cut short, guarded—a welcome laced with challenge.

I approached the table, and two councilmen shifted their chairs aside, clearing my path. "You're concerned with the Cragg's defenses, but through our alliance, you have the might of dragonkind."

"The union is not yet sealed." His frown deepened, though his voice softened a shade.

"I've given the Dragon's Kiss to Radaan." My cheeks flushed as I spoke, the words like embers in my throat. "My dragons are yours, King Kallias. I'll write to my father."

The corner of that handsome mouth twitched, a flicker of intrigue at my boldness. I leaned over the map, stretching forward to trace the watchtowers with my fingertip, my gaze falling away from his piercing stare as heat crept up my cheeks.

"Five dragons would be an easy concession for Draconia. Keep two companies stationed at each tower, but position a rider at every other one. They can make the flight swiftly, sound an alarm, and stir up enough presence to hold a line."

I forced down the knot in my throat as Tallon muttered something behind me, his voice like a burr against my thoughts. I straightened, wrestled my nerves into submission, and fixed a polite mask over my face. Kallias returned his focus to the map, eyes distant and thoughtful.

Shame prickled at me. I'd overstepped, spoken too brashly. It wasn't my place to dictate strategy or troop placements; that was the war council's domain. I was here as a bargaining chip—a princess promised to secure alliances and produce heirs—not to meddle in the kingdom's defenses.

Not a strategist. A figurehead. A pawn.

Kallias lifted his gaze, meeting mine with an intensity that broke through my self-reproach. "And what accommodations do five dragons require?"

Relief washed over me, and my shoulders eased, the tension melting away at his question. "They need open sky, space to hunt." I held his challenging stare, an unexpected thrill sparking in me. "And I understand the Craggs have an abundance of goats."

"My father will be mortified you offered the goats." Fyrn snickered as she led me back to my quarters.

"Claydon'sol has assured me he's found the finest buck to sire the next generation."

"Ah, yes. He prattles on and on about their coats. Apparently, their pelts and fibers are worth far more than their meat. Still—I must say—I'm happier here than in our manor."

I raised a brow, curious.

"It doesn't reek of livestock here."

A laugh burst out, and I shook my head at her antics.

Claydon'sol lingered at court to secure a suitor for Fyrn, but she was proving to be quite the free spirit. To his credit, he allowed her to have the final say, and so far, she'd found none to her liking.

"Just two more nights of his musings," she assured, giving my arm a gentle pat, "then he'll be off to manage the manor, and we'll be gloriously goat-free."

"You're staying, then?"

"I have a season pass. If I don't find a husband by winter, I'll return home." She gave an exaggerated sigh, then flashed a playful smile. "That gives me months to peruse the goods! Oh!" She glanced over her shoulder at our guards, then down the corridor. "Would you like to watch the prince spar?"

Unease stirred beneath my skin, thick and unwelcome. The last thing I wanted was to spend another moment penned in a room with him. I'd sooner track down Claydon'sol to discuss goat pedigrees than endure more of Tallon's smug smirks.

"The king has ordered His Highness to spar with him every day this week."

A strange thrill fluttered low in my belly, one I quickly crushed. Why did the thought of watching Tallon fill me with dread, yet the idea of seeing his father sent my pulse racing?

Did they exchange blows outdoors beneath the searing sun or inside, where light filtered through high windows? Would Kallias shed his mantle, his yoke of authority? The way his clothing draped over his broad frame and trim waist was a silent testament to his strength—strength that hadn't faded with age.

My mind drifted back to the warmth of his calloused hand brushing against mine, its roughness a memory I couldn't shake.

"If you'd rather not–"

"No." I forced the word out, shaking off the errant thoughts. "I'd love to watch Tallon fight, yes—very much."

Fyrn smirked, and I caught that glint of mischief in her eyes. Did she think my awkward stumbles were for the prince—when I was actually thinking about his father?

"Tomorrow, then, after the council meets." She hummed to herself as we continued along. "Tonight's dinner will be quite the affair. An ambassador from the Ivetti Islands arrived. Word is they've come just to witness your wedding."

I forced myself to soften my words, though I wanted to bite them out. "The wedding isn't for months." I knew what I was—understood the role I'd been given. But now that I learned Tallon's true colors, I couldn't stomach the idea of marrying him. Would we end up like his parents in a cold, distant arrangement? Strangers beneath the same roof? The thought made me feel hollow.

"Don't fret," Fyrn mused. "They're the only ones arriving so early."

When we arrived at my rooms, my gaze drifted to the carved dragons adorning the door's dark wood. Their wings swept up in graceful arcs, frozen in a moment of flight, yet bound to the surface. My heart twisted, envy stirring at the freedom in their poses.

"They'll be grounded by storms if they wait any longer," I said.

The Ivetti Islands lay close to my home, a scattered chain tossed westward across the sea. The whirlstorms hit Draconia first, moving on to churn over Ivetti waters for weeks, sometimes months. If the ambassadors waited, they'd be stranded, unable to attend at all.

"Do you know their ambassador?"

I shook my head. "I haven't. Only Princess Kittiana—she's visited a handful of times, though it's unlikely she'll leave the islands now."

Fyrn's eyes brightened, and she nudged my shoulder with a cheerful grin. "Then tonight, you shall."

She dipped into a playful curtsy, her blonde curls bouncing, then turned down the corridor. I drew in a deep breath and entered my room, closing the door behind me.

"How was it?" Scythe blurted, rising from the chaise.

Edith hushed her with a stern glare, standing as her sharp gaze swept over me, searching for any sign of distress or need.

"It was," I hesitated, recalling Tallon's push against his father and Kallias' calm attentiveness, "intriguing."

Scythe's face brightened as she hurried toward me, her hair flying behind her. Edith glanced at her wisps and patted her own gray hair down as if it made her feel unkempt.

"Edith, I'm parched."

She exhaled a resigned sigh and shook her head, already knowing why I was dismissing her. "I'll fetch some refreshments before we prepare you for the evening meal."

Scythe grinned like a fool, staring after her as she slipped out the servant door. "Tell me, tell me!"

She seized my hand, dragging me toward my bedchamber. We collapsed atop the plush blankets, laughter spilling from us as we tumbled in an awkward heap.

"You want to hear of old men discussing borders?" I teased, spreading my arms wide in a theatrical gesture.

"No! Only the exciting bits!"

She threw herself at me, pinning my arm beneath her. I squealed, struggling to free my limb as she settled in, propping her head on her hand.

"Tallon fought with his father again."

"That seems to be the trend." She hummed, nodding.

"I don't understand why he pushes him. Kallias is right! They just–"

"*King* Kallias?"

My mouth snapped shut, brows dropping into a glare.

She waggled her eyebrows. "Oh, do go on."

"*King* Kallias had a point. The ink on the Velli treaty is still fresh, and they're wise to proceed with caution. Until I'm married and the alliance sealed, they have nothing to deter an invasion. They need dragons, so I'll write Father and request a fleet."

She bolted upright, back straight, eyes wide with disbelief. "You *want* dragons in Radaan?"

"They'll be tucked away in the Craggs, far from the townsfolk, and with all the goats they can eat." I chuckled. "It'll be more like a vacation for them than anything."

"I don't doubt your father would send them." She sighed, sinking back against the bed. "I'm just concerned for the Radaanian citizens."

"I'll warn Kallias. He'll know what to expect."

"You should've seen the way people ogled Gyrak. No sense of self-preservation."

"Radaan is used to horses, cattle, and sheep."

"They're soft."

"No." I closed my eyes and laced my hands behind my head. "Radaan's fresh from war. They crave peace—Kallias craves peace. They've fought and bled for their land. Radaan's people are proud, courageous. They may not be accustomed to dragons, but they are not soft. They're just not Draconis."

Silence reigned, and Scythe's curiosity buzzed in the air. I rolled over to face her, locking eyes with her gleaming gaze.

"You called him Kallias again," she said.

I groaned and grabbed a pillow, aiming it at her with a laugh. She shrieked and ducked, grinning as she dodged my assault.

"He's my future father-in-law! I can call him by his first name!"

"Oh, but the way your eyes sparkle and glow!"

I chased her across the bed, whacking her with another pillow.

When Edith returned, we were a hysteric heap of laughter, my bedchamber in disarray.

When I entered the dining hall, I fought to keep my face neutral as Tallon offered me his arm. My gaze drifted to Kallias, who stood with a group of individuals engaged in easy conversation.

The Ivetti ambassador, a woman in a long flowing garment that trailed along the floor, wore a strip of matching cloth around her neck that cascaded to the ground. It was far more modest than the attire her people wore—or rather, *didn't* wear.

Behind her stood a guard clad in trousers and leather armor, a typical Ivetti choice. His arms, covered in intricate markings, hinted at their customs and rich culture.

"Neighbors of yours?"

The question, framed in his dismissive tone, irked me. He judged them based on appearances, unaware of their true nature. The Ivetti were among the most generous people I knew, their kindness extending far beyond what most understood. The only thing that kept other nations from threatening their island home was the whirlstorms, which made any siege impossible.

"Friendly ones, unlike yours," I muttered.

He chuckled. "Vellos is friendly enough—if you know how to win them over."

I stiffened as I realized he was steering us away from them—toward the dais. "We should greet the ambassador lest we fail to win them over," I suggested, my tone sharper than I intended—though with Tallon, some force seemed to be necessary.

"Kallias will take care of it."

He ascended the first step, and it took every ounce of restraint not to wrench my arm free and march straight to the group.

"This will be your kingdom one day. Perhaps you should develop some relations," I hissed, my smile concealing my irritation.

"You're right—"

He gave my relief no chance to take root.

"—it will be *my* kingdom one day."

He led me up the stairs and to my chair, waiting until I sat before shoving it in, pinning me against the table. I grunted, bracing against the wood to keep from being crushed.

His breath tickled my ear as he leaned down to whisper, "You would do well to remember that."

My fury flared like dragon's fire, hands trembling as I pressed them into my lap. Tallon's chuckle stoked the flames, turning my vision red. At that moment, Kallias stormed up the dais, his presence and indignation sweeping toward us like a raging whirlstorm.

Tallon moved to sit beside me, but the king strode around the table and snared his arm, hauling him upright. I kept my gaze down, unwilling to make a scene. Nobles exchanged glances, their attention shifting between the ambassador and the rising tension between the royals.

The two exchanged angry words. Then Kallias released him, watching as his son adjusted his overcoat. He sank into his seat next to mine, face flushed crimson.

Unease spiraled within, and I wasn't sure if I should feel angry, grateful, or if the letter to my father would request my return. I understood the logistics of *why* this alliance needed to happen, but I hadn't anticipated the reality. Tallon wanted nothing to do with me, and Kallias would always have to be the one to rescue me.

I expected some mutual understanding between us—that even if he found me unattractive, too vocal or opinionated for his tastes, we could make this work. We didn't have to fall in love. I could find Radaanian friends, people to care for, but we needed compatibility. Tallon, however, was proving to be a hard match in that regard.

The king found his seat, and I fought to ignore the seething hatred emanating from his son. A servant set a plate in front of me—piled with greens and earthy vegetables, glistening in oil and vinegar. Only when Kallias took the first bite did we begin to eat. The murmur of voices in the hall rose to a pleasant backdrop amidst the tense silence that clung to the dais.

Nobles approached between courses, discussing various topics, while Tallon remained aloof, listening to a young man discuss a horse race in the western region. It took me two courses before I noticed the Ivetti ambassador's untouched plate.

A tight knot formed in my stomach. No one had considered their customs.

In public, they never ate until their first bite was given. The act was a sacred gesture, woven into their faith. She would return to her quarters and eat alone, but here, she would not eat without a companion to share her food with.

I searched the room for her guard, spotting him at the far wall, blending with the other attendants—except Greaves, who lingered in the king's shadow.

Kallias met my eyes, head tipped as if sensing my concern.

My jaw tightened. As an ambassador, she deserved respect. She would have offered her food to the noblewomen beside her, but clearly, they had declined.

I twisted my hands in my lap, the pressure of indecision rising. Walking away from Tallon before the meal was finished would be a grave insult. Yet, this was my future kingdom, and Radaan needed allies. In this setting, leaving would cost me respect. But it was equally disrespectful to let an ambassador go hungry.

It should have been Tallon's responsibility—or even Kallias'—to ensure she had someone to share her meal. Who was in charge of international relations? I'd give them a piece of my mind when I found them.

The woman kept her gaze fixed on her plate, a polite smile masking her discomfort. She nodded at something said to her, but the flush on her face could have been anger, burning her cheeks a bright red.

I forced my chair back with a sharp scrape, then ducked my head to mask my cringe as I pushed to my feet. Every eye followed my movement, but I met Kallias' calm blue gaze as he stood with me. Tallon followed, after a long breath, and the conversation ebbed to murmurs.

"What are you doing?" the prince growled, his voice low and dangerous.

I shivered, feeling the heat of his ire, like standing too close to a ravenous wolf ready to snap.

"Your duty!" I hissed. My eyes snapped to the king before I sank into a shallow curtsy. "I beg your leave."

Kallias' gaze flicked to Tallon, and after a brief moment, he dipped his head, granting me release. I turned away from the table, my palms slick with sweat as the murmurs in the room softened to whispers. With a practiced smile, I lifted my chin and descended the stairs, grateful for the split in my dress. At least I didn't have to worry about tripping.

As I passed between the rows of tables, all eyes were on me, the weight of their stares making me feel like I was walking through a performance. The ambassador caught my gaze and, realizing where I was headed, rose to her feet. She smiled, her teeth a sharp contrast to her dark complexion. Her black hair cascaded in intricate braids, hanging over her shoulder and down her back. She curtsied as I stopped before her.

"Le'hoim bless you," I greeted, dipping my head in respect.

"Blessed be you, Princess Nienna, the Dragon's Heart." Her voice was soft, melodic, and as she met my gaze again, her dark eyes sparkled with gratitude. She reached for her plate and extended it toward me. "Would you share my bounty?"

"Many thanks."

I surveyed the food before plucking a single grape. As I chewed, I did my best to keep the sound as quiet as possible. It seemed every noble had fallen silent, their eyes fixed on the exchange. Surely, even Kallias across the room could hear the soft click of my teeth as I swallowed.

"Blessed be." I dipped my head again, and the ambassador curtsied, echoing my words.

It was a simple gesture—yet no one had seen to it or made proper accommodations. As the future queen, it would be my responsibility to ensure even the ambassadors of other nations felt welcomed here. Everyone deserved care, respect, and hospitality.

I turned back toward the dais, my gaze drifting to Kallias. His brow furrowed, a deep crease marking the space between his eyes. Tallon had returned to his seat beside him, but he remained standing, his attention fixed on me as I approached.

He was kind—had shown me nothing but warmth. He wouldn't turn me away.

I paused at the base of the stairs, waiting for his signal. When he nodded, granting me permission to ascend, I measured each step with practiced care. As I reached the top, Tallon, with much reluctance, rose to assist me, but I hardly noticed as I sank into my chair. Kallias resumed his seat, the world around us returning to its quiet hum as if nothing shifted.

As if I hadn't just salvaged the dignity of a kingdom that wasn't mine yet.

My hands trembled as I ascended the spiral staircase, doubt twisting in my chest. If Kallias was elsewhere, I'd step out for a breath of fresh air before retreating to my rooms. But if he lingered on the balcony, I planned to offer an apology for my impulsive actions.

It gnawed at me throughout the rest of the dinner. I should have spoken to him first, rather than taking matters into my own hands. I wasn't part of this kingdom yet, held no claim to its customs. My actions had been an overstep—and I feared I'd made him look foolish.

I couldn't care less if Tallon had been embarrassed—but Kallias? He was far more perceptive than his son, more capable of understanding the nuances of diplomacy. He didn't deserve that.

The frogs vanished beneath my boots as I reached the end of the stairwell. I paused at the balcony door, steadying my breath, then pushed it open and scanned the rooftop before stepping into the twilight. The sight that met me froze me in place.

Kallias leaned against the stone wall facing me, elbows braced, his head tilted back, eyes closed. With the strain of his posture, his overcoat pulled taut, the top button undone. His legs stretched out, crossed at the ankles, as if he had all the time in the world.

The door clicked shut behind me, and he jerked. His cornflower blue gaze locked onto mine, sharp and unreadable, his expression set with a hint of irritation. He straightened with slow deliberation, rolling his shoulders, and the air thickened with unspoken tension.

I forced my composure back into place and sank into a deep curtsy. "My apologies for tonight, Your Majesty. I should have sought your–"

"Rise." His voice was tight, his jaw clenched as he towered over me.

I cringed inwardly, wondering if I'd undone the fragile goodwill between us.

"Was it not 'Kallias' yesterday?" he asked.

I stole a glance at Greaves, who chose that moment to examine his nails.

"I owe you my thanks," he said.

When I straightened, my hands clasped in front of my dress. The fading sunlight caught his silvering hair, setting it ablaze with a soft glow. His hand twitched at his side, a brief wince crossing his face before he averted his gaze, fixing it on the patchwork fields stretching into the distance.

"It was a misstep—one you remedied." He exhaled long and slow, then turned to me, nodding once. "You have my thanks for saving our reputation with the Ivetti."

"Their princess visited Draconia in the quiet season. I know their ways well."

"Perhaps I should put you in charge of cultural relations," he said, slipping his hands into his pockets and shifting his weight onto his heels.

The ease in his stance, paired with the teasing smile tugging at the corners of his mouth, made him appear younger. I couldn't suppress the grin that tugged at my own lips.

"I would love to help," I said, my excitement clear. The thought of meaningful work, instead of endless socializing, would be a welcome breath of fresh air.

"I jest."

"No! Really," I protested, watching his smile fade into a thin line. The shift was as abrupt as a door slamming shut. "If Radaan is to be my home, I have a duty to help in any way I can."

He turned away from me, his expression hardening as he walked toward the wall. His hands remained in his pockets, but the ease of a moment ago had vanished, replaced by a quiet tension.

"I apologize if I overstepped." I stepped closer, uncertain where things had gone astray. One instant, he was open, almost tender; the next, he shut me and the world out.

"You did nothing wrong." His voice was tight, and a forced smile twisted his lips as he exhaled a heavy sigh.

Silence stretched, thick and unyielding. I leaned against the wall, closing my eyes. The wind lifted my hair, pulling it away from my face, and I smiled, letting the breeze wash over me. For a fleeting moment, I soaked up the memory of flying.

"Goodnight."

I hated the way my chest tightened as he took his leave, the soft rhythm of his steps swallowed by the rising wind. It felt as if I'd done something terribly wrong.

Chapter Eleven

KALLIAS

The way her gaze trailed me, eyes wide, lips parted—that blue stare studied my body with such curiosity it woke something–

"Do you need help with the buttons?"

Greaves' low voice jarred me from my thoughts, and I glanced at his reflection in the mirror.

He was unbuckling his armor, preparing for the night. Eldeiade never shared a room with me—only Greaves. After the second midnight assassin, I decided to give him a bed in my quarters rather than force him to sleep on the floor.

As his hands worked at the leather straps, he raised a dark eyebrow, daring me to confess my thoughts.

My fingers hurried to their task—I didn't require his assistance. "Tallon's negligence was unacceptable." The words slipped out, sharp and unforgiving.

In the solitude of my rooms, I could speak freely, and if there was one person I could trust with the truth, it was Greaves. He'd been by my side since my reckless youth, always cleaning up the chaos I created, the trouble I got us into. He never faltered and remained steadfast whenever I needed him. In battle, he saved my life more times than I could recall—and I repaid that debt just as often.

"The ambassador didn't seem offended," he offered, setting his chest piece on the stand beside his bed.

I sighed, shrugging off my overcoat, then draped it over a chair. "She shouldn't have been so forgiving." I yanked at my tunic's ties, frustration creeping in. "It's the one duty he asked for. The single task he seemed fit for."

When his mother died, I pushed Tallon to take a position in the palace. It was my attempt to move him through his grief. I wanted to give him purpose.

"You keep telling me he's young. Let him mature," he said.

In the mirror, I caught his indifferent shrug as he pulled off his tunic, revealing the scars he earned defending me. I kept offering the same excuse for my son, that he'd grow up—that his childish antics would fade with time. But I wasn't saying it for Greaves alone. I thought that perhaps, with enough repetition, I might convince myself, too.

"Princess Nienna will age him," he added. "Let her help him find his maturity."

I shot a glare at his back as he slipped on a clean tunic and settled on the edge of the bed.

He paused, catching my stare, then sighed with resignation. "Don't start," he muttered.

This argument had circled between us since her arrival. Nienna carried herself with the tact expected of royalty, a confidence that gnawed at my soul like a plague. She was prepared—poised to inherit the weight of the crown. Somehow, she navigated the court's tangled politics with ease, despite never setting foot beyond her island.

Nienna had the resilience of fire and the calm of deep waters. Her spirit, fierce and unyielding, clashed with Tallon's attempts to break it—she defied him at every turn. She would never fade into the shadows while he ruled—and that defiance filled me with hope.

But she deserved more.

I arranged her betrothal to secure Draconia's alliance and its powerful dragon fleets, all for Radaan's protection. Tallon was my only option, the single heir I had. The generals and I knew the treaty with Vellos would only hold long enough for them to amass their strength for a fresh assault.

The war crippled both countries. Vellos wanted the space to breathe, to grow bold, bide their time for another strike. I wished for a lasting peace that might secure a better future, and Nienna was the only bridge to that promise.

What else was I to do for Tallon? After his mother died, I tried every path I knew—gentleness, which he rejected; bribery—he scorned me. I even turned to discipline, and he mocked it. In the end, I dealt with him the best way I could: I let him live his life as he pleased, and I lived mine.

If he threw away this alliance, I would keep my word and cast him to the Untamed Valley. Those northern wilds seethed with creatures twisted by pestilence, inhabited by only the hardest of souls. There, outlaws ruled by the sword—a brutal land for a reckless heir.

"She understands her role," Greaves murmured. "She's a—"

I cocked my head, the movement slow and deliberate enough to cut his words short. "She is more than a tool."

"A spitfire, but a tool all the same. She understands her worth, Kal, recognizes why she's here—and now she knows Tallon. Let them forge their way. She is no Eldeiade; she won't–"

"Enough." I tore the tunic from my shoulders and tossed it aside. "See to my door."

At my dismissal, he grumbled under his breath, then left, taking up his watch outside my quarters.

The sound of her name still cut me years after her death. No agony compared to the fate of marrying someone who loathed your every breath, who cursed your presence and ridiculed your voice.

Allowing Tallon to be raised under her venomous influence had been a mistake. Even so, I couldn't wish a union as mine—a life of contempt hidden behind titles and vows—for him.

Or Nienna.

Jarion pleaded for his favorite ship engineer to receive training abroad. The council meeting veered far off course. It began with a motion to ease the fish tax—an attempt to bring more variety to the common folk—and somehow wound its way to the question of funding a family's vacation under the guise of professional development.

But the engineer wasn't the one who held my attention.

My gaze kept drifting to Nienna, who sat rigid with her hands clenched in her lap, her knuckles pale as bone. She maintained a soft smile, but her eyes were leagues away, locked on the foot of the table. Fyrn'sol and Tallon flanked her on either side, and she bristled as Fyrn dipped across her to murmur something to Tallon. He threw his head back, laughing loud enough to draw Hector's icy glance. The southern general had no love for my heir and showed as much with a narrowed stare.

A dark lock fell over Tallon's brow as he leaned past Nienna to reply. Her sea-blue eyes flashed to mine, the politeness in her smile faltering for a heartbeat. Her gaze all but begged for reprieve, some signal from me that I *saw* her, understood her isolation. Surrounded by her betrothed and a noblewoman's kinship, she sat adrift, lost in the press of voices around her.

I knew that feeling all too well.

"Princess Nienna." Withering son of a jester—what was I doing?

Her eyes brightened, a spark lighting in that endless blue, and her smile curved higher. "Yes, Your Majesty?"

Beside her, Tallon turned, an intrigued smirk tugging at his mouth.

"Your people sail the seas, do they not?"

"They do, though..." She hesitated, a glimmer of eagerness breaking through her composure. "May I offer a suggestion?"

My lips twitched at the corner as she leaned in, her interest unmistakable. Here she was, the woman trained and raised for this moment—full of ideas, with solutions burning on the tip of her tongue.

"Please do." I inclined my head, inviting her forward.

She rose with grace, adjusting her gown of deep green—the shade, perhaps unknowingly, adding a sense of belonging to her presence here in Radaan.

With each step toward the map, life seemed to pour into her. A faint blush warmed her cheeks, and she ducked her head as if to hide it before pointing to a scattering of islands across the southern sea.

"The Kulletti," she began, voice steady with a trace of pride, "are known for their seafaring. Surely you trade with them already—their ships are renowned far beyond these waters."

Jarion hummed, tapping a finger on the table. "They are iron-bound, built for war. We need vessels for trade."

"You've seen their merchant ships, Sir Jarion." She softened the correction with a smile that disarmed him, drawing a reluctant nod in agreement.

"They have fishing vessels twice the size of the ship we sailed in on," she said. "Big enough to catch a whale and haul it back to port."

"And you've seen them?" Tallon strode up behind her. "They've never reached our shores?"

His habit of stepping up whenever she spoke wasn't growth—it was the need to loom over her, to remind her of her place, or so he thought.

"I've flown on dragonback, Prince," she replied, eyes fixed on him with a glint of ice beneath her court-practiced smile. "I've seen a great many things you haven't."

My lips pressed together as I watched their exchange unfold. Tallon's expression remained smooth, untroubled, as he shrugged and flicked a strand of hair from his face.

"That island chain is too distant for a mere engineer." He tossed the words with a sidelong glance at the map, barely sparing it a look. He knew its markings well enough—he wasn't that negligent—but his dismissal stung with deliberate disrespect.

"Her suggestion has merit."

At my comment, Tallon's smirk fell from his face. Betrayal colored his features as his brows lowered and his jaw clenched. I was taking her side, putting him in his place in front of the council—which wasn't new, but was never well received.

"The Kulletti are unlike any people you've known," I continued. "Your engineer will need to study their customs. Prince Tallon shall ensure he has what he needs for this task—as is proper for his role as foreign diplomat."

My words landed as I intended—another blow to his pride. His shoulders drew back, his black and red overcoat pulled taut, a show of defiance he hardly concealed.

Nienna's lips parted, as if she had more to offer, but uncertainty flickered over her features. She glanced at me, words held at bay. I leaned in my seat, my gaze trained on Tallon, shuttered yet sharp. His nostrils flared, the bruised look of an unbroken stallion flashing across his face. With a forced smile, he turned on his heel, striding away from the table.

His newest shadow, Flinn'dor, rose and bowed before trailing after him. My eyes narrowed as I watched my son's retreat, noting the company he had begun to keep. Fyrn, too, cast a glance over her shoulder, her gaze lingering, before shifting back to Nienna.

"The Kulletti it is," Jarion declared.

Sweat already beaded on my brow as I shrugged out of my overcoat. A servant took it, then arranged my mantle on a stand, stepping aside to blend into the arena's wall.

I rolled my shoulders, relishing the freedom. The overcoat was stifling, tempering my bulk into a form more suitable for court. But each movement in it was measured, constrained.

The battle hall was a sand-filled pit with an open roof, letting in the harsh midday sun. Once a place of noble entertainment, it stood silent, the two-hundred seats empty. I drew my sword, the rasp of steel cutting through the air.

Tallon's mother relished the violence, encouraged it even, filling the hall with bloodthirsty crowds.

Now, it was a place for a father to discipline an unruly son.

When I returned with the signed peace treaty, I hoped for an end to bloodshed. I had done my duty, seen too many soldiers die. The mockery of battle had no appeal anymore. I retired the royal combatants, sending them away, despite Tallon's complaints.

I swung the sword in a wide arc, following through with a lunge. My right shoulder twinged, an old ache from when it had nearly been hacked off by a Velli warrior. I ignored the sharp reminder and fell into the flow of practice, each move as instinctive as breathing. The door slammed shut behind me, but I didn't look up.

The sun had passed its zenith. When I finished, I would take a reprieve—a cold bath, a necessary one, given the way the heat clung to my tunic, sticking to my chest and chafing my skin as it dragged across my back.

"You've brought this on yourself." I grunted, the words slipping from my mouth as the steps neared. Soft footfalls, the kind that made me wonder if Tallon had opted for something less ostentatious today.

Without looking up, I thrust the sword into the sand and tugged at the hem of my tunic. Sun be cursed, I cared little for formality at the moment—no one else was here to witness my lapse.

Greaves coughed, or rather, choked, his gaze fixed somewhere behind me. I turned, barely restraining a flinch.

It wasn't Tallon who entered.

Chapter Twelve

NIENNA

The breeze grazed my parted lips—a whisper of coolness, or maybe just the sound of my own breath catching. Flames licked at my skin, spreading a warm blush over my cheeks and ears, staining them a vivid scarlet.

And yet, I could not tear my eyes from Kallias' body.

Broad shoulders thick with solid, corded muscle, each line of his chest and capable arms stark under the midday light. His wrists were caught in his sleeves, drawing my gaze lower, where the taut ridges of his abdomen rose and fell with quiet power. A faint dusting of dark hair brushed across his skin, the trail disappearing into his trousers' waistband.

He whipped the tunic back over his head in one fluid motion, the fabric whispering over his torso as he stretched and flexed. I snapped my mouth shut, caught between fleeing and pretending I hadn't just ogled him like a stunned courtier.

The shirt fell past his navel; the hem skimming his hips, and some small part of me wanted to demand he take it right back off.

Those eyes locked onto mine, and I struggled to swallow around the dryness in my throat, forcing a smile. His brow furrowed, gaze flicking to my guards, then to me with the intensity of a hawk zeroing in. With a swift jerk, he tugged his sword from the sand and strode forward.

I pressed my damp palms against my skirts, moving closer to the iron fence—a slim barrier between me and the arena's sandy drop. My mouth felt parched, and I traced my lips with my tongue, a small, nervous gesture that caught his eye.

"Good day."

"Where is Tallon?"

Our voices overlapped, but his cut through, overpowering my cracked tone with ease.

I gripped the handrail to steady myself. "I was told he'd be here." My eyes slid down, almost involuntarily, to where the linen clung to his bronzed skin, the fabric skimming each carved line of muscle—leaving little to the imagination. "Fyrn'sol told me he would be here." The words tumbled out again, and I cursed my own repetition.

Think of Fyrn—clever, graceful Fyrn with her golden hair and eyes like a midsummer sky.

But my attention kept drifting to Kallias, to the way his presence seemed to fill every corner of the arena.

His sharp gaze pinned me, slicing through me as if he could hear my thoughts. My smile wavered, brittle under the intensity of his scrutiny. Those piercing eyes, dazzling yet shrewd, weighed each word I spoke, as if testing their truth. Heat prickled over my cheeks, deepening the flush that must have looked painfully incriminating.

Surely, he did not think I sought him out?

Not that I could complain, considering the state I found him in.

The arena's entryway crashed open, and I gave Radaan's gods a silent prayer of thanks as Tallon strode in.

"Father," he drawled, fingers pushing back his dark hair.

Fyrn'sol beamed as she trailed him, her eyes flicking between me and Kallias. She rushed toward me as Tallon flashed a vicious grin, then altered his course to the arena's stairs.

Fyrn dipped into a quick curtsy, then tugged me aside. "Come along," she whispered.

She guided me with a firm hand, but I couldn't escape the press of Kallias' gaze until I turned away, forcing myself to focus on each step.

"I'm so sorry," she murmured as we reached the front row. "I didn't realize you'd head straight here!"

Embarrassment shifted to frustration. As a princess, I expected her by my side, guiding me when the time came. Instead, I entered an empty arena and glimpsed a man's bare chest—an image now seared into my mind.

I blinked, but Kallias' physique refused to fade. Each flex and ripple just as clear as before. I forced my attention onto Tallon, determined to banish the memory. Fyrn wasn't to blame, and I had no right to dump my guilt on her.

The prince strolled across the sand toward Greaves, his steps slow and deliberate. The guard tracked him with a steady gaze, but remained still, a silent sentinel whose loyalty lay with the king alone—not a mere servant to be summoned.

Clad in his customary black from collar to boot, my betrothed moved toward the arena's shaded half, sparing himself the worst of the sun's heat. Yet, if Kallias maneuvered him into the sunlight, he'd soon regret his choice of attire. As he shrugged off his overcoat, I found myself comparing the two men. They were as different as night and day: Tallon, all dark hair and sharp angles, lean and wiry, with narrowed green eyes that missed nothing; Kallias, silver-threaded and powerful, his frame broad and steady, every inch of him a testament to hard-won strength.

Act like an heir, or I'll treat you as the bastard you are.

Fyrn chattered on about an upcoming social she was organizing, her voice a cheerful hum. My gaze drifted past her, drawn to the men, and the unspoken tension between them. I wondered how much legitimacy ran through their private words.

The king never showed his hand, always controlled and precise. Even in moments of anger, he kept his temper leashed, like a tiger restrained by a length of chain. He served a god of truth, his loyalty bound to honesty. Did he know of Tallon's questionable lineage? Had he guessed? Surely, if he knew for certain, he would have ensured another heir by now. Perhaps he harbored doubts—or maybe, as Scythe suggested, it was merely a slip of phrasing.

But Kallias didn't slip.

"I would be delighted for you to attend."

Fyrn's words jolted me back, just as Tallon stalked toward the weapon rack. He selected a sword, the cold gleam of metal catching the light.

"Yes, I'd love to," I replied, hoping to sound collected despite my wandering mind. "When was it again?"

"You didn't hear a word I said, did you?" she teased, arching a brow.

Fyrn cast me a sly grin and tilted her head toward the arena. "Quite the distraction, isn't he?"

Oh, sea beneath—she caught me staring. The ground felt unsteady beneath me. "I assure you, I wasn't–"

"Oh, Princess," she interrupted, her smile widening. "He's your betrothed. If anyone's allowed to appraise the goods, it's you."

Relief flooded over me, and I forced a nervous grin, pretending that, yes, Tallon was indeed the object of my interest. "My apologies. When is your gathering?"

"Tomorrow, after the council meeting," she replied. "The Gad family will be there—they're quite influential along the border and share your taste for art." Her tone held a gentle nudge, urging me to seize the opportunity for connection.

Still, if Kallias—no, Tallon—was to spar after the gathering, my attention would rather lie here, in the heart of the arena.

Sacrifices would have to be made.

"Send for me, and I'll be there."

The prince now strode up to his father, shoulders squared. Tension coiled between them, sharp words barely audible, and Kallias shook his head, his jaw set like stone.

"Where are the others?" I whispered, scanning the barren room once more. Dust clung to the empty seats, the silence thick and oppressive.

"The king disbanded the fighting games after he returned from the war," she said. "Queen Eldeiade loved them. She scheduled one every time he visited, but he never attended."

"Did she not welcome him home?" I asked, my shock evident.

Surely, the absence of affection didn't mean she would ignore him so thoroughly. The notion that she would dismiss his visits in favor of something he despised troubled me. If I were married to a king like Kallias, I would be by his side every moment he returned from the battlefield.

"I only visited with my parents then," Fyrn continued, her voice dropping lower as she leaned closer, her curls brushing my shoulder. "But she accused him of treating her like a womb, nothing more. So, she staged the games to keep him at bay."

My lips dipped in a frown, thoughts tumbling over themselves as my gaze returned to the arena. The men stood ready, locked in tense fighting stances. I'd witnessed the Dragon Riders spar enough to recognize Kallias as the superior swordsman.

"I doubt that," I murmured.

My words felt almost too blunt, but they could not be helped. The king was too proper, too kind. I had seen him honor me in ways no one else had. He recognized my worth, allowed me to speak at the council even when he didn't need to. He'd been nothing but respectful, and I couldn't fathom him treating any woman as less than she deserved.

Tallon made the first move, lunging with an overhead strike. The clash of steel echoed in the arena. They fought with naked blades?

"Me too." Her tone carried a quiet bitterness. "You should have seen how she treated people. She only showed love to her son—tried to keep him from the king as much as she could, and he stayed away. They were almost never together."

My heart tightened at the thought. Would Tallon treat me the same way? My parents loved each other fiercely—and often enough that my brother and I would hide to avoid their overt displays of affection. I came from a home where love was a blessing, not just a duty. And yet, I was marrying into a family so broken, so distant—one that seemed to loathe the very idea of connection.

Kallias parried Tallon's strike, letting him take the offensive. Blow after blow rained down, each met with calm, almost shrugging off the attacks.

How many verbal blows had the king deflected from his late queen? How many insults had he endured and dismissed as effortlessly as he shrugged off Tallon's attacks? Would I be expected to do the same?

The thought turned my stomach. I had agreed to this union for an alliance, for the good of my people—but also for myself. It was my choice, despite the burden of duty.

But what if that meant living in a world of isolation, in a marriage where love was merely a formality? If I broke the engagement, I knew my father would welcome me home—but what would I return to? A sullied reputation, the stain of a princess who ran from her fate, from her father's blood oath? I'd be branded a failure, a coward, no matter what my heart truly desired.

I could escape a miserable married life, but at what cost? Not only for me, but for the Radaanian people, for Draconia. This alliance was critical for both sides. I might not have witnessed the full horror of war, but I saw Kallias picking up the pieces of his nation, rebuilding what had been torn apart. He wasn't just a king—he was trying to create something new from the ashes of destruction.

And Tallon? He would raze it all to the ground without a second thought.

Kallias' sword swung out with precision, twisting Tallon's blow back onto himself. It was as though, in that instant, he finally had enough of his son's reckless assault. Like a wave crashing against rocks, he surged forward, closing the distance with relentless force. The prince stumbled, retreating, his strikes now panicked and wild as he tried to parry the unyielding barrage.

Fyrn gasped, her breath catching as Tallon faltered. Panic flashed across his face, a raw expression I'd never seen on the arrogant young man. He caught himself, then retreated farther, his footfalls quick and desperate, no longer attempting to defend himself.

"Bare blades?" I choked out. One wrong move, and the royal bloodline—if it even was—could be severed for good.

"The king demands it," Fyrn murmured, her gaze glued to the arena. "I think he believes wooden staves are too soft after the war."

Of course. He bore witness to the carnage of battle, the lives lost—he would see this fight as more than a training exercise. There was no place for softness now.

A low snarl cut through the tension, and my lips parted in surprise as I realized it came from Kallias. He lunged again, not giving Tallon an inch. Each strike, each thrust, was deliberate, precise, and as swift as the wind. The king wasn't relying on brute strength; he read his son's every feint, every attempt to deceive him, and countering with a speed that only came from years of relentless practice. The kind of practice that separated warriors from mere men.

He smacked Tallon across the head with the flat of his blade, the slap echoing.

Fyrn let out a soft, empathetic whimper as the prince crumpled to the sand. But my gaze never left Kallias. He stepped back, giving him room to rise, his chest rising and falling with measured breaths. His sword tip dug into the sand, and the breeze ruffled his silvering hair. He ran a hand through the strands, pushing them away from his brow, muttering something too low for me to hear.

Tallon's reply was a venomous snarl. White-knuckled, Kallias gripped the hilt, spinning around, and stalked back to the arena's center.

Greaves, standing at attention against the wall, gave no indication of concern. It was clear he knew Kallias could handle Tallon with ease.

"He should be more careful. He's bleeding," Fyrn whispered.

It was true. Blood trickled down Tallon's cheek, and he wiped it away with disgust before forcing himself to his feet. His gaze flicked in our direction, but his anger was all-consuming. With a grimace, he stormed toward Kallias, his features a mask of rage.

"One slip-up, and his son's face could be scarred forever," she murmured.

I blinked—she thought the king had been careless. I bit my cheek, holding back my rebuke. Ronan and my father had sparred enough that I knew Kallias' every step was deliberate. His blows were controlled, his movements calculated. He was letting Tallon waste his energy, waiting for him to become overly confident, then striking when the moment was right.

That strike hadn't been careless—it took the utmost care.

"At least you wouldn't have to marry him," I scoffed.

Her lips twitched in a smile, but it didn't reach her eyes. Her gaze remained fixed on the prince, and guilt twisted my heart. I winced, knowing she was his friend.

"Surly Kallias won't let that happen," I added, attempting to reassure her.

"I hope not. He never seems to care for Tallon, though."

I frowned at Fyrn's casual use of Tallon's name—she was his friend, no doubt, but the informality struck me as odd, and I thought back on previous conversations, trying to recall if she used it before. Perhaps he'd given her permission to speak so freely.

The prince, predictably, didn't learn. Blow after blow, he drove at Kallias, each attack leaving him more frustrated than the last.

The bout ended as fast as it started. The king spun behind, slamming the sword's pommel between his shoulder blades. Tallon collapsed, and Kallias growled something under his breath. This time, he didn't step back. He loomed over the prince—a silent challenge. Clearly, Kallias was trying to teach him a lesson. But he refused to yield.

"Again!" Tallon barked, voice thick with frustration.

Kallias paced to the center, and Tallon rose—his movements slow, measured. My brow pinched at the pure malice in his glare. Then he lunged.

The king, though surprised, was not caught off-guard. He twisted, avoiding the sharp edge. But Tallon, quick and desperate, hooked an arm around his neck and used the momentum to slam his hilt into his right shoulder.

Greaves, ever stoic at his place near the wall, flinched. A grimace pulled his face taut.

Kallias doubled over, gritting his teeth with a wince as he rolled the prince to the ground, his weapon a flash of silver as it hovered just above Tallon's throat. Fyrn gasped as the blade hung there, suspended in an eerie stillness.

This was wrong—and not because Kallias had my betrothed at sword-point. Unease slithered through me like cold fingers, my pulse quickening. This wasn't just a sparring match anymore. It wasn't tension between mentor and student, or father and son.

It was darker.

Wrath billowed off Tallon in waves as he lay in the sand, panting and disheveled. The bitter animosity radiating from him felt like a storm gathering—unrelenting and vicious. He spat something, and Fyrn and I leaned forward as if we might catch his words. Kallias' gaze flicked toward us and I shrank back with a nervous swallow.

"No." His command sent a ripple through the arena, and Fyrn recoiled into her seat.

The irritation pulling at her brow didn't escape me. "What did he say?" I asked.

"I only heard the king," she murmured, but her eyes betrayed her—shifting with something unsaid. There was more she refused to say.

Kallias turned on his heel, storming toward Greaves, who was already retrieving his mantle from the stand.

Tallon's glare whipped to me, filled with the promise of vengeance so vehement it chilled my blood. A low hum of warning buzzed in my chest. I'd done nothing to provoke such fury, such ire. I straightened, lifting my chin in silent defiance. He could take that attitude and redirect it somewhere useful—like actually learning how to wield a sword.

Without waiting for the prince to rise, I stood, my movements deliberate. I dipped my head toward him, acknowledging his humiliation—then strode past Fyrn, who scrambled to her feet, and walked away. My pace didn't falter. I was no longer interested in whatever game Tallon thought he was playing. I wasn't impressed.

The evening meal passed in a quiet haze. The prince and I shared the same space, but the silence between us was a wall too thick to breach. Surrounded by a crowd, I was utterly alone. Besides Edith and Scythe, I knew no one here. Fyrn was across the room, wrapped up in conversation with some young women, all of whom kept sneaking glances at the dais.

Or rather—at Tallon.

I couldn't understand why it annoyed me that they found him attractive. He had a certain boyish charm—bright green eyes and dark hair that fell across his brow. Yet I knew the darkness behind that gaze. The cruelty. The anger. It was impossible to reconcile the man he was with the face that captivated others. I hated I was destined to marry him, and I resented the fact that all the noblewomen saw something I didn't.

When Kallias rose from the table, I watched him go, timing my escape by the seconds. As soon as I deemed it safe, I excused myself and practically fled the hall. It took more effort than usual to shake my guards, requiring me to insist on my freedom to roam—punctuated by a lofty chin raise that lacked conviction.

I managed to navigate the route to the rooftop, my steps quickening as I neared the stairs. The sun, the warmth, the wind on my face—it was what I craved.

And perhaps, the king's company.

Hiking my skirts, I pushed forward and cleared the door to the balcony—only to find it empty.

Disappointment settled deep, and my shoulders sagged as I made my way toward the short wall. The sky was darkening, the fading yellow light bleeding into deep blue. No vibrant colors this evening, just the slow retreat of daylight—mirroring my heavy mood.

With a soft grunt, I hoisted myself up, letting my feet swing over the edge. Overgrown and wild, the garden below bled into a thick forest that bordered the untamed fields. The scene reflected the disarray inside me, the untended chaos of thoughts I couldn't quiet.

I don't know how long I sat there. Time seemed to stretch and bend. Eventually, the weight of my unease lifted, as if carried away on the breeze. My hair whipped around my face, and I closed my eyes, listening to the rush of wind as the sun disappeared beneath the horizon. Stars blinked to life far above, familiar and constant, though now viewed from a different angle—just like everything else.

"I didn't realize today was so trying."

Kallias' voice snapped me from my thoughts, and I gasped, twisting to face him.

"If you throw yourself to your death, please wait until I leave," he said with a smile tugging at the corner of his mouth, offering me a steaming mug. "It will look less like I pushed you."

I laughed and took the cup, fingers brushing his warm skin. The connection sent butterflies skittering low in my belly, and I pulled away, sniffing the drink.

He raised an eyebrow, sipping his own. "It's cider."

Steam curled beneath my nose as I brought the mug to my lips. Hot, sweet, comforting. It smelled like him. Cinnamon. I hid a grin, glancing out at the darkening fields. The sip was smooth, warmth spreading down my throat, filling my chest—tangy apples with a touch of sweetness.

I nodded, satisfied. "Thank you."

"Once I saw your guards roaming the halls, I thought refreshments were in order."

"How did you know I'd be here?" I teased. "I could've been anywhere."

He braced against the wall beside me, scanning the garden below. "I come here to be alone. It's my sanctuary when days are trying."

I shifted, ready to get down. "I didn't mean to impose–"

"Don't," he interrupted, raising a hand. "Please stay. It seems our days have both been more ill than good."

I settled back into my seat, curling around my cup, trying to leech the heat from it but also protect it from the wind. Silence lapsed between us, and I wondered which part of his day was the worst. Was it the council meeting where he had to face down his son? Or the sparring ring? There was so much to being a king that I wasn't privy to—perhaps it was something else.

"How's your shoulder?" I asked.

He scoffed, rolling it in a half-shrug. "A hilt hurts less than a blade through the socket. Tallon knew I favored it."

"That sounds... unpleasant." I grimaced. "Vellos?"

"The battle of Ereth'nor. We were outnumbered three to one." He blinked, his expression softening.

I leaned forward, resting my chin on my hand as I watched him. "And yet, here you are."

"I'm harder to kill than most." He tipped his cup toward me, eyes glinting. "Best keep that in mind."

I pressed a palm to my chest in mock horror. "I would never! Besides, my dragons are far too distant to carry me home."

"Not you." His gaze flickered, a slight wrinkle creasing his brow before he looked away. "Tallon's too eager for the throne. But I jest." His eyes held a guarded light as he watched me over the rim of his mug, as if weighing my reaction.

"The throne, not the yoke," I murmured.

"He will mature."

"Are you convincing me or yourself?" I bit down on my lip. What was it about this man that caused me to blurt out such things? He put me at ease, made me feel seen. But he was the *king!*

"You don't care for him."

Something sat on the edge of my tongue—denial? An excuse for my outburst?

His brow lifted, a spark of challenge. "Truth, remember?"

I clamped my mouth shut, watching him. His eyes held a glimmer, as if he'd known my answer long before I spoke it, and his lips edged into a faint smile. He wasn't upset.

"No." Admitting it brought a strange sense of relief. "I don't care for his attitude or the way he treats me. I was raised better, and expected more from him."

A muscle ticked in his jaw, though he kept his eyes steady, willing me to continue.

"He's rude, immature, and full of himself. I've tried, again and again, to prove my worth, yet he shuns me at every turn. I can't see us finding happiness in marriage."

He looked away, back to the dark fields, his face cast in shadow as the night deepened. Crickets chirped, their happy tune mocking my turmoil.

"He asked to be released from the alliance," he said.

I drew in a sharp breath. I hadn't dared suggest that, determined to fulfill my duty for Draconia's sake. For Tallon to request my dismissal—retract his father's blood oath and the very foundation of our treaty—would push Draconia and Radaan to the brink of war.

"Radaan needs this, Nienna." His tone steadied, though his voice remained tight, guarded. "If we don't secure this alliance—and the marriage that binds it—the Velli will attack within a year. They won't stop, and this time, I'm not certain we can hold them back."

His jaw tightened as he exhaled a weary sigh. He was risking everything by telling me Tallon requested to dissolve the contract—all for the sake of honesty.

"Kallias—"

His gaze darkened, a perfect mirror of the night sky as he searched my face.

"—I will marry Tallon. Draconia needs food. Our dragons deserve better hunting grounds. My duty isn't to him, but to our kingdoms. I know where I belong, and it's here, at Radaan's side."

His eyelids drifted shut as if my words pained him, and he turned away.

"If I may be blunt?" I asked, hating the invisible weight he shouldered—even though I was the one marrying Tallon.

He nodded, draining his mug.

"I've heard there was little love between you and the late queen."

His eye twitched, and his posture shifted—the stiff set of his shoulders, the subtle bracing of his stance. There was more to the story, more than he wanted to share, and I needed to uncover it.

"Perhaps you could offer guidance."

"Marriage advice?" His scoff came short and dry.

"From one loveless union to the next." I beamed, though the words cut a gash through my heart. Love was never an expectation, but I had hoped, at least, for a partner I could tolerate.

"I fear I'm rather unqualified." He held out his hand, a silent gesture for my cup.

"That's where you're wrong." I drained the last sip and swung my legs over the wall, dropping beside him. The warmth radiating from him brushed my skin like a stolen comfort. "You can teach me how to win Tallon's heart. You're the most qualified—unless *you* were the one who pushed the queen away?"

A flicker betrayed him, a brief twitch at the corner of his eye. His tell. I extended the cup, grinning in challenge.

He squinted, then sighed, and took it from my grasp. His fingers grazed my palm, the touch lingering just enough to notice.

"Come tomorrow night." He shook his head, a reluctant smirk tugging at his lips. "I'll share my pearls of wisdom. Though I doubt you'll find them valuable."

"I shall string them into a necklace."

I laughed, retreating toward the door. My steps were lighter, my chest unburdened. It wasn't the crisp air or even the time with him—it was the invitation. He wanted me to return.

And that was just silly.

Chapter Thirteen

NIENNA

The canvas loomed before me, its surface a taunting confession. My fingers twitched, itching to hurl it into a hearth—even in the sweltering summer heat, where no flames danced. Obliteration was the only solution.

Rough lines and jagged strokes seemed to pulse with accusation. The strong, sinewed figure caught in charcoal was unfinished but damning. The face remained blank, yet the wrists were bound in the sleeves of a garment.

"What are you sketching?" Fyrn's voice pierced the silence behind me.

My breath hitched. Too late. Her sharp eyes had already seen it. Suppressing the sting of panic, I reached for the canvas, letting my features settle into an indifferent mask.

"Nothing of importance," I muttered, fingers curling to claim it.

"Is that a man?" Dior'gad rose from her chair, pinching her spectacle into place as she squinted at the sketch.

Rachel, her youngest, perked up at the question. She darted to my side, quicker than her mother's limping steps, and leaned in to inspect the damning lines.

At nearly fourteen, she would soon be seeking a match of her own, but for now, Dior'gad shepherded her through palace halls, assessing the options.

The girl frowned, tilting her head as though a different angle might reveal the truth. "I don't see it." Her lips puckered in thought, her curiosity as sharp as her mother's scrutiny.

"Rachel! Princess Nienna—is that man naked?" Dior'gad's voice rang with both scandal and intrigue.

Heat rushed to my cheeks as I gripped the folds of my skirt, my palms damp. "I was only working on proportions," I stammered. "It's crucial to understand the balance of the human form in art."

Did that sound believable—or worse?

"If that's the case," Dior'gad sniffed, "you've exaggerated his shoulders, his chest is overdone, and Veridis be praised, no man possesses that many abdominals."

One did. Six visible muscles carved his stomach, with faint diagonal lines connecting them to his back. The memory of that perfection lingered, burned into my mind like the charcoal that had captured him. A reminder I couldn't erase, no matter how much I tried.

But I could dispose of the canvas.

"You're right, the proportions are off," I said, nodding with feigned agreement.

Fyrn narrowed her eyes, that sly grin creeping across her face. She knew I was lying—and I would pay for it later.

"I'll get rid of it and start fresh. It was a pleasure, Dior'gad."

Even Rachel couldn't hold back a giggle as I took my leave.

"I'll visit later!" Fyrn called after me.

I offered a brief nod before stepping out into the hall, clutching the canvas close. A deep breath of relief filled my lungs.

None of them knew. They didn't know I had drawn the king with his tunic off. If they did—my reputation would be ruined. It was improper for me to even perceive what his bare chest looked like, let alone capture it in art.

I hurried down the corridor, my guards falling into step behind me. It was my own fault for letting my mind wander. Dior's complaints about the lack of trade from central Radaan had worn thin. I understood her point, but after her sixth lament about lavender from their fields, I nearly suggested she hire a new overseer to source better seeds.

Her constant droning had set my thoughts adrift, my hand absentmindedly sketching that damnable image.

The drawing room felt miles from my quarters as my boots sped against the rugs, urgency driving me forward. My guards were nearly jogging to keep pace, their footsteps echoing in the halls. I approached an intersection, unsure whether to turn left or go straight. A wrong move would mean retracing my steps to ask for directions or worse—relying on my guards.

I spun around the corner—and collided with a wall of metal and cloth.

The canvas slipped from my grip as I tried to catch myself. Its corner caught the toe of my boot, sending it skidding out of reach. I yelped in surprise, and the man I collided with grunted under the impact, and someone's strong grip seized my arm to steady me.

"Princess."

The chains of Kallias' mantle tangled in my hair, and I gasped as he pulled away to put proper distance between us.

"My hair!" I whimpered, stepping on his toes as I followed his retreat.

Greaves released his hold and took a step back, giving a brief bow for touching me.

Frantically, I worked at the gold chains. The loops felt endless, and my fingers trembled, only tightening the mess. "I'm sorry!"

"Wait." Kallias grunted, shifting his boot beneath mine to remind me I still stood on his toes.

I mumbled an apology and shifted back, my head near his chest. His hands moved through my hair, pulling the chains free with gentle tugs.

"I should've slowed down. I apologize." My voice stumbled as I noticed the deep green brocade of his overcoat. Gold embroidery of flowers and leaves traced the fabric, fitting his broad chest and tapering waist. The scent of spices surrounded me, and my stomach twisted with nervous energy.

"In a hurry?"

I opened my mouth, but nothing came out. His fingers, long and callused, worked with precision. A sign of his noble heritage, but a testament to his work ethic.

My gaze dropped to his black boots, then to my light blue dress brushing the tops of them.

Too close. I stood far too close. Anyone passing by might see us like this—my reputation undone over a careless sketch.

"Princess." His rough fingers released the final chain, and it fell against his chest as he placed a hand on my shoulder. "Are you well?"

I forced a smile and stepped back. His touch fell away, but his brow remained furrowed, lips pressed tight with concern.

"I'm fine. I was just heading to my rooms. My apologies."

"The third apology in as many minutes." His face softened, the crease between his brows fading. "You're forgiven."

I let out a breath, trying to push the knot of nerves with it.

Then he bent down and picked up the canvas.

A wave of horror surged through me, and my cheeks burned. He straightened, glancing at the sketch as he passed it back to me.

"I didn't know you drew." His voice faltered as I reached out for it, and that familiar crease of confusion reappeared as he tilted his head. He brought the canvas closer, studying it with narrowed eyes. I prayed to every god I knew that the earth would open and swallow me whole.

"Just a sketch," I managed, voice tight.

Greaves cleared his throat, and I caught the way he blinked, lips pressed together as though to hold back a smile. My face flamed, and sweat gathered along my brow.

"Just a sketch," I repeated, more forcefully this time. "Nothing worth calling art."

His piercing gaze locked onto mine, but his expression remained unreadable. Yet the weight of his stare carried a thousand questions.

Did he assume I'd drawn another man? Would he think me unchaste, disloyal? Was he worried about a bastard heir? If he knew I'd been close enough to sketch a half-naked man, as a princess–

"The battle for the foothills," he said.

I blinked, confusion warring with panic. My fingers tugged at my skirts, and I tried a smile, but it faltered and disappeared.

"The scar across my chest is from the battle for the foothills in the northern mountain range," he continued, handing me the canvas. "Nearly lost my heart that day."

He watched me closely as I grabbed it and hugged it close, not caring if charcoal smeared my blouse. Did he find this amusing?

"I don't know what you mean." My throat tightened as I met his gaze, chin raised.

"I think you do." His eyes flicked toward the guards, and his expression went unreadable as he straightened. "But you seem to be in a hurry. I won't keep you."

"Thank you," I muttered, stepping around him. The words caught in my throat, and I moved with haste, letting the tension in my muscles carry me away. I didn't say another word as I fled the scene, though I thought a great many curses.

"It was quite a nice picture."

"Scythe!" Both Edith and I hissed in unison.

The younger handmaiden flinched and gave a sheepish smile. Edith poked at the canvas, already burning in the hearth, scattering ashes back into the flames. I sprawled across my sofa, my arm over my eyes, waiting for my pulse to return to an acceptable pace.

"Perhaps you should refrain from drawing men."

Edith's voice hummed with a reprimand, but I didn't dare lift my gaze. When I'd rushed in, demanding the sketch be destroyed, she had taken it without a word. Her stare alone could've withered grass.

I lay still, listening to the crackle of the fire, trying to ignore the weight of Edith's words. The tradition of waiting three seasons to wed had already begun—enough time to prepare for the wedding, for Tallon and I to become acquainted, for us to prove we were trustworthy.

And, perhaps most crucial of all, for me to prove I wasn't with child.

Purity mattered to royals. Reputation was everything. And yet, yesterday, I stared at the king in his undress, then approached him afterward—the guards had to have witnessed. Who had they told? Scythe remained silent, so the servants hadn't spread the word.

But Kallias? He'd practically broadcasted that not only had I seen him bare, but I'd drawn him. Models posed for hours while trained artists worked. How long did they think I studied the sculpted planes of his torso? Had they imagined I mapped every dip, every curve, scrutinized the trail of hair that led down–

"Shall you wear a brown dress for the evening meal?"

I could always rely on Edith to pull me from my spiraling thoughts.

"Brown is so drab," Scythe groaned, heading into my dressing room in search of something brighter.

"Princess," Edith's voice dropped to a whisper, meant only for me.

I straightened, pressing my lips tight. "I know."

"Is there another man?"

My gaze sank to the floor. I rubbed at my cheeks, willing them to cool. The heat of the blush from earlier was still there, lingering.

Kallias' blue eyes flashed before me, his tunic tangled around his wrists. His bare skin shimmered in the midday sun, his expression a mix of shock and confusion.

"No." I cleared my throat, meeting her sharp gaze. "There's no other man."

I was bound for Tallon, no matter my feelings. He wasn't hard on the eyes, but it was his spirit I loathed. I still had a chance at happiness, even if I had to force myself into it.

"You are a princess, Your Highness." Edith sighed, sitting beside me. She took my hand, her touch warm and steady. Always so proper, never letting her affection as the nanny who raised me show too much. "He is young. Give the prince time. Your marriage does not have to be loveless."

"I have tried, Edith." Tears burned at the backs of my eyes, but I wiped them away. I wouldn't cry over a boy I didn't love. "He's vile, and he doesn't care about me, this alliance, or Radaan. He fights me and tests me at every turn, leaving his father to clean up his mess."

Her expression softened. "He will mature. Nineteen is young for–"

"A royal." The words snapped out before I could stop them. Immediately, I regretted the harshness in my tone, but I couldn't take it back. "If he were anyone else, at nineteen, he'd be expected to have sired a son and be raising a family by now."

"And you'd be called a spinster. You have matured too fast." Her words cut through the anger, calm and steady.

I shot her a glare. "You've been listening to Scythe too long."

"You're ready for marriage, for children, to lead." She sighed, her gaze never leaving me. "He is not. It will take him longer, but don't hold that against him."

I ground my teeth together, focus locked on the fire, resisting the urge to yank my hand from hers. There was no hope of a happy marriage with Tallon. I would do my duty, bear heirs. But I wouldn't fool myself into thinking I could be happy doing so.

"Everyone keeps telling me to give him time." I stood, moving toward the sounds of Scythe rummaging through my dressing room. "It seems time is all I have."

I buried my emotions deep and lifted my chin. I was a princess, and I would act like one.

Scythe picked a shimmering bronze dress, a compromise with Edith, who had insisted on brown for tonight because of the moons' cycle and the rotation of my wardrobe.

At dinner, every movement of mine caught the light, but throughout the meal, I avoided eye contact with both Kallias and his son.

When I excused myself, Tallon looked relieved, his usual smirk replaced by a lighter mood. I ignored him and went straight to my rooms.

No sneaking past my guards. No quiet escapes.

And certainly no balcony meetings with a man whose body still haunted my dreams.

Chapter Fourteen

KALLIAS

My stallion snorted, his nostrils flaring as a ball rolled into his path, chased by a boy no taller than my knee. His ears flicked forward, tracking the child as he darted after it, heedless of the towering beast in his way. Behind him, his mother's frantic voice rose above the bustle of the crowd.

"Pardon him, Your Majesty!" she cried, her back bent in a hurried bow. Her arms reached for him, but the boy slipped from her grasp and vanished into the throng, paying us no mind.

I chuckled, content. These were my people—their familiarity with me, even their disregard, spoke volumes. They were safe. Protected.

"Peace," I said, my voice carrying above the market's murmur.

She looked up, her eyes wide with relief. Her dress, frayed at the hem and patched over the knee, expressed long days and harder nights. The bonnet perched on her head, once white, bore streaks of earth and toil. She was of the working class, a woman whose son would one day inherit her burdens, just as surely as the sun would rise.

Greaves reined in his horse beside me, his keen gaze sweeping the crowd. The tension in his shoulders mirrored the weight pressing on my own.

I'd given so much—my blood, my peace, my very sense of self—to protect these people. And still, the sacrifice continued. Would they cower in fear when dragons darkened their skies? Or would they trust this decision? That it would keep them alive, ensure food for their tables?

"Elohios bless you," a woman called, her voice rising above the murmurs as I rode past.

"Blessed of Elohios," the chant swelled, spreading like a wave through the gathered masses.

My lips curved into a smile, but the sound twisted something deep within me.

The Radaanian people were faithful to their core. Survival had forged that bond. I'd led them through the war's fire, into this fragile peace. Many witnessed the Velli rip through our ranks. Others carried stories of that horror passed down by their dead. And then there was me—alive when I shouldn't be, rising again and again from wounds meant to end me, the light of Elohios blazing through my sunlit skin as proof of his favor.

I owed everything to my god. His wisdom lit my path. His strength bore the weight I could not carry alone. In return, I gave him all of myself—honesty, integrity, and the unwavering resolve demanded by my people and the god who chose me.

Yet, being placed on a pedestal under Elohios was an unease I could never shake.

The gold chains draped over my shoulders and chest felt heavier than their weight suggested, biting into my skin as if to remind me of the nation resting on my reputation.

We continued through the streets of Reem, the clamor of the marketplace blending with the steady clop of hooves on cobblestones. The mingled scents of baking bread and livestock filled the air. Greaves rode at my side, his ever-watchful eyes scanning the crowd, though the city patrol had been tripled.

I allowed the streets to guide the way, letting instinct and faith intertwine as I searched my heart for Elohios' subtle leading.

As I rounded the corner onto the broad avenue, a prickle of unease crept up my spine. My eyes swept the square, noting its familiar rhythm—the wary merchants haggling, workers lingering in the shade, little ones darting between stalls. But two women stood out. Their posture, too rigid, too controlled—something about them didn't belong.

They weren't Radaanian.

Children clustered around the pair, giggling as they tossed dice into a chalk circle. The usual murmurs of blessings faded under the noise of the street, blending with the rhythmic hoofbeats of my stallion.

The women's fine cloaks caught my eye, too pristine against the dust and heat. Torn at the edges, the fabric still clung to a quality of wealth. Their hoods were pulled back, revealing hair—brown and blonde—that looked too clean for the working class.

One woman shook a die in her hand, her fingers caressing the smooth surface as she blew on it, a motion practiced like a gambler's ritual. She tossed the die with a flourish, and a cry of dismay escaped her when it landed.

The children's laughter erupted around us, their high-pitched voices ringing through the air. They clutched their bellies, some collapsing onto the ground, kicking their feet in the dirt as if her misfortune were the greatest joke they'd ever heard.

Greaves pulled up beside me, and with a single glance, I knew he understood. What noblewoman would be caught on the filthy streets playing with children?

The woman's golden hair tumbled forward as her shoulders slumped, defeated. She struggled to rise, letting out an ungraceful groan, fumbling with the clasp of her cloak. Around her, the young ones bounced to their feet, their energy unrestrained as they crowded closer, laughing in wild circles.

Who was this woman, to draw my people's attention away from their king? The crowd's focus shifted, yet no one seemed bothered for long. They shrugged it off and returned to their routines.

She tugged at her cloak, undone and falling loose, and handed it to her companion. I caught a glimpse of her cheeks flushed with the midday heat.

"Sun above." The curse slipped from my lips before I could stop it.

Greaves made a strangled noise, his gaze darting over the crowd again, searching in vain for any guards who might be accompanying them.

I spurred my stallion into a brisk trot. The horse snorted at the sudden shift, its hooves striking the cobblestones with force as it surged forward. The woman's eyes flicked to me, sharp with surprise.

Her gaze, the color of the deepest sea, locked onto mine. Shock flashed across her face as her lips parted in surprise.

The woman beside her—a stranger—ripped the cloak from her shoulders with a laugh, then turned toward me. "Balls!"

I froze, eyebrows shooting up at her exclamation. My stallion came to a halt as I took in the scene.

Nienna elbowed her friend, who wheezed. They both dropped into a curtsy, hers being far too low for her station. "My king!"

Curse it, they were sneaking around Reem, pretending to be common noblewomen.

I cleared my throat, shifting in the saddle. One hand rested on the pommel, the other on my hip as I tilted my head and waited.

Hoodlums swirled about like a ragged cloud, keeping their distance but bowing in awkward, uncoordinated movements. Grubby hands grasped at Nienna's dress, pulling at her as they jostled her forward.

She flashed me a hesitant smile, swaying with their tugs. Her mouth opened, then closed, as though searching for something to say.

"It seems you're at a loss for words, my lady," I teased, letting her scramble for an explanation.

"I—I beg your pardon, my king. I've just lost a wager," she stammered, her face deepening in color.

The woman beside her grimaced and edged a step away.

"And who do I have the pleasure of meeting?" I inquired, voice low and steady.

She seized the woman's arm in a grip that could have snapped bone, snapping a smile that was more like a flash of teeth. "This is my handmaid–"

"Noblewoman Scythe," the brunette blurted, dropping into a curtsey that was a more forced movement than a graceful gesture.

I squinted at them, Nienna's grin faltering as a girl yanked at her skirts. "That's an unusual name," I murmured, trying to place the woman.

"You lost! You have to race us!" the girl demanded, ignoring my presence. She was small, her dress a tattered brown, a size too short. Her hand gripped Nienna's as though it might be the only thing keeping her tethered to the world.

"I couldn't beg your horse, could I, Your Majesty?" Her laugh wavered, betraying the nervous edge in her voice.

"'Tis a beast reserved for royalty, I'm afraid," I replied with a sigh. She wanted to play games, I would let her. Within Reem, Greaves and I could watch over her and protect her despite her lack of guards.

That, and I remembered her inexperience with horses.

"Drat."

Her mild curse surprised me. I raised an eyebrow as she huffed, then straightened her posture.

"If you'll excuse me, dear King," she spun from me—actually *turned her back* on me, "I have a race to win."

Her voice trailed off as I stared at her bare shoulders, glowing in the sunlight. I couldn't tear my eyes away, my focus locked on the way she tied her hair. A bead of sweat ran down her neck, following the curve of her shoulder before disappearing into the fabric of her dress. I gripped the saddle tighter than I meant to, watching a few tendrils of hair slip free.

The urge to sweep them away—and taste that exposed skin—struck me like a fist to the chest.

When she gathered her skirts, hiking them between her knees, the impulse to sweep her onto my horse and ride straight to the safety of the castle nearly overtook me.

The smile faded from my lips, replaced by a dry mouth as she yanked the hem through her belt, revealing her legs.

They were wrapped in fabric that caused the children to giggle and point. But the tan trousers clung to her like a second skin, shaping every curve as she adjusted the waistband.

As she twisted, the definition in her thick thigh caught the light.

A snort tore my gaze from Nienna's legs, and I snapped toward the 'noblewoman' at her side.

Who was she? And what lent her the confidence to snicker at me as if she'd spotted me ogling the princess' body?

Good gods. I had.

Heat washed over me, thick and shameful. I cleared my throat and straightened, one hand resting on my belt.

Nienna glanced over her shoulder, brushing a curl from her face. Mischief gleamed in her eyes as the children lined up beside her.

"On your call, my king?"

My king.

A tight knot formed in my chest. What was wrong with me?

"On three," I muttered, pushing the thought aside.

She crouched low, hands pressing into the dirt. The crowd, thin but watchful, shuffled back, clearing a path.

"One, two—"

She wiggled her rear, boots digging into the earth.

"—three."

I strained to keep my voice steady as they bolted forward, a blur of whoops and laughter. Nienna's legs ate up the distance, though she hesitated, darting after the children who weaved through the crowd.

I turned to Scythe with a sigh. "She hasn't the faintest idea where she's racing to, does she?"

"Not a clue." She grinned, clutching the cloak tighter to her chest.

"Greaves." My bodyguard and friend took a deep breath, his only complaint as he spurred his horse into a trot, following the ruckus of children and a full grown woman that were racing through the streets.

At dinner, Nienna seemed at ease for the first time in days. As Tallon approached to claim the seat beside her, she glanced my way and smiled—a real one, the corners of her eyes crinkling with warmth. That smile was her tell, unguarded and genuine, unlike the polished façade she wore for court.

The afternoon run through the city had lifted her spirits, and I knew why. Reem's bustling chaos offered her a reprieve from all the suffocating expectations. I understood the need for escape. She was adjusting to life here, and the demands of court were a burden on anyone. I sought out common folk just the same, but I had many more years to learn how to blend in. For her, new to this world, a stolen afternoon outside noble eyes had been a gift.

Greaves, however, saw it differently. As we turned in for the night, he made his opinion known.

"You need to triple her guard," he muttered, tucking his favorite knife under his pillow with a sharp, deliberate motion.

"And what good would that do?" I asked, pulling my tunic over my head and tossing it onto the chair. "You've seen her slip past them more times than I can count."

He grunted in agreement. The thought trailed after me as I prepared for bed. She didn't need more guards—another squad of well-meaning sentinels wouldn't stop her. What she needed was a shadow, someone like Greaves, sharp enough to anticipate her moves and stubborn enough to keep up.

The man himself had shadowed me for years. Loyal to a fault, he was more than a bodyguard—he was the friend I hadn't known I was missing, the one who remained steadfast when the world turned its back.

He had seen me at my worst. After Eldeiade took what she wanted and left me hollow, he endured my fury in the sparring ring without complaint. When Tallon was born and she refused me even a glimpse of him, Greaves witnessed my shame and never spoke a word.

"She needs someone to stop her before she does anything reckless," he said, his voice low but firm.

I couldn't help but snort. "Have you ever managed to hold me back?"

His huff carried a blend of humor and resignation as he sank onto his bed. "I'd like to think I've saved you from yourself more than a few times." His gaze lingered, steady and unyielding. "You need to be careful, Kal."

I dipped a cloth into the basin, letting the cool water seep through my fingers before pressing it to my face. The deliberate act bought me time to formulate a reply. He wasn't worried about my safety. He'd seen too much—watched me endure Eldeiade's manipulations—and he was too perceptive to miss the way my eyes followed Nienna.

A queen in the making, forged from strength and poise. She was what Radaan needed, what the people deserved.

What I could never claim.

"I *am* careful," I said, keeping my tone calm.

Climbing into bed, I avoided his eyes. His silence stretched, heavy with unspoken words, until he sighed and shifted, the cot creaking beneath his weight.

The room fell quiet, but sleep eluded me. The night thickened, shadows pooling in corners while my thoughts spiraled. Her sketch haunted me. I remembered how her gaze had rested on me in the arena. That look—it had to be shock. Surely, that's all it was.

I knew the customs of her people. Draconis were far from prudish, but their noblewomen were treasures, their virtue guarded. And yet, I had stood there in the sparring ring, stripped to the waist.

And I'd made enough of an impression for her to draw me.

Her lines, clean and deliberate, marked the canvas with a precision that betrayed practiced skill. The curves of the torso were mine, though the face remained a hollow void, the legs unfinished. Yet, cutting across the chest, she had etched the jagged scar—a brutal relic of the battlefield.

How many more scars had she noticed?

Sleep refused to claim me. I tried to ground my thoughts to the harvests in the south or the watchtowers guarding the eastern frontier. I thought of the Untamed Valley and the great crater that scarred the land. Anything to keep my mind from *her*. From the bead of sweat that had slipped down her neck, catching the light, or the way her trousers hugged her frame.

Did she have to wear fabric so close to her skin's tone? Couldn't it have been black? Red, perhaps?

An unbidden image flared—a sheer tunic, crimson trousers clinging to her figure. Heat coiled low in my stomach, and I cursed under my breath, biting back a groan as I turned again in the bed, kicking at the tangled sheets. Why were my rooms so hot?

Greaves grumbled from the cot, his words muffled by the pillow. "Fight it out or walk it off?" He didn't bother lifting his head.

"Sleep," I barked, scrubbing a hand over my face.

I would have sleep.

My finger tapped against my thigh beneath the council table, the anxious motion concealed from view. My gaze drifted to the empty chair on Tallon's right, the left now occupied by his newest companion. Verard'gog—a minor landowner from the Craggs. It seemed all of his guests hailed from the east these days.

Nienna had avoided me for two nights. Two.

Not that I could offer her much in the way of marital advice. What wisdom could I share, except what *not* to do?

Look your husband in the eye when he speaks. Listen when he rambles about the strain between nations. Don't scream and strike him when he tries to kiss you.

Unbidden, shame unfurled in my chest, raw and biting. Memories of Eldeiade's tirades clawed to the surface. Her voice, rising like a whip crack, accusing me of treating her like an animal, only to demand an heir in the next breath. The venom in her words as she tore at me in private, unraveling everything I tried to hold together.

Nothing was ever good enough for her.

I swallowed hard, forcing the thoughts aside. They lingered like ghosts at the edges of my mind, but the council's murmur drew me to the present. Still, the bitterness remained, a familiar taste I couldn't quite spit out.

It wouldn't be Tallon enduring those tirades and verbal abuse. No, it would be Nienna.

The thought twisted through me as Lieghton'son droned on about the drought plaguing his province. He proposed trenches from the Fillyen River, while Har'mon railed against it, arguing it would devastate his wheat fields. Their voices blurred into the background, eclipsed by the rising tide of my own irritation.

Where was Nienna?

At a social gathering, perhaps, immersed in the labyrinthine games of court? Was she seated among noblewomen, nodding as they spoke of her "luck" in securing a match with Tallon?

My son chuckled low, his shoulders shaking with quiet amusement at some remark from Verard. The nobleman's gaze flicked to mine, and for a moment, the shrewd smirk that followed slipped past his polished mask.

Perhaps she was alone, sketching—a refuge from the deceit and hollow courtesies that poisoned our world.

Was she drawing me again? Filling in the blanks of her unfinished sketch? A smile tugged at the corner of my lips. I shifted in my chair, angling my head to shield the traitorous expression from view.

I was a blasted king, smiling over a princess drawing me.

Throne or not, I had never allowed the burden of my years—or my crown—to drag my body into disrepair. Sparring with Greaves and the occasional disciplinary bout with Tallon kept my strength honed. I was no longer a young man, and the hard lines of my youth had softened, but they hadn't disappeared. Clearly, they were sharp enough to inspire a virile, golden-haired woman to commit them to canvas.

"—Velli within the week."

The name struck like a cold wind, scattering the warmth of her memory. *Velli*—my enemy and the architect of half my troubles—demanded my focus.

"His rooms are prepared." My voice dipped, deliberate and firm. These were not friends. *One* ambassador, permitted under the treaty, would now reside within these walls—his quarters placed at the farthest end of the palace, as distant from Nienna's as possible.

"It would serve us well to extend an olive branch, Father." Tallon's gaze locked on mine, a glint of challenge in their depths.

I frowned, my disapproval clear.

"Perhaps a ball in his honor," he said.

"A *ball?*" General Darius spat the word, his voice rough with disbelief.

Across the table, Fallione stiffened, his fists tightening as his gaze drilled into the map, as if sheer focus could temper the bite he no doubt wished to unleash.

"Yes," Tallon continued, unflinching, the corner of his mouth lifting into a smirk. "A formal occasion, General. Nobles dressed in finery, exchanging pleasantries. Though I imagine you might find little to discuss beyond soldiering—bland topics for a dance."

"You weren't there, *boy*, when Vellos–"

"There isn't enough notice." My tone cut through the tension before Darius could step too far. Tallon's goading had worked, but the general should've known better. "A few days won't suffice to prepare."

"Just a small one." Tallon brushed a hand through his dark hair, revealing the sharp angles of his face, features gleaming with an intensity that bordered on defiance. "Say the word, Father. I'll handle it. Foreign relations are my domain—let me do my job."

It was the first time he'd ever shown enthusiasm for the duties laid upon him. His smile, more a baring of teeth than a sign of goodwill, carried a challenge I did not trust. The calculation in his gaze made my chest tighten, but I couldn't ignore the truth. Radaan didn't belong to me alone. It was his kingdom, too.

The lantern's glow flickered across his face, and for a moment, his eyes gleamed like a predator's—too much like the Velli.

But this was my son. My only heir. Without him, the throne held no future. If he wanted to test himself, I wouldn't stand in his way.

"Done," I said. "Set it for the day after his arrival."

Fallione's jaw tightened as his eyes closed, a practiced gesture of restrained fury. Across the table, Darius sank into his seat, muttering curses under his breath while shaking his head.

"Thank you," Tallon replied, his tone laden with anything but gratitude. "Who's the ambassador?"

A groan rippled through the room. My own eyes closed against the dull throb of frustration. He listened only when it served his purpose, a trait inherited straight from his mother.

"Egath," I said at last, the name heavy on my tongue.

Egath, son of Wrath. The warrior whose blade came within a whisper of my heart at the foothills. The descendant of the man I killed.

"Done!"

Tallon shot to his feet with far more enthusiasm than the topic deserved. Verard rose with him, both offering a curt excuse before taking their leave.

The heavy thud of the doors shutting echoed through the chamber. Silence reigned until Darius turned a scowl on me, his disapproval written in the hard lines of his face.

I met his glare with indifference. He had no heirs. War consumed his every moment. He wouldn't understand.

Not that I did either.

That night, I distanced myself from Nienna. My mask remained a quiet defense against the swirling tension in the room. The Velli were coming—into the very heart of Radaan, the one place I had kept them out of. The safety of my people, the sanctuary I had fought for, would be exposed to their bloodlust.

Even as I avoided her, I could *feel* her presence. The sound of her voice, the warmth in her gaze—it was a balm to my fractured soul. She embodied everything pure and unbroken—the fire in the Radaanian people that refused to fade. As long as she was safe, perhaps it would be enough.

Tallon rambled on about the ball, dismissing every suggestion Nienna made with a scoff. She tried to offer encouragement, but he shut her down each time, his laughter biting, his words belittling.

The way he treated her stirred a cold anger in me, a bitterness I knew all too well.

I couldn't stay. I rose, the chair scraping against the stone floor. As I left the dining hall, I felt her gaze following me, sharp with questions. She wanted to ask, but the company wouldn't allow it.

When we ventured past the private kitchen in our wing, without a word, Igor handed me my cider, a grin flickering across his face. I moved on, passing the cup to Greaves, who took a sip as we walked.

When we reached the pond stairwell, he offered me the mug, nodding as if it passed his inspection.

"I swear you drink more each time," I muttered, eyeing the half-filled cup.

"Some poisons are measured by quantity, not potency." Greaves sighed, taking his position by the door. "I do it for your sake."

With a snort, I strode to the stone wall and leaned over, the chill in the air biting at my skin. I counted the months in my mind until the harvests ended. The south would keep their land producing year-round, while the north would begin with cold-hardy greens. But the warm-season crops would finish in a few months.

We needed our men in the fields, not fighting wars.

Unease churned in my gut. No dragons arrived yet, and the whirlstorms added uncertainty to the delivery of Nienna's letter. A Velli stood on Radaan soil. I despised the thought of those monsters in my kingdom. They made me feel exposed, fragile.

And I loathed it.

If the Velli moved, I'd have to pull my men back to the Craggs. The loss of manpower to work the harvests and bring in food might balance out with the bodies left in the mountains. Another war wasn't an easy choice, but perhaps it was necessary.

The door to the roof groaned open, pulling me from my thoughts. I breathed in, forcing my mind to calm as I turned to face her.

Nienna peeked through, her silhouette bathed in the warm glow of the palace. Dusk had already settled, and the crickets sang their evening chorus.

"If you would rather be alone…" she began.

I ignored the rest of her words, focused on how her eyes softened with concern. She fretted about me. A princess, worried for a king.

"Come," I said, gesturing with a tilt of my head. Her frown eased, replaced by a hesitant smile as she crossed the threshold. She wore a red dress, the deep hue like blood.

It did not bode well for my evening.

The garment hugged her curves as she walked, swaying over black boots.

"You're worried."

Her attention did not drift to the fields or the sky above. She didn't peer down at the queen's garden, tangled and forgotten. No, her eyes—darkened by the fading light—focused on my face as she stood beside me.

I met her gaze, taking a slow sip of my cider, now lukewarm. "I don't worry—I prepare."

"What are you preparing for?"

A thrill ran through me when her stare lingered on my mouth.

Sun above, it had been too long since a woman looked at me that way.

"Everything."

It came out more of a grunt than I intended, and my attention shifted to the fields again. She made a thoughtful noise, letting me simmer while I studied the borders. An oxcart had wandered too close to the wheat field. Its wheel trail cut through the chaff, leaving a disorganized path.

Daylight dimmed with the setting sun, yet she stayed beside me, leaning against the wall, silent but watchful. She didn't press for conversation, nor did she pry. She was content with just being.

"Why are you here?" The question gnawed at me, buzzing like a fly too close to my ear.

The Velli's arrival weighed heavily on me, and the absence of dragons was unsettling. My hunger for her was an unfamiliar ache. It all left me feeling young, unprepared.

And I was taking it out on her.

"I want to be."

I blinked, frowning as I studied her dark silhouette. Her face was turned upward, eyes closed. The breeze tugged at her wavy hair, her presence still, serene.

I grunted, reaching for my empty mug, eager to escape the burden of the night—of everyone's company, even hers.

"You owe me marriage advice."

"I have none to give." The words snarled from my throat, biting as I hated myself for lashing out but couldn't stop. "My marriage was a torturous, miserable affair. I wouldn't wish it on anyone."

"Kallias."

I froze, my boots anchoring to the cool, sparkling sandstone. My gaze shot to Greaves, a silent plea for his aid.

Her voice—commanding, demanding—struck deep. It was the essence of a queen addressing her subject, the tone of a lover scorned.

The man exhaled, his brows rising as he stared at the ground. I'd opened that door, and now I had to face the consequences. My response would either drive her away, shattering whatever fragile connection we'd built, or it would break down another wall between us.

She was Tallon's betrothed. A union forged in the name of alliance. She was safe from me, as I was from her.

Her hand found my shoulder, searing through the thick fabric of my overcoat. "It's one Velli. Your people are safe."

Elohios above, how did she know?

"This is the single place I swore they would never set foot in again." The words grated from my throat. "You've never seen them fight, Nienna. Never felt the power they wield."

Bile crawled up, remembering the soldiers torn apart in front of me. Velli drank their blood as though it were water. Men stripped of their will, forced into combat against comrades. Faces of those I had known—fighting by my side—dying on my sword, their bodies puppets controlled by the enemy. She never–

"I haven't." Her voice, soft and steady, pulled me from my recollections. She caught my hand, her grip warm. "Tell me."

And I knew she would listen. She would sit with me all night if necessary, letting me relive my worst memories. She would bear it, share it with me. But she shouldn't. She was too pure, too innocent. She didn't need to carry my nightmares. Radaan's burden was mine alone to bear.

"My advice for tonight is this," I said, easing her fingers off, ignoring the brief flicker of hurt in her eyes. "Do not touch a man who is not your betrothed."

Her hand jerked from my shoulder, and she sucked in a breath, stepping back. I ground my teeth and stormed for the door, leaving her alone in the darkening silence of the roof.

Chapter Fifteen

Nienna

"You're wrong." I snapped, storming through the door and slamming it behind me. Not that it slammed—there was something maddening about how smoothly it closed, as though it refused to match my frustration.

Scythe jolted upright from the sofa, her eyes wide and disoriented. "I'm never wrong!"

"He doesn't like me." I threw my hands at the back of my dress, fumbling with the lacing. The cords were out of reach, teasing me as my anger mounted.

"Trust me," she said, trailing behind as I stormed to the bathing chambers, "he ogled you like a sticky bun, just waiting to devour you!"

"Well, devour, he did—a dragon with its meal."

She froze, her grin flashing as she reached me. "That good, eh?"

"Ugh!" I shoved her away, struggling with the dress. The laces snagged, and I yanked it over my head, getting it caught on my shoulders. "He was upset tonight, so I thought, what's the harm? I should make sure he's all right."

"You. Seeing if the *king* was fine?"

I seethed as she giggled, tugging at the laces.

"We were enjoying each other's company," I muttered from beneath the dress now tangled around my head.

"Oh?"

"—in silence! And I simply asked what was wrong."

"Mm-hmm?" She yanked a lace loose with a quick tug, the snap echoing through the room, followed by a quiet whimper.

"I put my hand on his arm–"

"You touched him?!" Scythe's voice was a delighted squeal as she jerked the dress off my head, sending herself stumbling backward. "Was it like when you and the prince touched?"

I spun away, anger clawing at me. Every touch with Kallias was a spark, a warmth that spread through my chest—the first rays of sunlight after a storm. With him, there was always certainty. Safety.

"He scolded me—"

Scythe winced, her breath catching as she rushed over to pull the pins from my hair.

"—like a child."

That was the worst part. We built something solid between us—an understanding, a friendship, as much as a man and a woman could have while being promised to his son. And yet, he rebuked me as though I were a toddler who reached for the cookie jar without permission.

He could go nurse his wounds and bear his burdens alone, if that's how he would treat me. I was just trying to be polite, a friend.

"I'm sure he didn't mean-"

"He's the king, Scythe. He means everything he says."

Curse Elohios and the honesty he demanded. Kallias was nothing if not truthful. If he did not want me touching him, that was fine. I wouldn't.

And I would not let him touch me.

The next days dragged, a sickening blur of both haste and stagnation. Days rushed by as preparations for the ball consumed everyone. The Velli's arrival loomed, and Fyrn was immersed in the planning, her time spent almost entirely with the prince. The way she fit in with him gnawed at me. I tried to join them once, but it was clear that Tallon wanted nothing from me. I'd pulled each trick I knew to gain his respect, yet still, he brushed me aside.

The evenings were worse.

Kallias avoided my gaze, though I could feel the weight of his stare whenever I retired. I knew he watched. So, I sauntered, chin lifted, a princess in every step. Let him watch me walk away, knowing I wouldn't be joining him on his roof. Knowing that he should have taken more care with his words.

No. Kallias was always careful. Each word measured with purpose. I set my book aside and settled into the chaise, mind racing. That night, he'd been weighed down, burdened by more than just the crown. The pressure of it all made him snap—but still, he never lied.

When he told me not to touch him, was it for my sake, or his? His gaze lingered, sharp with something I couldn't quite place. Scythe said he looked like a man starved the day I raced in Reem. She wouldn't tease me if she didn't believe Kallias had feelings.

Did he forbid my touch to protect me from other men, or to keep me away from him? I studied my palm, fingers tracing the lines. Had it calmed him, soothed him? Or had it stirred something dangerous beneath the surface?

"I know some witches who could read those," Scythe offered, smirking over her book.

"What?"

She grinned. "The lines—on your hand."

"Witchcraft is frowned upon," Edith hissed, pausing in her mending. A cloak—mysteriously torn—lay in her lap.

My eyes rolled, and I was about to speak when a knock interrupted.

"Your dress!" Scythe chirped. She bounced up, jostling me, causing my book to hit the floor. "It's going to be beautiful!"

I stooped over to retrieve it while Edith went to answer. She took the package from the messenger, closing the door with a harsh frown. She faced us, brow furrowed as I dangled off the chaise, grinning up at her, then placed it on the table, eyeing it as if it might bite.

"What's wrong?" I asked.

"It's awfully small."

Scythe crawled over me, shoving me to the floor, eyes wide with excitement. "You haven't even opened it!"

"It's *my* dress!" I laughed, picking myself up off the carpet.

Tallon chose it himself, and on the heels of being shunned by his father, I was eager to garner some bridge between us. If wearing his selection accomplished that, I'd do it. A chime echoed in the distance—we didn't have much time to prepare.

Scythe tore into the box, then froze. "Where's the rest of it?"

All color drained from her face, her usual energy muted. Edith stiffened, her expression sharpening into a cold mask of fury. My chest tightened. I set my book aside, glancing between them. Dread coiled in my stomach as I approached the table.

"Where's the rest of it?" Scythe choked out.

Her question wasn't an exaggeration. Most of the dress seemed to be... absent.

I steeled myself and pulled the garment from the box. The fabric, no more than a whisper, shimmered under the light. Tiny black gemstones caught the glow like spilled ink against transparent crimson. The material reminded me of blood—sheer, yet vivid. Two daring slits ran up the front, slicing from ankle to waist in the bold style of Draconia. The neckline plunged scandalously low, the shoulders designed to drape over my arms, exposing my collarbone.

If it didn't fit, I'd have nothing else.

To wear it would feel like wearing nothing at all. The fabric offered no lining, no backing—just translucent red gauze stitched with black gemstones that would catch the light and every prying eye.

The three of us stood in silence, staring at the indecent garment. Edith's hands clenched the table's edge, her knuckles white. Scythe's jaw hung open, and for once, she seemed at a loss for words.

Tallon promised to find the perfect dress. He left no time for alternatives, no chance to commission a gown or even alter one I already owned. This was it. The only option.

My thoughts churned. Was this humiliation planned, a way to shame me in front of the court? Or was it meant to flaunt what he believed was his?

My pulse hammered, anger and defiance warring within. I wasn't a pawn, and I wouldn't shrink beneath their stares. If he desired me to be on display, then I'd make sure they looked.

I chose to flaunt it.

Heat crawled up my neck, flushing my face as my hands dampened with sweat. I had to piss.

But I straightened my spine, lifted my chin, and walked the corridors as if they were already mine. One day, they would be.

The dress revealed my thighs with each stride. Beneath it, black trousers hugged my legs like a second skin, as was the custom for female Draconis. It did little to quell the sensation of being exposed.

The fit was precise, a testament to Tallon's interference. He hadn't chosen this dress on a whim; a seamstress tailored it to my measurements. The timing, the craftsmanship—every detail screamed of deliberate planning. It was his doing, and I would wear it.

A strip of black fabric wrapped across my chest, barely concealing my breasts. I prayed it held through the night.

Radaanian women were modest, with their poofy-sleeves and high collars. Tonight, I paired my ensemble with towering boots, their sharp heels adding inches to my height. The taller I was, the more I could look down on Tallon—and ensure I'd never let him dictate my wardrobe again.

Gasps rippled through the halls, punctuated by the occasional stifled cough. Noblewomen clutched pearls while servants darted glances, their expressions caught between awe and scandal. My guards, stoic as ever, kept their gazes fixed ahead, helmets obscuring any hint of disapproval—or curiosity.

Boldness fueled by anger propelled me toward the herald. He hardly glanced up before his jaw slackened, lips forming a comical *O*. His wide eyes bulged as though they might tumble from their sockets.

"Princess Nienna of Draconia," I snapped, my tone as sharp as the steel on the guards' belts.

"Of course! Beg your pardon, Your Highness!" The herald jerked his gaze away, fumbling with the parchment in his trembling hands. He squinted at it as though confirming I belonged there. "Yes, yes—here!" His foot caught on the edge of his robe as he scrambled to the ballroom door.

The guards moved to open it, one lagging behind as the heavy panels creaked apart.

Curse this dress.

"Announcing Priestess—Princess Nienna of Draconia!" The herald's words cracked, wobbling into an undignified screech.

"The Dragon's Heart," I corrected, my voice cool and commanding.

Sweat gleamed on his brow as he darted a panicked glance my way, then back at the stairs. "The Dragon's Heart!" he managed, his tone rising an octave higher.

The staircase across the room remained empty. No one to distract the audience. Every eye would be on me.

This was not the time to stumble.

I lifted my chin, determination anchoring my steps as I descended the staircase. Each movement was deliberate, measured. The carpet muffled the sound of my boots, its plush weave deceptively soft underfoot. I kept my gaze forward, refusing to meet the sea of stares until I reached the landing.

When I last stood on this landing, it was to announce my betrothal to Tallon. The memory clung to the air, a ghost with harsh edges, heavy and acrid.

This time, the urge to kill him settled in my chest, cold and clear.

I pivoted on my heel, turning toward the crowd.

A musician faltered, his fingers stumbling over the strings. The jarring note sent another toppling backward, his chair saved from collapse by a quick-handed companion. Gasps rippled across the expanse, colliding with the awkward shuffle of instruments as the ensemble scrambled to regain their rhythm.

Heat scorched my ears, but something deeper, hotter, burned within. Fury kindled beneath my skin, propelling me as my gaze swept the room. I searched for Tallon's mocking green eyes.

Instead, I met blue.

Kallias stared back, his rage tangible, a roaring inferno that made my own anger feel like a matchstick's flicker. His head and shoulders rose above the sea of faces, his clenched jaw and storm-darkened eyes unmasking him completely.

Tallon emerged from the throng, standing just beyond the last step, his hand extended as if welcoming me to my own humiliation. A smirk tugged at his lips, the gesture almost boyish, ruined by the stray lock of hair falling against his brow.

The dress was a message—a statement meant to disgrace me.

So I'd wear it like a crown.

A cocky grin stretched across my face, false confidence masking the simmering fury beneath. I prowled down the steps, each stride calculated, hips swaying with defiance. Let them stare—feast their eyes. If Tallon wanted a spectacle, I'd give him one they'd never forget.

At the base of the stairs, I paused, tilting my head as I met Tallon's outstretched hand with a raised brow.

"This is your grand reception?" My voice cut through the air, pointed with mockery. "I expected better."

His smirk faltered for a heartbeat before venom glinted in his eyes. He withdrew and gestured toward the towering stranger at his side.

"Allow me to introduce Egath, *future bride*," Tallon said, voice clipped. "Egath, meet Nienna."

The man was tall. Even with my boots giving me height, I was a head shorter. At first glance, he seemed ordinary—dark hair, emerald eyes like Tallon's, nothing menacing. Then he smiled.

My blood ran cold.

His teeth were razor-sharp, filed to points that gleamed like ivory daggers under the chandeliers. He held his hand out—a shark stalking its prey.

"The pleasure is mine, Princess Nienna," he said, voice smooth.

How he spoke so clearly with a mouthful of daggers remained a mystery, one I didn't care to solve.

I refused to flinch. "The Dragon's Heart," I stated, extending my hand with regal detachment.

He took it, grip firm, eyes predatory. He lifted my palm to his lips, the brief touch deliberate. His gaze fixed on mine, his expression amused and calculating.

"Ah, yes. The dragons." His voice oozed mockery, the grin spreading wide, grotesque in its indulgence. "When do they arrive again?"

I fought the urge to wipe my hand against my skirts. "When I need them." I spun on my heel, eyes scanning the hushed crowd. "Where are the drinks, *husband to be?*"

That was just the start. The night dragged on, each minute heavier than the last. My feet screamed in protest, my throat dry as dust, and no amount of wine eased the burn. I avoided food, afraid my nerves would betray me. I wore a mask of bravado, pretending to be cocky, confident—Tallon's equal.

But Kallias remained a constant presence. He worked the crowd like a dragon, always in sight, ever within earshot. From the corner of my eye, I caught his gaze sliding over my transparent dress. He lingered on the curves of my body, eyes tracing upward in a slow, deliberate motion, a gesture that stoked the fire behind my façade.

I stood before the nobles and dignitaries, drawing strength from the weight of his gaze. My voice held steady, distant, as if anchored by his watchful presence. He was listening to every word.

Then, the exhaustion hit. It swept over like a storm, dousing the last embers of my resolve. The energy drained from my limbs, leaving me hollow, and my mask faltered. No one dared approach me—not even Tallon, who kept his distance more often than not.

Fyrn avoided me too, likely ashamed of my choice of dress—and ignorant of the fact that the prince selected it.

I slipped into the quiet corridors, my frustration mounting, and leveled a sharp glare at my guards. "I don't have the energy to escape tonight. Leave me be."

Of course, they refused.

For once, I didn't try to evade them. I found a secluded hall, sank to the carpet, and tugged off my boots. Relief flooded through me as I massaged my aching feet. After a moment, I continued on, padding barefoot down the corridor.

I trudged up the stairs, the cool touch of tadpoles and frogs in the wrought iron offered a reprieve. The guards clattered, their armor clanging with each step.

Cold night air wrapped me in a welcome embrace. I let the door swing shut, leaving my guards behind, then dropped my boots in a careless pile. When I reached the wall, I climbed on, letting out a quiet moan as I stretched out, propping one leg up while the other dangled over the safety of the sandstone.

Every muscle in my body screamed with the effort to relax, the tension from the evening clinging to me like a second skin.

It was mere breaths before the door opened again, and I rolled my head to the side. Kallias stood, his broad frame outlined by the lantern light, casting him in shadow. I sighed, returning my gaze to the stars glittering in the black sky.

A hushed voice broke the stillness, followed by the loud clank of armor as my guards retreated. Footsteps heralded Kallias' approach, and when he stopped, I drew in a deep breath and pushed upright.

I swung my legs inside the wall and braced my hands between my thighs, leaning forward. "Do you approve of your son's choice of dress?"

A soft creak betrayed the tension in his fist as it tightened around the hilt of his sword. I met his gaze—dark, brooding.

Definitely the wrong thing to say.

"You had every eye on you tonight," he rasped.

"I know I had yours," I said, a bitter laugh escaping. The mask was slipping. I was done pretending. Exhausted from the act. If he wanted me, he'd take me at my worst—or leave. I didn't care if it was his roof.

"You have other dresses."

"Telling me how to dress now?" I taunted.

"I could tell you what not to wear."

"Next time I get dressed, I'll be sure to invite you," I shot back, leaning against the stone. "To ensure my outfit is approved."

"Greaves," Kallias bit out, the name sharp as a command.

I raised an eyebrow, glancing past him. The man shifted, uncomfortable, but when our eyes met, he dipped his head and retreated into the palace. The roof felt quieter now, just the two of us.

"Why did you wear it?"

"Questions, questions," I murmured, tipping my chin, letting my hair spill down. The movement threw off my balance. I gasped, my nails digging into the stone. Kallias closed the gap between us, his arm wrapping around my waist and pulling me against his chest.

"How much wine did you have?"

I smiled, fingers tracing along his sleeve. Winds and seas, the man smelled incredible. Cinnamon and spice encased him, warm and familiar, with a touch of wood and a hint of musk.

He felt good too—solid muscle beneath fine clothing, heat radiating from him. His arm around me was firm, the closeness pinning him between my legs. The position sent flaming butterflies through my core.

"A bit of advice," I murmured, my gaze drifting over his face. "Don't touch a man's betrothed."

His jaw tightened, and I watched it, intrigued. A shadow of stubble darkened his cheeks, and his lips pressed into a tight line.

My own felt dry. I ran my tongue over them, almost without thinking.

His hand twitched at my back, and I leaned away. But instead of letting me go, he tightened his hold, drawing me in closer. His belt buckle jabbed into my thigh, and his gaze followed my tongue as it slid behind my teeth.

"I don't think you're in any condition to sit on a roof," he said, tugging me off the wall.

I stumbled against him—not from the wine, but because my feet had given up.

His hands steadied me at the waist, keeping me balanced—and keeping a careful distance. His dark eyes locked on mine, cutting through the night. A mix of concern and desire flickered there, the same hunger I'd seen in too many men tonight.

I reached to cup his jaw, but he shied away.

"Why do you get to touch me, but I can't touch you?" I asked.

"You don't know what you're doing. The wine's talking."

It hit me like cold water. I stepped back, the sudden clarity grounding me. Drawing from a strength I didn't realize I had, I met his gaze with a cutting stare. "I know exactly what I'm doing—what I crave. But I don't think *you* do."

"I came here to make sure no stray nobleman pursued you." He lifted his chin, arms crossing over his chest. "Every man in that room watched you. They're not all honorable."

"And your eyes never left me. You hovered, watching every conversation, waiting to intervene if needed. You followed me up here. Yet, you push me away. You'd think by running a kingdom you'd know how to get what you want!"

"I can't have what I want."

I recoiled, snapping my mouth shut. He ground his teeth together and glared at me, offering no more. His nostrils flared with his breaths, chest heaving—his mask long gone.

I swallowed, my words dry and cracked. "You came after me tonight. You sought me out. Yet you push me away."

He said nothing. His piercing blue gaze drifted over me, scanning my dress, tracing every curve. It sparked something deep inside—a fire that grew from ember to full blaze. Ravenous. He took in my ample hips, then traveled along my waist, lingering at my chest. I made no move to shield myself, refusing to cross my arms. His eyes climbed higher, pausing at my mouth, and stayed there.

His gaze burned into my skin, each look a touch, slow and deliberate, sending heat crawling across my flesh. I bit my lip. A muscle flickered in his jaw as he studied me.

"Sea beneath," I whispered. "You cannot have what you want."

My mind screamed—this wasn't right. He couldn't mean it. When his eyes locked with mine, they *burned*.

Gods, to be viewed like that. To be seen as something worth claiming, devouring. Yet he held himself back, tethering that hunger, forcing restraint.

I wanted him to lose that control.

Tallon never looked at me that way. Never would.

"You are my son's *betrothed*." Each word dragged from him, heavy and reluctant. I was off limits. The blood oath bound me to the prince. If we crossed that line—if I *let* him—the alliance would crumble.

Radaan's fragile peace would splinter. His lands would face war again, and my dragons wouldn't come unless they came to destroy. The people's faith in him would wither, blaming him for a broken treaty.

"And you are the father of my betrothed." The words scraped from my dry throat, my pulse hammering against my ribs. Saying it didn't quell the blaze rolling through me. I swallowed, and propped a hand on my hip as I studied him.

His snug overcoat buttoned over a pristine white tunic. The neckline had loosened, the fabric tugged as though he'd yanked at it to breathe. The gold chains of his mantle glinted in the starlight, draped over his broad chest. His arms remained crossed, but the strain on the seams of his sleeves told a different story, as if the tension in his muscles threatened to burst through.

The coat narrowed at his trim waist, hinting at the power concealed beneath. A dark leather belt, fastened with a gleaming gold buckle, rested against black trousers tailored to perfection. The fabric hugged his thighs, muscular and solid, commanding my gaze until I bit the inside of my cheek to keep from staring too long.

Those thighs alone could ruin me.

Dark boots wrapped his calves, buckles gleaming. Even here in the palace, where fashion dictated concealment, he tucked his pants into his boots like a soldier—unyielding, vigilant.

My gaze traveled upward, absorbing every detail as if I were committing a masterpiece to memory. When my eyes met his face again, his hand shifted, thumb hooking into his belt with an easy confidence that sent a flush crawling up my neck.

"Like what you see?" he asked, voice husky and low.

I'd seen handsome men before, from the polished nobles with their aristocratic features to the unyielding strength of the Spire's warriors. Yet Kallias eclipsed them all—a league of his own.

His glacier-blue eyes held mine, a storm of restraint and yearning. I had to leave. To stay any longer would push us both to the edge. He was far too disciplined to act on his desires. A king couldn't always have what he coveted.

"I don't just *like* it," I breathed, not daring myself to raise my voice. "I burn for it."

His breath hitched, sharp and audible, as if I struck him. The fire in his eyes flared brighter.

Then I ran.

Like a child fleeing from ridicule or punishment, I fled into the palace. I didn't look back, refused to meet his searing gaze again. Greaves stood sentinel near the door, an immovable shadow as I swept past him and down the stairs.

The quiet corridors offered no solace, only the soft echo of my steps as I jogged, my heartbeat a frantic drumbeat in my ears.

I was no lovesick girl. I was a grown woman who'd said too much. Yet it wasn't just my mistake—his words fanned the flames too.

But his truth lingered, haunting me. *I can't have what I want.*

He wanted me. The thought stopped me cold in the middle of the hall. My lips curved into a smile before I could stop them, a giddy laugh slipping free. He desired me—truly. The thrill of it sent a spark through my veins, leaving me breathless.

Then it hit me—I'd left my boots behind. The absurdity of it broke whatever tension clung to me, and I chuckled, soft and incredulous. Barefoot, I padded toward my room, the cool stone floors grounding me as I held my secret close to my heart.

Chapter Sixteen

NIENNA

E dith's sharp gaze bore into me, and I felt every ounce of her displeasure. She'd been watching me all morning, her eyes heavy with questions she hadn't voiced. I avoided her scrutiny as best I could, burying myself in a thick tome about Radaan's districts.

Her expression said everything. She noticed my state last night—bootless, cheeks flushed—and drew her own conclusions.

I let her.

What could she do?

The rooftop confessions still lingered, a slow burn within. They made me feel alive, more like a woman than any whispered promise ever had.

He wanted me.

The thought refused to leave, circling back, an unbidden dream. My fingers slackened on the book I held, the paragraph before me unreadable despite my repeated attempts. My mind wandered instead to the way Kallias' trousers clung to his thighs, powerful and unyielding. I never imagined legs like that on a man—thick and solid, carved like the roots of an ancient oak.

The book slipped from my hands, tumbling to the floor with a heavy thud. I scrambled to retrieve it, my yelp echoing in the quiet room.

Edith sat poised in her chair, her knitting forgotten as she fixed me with a knowing glare. Her gray brows pinched together, suspicion sparking in her eyes. She thought she knew.

She'd assume it was Tallon.

No one would guess it was his father.

Scythe burst through the door, boots swinging from her hand like trophies. "Found them!"

"Where were they?" Edith asked, before I could muster a word of gratitude.

"Ballroom," she said. "Gwyn swears half the guests left their shoes behind. Must've been quite the evening."

She turned her back to Edith and strode toward my dressing room, her steps purposeful. As she passed, she shot me a quick wink. Trust Scythe to cover for me without asking questions.

I had no engagements today, no summons from Fyrn. I wasn't sure if her absence was due to my attire the previous night or the Velli guest. Either way, the reprieve suited me just fine.

A shiver skated down my spine as I remembered the ambassador's smile. At first glance, he almost passed for normal, even handsome—until he opened his mouth. What drove someone to file their teeth to points? Necessity? Religion? The thought curled in my stomach.

"I'm certain you've taken ill," Edith murmured, her knitting needles resuming their rhythm. Her narrowed eyes didn't match her calm tone. "First flushed, now pale as a ghost. Perhaps it's best if you skipped dinner."

"I'm fine," I said too quickly, my voice betraying me. I couldn't risk missing him—Kallias. Not after last night.

The memory of the rooftop swirled, vivid and heady. He dismissed Greaves to be alone with me, something he'd never done before. Would he dare again? I swallowed hard, anticipation quickening my pulse.

Edith grunted as Scythe began humming, her tune light and aimless while she set out my evening attire. I resigned myself to a dull day, determined to remain as unremarkable as possible until dinner.

As I dressed, nerves twisted in my stomach. The gown I chose was far more modest than last night's daring ensemble. Deep emerald velvet swept to the floor, its high neckline brushing my collarbone. The bodice hugged my figure, leaving little to the imagination. Sleeves clung to my arms, and the flat black boots beneath the hem promised a mercifully steady footing. No risk of twisting an ankle tonight.

Edith worked with deft fingers, pinning my hair into a cascade of soft waves that spilled down my back. She stepped away, her sharp eye assessing every detail, before a small smile broke through her usual sternness. "Beautiful."

My shoulders eased, tension slipping away under her rare praise. Edith could be severe, but she'd been my nursemaid for as long as I could remember. If anyone could make me feel beautiful, it was her.

"Thank you," I murmured, rising to smooth the folds of my dress.

My pulse quickened. Would Kallias wear his signature evergreen tonight? The thought of our colors complementing each other sent a flutter through me.

Ridiculous. Silly. And yet, I couldn't quite squash the hope.

The walk to the dining hall gave me ample time to strategize. Shedding a pair of guards had been manageable before, but parting with six—my new entourage—felt like planning a battlefield maneuver. Their boots thundered against the stone floor, the sound swallowing the quieter murmurs of the palace corridors.

When I arrived, I forced my breathing steady, repeating the courtly mantra: masks on, feelings hidden. This was a game, one I'd played before. Still, the sheer number of guards shadowing me gave me pause, their presence a wall between me and freedom.

The heavy doors swung wide, and the scent of Radaanian fare hit me—a blend of greens and savory gravy that stirred memories of simpler evenings.

Then his gaze met mine.

Across the expanse of the hall, Kallias turned. Distance blurred the details of his face—whether his jaw carried a shadow of stubble or remained smooth—but I felt the weight of his attention like a touch. A shiver ran through me, unbidden, as I recalled his words from the night before. My reply burned alongside them, a secret stretched taut between us, fragile as spun glass.

I forced my feet forward, drawing a steadying breath, and fixed my eyes on the dais. Tallon sat at his father's right, and next to him, the Velli.

The heat ignited by Kallias' gaze iced over. Had the prince replaced me with that creature? Egath's presence radiated an unsettling authority, his sharp features a reminder of everything I didn't trust. Where would I sit now? Did the prince even comprehend the consequences of such a slight?

At the base of the dais steps, I hesitated. Kallias' gaze hadn't wavered, his steady scrutiny a lifeline. He intervened for me before, his quiet authority speaking louder than Tallon's empty gestures.

With a cool exhale, I climbed the steps. My resolve firmed, one thought anchoring me: I would not falter, no matter who sat where.

"Tallon." The stern timbre of his voice rumbled, commanding immediate attention.

The prince abandoned his conversation mid-sentence. He scrambled from his chair and hurried down the steps. His enthusiasm might have impressed me if his first words hadn't been, "Egath has a trick to show us."

Egath's smile remained polite, almost soft, but his eyes told a different story. A cold thread coiled in my chest, though years at court had trained me well. I returned his expression with a practiced grin, hollow but convincing.

I'd grown up among dragons. What was one man with filed teeth?

As we neared my seat, Egath rose. To my dismay, he slid into the chair beside mine, his presence a shadow at my elbow. Dread settled like a stone in my belly, but I took my place between Tallon and the Velli with the precision of a chess piece moved into position.

"Good evening, Your Highness."

His voice, smooth and measured, still caught me off guard. I half-expected him to hiss through those unnerving teeth.

"Evening, Egath." I unfolded the napkin in my lap, keeping my movements deliberate. "I trust your day went well?"

"Well enough." He leaned forward with a casual disregard for decorum. His elbow pressed into the table, propping his angled chin on one hand. "The palace is charming, though I was disappointed to learn the city remains off-limits."

His relaxed posture and loose manners grated against the rigid formality of the dining hall. Perhaps the Velli favored such informality, but it went against the practiced etiquette drilled into me.

I made a note to research his culture further. Gods knew the foreign advisor would be no help.

With any luck, the meal would begin soon, though the delay as Greaves sampled Kallias' plate meant more of this dreadful small talk. My fingers tightened around the silverware, but I smiled as if nothing was amiss.

"I'm sure my father would–"

"Article Twenty-Three of the Treaty of Me'orn." The king's voice cut through the prince's protest like a blade, low but commanding. "The people of Vellos are forbidden entry into Radaanian cities without written permission from the king."

Tallon flinched but kept his eyes averted, his gaze fixed somewhere beyond his father's stern face. I leaned to see over his shoulder, the subtle movement catching Kallias' firm expression. His jaw clenched, and a muscle ticked near his temple, but he smoothed it with a deliberate blink before turning back to the noble at his left.

That small, silent gesture spoke volumes. It was a reminder, a reassurance—his promise to intervene when his son overstepped.

Tallon sighed, the sound heavy with defiance, and offered Egath a crooked, mocking smile. The message in that grin was unmistakable: *Wait until I'm in charge.*

Fortunately, Kallias was far from yielding his crown, his health and resolve still formidable.

The Velli chuckled, slouching in his seat with a calculated nonchalance. "Ah, therein lies my problem. One might think of this place as a prison."

His arm draped over the back of my chair, and I stiffened. The unwelcome closeness sent a shiver crawling up my spine, but I resisted the urge to recoil. Instead, I adjusted my posture, maintaining the illusion of poise while inching away from his touch.

"The ink is barely dry on the treaty," I replied, my voice steady though my jaw tightened. "Radaan will need time to adjust. Surely, you wouldn't allow Radaanians to roam Velli soil unchecked."

Egath's grin widened, sharp and too knowing. "Then the blood on your marriage oath must be ready to drip off the page!" His laughter boomed, Tallon's joining in. "And I daresay we'd welcome any Radaanians on our soil. In fact, send them."

The undertone in his words prickled at my awareness, a veiled threat I couldn't quite decipher. Frustration simmered under my skin, my ignorance gnawing at me. Before I could respond, the servants arrived, carrying bowls of steaming tomato soup laced with delicate noodles and fresh basil.

Tallon waved a hand over my bowl, his tone too light to mask his eagerness. "Show me your magic now."

I glanced between them, suspicion curling in my chest.

Egath inclined his head, his movements fluid and deferential, though the smugness in his expression betrayed him. "I was waiting for Princess Nienna's arrival. She wouldn't want to miss such a spectacle."

His outstretched hand hovered in invitation, pale and steady. "May I?"

My gaze fixed on him, narrowing as the weight of unspoken warnings pressed against my thoughts. "I'm unfamiliar with Velli magic," I said, my tone cool. "Perhaps another time would be more appropriate."

A polite refusal. No, I would not offer him my hand or let him work his magic on me. My bond with dragons made me a poor vessel—I dreaded to imagine what this man's magic might inflict on my body.

"What are you so afraid of?" Tallon's voice curled with mockery as he draped his arm across the back of my chair.

The sudden weight at my shoulders had me wanting to bolt. Panic swelled, but I forced myself to sit still. I was a princess. Even if my insides twisted with dread, I wouldn't let them see me falter.

"Egath has had a long day. I'm sure he–" The words choked off as my throat tightened.

"Raised among dragons—don't you remind me of that constantly?" the prince jeered.

The ambassador leaned forward, his sharp grin glinting like a blade. "Gracious! And now you fear a touch of Velli magic?"

My gaze dropped to my soup, steam curling from the surface. Noodles bobbed in the broth, taunting me with their stillness while rage churned within. *How dare he.* Tallon's lack of tact, his audacity to side with this smug foreigner against his future queen, and he plays the fool.

Heat scorched my cheeks as I bared a vicious smile, pushing back my chair just enough to extend my hand. "You're right. Compared to dragons, you're hardly worth fearing."

Egath's grin spread like rot, slow and vile. His cold fingers brushed mine as he rolled my palm upright, his touch dry and unsettling. My instincts screamed to pull away, but I held firm.

His voice dipped into a measured hum as his fingertip traced the delicate skin on my wrist. "You know so little about Vellos, don't you, Princess?"

"Easily remedied," I murmured, my gaze flickering between his eyes and the pale finger gliding over my veins.

"I take it upon myself to teach you," he continued.

A faint tickle built beneath the surface, a sensation that sank deeper with each pass. The itch crawled inside my bones.

"The Velli wield magic granted by Baenfior, God of the Abyss," he explained, his tone rich with reverence. "In a land where survival demands sacrifice, he gave us blood magic. All possess it, but not all can wield it."

His finger moved faster now, a hypnotic rhythm. My stomach turned as I watched the vein beneath my skin writhe, slithering toward his touch like a living thing.

"Some of us," he continued, "draw power from blood—strength stolen at the cost of another's life. Others control beasts with a single taste. Magic always demands a price, does it not?"

The vein squirmed, and my breath caught. I jerked my hand back, but Egath's grip tightened, his forest-green eyes gleaming with malice.

"If only I had a drop of your blood—the things I could do."

"Ambassador Egath—"

Kallias' voice cut through the tension, steadying me. Without thinking, I leaned toward it.

"—would you recite Article Thirty-One of the treaty?"

The man snapped out of his trance, his gaze flicking up. The polite smile reappeared, though it seemed hollow. "No Velli shall ask for Radaanian blood."

"Due to the breach of trust, I request you to retire to your rooms." Kallias' tone was flat, final. There was no question in his words.

Egath released my hand, leaning back and dropping his arms into his lap. Relief washed over me, but I kept my expression neutral, unwilling to show how eager I was to escape his grasp.

"She's not Radaanian yet, and I didn't ask for her blood," he said. "I would never violate the treaty our men fought so bravely to establish."

The reminder of war hovered in the air, thick and heavy. I kept my gaze fixed on the soup, but out of the corner of my eye, I saw Egath's movements, every subtle shift. The surrounding conversations fell silent, eager to catch whatever fragments of our exchange they could.

"You straddle the line, Ambassador." Kallias' voice was measured, but the warning beneath it was clear.

Egath rose, his smile tight, but his words wrapped in false contrition. "My sincerest apologies, Princess Nienna, and Your Majesty." He bowed, then continued, "I am weary from my travels; an early night would be best."

Without waiting for a response, he turned and walked around the table, descending the stairs. The nobles' stares followed him, whispers drifting as they tried to gauge his intentions. Was he making a statement by leaving before the first course? Or was it just coincidence?

"The war is over, Father," Tallon growled.

Kallias' cold eyes never left Egath, tracking his every movement. The Velli's chin was held high, a subtle smirk dancing on his lips as he passed through the crowd and toward the doors.

"The war is over, but peace is maintained by vigilance," Kallias murmured, his words barely more than a breath as the door closed behind Egath. He picked up his spoon, dipping it into the soup without another glance at me.

Tallon huffed and followed suit, but my focus remained on the bowl in front of me. The red liquid swirled, and my wrist itched, as if Egath's fingers still traced the veins.

There would be no eating for me tonight.

Six guards trailed me, their armor clanking with every step. Subtlety had long since fled. I'd left the evening meal early, unable to stomach more than a few bites before nausea twisted my insides.

Rubbing my wrist, I moved through the castle's winding corridors, confident I could reach the roof without assistance. The hem of my green dress swished against my boots, and the long sleeves clung to my arms, stifling in the castle's heat. Far more clothed than I had been the night before.

I'd nearly talked myself out of it. After our last conversation, I wasn't sure approaching him so soon was wise. Yet, if anyone could ease the discomfort of having a Velli in the palace, it was him.

It should have unsettled me that, when troubled, I sought his presence, craved his proximity. But Kallias was always there—steadfast, ready to shield me—even from myself.

I climbed the wrought-iron stairs, wincing at the sound of my guards' footsteps echoing behind. Halfway up, the balcony door swung open, and Greaves' fierce gaze met mine. I flashed him a quick, apologetic smile. His frown softened as a hint of resignation passed over his face.

"You're relieved," he said, his voice low and smooth—deeper than I expected from a man who spoke so little.

The guards stopped at the landing as I reached the top. I nodded my thanks to Greaves. He grunted in amusement and held the door open for me.

Kallias stood by the railing, a steaming mug beside him. The sun had long set, leaving the fading glow of twilight. Above us, the stars blinked into view. The tension that had knotted me all day began to unravel, and I let out a breath.

He was just... *right*. Kallias was my anchor, steady in any storm.

Tonight, his overcoat was absent, leaving his broad shoulders exposed. The golden chains of his mantle gleamed against the stark white of his tunic. He didn't turn to greet me but nudged the mug further away, as though to make room for me.

I approached, a nervous flutter stirring in my belly—a different kind of unease. The air between us felt charged with an unfamiliar tension, the kind that made every step seem heavier than the last.

The mugs still steamed, evidence he hadn't been there long. His cup, slightly drained, rested between his large hands. I picked up the second one, scrunching my nose as the bitter aroma hit me.

"This isn't cider," I said, frowning at the scalding liquid. The scent was sharp, acrid—far from pleasant.

He chuckled, a deep, resonant sound that sent a shiver up my spine. "No. Tonight, I needed something stronger."

I squinted, but he smirked, raising an eyebrow before taking a sip.

"What is it?"

"Don't trust me?" His voice dropped low as he shifted to face me, leaning against the wall—cocky, unbothered.

Besides Fyrn, Kallias was the only one I trusted in this palace. I growled in frustration, lifting it to my lips, holding my breath as I took a sip. The sweetness coated my tongue before a rich, nutty flavor hit. But when I swallowed, a bitterness lingered, unwelcome.

I clicked my tongue, studying the cup without meeting his gaze.

"Well?" he asked, amusement clear in his voice.

Another sip, and the same sweetness followed by an acrid aftertaste. "It's... not very good."

He laughed, and I smiled at the ease between us. Here he was, the king, letting me mock his drink of choice without rebuke. He accepted me as I was—unfiltered, unpolished—and found humor in it.

"Kahve," he explained, reaching to take the cup.

I pulled it away, sheltering it from his grasp. When I took another sip, I winced at the taste.

"It's a tea made from beans, not leaves. Grown in the south, a difficult plant to cultivate—luxurious."

"Reserved for special occasions?" I asked, though I was unsure I could stomach more. Even if I didn't like it, it meant something to him, and I would drink the whole thing just to prove I could.

"It energizes me," he said, his eyes twinkling, "and calms me, in a way."

"Bean tea versus leaf tea," I teased, grimacing as another sip burned down my throat. "Beans must be stronger." Who would have thought?

He shook his head, but his gaze dropped to my wrist, where Egath had gripped it. His eyes darkened. Without a word, he held out his hand, and I gave him my wrist without hesitation.

The strange sensation—the phantom touch—still lingered. A restless squirm beneath my skin that wasn't quite normal. A twitch.

His thumb traced the blue veins, his gaze flickering up to meet mine, and his brow furrowed.

"You're safe here," he murmured.

With you, I wanted to say. *With you, I'm safe.*

"He won't hurt you—or any Radaanian—while the treaty stands."

The words hit like a blow. The treaty, the fragile thread that held Radaan's safety in place. One that relied on my marriage to Tallon and the promise of dragons patrolling the mountains.

No matter how right Kallias felt at this moment, or how I longed for him to pull me closer...

I was not his.

A rush of heat bloomed in my cheeks, and desire clawed at me, threatening to spill over. I pulled away from him, afraid I might act on the hunger gnawing at my sanity. I took another sip of the vile drink, staring over the dark fields. They stretched out in a patchwork of navy and gray, silent and still.

Kallias didn't speak. We stayed there in the quiet, staring out at the sleeping fields, long after our mugs had gone cold and empty.

Chapter Seventeen

NIENNA

I could *not* sleep.

No matter how I twisted beneath the blankets, my thoughts spiraled back to Kallias—the feel of his calloused fingers brushing my wrist, the shiver that followed. I tried to focus on Fyrn and her visit tomorrow, or the looming misery of a life bound to Tallon. Even Egath crept into my mind, with schemes forming on how I could show him I wasn't to be trifled with.

But none of it held. My thoughts circled back to the moment on the roof—Kallias' arms locking around me when he feared I might fall. I could still feel the solid strength of him pressed close, the warmth radiating from his body. His scent lingered in my memory, rich with spice and the faintest trace of woodsmoke.

A groan tore from my throat as I buried my face in a pillow, muffling a silent scream.

Why couldn't I stop thinking about him? Why couldn't I just *sleep*?

At the foot of my bed, Edith's small breaths filled the quiet, soft and rhythmic. She didn't snore, a minor blessing, but her even exhalations told me she slept deeply enough not to notice me—if I stayed silent.

My chest burned with frustration, then I tossed the pillow aside and slid out of bed. The night's chill sank into my skin. My slippers waited nearby, their soft lining a welcome warmth against the cold floor. I slipped them on, wincing at every creak of the wooden boards.

Was it still night, or had morning crept closer? I couldn't tell.

A glance at Edith, undisturbed, solidified my resolve. I didn't want to wake her. If she caught me, she'd insist on a tonic as dreadful as that bitter bean tea Kallias gave me earlier. I shuddered at the thought.

After I found my thin blue cape draped over my chair, I fastened it over my nightdress. The fabric whispered as it settled over my shoulders, offering little protection against the icy air. But it would have to do.

The palace was a labyrinth I didn't know well enough to navigate without risk of encountering servants, but the nobles would be asleep by now. Most of the staff working at this hour would stick to tasks out of sight. If I was careful, I could avoid anyone while I wandered.

I spared only a fleeting glance at the hidden passage behind the dresser before turning to the narrow door in my dressing room. It was the servants' current route, and as the hinges swung open without a creak, I had to admit it was a convenient improvement.

A single lantern sputtered in its bracket, casting uneven light that flickered over the narrow walls. I hesitated at the threshold, biting my lip. Scythe would have loved this—she'd have taken the hidden passageways simply for adventure's sake. I only needed to stretch my legs and quiet my mind.

After a steadying breath, I stepped into the cramped corridor and eased the door shut behind me. The soft click didn't carry, and Edith did not stir. With a smile, I moved, the thin soles of my slippers making no sound on the smooth floor.

The walls pressed close, brushing my shoulders, and the ceiling hung low enough to make me stoop. The confined space clawed at my nerves, but I reminded myself that the servants walked these halls every day without complaint. If they could manage, so could I.

At first, my steps were tentative, passing intersections shrouded in shadows. I needed to slip past the guards stationed near my chambers before venturing into the main corridors, where the space felt less suffocating. My breath hitched as a faint sound reached me—a soft scrape, or perhaps just my imagination. I froze, tilting my head to listen, then continued when silence enveloped me again.

The farther I moved, the more the confinement gnawed at me. These corridors were clean. No scurrying mice or even a stray cobweb broke the stillness. When I judged I was far enough from my rooms—and those perpetually alert guards—I angled toward the main hall.

When I reached a small door, I pressed my palm to its worn wood and inched it open. Light spilled through the gap, stark and blinding after my time in the dim passage. The mirrored lanterns cast harsh reflections, illuminating every detail. I squinted as I peeked out, my gaze roaming over the ornate decor—polished floors, trailing plants, and paintings that lined the walls.

My attention caught on a vivid depiction of a woman sipping tea in a lush garden. The deep greens of the foliage and the striking red of the flowers felt familiar and I tried to place them. I clutched my cloak tighter and slipped out, easing the door shut.

My heart thudded against my ribs, its frantic rhythm spurred by the thrill of solitude. No guards shadowed my steps, no Greaves watching over me and Kallias. It was just me, alone in the quiet halls. I bit down on a smile, willing my breath to even out. Every sound mattered now—I needed to listen for footsteps, to hide if necessary.

Heat crept into my cheeks as I ignored the state of my attire. Scythe, of course, would've helped me dress without a word. Edith would have woken with a start, summoned an entire escort, and glared at me all the way to the garden.

My fingertips brushed the vines snaking up the walls, their paths guided by artful hooks. One plant held my gaze—a sprawling specimen with variegated leaves striped in green, white, and faint pink. The delicate patterns reminded me of Veridis' temple. I snorted at the absurdity of it—pink leaves.

The palace glowed with serene warmth, its rich hues and vibrant greenery exuding life. A gilded frame caught my attention, cradling a painting of a fair-haired boy darting through a sunlit forest. A stag lingered in the background, its gaze protective, while a rabbit peeked from behind a tree. I leaned closer, letting out a breathless laugh at the rabbit's scrunched nose. The artist even captured its amusement as perfectly as the boy's joy.

Something thudded, and the spell of peace shattered. I spun, heart jolting, as a hushed voice followed the noise.

Sea beneath! I snatched a fistful of my nightdress and sprinted down the corridor. My feet barely touched the polished floor as I wove through the halls, each turn a desperate attempt to lose whoever—or whatever—was behind me. My lungs burned, ears straining for any hint of pursuit.

I rounded another corner—and collided with a solid form.

A startled yelp escaped me as I grabbed for the man's tunic to steady myself. He staggered but righted us, his hands firm on my elbows. The faint scent of warm spices filled the air, reaching me before I dared glance up. My face ignited with embarrassment, a blush burning hot under my skin.

"Should I call for the guards?" Kallias asked, the question a deep rumble. His gaze pinned me as I struggled to find words. "Or are you running from them again?"

A nervous laugh tumbled out as I winced. "I think it was a servant this time."

His hair was disheveled and his tunic—deep green and half-laced—revealed the shallow curve of his chest.

Before I could dwell on his state of dress too long, a soft curse sounded from down the hall. Kallias turned, his hand sliding to the small of my back.

His eyes locked with mine, alight with a mischievous glint. "Care for a walk?"

"Why else would I be out here?" I countered, my own smile teasing.

Without another word, he guided me forward. The heat of his palm burned through my cape, a phantom warmth that spread to my skin. My heart thundered—not just from the adventure, but from the sensation his simple touch aroused.

The palace's labyrinthine corridors posed no challenge to him. Kallias moved with purpose, his confidence in every step evident as he led me deeper. Each turn came with a light press of his fingers against my arm, an effortless command I couldn't ignore. A quiet laugh slipped from me as his pace quickened, the thrill infectious.

"Who are you running from?" I whispered, tilting my head to steal a glance at him.

His face seemed almost alive with boyish energy. Blue eyes glittered with amusement, and his rare, unguarded smile carved warmth into his features. "Greaves."

I couldn't help but snicker. Whatever plan he'd crafted to avoid his ever-present shadow had worked. At the end of another passage, he shoved a door open and nudged me inside. The room swallowed me in darkness, the only light spilling in from the hall.

"One moment." His tone was soft, unhurried, though his movements were swift. He found a lantern on a nearby table, his hands deft as he struck a flame. The warm glow illuminated his features, then he leaned against the door, pushing it shut with a quiet click.

"He would've noticed the..." His voice faltered, words dying mid-sentence as his gaze swept over me.

I froze, clutching the edges of my cape tighter. The blue fabric hid what the thin white silk beneath did not. His expression shifted, the playful warmth replaced by something darker. The wrinkle between his brows deepened as if he only now realized the precarious intimacy of the moment.

Silence settled between us, heavy and awkward. My cheeks burned under his scrutiny, and I turned, focusing on the room he'd chosen for our escape.

Books lined the walls from floor to ceiling, their spines a rainbow of muted tones in the lantern's glow. Shadows pooled in the corners, adding a mysterious air to the space. A small sofa sat at the room's center flanked by modest tables, its fabric worn with use.

I kept my gaze on the shelves, my fingers skimming the edge of a table as Kallias approached me. Anything to hold my attention away from him.

His low murmur broke the stillness, "I should've warned you—"

Warn me? Of the dangers of slipping into a darkened room with a man who haunted my dreams?

"—the kahve might keep you up," he continued, stepping closer.

His tone softened, but the tension in his frame remained. I forced myself to meet his eyes, though the guarded expression there stung. The light-hearted man from the halls had vanished, replaced by someone measured, his feelings hidden behind a mask I longed to tear away.

"What do you do when it keeps you awake?" I asked, the question barely audible as I clutched my cape tighter, the fabric creasing beneath my fingers.

Kallias studied my face, his gaze lingering. When he cleared his throat, he gestured to the shelves. "I read. It quiets my mind. Care to join me?"

The thought of reading beside him felt anything but calming. Yet my head betrayed me, nodding in agreement.

"Choose whatever catches your eye," he said, moving past me to pick up a book from a nearby table. He lowered himself onto the sofa, the cushions shifting under his weight. "This is the northern library. Most of these are about legends or history—dry enough to put even the restless to sleep." He crossed an ankle over his knee, then opened the tome to a page marked by a delicate black feather.

I swallowed the lump in my throat and turned toward the shelves. Anything would be better than thinking about my sheer nightdress or the magnetic pull of his presence.

The books bore worn spines, their titles embossed in fading gold. They smelled of leather and ink, a comforting combination. How many of these had he read? How many sleepless nights brought him here to find solace in their pages?

I skimmed the rows. *'History of the Aenor.' 'History of the Agolaths.' Apostos. Azarat.* The titles blurred into monotony. Skipping a few shelves, I crouched to scan another section, the flickering lantern light casting long shadows across the bindings.

'Tale of Isa and Vane.' 'Tales from the Crater of Gods.' My fingers paused on the latter, its dark cover inviting in a way the others hadn't. "The crater?" I called out, pulling it free.

Kallias didn't look up. "A meteor struck the northern lands long ago. The area's... unique. Life there flourishes in strange ways—enough to inspire stories of mammoths and other curiosities."

I cradled the book, flipping it open as I wandered to the sofa. "The tales within these pages have been recorded from firsthand accounts and verified by multiple sources," I read aloud, settling on the farthest edge of the cushion. Its plush fabric enveloped me as I perched, unwilling to relax too much.

"Keep your wits about you with that one," he said, throwing an arm over the backrest.

I kicked off my slippers, tucked a leg beneath me, and stretched the other in his direction. He glanced at it, then swallowed before his attention returned to his book.

That's when I noticed. He looked... different. His usual mantle, adorned with golden chains and gleaming pauldrons, was absent. Instead, a simple dark green tunic embroidered with gold thread softened his appearance. Black trousers tucked into polished boots gleamed in the lantern light.

For once, he wasn't the king of Radaan. He was just Kallias.

I adjusted my cape over my lap, then stared down at the open book in my hands. Draconia held its own myths of merfolk, sea serpents—entire worlds beneath the surface. What mysteries would a crater offer?

I read the same paragraph over and over, unable to absorb a single word. After a few moments, I flipped the page to keep up appearances, then stole another glance at him. He tilted his head at something in his book, his lips pressing into a thoughtful line. His finger traced the page's edge before he turned it, the subtle movement drawing my attention. My heart thudded in my chest, heat rising to my cheeks. I skipped to another page.

"You're a quick reader," he said without looking up.

I peered over the rim of my book, hiding behind it like a shield. "It's interesting," I blurted, my response tumbling out too fast.

He smirked at his own book. "As the first three pages describing the levels of stone are. What's the third level again? Quartz?"

My teeth grazed my lip, my cheeks burning as I scoured the inked words for anything resembling an answer, but the letters swam. Glancing back up at him, he flashed a knowing smile and his brow raised in challenge. I clenched the tome tighter.

Caught. Again.

"Perhaps this isn't the right book for me," I muttered, snapping it shut. My fingers curled over the cover, as if holding it too tightly would betray my nerves.

"If the garden paths are more to your liking, I'm sure Greaves–"

"No!" The word burst out before I could temper it. Heat climbed up my neck as I bit my lip, wishing I could snatch it back. "I mean... no. I'd rather stay here."

The mantle was gone tonight. No crown, no weight of the throne. Just Kallias. And I didn't want to lose that.

His dark brow arched as he shifted, uncrossing his legs and leaning forward. His book now rested forgotten on his knee. "Surely you're not nervous."

A laugh caught in my throat, dry and unconvincing. Butterflies stirred low in my stomach, their wings igniting flames that raced through my veins. A vivid, shameful image of myself straddling his lap seared my thoughts, leaving my cheeks unbearably red. "Not at all," I croaked.

His chuckle was deep, rich, and far too knowing. I shifted my feet, but before I could tuck my foot beneath me, he snagged it. My breath hitched as his fingers wrapped around my ankle, warm and rough from countless battles. He didn't tug, but the unspoken command was there. I relaxed into his hold, and he pulled it into his lap with deliberate care, settling my heel against his thigh.

His gaze locked on mine, unwavering, a challenge burning in his eyes. My pulse thundered as his palm slid up, slow and unhurried, trailing heat along my calf. The motion was infuriatingly steady, each inch of contact unraveling my composure. A whisper in the depths of my mind told me I should protest, wrench my leg away, but the truth sat heavy between us—I wouldn't.

I couldn't.

It was just my ankle for the love of the sea.

His hand stopped beneath my knee, fingers cradling the back of my calf. The room felt charged, the air electric—and I reveled in it. His breaths came quicker now, his lips parting as his focus narrowed. That gaze—blistering, unguarded—pinned me in place.

My heart slammed, warring between right and wrong. I should stop this, shove his hand away, create the distance that decency demanded. But instead, I shifted, sliding my foot a fraction deeper into his lap. His jaw twitched, and the slight clench of his fingers warned me not to push further.

Good. Let me unnerve him.

I raised my book again, burying my nose in its pages. Pretend. I could pretend we were two strangers sharing quiet moments in the dim light. Pretend the heat pooling in my core wasn't because of him.

The words blurred before my eyes, swimming in meaningless swirls. Still, I turned pages at a steady pace, faking interest in tedious descriptions of stone layers and crater flora. Kallias hadn't been wrong about the dry content—it did little to distract me. Especially with his thumb stroking along my skin, a lazy, maddening rhythm that made focus impossible.

My eyes darted toward him over the book's edge. His own expression betrayed nothing but concentration, brow furrowed as he absorbed whatever legend or history that had captured him. The gold embroidery of his tunic caught the lamplight, the deep green softening his sharp features. His silver-threaded hair, slightly mussed, lent him an air of ease. Dignified. Put-together.

Like he knew how to handle a woman.

He flipped a page, his long fingers precise and deliberate, and then his gaze found mine.

The intensity there stole the breath from my lungs. His thumb stilled on my leg, a silent acknowledgment that we'd crossed some invisible line. Neither of us spoke. Neither of us moved. His eyes searched, daring me, waiting for me to decide.

I shifted my foot again, brushing the edge of his belt buckle. His hand rose with the motion, stopping beneath the bend of my knee. His grip tightened. Not harsh, but firm enough to let me feel his restraint. The charged silence thickened, words unnecessary as his thumb resumed its agonizingly slow sweep.

"Nienna."

The way he spoke my name terrified me. It wasn't just a word—He rasped it like a starving man. My name was a command to stop, a desperate plea for more. It was a prayer to his god for mercy. Hunger roughened his voice, fraying its edges like an unraveling thread.

I tore my leg from his grasp and scrambled to my feet. My heart pounded against my ribs as I fumbled to shelve the book, my fingers trembling so violently I almost dropped it. Blood roared in my ears, drowning out all sound until his hand landed on the shelf beside me. The warmth of his presence radiated against my back, crumbling the last remnants of my composure.

"Was it not to your liking?" His breath skimmed the nape of my neck, coaxing a shiver down my spine.

My fingers grazed the spines of books without focus, pretending to search. My grip faltered as I clutched one, its title a blur. "I... couldn't give it the attention it deserved."

"And what has you so distracted?" His voice dropped lower, a coaxing murmur that slid beneath my skin.

Every sensible instinct screamed at me to flee, to demand distance, to uphold decorum. But duty had shackled me all my life—telling me how to act, what to wear, even how to breathe. For once, I wanted to choose for myself.

I spun, pressing my back against the shelves. My cape fell open, revealing the thin fabric of my nightdress beneath. His gaze roved over me, tracing every curve with a precision that stole my breath. His eyes followed the dart of my tongue as I wet my dry lips.

My breaths hitched, shallow and unsteady. The corner of his eye twitched once—twice.

For the first time, I reached for what I wanted. My trembling hands gripped his tunic and tugged. The strength in his posture wavered as he leaned closer.

"Please," I whispered. My fingers slid to his belt, clutching the leather like a lifeline.

"Please what?" He closed the distance by a fraction, his arm trembling with restraint, the tension crackling between us like a storm about to break.

"You know." My voice shook, an accusation heavy with longing.

Heat rolled off him in waves, his need a palpable force. "Say it."

His command was a blade, cutting through every ounce of hesitation I had left. This was Kallias, not some boy or mere noble. He wanted me to ask this of him. He needed to protect me, provide for me.

And I would let him.

Just once.

"Kiss me."

The dam broke. His lips crashed to mine with a growl, his restraint snapping like a brittle twig. The shelf rattled beneath the force, books tumbling around us. His hand cupped my chin, tilting my face up as his mouth claimed mine. Sensation blazed through me—a wild, electric fire that consumed every coherent thought.

I moaned against him, my fingers twisting in his tunic as his tongue traced the seam of my lips. When I opened to him, he deepened the kiss, plunging into me with slow, deliberate intent. A heady mix of spice and heat flooded my senses. My knees buckled, but his arm at my waist held me firm.

One hand slid down to my thigh, lifting it to hook around his hip. He pressed into me, his solid frame anchoring me as more books clattered. The pressure of his leg between mine sparked something primal, and I moved against him, desperate for more. His groan vibrated through my chest, igniting a reckless need that left me gasping.

"Don't you dare stop," I snarled, tugging him back when he pulled away.

He chuckled against my mouth, his kiss slowing, steadying me even as my pulse hammered. With a swift motion, he grasped my thighs and hoisted me up, pinning me against the shelves. I hissed at the pleasure of him pressed against me, and threw back my head, knocking books askew and to the ground. His lips moved to my neck and I threaded my fingers through his hair, moaning against the kisses he trailed down my skin, tugging him closer.

The library door flung open.

I gasped. Kallias froze, his hands tightening around my legs as his head whipped toward the intruder. Shame burned through me as he lowered me to the floor.

Greaves stood in the doorway, closing it behind him with measured precision. His expression remained impassive, though his gaze flicked between us. He stepped aside to stand at the door, boot propped against the base to keep it from opening. With a rigid set to his posture, his hand rested on the pommel of his sword. He said nothing, only turned his attention to the far wall, ignoring us.

I had been caught in the act—kissing the king of Radaan, not the prince. Heat clawed up my throat, and my stomach twisted into a violent knot. My hands trembled uncontrollably, my legs unsteady beneath me. If Greaves spoke of this—if word spread of what I had done—the alliance would crumble. I'd be branded a disgrace, sent back home to rot in shame. Marriage prospects would vanish, leaving me to wither away in a locked tower of regret and isolation.

Kallias' fingers brushed against my temple, tucking a loose strand of hair behind my ear. His palm cupped my cheek, the faint tremor in his touch betraying the composure on his face. Tears blurred the world, but I could still see the tight line of his jaw, the frustration hardening his features. Without a word, he turned, each step deliberate and heavy with unspoken meaning. He reached the door, yanked it open, and strode into the hallway. The echo of his retreating footsteps filled the silence.

Greaves hesitated. His unreadable gaze flicked to mine, offering a subtle shake of his head before he followed the king, his boots clicking softly on the floorboards.

The door thudded shut.

I stood amidst the chaos—books scattered like broken promises—and wrapped my arms around myself, trying to hold together the pieces of my unraveling world. My knees gave out, and I sank to the floor, the hard edges of fallen tomes pressing into my thighs.

What had I done?

My lips still tingled, a bittersweet ache.

My first *real* kiss, and I'd given it to the wrong man. Again.

Chapter Eighteen

KALLIAS

I was more alert now than when I'd left my quarters, guilt clawing like a jagged hook in my chest. Greaves hurried to keep pace behind me, his boots a faint echo in the corridor. The roof called to me with its cold silence and the promise of solitude, but I pushed the thought aside. Like a wounded animal, I craved the dark comfort of my own space to tend to my wounds.

Pay my penance.

Shame made it hard to keep my head held high. I knew better. I never should've brought her to the library. Never should have allowed myself to be alone with her. Why she seemed to be attracted to me, I couldn't fathom—but Elohios knew how much I wanted her.

She wasn't mine to want.

I reached my chambers and threw the door open with more force than intended. The loud crack made me wince. I despised losing control. There was nothing worse than leadership that couldn't control their temper—or desires. A man ruled themselves first, or they ruled nothing at all.

Greaves entered after me, quiet and composed. I yanked my tunic off and tossed it aside before attacking the buckle at my waist. My silence spoke for me—there was no excuse for what I'd done. None that I dared to offer. The clasp resisted, and with a frustrated breath, I stilled my hands and closed my eyes.

At least it had been Greaves who found us. His loyalty was unshakable. He wouldn't speak of my lapse in judgment. That much I could trust. But did Nienna know that?

A fresh wave of dread surged through me. Did she think her reputation was ruined? Had I left her to believe the worst?

My eyes snapped open as Greaves poured water into the basin. The water's soft slosh seemed too loud in the room's silence. He prepared for me to wash and retire to bed—where I should have been all along—not stealing moments with my son's future wife in the dead of night.

The buckle finally gave, and I let it hang loose as I sank onto the edge of my bed. My fingers threaded through my hair, but the memory of her touch made my chest tighten. I dragged my hands down my face, pressing them over my mouth as I met Greaves' pointed glare.

"You realize how old you are?" he asked, tone sharp, arms folded as he leaned against the dresser.

"I haven't forgotten."

He grunted, unimpressed, but said no more. I *should* have had more restraint. I was old enough to know better. It had been nearly twenty years since I'd last lain with a woman, not for lack of offers. A few courtiers had tried their hand, but after Eldeiade... I had no desire to entangle myself in that again. Or so I thought.

I stared at the floor, hands cradling my head. Nienna had to know it was a mistake. A lapse. One no one could ever discover. If she let it slip to her handmaid, and the rumors reached my staff, everything would crumble. Tallon would demand I send her back to Draconia with her reputation in tatters, and risk sending their dragons in righteous revenge. My name—Elohios-blessed—would rot under my own hypocrisy. The nobles would turn. My generals would abandon me. I would fall, undone by my inability to control my desires.

Cold water hit me like a thunderclap. I jerked to my feet, sputtering.

Greaves stood there, empty pitcher in hand. His raised brow and faint shrug offered no apology. "Perhaps now you'll get some sleep," he said.

I glared, muttering something about finding a new bodyguard, but peeled off my soaked clothes and donned dry trousers. Greaves took up his post by the door, arms crossed, as though I couldn't be trusted to stay in my bed.

I climbed under the covers, turning my back to him. My fingers combed through damp hair, smoothing it away from my face, but rest wouldn't come. My mind circled endlessly, trapped in a storm of guilt and regret.

She wasn't at the council meeting. The droning nobles argued over flax taxes, but the words slipped past me. My shoulders stiffened beneath Radaan's mantle, the fabric's ornate trim biting into my skin. Its heaviness mirrored the guilt coiled deep in my soul, pressing harder today than ever.

No one else knew. Yet every glance in my direction felt like a blade, sharp with unspoken accusation.

Her absence struck like a missing heartbeat. Tallon, however, was present—lounging with Verard'gog, his indifference to governance plain. The place to my right remained empty. His chair. One day, I imagined, he might sit there and actually care about such matters. But today, the thought rang hollow.

At least Nienna understood duty. Though new to Radaan, she had a grasp on the kingdom's needs and an unflinching loyalty to its people. She'd make a worthy queen.

Her body, soft beneath me, flared in my thoughts. The memory burned—the press of her lips, her quiet moans.

Don't you dare stop.

A grimace twisted my face. I pinched the bridge of my nose, forcing my focus back to the present. Safer ground for a treacherous mind.

"The tax on wool is far less! And what about the goats Claydon'sol raises? Is he even taxed?"

"The Sols pay their share, as required by law," I answered, sharper than intended.

"Wool is scarcer and more labor-intensive. You can't compare them." Another noble's protest rippled through the chamber. Their squabbling sent jabbing pulses behind my temples.

Tallon chuckled. My glare snapped to him. He faced Verard, entirely disengaged. The sight stirred an impulse to drag him into the debate, though I knew it would only end in embarrassment—for us both.

Even basic tasks, like preparing for the Velli reception, had proven beyond him. His choice of attire for Nienna was a mockery—but she owned it. He meant to humiliate her, but instead, every eye in the room was drawn to her bold defiance.

Elohios help me, I couldn't look away. The sheer fabric clung to her, a second skin that left nothing hidden.

Shame pressed harder. I straightened, drawing the room's attention. "Council's dismissed."

Confused murmurs rippled around me, but I didn't wait for questions. I strode from the chamber, each step heavy with unspoken turmoil. Darius moved to follow, but I waved him off. If I let him, he'd drag me to a healer who would offer nothing but useless remedies.

Tallon watched as I passed, his head tilted in mild curiosity. I never dismissed early—always listened to my people's concerns, as a king should. His gaze prickled, but I kept moving.

My pauldron slipped, and I stood straighter, righting it. Could nothing go right today?

The corridor loomed quiet, the routine of my day shattered. Normally, I would spar or visit the temple after council sessions. Neither appealed now. Sparring would earn me bruises and Greaves' wordless disapproval—a lecture delivered through blows.

My steps slowed. Where was Nienna?

Greaves drew even with me. "Are you well?"

"Just a headache," I muttered, though we both knew better. "Perhaps I'll send for the healer."

"You don't need a healer," he said. "You need the temple."

The corner of my eye twitched, but I couldn't refute him. He was right. My guilt dragged behind me like a shadow, and until I apologized to Nienna, and righted things with my god, there would be no relief.

I exhaled, a pointed signal of my displeasure, before pivoting and heading toward the temple district.

He fell into step behind me without further protest, his silence more valuable than any apology. For all his infuriating habits, Greaves understood his role as well as I did. In public, he knew his place, offering his opinions only when protocol allowed. In private, however, he exercised a certain freedom, though he compensated for it by holding his tongue when it mattered most.

Last night, his disapproval had been palpable, his expression a silent accusation. Yet even in my chambers, he refrained from speaking aloud what we both knew—I made a mistake. He didn't need to say it. His words, when offered, were rarely soothing, but I relied on him regardless—just as Radaan relied on me.

My son was a problem without a solution. His upbringing bore the weight of my failures. I had exhausted my arsenal of reprimands. Threats of banishment, sparring matches—they were meaningless gestures, like scolding a child for playing too rough. Assigning him to dull diplomatic duties or limiting his wine only underscored the futility. None of it would forge the man Radaan needed him to become.

A dull ache pulsed in the back of my neck, tempting me to rub the tension away, but I resisted. There was no escape from this, no reprieve from the consequences of my choices. This was the hand I had been dealt, and I would see it played through.

At least Radaan had Nienna

Tallon had Nienna—assuming he didn't push her to the breaking point and drive her back to Draconia. Yet she had already shown more resilience than that. She didn't run—she wouldn't. She loathed him, yes, but she stayed. Not as a lover or equal, but as a general waging a private war. She calculated her moves, wielding every flaw and misstep of his as a weapon.

For now, I would be her shield while she fought her battles against him.

The palace gates gave way to sunlight, and a faint relief loosened the invisible chains binding my shoulders. The warmth of the sun seemed to scrape away the guilty shadows clinging to my thoughts. My jaw, tight moments ago, relaxed as I inhaled the garden's sweet air.

Startled workers glanced up at my unexpected arrival, their tools stilled. I waved them back to their duties with a small smile. They had work to do, and my presence shouldn't unsettle them. At least their roles were straightforward, their purpose unclouded by the burden of fractured family ties.

The temple loomed ahead, its arches stark against the morning sky. Two priests glanced my way, then quickly ducked into the shadows of the alcoves. Only Greaves would hear my confessions here, my prayers bleeding into the silence of stone walls. Only he was privy to my sins.

And a certain princess.

Greaves moved to unfasten my yoke, his fingers deft against the heavy clasps. My jaw tightened as I debated whether to kneel before Elohios with the mantle weighing on my shoulders. A man's desires drove me, but it wasn't just a man who failed—it was a king. My recklessness jeopardized more than my own reputation. I gambled the fragile peace I fought for and put Radaan's people at risk.

"Leave it," I said.

Without hesitation, Greaves began re-securing the clasps. To rise from my knees while bearing the mantle would be awkward, but the struggle felt appropriate. Kingship demanded balance, a sacrifice of personal desires for the greater good.

He stepped back as I approached the altar, leaving the rug behind. Comfort had no place here. The chill in the chamber pressed against my skin, no longer the soothing calm I once knew, but a cold judgment. Elohios' stone gaze bore down from above, sharp and unyielding, dissecting every corner of my soul.

I compromised a woman.

When I lowered to my knees, I grunted, the mantle pulling at my shoulders.

I betrayed my son.

My head bowed, shame dragging it down as if the act itself might absolve me. A faint breeze stirred the air, icy tendrils snaking around me and biting at my exposed skin.

I risked everything: Radaan's people, the alliance with Draconia, the very peace I fought to preserve. My selfish actions could have set a war in motion—one we would not survive.

"Forgive me." My voice wavered in the vast, empty chamber. Injustice seeped into my choices, deceit tainting truths I left unspoken. To rule through lies would unravel everything I built. Other kingdoms thrived on treachery, but Elohios blessed me for my honesty and the justice I upheld.

The breeze stilled. I waited, straining for any sign of forgiveness. None came.

I inhaled, steadying myself, and began another prayer, this one voiceless, meant for no ears but the god's.

Bolster my strength. Sharpen my resolve. Remind me of my duty. Spare me the temptation she stirs within me. Remind me that she is not mine-

A laugh, light and melodic, broke the silence. Nienna's. It rippled through the still air, mocking my plea. A second voice joined hers, feminine and cutting, scattering my focus like leaves in a storm.

At least I found her.

Would she have confided in Fyrn'sol? I trusted her instincts and her ability to act with grace, yet no amount of tact could erase what I did. A princess pressed against a bookshelf, kissed as though the world burned around us—it could have been her escape from Tallon.

My breath escaped in a sharp hiss. I didn't want her tethered to him, left to endure the fate he offered. But there was no alternative. If she left, Radaan would crumble.

Grant me wisdom. My thoughts twisted into a final plea, the words heavy, raw, and unanswered.

The dinner felt as wretched as every other—though tonight, each barbed remark Tallon aimed at Nienna ignited an urge to lash out. My hand curled under the table, nails biting into my palm. The Velli ambassador sat smug and calculating, his very presence a provocation. When he joined in, testing Nienna's limits, my patience frayed, anger simmering close to boiling over.

To my left, Griar'tal droned on about breeding a new line of horses, his voice an irritating hum against the tension at the table. My focus remained fixed on Nienna, watching for her response to Tallon's latest volley.

"I would love to travel. I should see the kingdom I will become princess of," she said, her tone sharp enough to cut. A determined attempt to force an invitation.

Egath chuckled, his jagged teeth glinting. "You'll be queen one day, my dear. Better to conserve your strength—for heirs."

My grip tightened on the silverware. I stabbed a potato, the motion deliberate, though it did little to steady me. To Tallon, Nienna was nothing more than a vessel for his ambitions—less than Griar'tal's prized stallions, a broodmare for his legacy.

"A queen should be as capable as a king, wouldn't you agree, Your Majesty?" Nienna's gaze locked with mine, dark and imploring. Her silent plea sliced through the tension—a wordless request for reprieve after enduring an evening of relentless jabs.

I held her stare and inclined my head, my voice measured. "The kingdom's strength depends on both the king and queen. Take her. Let her out of the Golden Palace."

The words tasted bitter. The thought of her leaving—especially under Tallon's care—twisted my gut, but for her sake, I relented.

"If King of the Plentiful Plains suggests it, then you must, Tallon." Egath's grin widened as he leaned forward. "I'm well-acquainted with the Craggs. I'd seek permission to accompany you."

The mention of the mountain range froze me. The Craggs? Now? He never showed interest before, and unease prickled under my skin.

"I will consider your request," I replied, knowing I wouldn't. "But I suggest you stay with Claydon'sol while you visit." The man was no genius, but he would keep Nienna safe.

Tallon faced me, a predatory smile pulling at his lips. "Accidents happen in those mountains, Father. You bear the scars to prove it."

I eased back, studying him. His words weren't mere petulance. They carried a darker edge, a warning I wasn't ready to dismiss—not with Nienna involved.

The princess leaned forward, her posture demure, her expression schooled into the perfect mask. Her smile, restrained yet polite, suited the occasion, but her eyes betrayed her desperation. She wanted this—needed it.

Did she hope to spend more time with her betrothed? Doubtful. Avoid me? Possible. Or did the prospect of freedom beyond the palace walls call to her? Probable.

I forced my attention back to Tallon, the uneasy knot in my chest tightening. His emotions always bled through his façade, much like his mother's. He was too unguarded, too reckless.

"I'm due for a visit to the Manor in the Mountains," I said, watching his lip curl in a silent snarl. "We'll leave in two weeks."

"Thank you!" Nienna's voice brimmed with relief, her triumph unmistakable.

Tallon stiffened, his fork plunging into a carrot with a force that sent the vegetable skidding. His gaze flicked to Egath, and the unspoken exchange between them set my nerves alight. What was he plotting? Seeking assurance? A plan?

Without a word, he pushed to his feet and tossed his napkin onto the table. His departure was as abrupt as it was insolent, though he spared the bare minimum courtesy. "I beg my leave."

His boots thundered against the marble steps, drawing a few glances from visiting nobles. Those unfamiliar with his tantrums watched, wide-eyed. The rest ignored him.

With his chair vacant, my line of sight to Nienna was clear. Her back remained rigid, her composure strained. Egath's hand brushed hers, and she recoiled, a flicker of discomfort flashing across her face. His murmured apology barely concealed his amusement.

Rage coiled hot and sharp in my veins. I drowned it with a swig of wine, though the desire to challenge the Velli to a duel lingered, gnawing at my restraint.

Whatever Griar'tal had to say, I doubted I would concentrate on any more horses tonight.

Chapter Nineteen

NIENNA

I couldn't endure another moment. Kallias sat so near, his presence tangible, yet a chasm stretched between us. The unspoken confessions simmering within me—questions I longed to voice—clawed at my resolve. Egath's silent proximity only sharpened the edge of my discomfort. A phantom stirring curled through my body, a sensation foreign and unsettling. I didn't know enough about the Velli to determine if it was imagined or if Egath, tearing into his steak with disinterest, was the source.

Either way, I was done.

"I beg your leave, Your Majesty," I murmured, pushing to my feet.

Kallias rose as well, setting off a ripple of movement through the hall as every guest followed suit. His calm, steady gaze held mine, and I froze under its weight.

"It's been a long day," he said, his voice smooth and deliberate. "I will retire as well."

Lowering my head, I stepped aside, hiding my turmoil. Before I could round the table, Kallias excused himself from his companion and extended his elbow.

The gesture was perfectly proper, nothing unusual. I swallowed hard, laying my palm on his arm, fighting to steady my breath. This wasn't improper. It was customary for him to escort me in place of Tallon. Yet Egath's sharp, lingering gaze burned where my hand rested. His smirk hinted at knowledge I preferred he didn't possess.

Kallias led me out, and the impact of every stare pressed against my back. My pulse raced to a breakneck speed, drowning out the murmurs of the room.

Calm. This was normal. Acceptable.

The moment we cleared the dining hall, my fingers twitched, itching to pull away. The memory of last night blazed hot, leaving a pile of humiliated ashes in its wake. He hadn't spoken to me since, aside from dinner. I knew why.

It was a mistake.

I initiated it, and he might have welcomed it, but I should have shown restraint. His arm beneath my hand radiated warmth, his closeness smothering. I wanted to tear away, lock myself in my room, and bury the shame.

But he turned, guiding me down a different corridor. Confusion prickled, and I glanced around, recognizing the path but puzzled by his choice. Why wasn't he taking me to my quarters?

Unless he didn't see it as a mistake.

A cursed flicker of hope kindled in my chest, and though I tried to extinguish it, my denial only fanned the flame.

He hadn't spoken—was it restraint or hesitation? Was he leading me to privacy, where words weren't necessary, where actions might resume what we'd begun?

Greaves followed at a measured pace, dismissing the guards who attempted to fall in line. His presence was deliberate, his loyalty assured. Had Kallias sworn him to secrecy, making him an accomplice in this unspoken arrangement?

The air thickened with the warm scent of cinnamon and cloves. Servants bustled past, bowing as they carried trays and supplies. Overgrown vines spilled from planters along the walls, their leaves twisting toward the glittering sandstone that reflected a soft golden light. Towers of greenery filled massive pots, and the entire hall exuded a rare, lived-in warmth, far from the cold grandeur of the noble courts.

The spice in the air deepened as we approached a door propped open. Servants flowed in and out with ease, greeting Kallias with familiarity. His replies were warm, his voice low and genuine, each word carrying a quiet reverence for his people. He *knew* them.

He was a good king.

I would ruin him.

The thought tightened my throat, splitting my emotions. Horror at the damage I could cause tangled with a giddy thrill. He was everything a ruler should be—honest, moral, beloved. Yet I tempted him. My presence alone had the power to erode his perfection, to stain his legacy.

The idea left me breathless.

Kallias rounded the corner, stepping into a room heavy with heat and moisture. My grin widened as my gaze landed on the snug kitchen carved into the wall. It was tiny—smaller than my dressing room—but alive with activity. Steam curled from several pots bubbling on a modest stove, the humid air thick with the mingling scents of simmering spices.

A wiry man in a stained apron turned from a towering spice rack crammed with jars of powders, pastes, and seeds. Herbs dangled from the ceiling, their leaves wilting in the oppressive humidity.

"Your Majesty!" The cook bowed, his bald head gleaming with perspiration. When he straightened, his eyes widened, landing on me. "And Your Highness!"

Kallias chuckled, a sound low and rich. "The usual."

"Of course!" the man chirped, darting around the cramped kitchen. His movements were quick but practiced, and I couldn't suppress a laugh as he rummaged through a cabinet, producing two simple gold mugs—ones I'd grown accustomed to.

Kallias gestured toward him. "Nienna, meet Igor, the man responsible for our cider."

"It's delicious. Thank you."

Igor's face lit up, and he bowed again. "It is my *honor!*" With a flourish, he ladled deep amber liquid into the mugs, his focus absolute. He handed them to Kallias, who offered one to me.

I wrapped both hands around the metal, the warmth seeping into my chilled fingers. The steam carried a medley of spices—cinnamon, clove, and the faintest hint of apple. I brought it closer, inhaling deeply, the fragrant vapors curling through my chest like a slow, gentle fire.

Or maybe the heat came from Kallias, standing so near and thoughtful enough to bring me here.

"Thank you, Igor." He nodded toward the cook and backed out of the room.

I followed, the cup clutched close, more for the butterflies it shielded than the warmth it offered.

As we moved farther from the kitchen, the corridors emptied, the clatter of staff fading behind us. Recognition stirred as I realized the path led to the balcony.

"I almost feel bad Greaves doesn't get any," I murmured as the spiral staircase came into view.

Without hesitation, he held out his mug to the man, who accepted it with a raised brow, swirling the liquid before taking a cautious sip. He grunted, pursed his lips, and took another, slower this time.

"I hope you burn yourself," Kallias muttered, though the corner of his mouth tugged upward. Greaves' only response was the faintest lift beneath his tidy, trimmed beard, the tiniest hint of a smile.

His bodyguard was calm, reserved, but Kallias burned in contrast. His heat wasn't confined to his temper or demeanor—it radiated through him, through every glance and movement. Though he wore a reserved mask, cool and deliberate, I could feel the wildfire just beneath, waiting to ignite.

"Why the frogs?" I asked as we stepped onto the winding staircase.

Kallias glanced at the carved tadpoles underfoot, his brows knitting together. "Deep in the Untamed Valley—some call it the Valley Beneath—there are sprawling bogs to the northwest. Miserable terrain. My mother hated the place and refused to visit. She said it stank, suffocated with heat, and demanded gills just to breathe. My father, though, saw beauty in all of Radaan. He commissioned a craftsman to capture the life thriving there."

My gaze followed the intricate details: lily pads resting on the steps, delicate flowers sprouting along the rails. "And did she change her mind after seeing this?"

"She did," Kallias said, tapping the carved shape of a flying insect on the support beam. His lip curled. "She insisted these be added—bugs the size of your palm that swarm and leave you scratching for days."

I recoiled with a cringe. That would ruin the charm.

His faint smile flickered and then faded as we reached the landing. His expression turned solemn as he opened the balcony door and stepped aside. With a bow, he gestured for me to pass. Warmth crept into my cheeks, my stomach twisting as I did so.

"Wait here."

From the corner of my eye, I caught Greaves throwing Kallias a sharp glare, but the king didn't acknowledge him. Instead, he shut the door in his face. When he turned to me, his expression shifted, the subtle hardness of the king's mask slipping.

The balcony was his refuge, where the pressure of his status lightened just enough to let me glimpse the man beneath. Here, he could be Kallias, not only the ruler of Radaan. Beyond this space, he could never separate himself from the mantle of kingship.

The cider tempted me, and I nursed the spiced drink as I wandered toward the stone balustrade, gazing out at the expanse. The sun had long since melted against the earth, streaking the horizon with the fading purples and deep indigos of dusk. Daylight hours were shortening. I'd heard of 'snow'—frozen flakes that fell from the sky in the depth of winter—and wondered if I'd ever witness such a thing.

Kallias leaned against the wall beside me, releasing a quiet sigh. The sound stirred something in me, my pulse quickening. I kept my focus on the distant fields, where a farmer, no more than a speck, led a horse along a narrow road.

"Nienna—"

"I don't usually see farmers out this late," I interrupted, unwilling to broach any topic he addressed with that grave tone.

"The second alfalfa harvest is underway," he said. "Farmers work long hours this time of year. That horse is limping, though. That's why he's running late."

I squinted at the faint figure, trying to make out the supposed limp. "How can you see that far?"

He didn't answer. Instead, he tried again. "Last night–"

"Do you think it'll snow this winter?"

He straightened, the tension in his frame palpable. "Nienna."

My chest tightened, pulse pounding in my ears as I met his gaze. His lips pressed into a hard line, and a deep crease carved itself between his brows. Dread flooded me with his pained expression, drowning the fragile hope I'd clung to.

"I'm sorry," I blurted, desperate to stop whatever words hovered on his tongue. "I shouldn't have..." The sentence withered before it formed, shame choking me into silence.

His attention roved over my face, lingering for a moment, as though searching for something unspoken. His hand rose, hesitated, then fell back to his side. "You are not responsible for what happened last night."

I gripped the mug, its warmth the only anchor against the tremor threatening to give me away. "If I remember correctly... I asked for it."

A flicker of pain flashed in his expression, smothered as quickly as it appeared. A small flinch, as if my words struck harder than any blade.

"And the responsibility falls on me." His hand found the hilt of his sword, fingers tightening, but he held my gaze. "I shouldn't have let it happen. I should have had more restraint. You deserve an apology—"

My heart stumbled over itself. "There's no reason to–"

"—and a promise." His brows furrowed into a grim line. "It won't happen again. I'll make sure of it."

The words shattered something inside me. My breath caught, the ache twisting deeper with every beat of silence.

A mistake. That's what I was.

"Greaves remains loyal to me," he continued, his voice colder now, each word another stone on the wall between us. "Word will not come from me or him concerning the matter." His mask slipped into place, locking me out.

I wanted to believe it shielded me from his true feelings, but the sting of accusation couldn't be ignored.

He wouldn't tell. Would I?

"I haven't told anyone," I murmured, though my stomach churned with his unspoken distrust. He thought I might. He believed I'd betray this secret—that I might trade it like coin, gossip for sport—when *my* reputation was at stake.

The cider soured in my mouth, its sweetness turned sharp and acidic.

He exhaled, his shoulders easing, and the sight sent heat rushing to my cheeks. Relief—his relief—only enraged me. How dare he only care for his crown's untarnished shine?

The insult burned hotter than my shame.

I placed the mug on the wall with deliberate calm. His gaze flicked to it, then back to me, wariness shadowing his features.

"I wouldn't whisper secrets that could send me to Draconia with my purity in question," I said, my voice as cold as the night air biting at my cheeks. The venom spilled freely now, my treacherous tears brimming but unshed. "I am not yours, Kallias. And you are not mine. Perhaps we should keep our distance to remember that."

Each word lanced through the fragile thread between us, severing it with precision. I refused to waver, even as my vision blurred, even as my heart fractured beneath the weight of unspoken truths.

A muscle jumped in his jaw as his teeth ground together. "I agree. You're bound to my son, and he deserves an unsullied wife."

My lip curled in a snarl, and my fingers twitched with the urge to strike him. How dare he say Tallon deserved *anything!* That snake deserved to rot in the bog.

Pain knifed through my stomach as I turned and stormed toward the door. I refused to be treated like a mistake—a stain. His apology and acceptance of blame meant nothing when the kiss still burned in my mind, scalding away every trace of composure. It unraveled me, made me long for something I could never have.

I yanked the door open, the hinges groaning under the force, and Greaves' keen eyes flicked over my face before shifting toward the balcony.

"He needs you," I hissed, shoving past him. My boots thudded against the stairs as I descended.

Anger warred with despair in my chest. Why couldn't Tallon be like Kallias? Why did *he* have to be the one my heart longed for? There were plenty of men who treated me with respect, some even considered more handsome by conventional standards.

Yet, Kallias *saw* me. Beyond my title and predetermined duty. He knew I'd never be content to live caged, birthing heirs on command. I imagined Tallon already had a governess hired to whisk my newborn babes away to teach them his ways. The thought poisoned my resolve.

I missed a step, my boot catching on the final one, and stumbled. Hot tears blurred my vision, and I clung to the railing, breathing hard.

I forced myself to stop. To breathe. The last thing I needed was to be seen weeping like a scorned lover in the halls. My grip tightened on the rail, and the cold engraved dragonfly dug into my palm, anchoring me.

This was my duty. My father trusted my honor. My mother had once been a stranger to him, yet their love grew with time. Perhaps I could learn to love another—not the king on the balcony.

The world tilted as a rough hand clamped over my mouth. I thrashed, heels scraping stone, and clawed at the fingers sealing off my scream. As the assailant hauled me to the side, my teeth sank into his finger.

"Whore!"

My breath fled when my back slammed into the wall, his body pinned hard against mine. Grit scraped my skin as Tallon's furious face came into view, his black hair wild, and his pale cheeks splotched red.

"You couldn't settle for me, could you?" His sneer twisted his features into something cruel.

I bucked against his hold, slamming my palms into his chest. "Get off me!"

"I bet you didn't tell him that!"

Teeth bared, I struggled against his weight. Better to face the snake. "I don't know what you're talking about," I growled.

"How long have you been sneaking around with him? Every night?" He seethed, hatred distorting his features.

My palm cracked across his cheek. His head snapped to the side, and his hand rose as if to return the blow.

"Go on, Tallon." I snarled, leaning into him. "I dare you."

He hesitated, then lunged. His fingers gripped my throat—not to choke, but to pin me in place.

Fury boiled in my veins. "You're risking *everything!*"

"I never wanted this marriage," he spat. Wine soured his breath as he leaned closer. "But my father demanded it. Signed me away to you, and for what? I don't need your worthless dragons!"

His words hit harder than the hand on my throat. Another rejection, this time delivered with venom.

He sneered. "Perhaps you planned it all along—what does he need me for if he can make another heir?"

"You're drunk!" I spat.

His fingers tightened with a warning squeeze, and my hands brushed his tunic, shying away from the press of his body. My grasp danced around his belt, searching.

"Perhaps, but I've more sense than my rutting father. I don't need you or *him*. Radaan is mine, and–"

I flicked my wrist, and the cold steel of his dagger kissed his throat.

"Back off."

He froze, eyes widening. The point pressed into his skin, and his hold on me slackened.

"A knife doesn't make you less of a whore," he hissed, taking a step.

I flipped the blade in my hand, catching it by the hilt. "Careful, *boy*. Your future wife doesn't take kindly to insults."

His hands trembled at his sides, and his face darkened with barely contained rage. I tilted my head and smirked, pretending his fury amused me.

Then I spun on my heel and strode down the hall.

My grip tightened on the weapon, its hilt biting into my palm. My ears strained for the sound of footsteps, but he didn't follow.

I forced my expression into something polite, serene. The dagger disappeared into the folds of my dress as I straightened my posture. The façade held firm, but inside, my heart ached, splintered into pieces too jagged to mend.

It was all a play I was locked in. Some drama that I starred in. Promised to a prince who hated me, trusted to marry him by a starving nation. A king that wanted me, but his kingdom's survival hinged on my union.

This wasn't a drama.

It was a tragedy.

Chapter Twenty

NIENNA

Scythe's smile vanished as I crossed the threshold of my chambers, the dagger slipping from my fingers to clatter against the floor. She rose from the chair where she'd been reading, placing the book aside. Her wary gaze swept over me, her composure cracking.

Before the first tear escaped, she pulled me into her arms. Her embrace was firm, anchoring me as my strength collapsed. My knees buckled, and I sagged against her, crushed by everything I couldn't say.

I hated Tallon. The thought of marrying him made my stomach churn, but my father's blood oath bound me. My duty demanded it, though my heart rebelled against every thread of that obligation.

"What happened?" Scythe guided me to the sofa in the receiving room, and I let her lead me, too drained to resist.

"It's all wrong." Tears choked my words, and I nestled my head into the crook of her neck as her fingers brushed back my hair, her touch gentle but grounding. "I never expected to marry for love—I've always known that."

My knees drew to my chest as I curled into her. "But why—why do I..." My voice fractured into a sob, Kallias' face flashing in my mind. His promise, his shame, Tallon's vile accusations—all of it lashed at me like a storm.

"You love him, don't you?" she whispered. She didn't name him, but she didn't need to.

The silence that followed screamed louder than any confession I might've given. I couldn't bring myself to say it, couldn't manage anything but another broken sob. It would have been easier to hate everyone here, to despise Fyrn, to see Kallias as nothing more than a man on the throne. If only Tallon continued on with his indifference—I could have endured.

But tonight shattered that fragile pretense. His attack revealed a darker truth—the prince would never leave me in peace. My future with him wouldn't hold even the hope of friendship. It would be a battleground every day—a war waged in silence and rage.

Could I endure that? A lifetime of bitterness and strife?

"Are we going home?" Scythe asked, her voice low, as if fearing the answer.

Home. Draconia. The familiar halls where I might wait for another proposal to tether me to a foreign kingdom—or resign myself to a solitary life without a husband or children.

Kallias rose unbidden into my thoughts. I saw him on the battlefield, his scarred chest bared, blood streaking his sword. A Velli blade pierced him, the steel sinking into his flesh with horrifying finality.

"I despise it here," I spat, forcing the image from my mind.

The lie tasted bitter, but we both knew it for what it was. I couldn't hate Reem, not truly. I was growing to care for its people, to appreciate its beauty. Radaan offered food and timber that could rebuild Draconia, strengthen them enough to push deeper into the Wild Shores.

But if I fled, Kallias would die. I knew it like I knew my own heart. Draconia could scrape by through famine. My people would endure, but his—they would pay the price in blood.

"I can't," I whispered. Then I wiped the tears from my cheeks and pushed myself upright, steeling my voice. Princesses did not break in their handmaidens' arms. "I won't."

Scythe studied me, her brows knitting together as worry flickered in her gaze.

"I refuse to abandon Radaan and allow them to be ravaged by war." The words trembled, but the resolve behind them didn't waver.

The unspoken truth hung heavy between us.

I wouldn't leave Kallias.

Fyrn's presence offered a reprieve from thoughts of the king, but even her company circled back to Tallon. It was the safe choice—the obvious one, given I was to marry him. She seemed determined to make it palatable.

"If you'd like, I could show you his sprinter," she said, her face alight with enthusiasm. "He's the fastest Radaan has seen in years!"

Horses. Boys and their horses.

"I'd rather hear about your goats." My sigh escaped as I cradled a rose, its velvet petals cool against my palm.

We wandered through the garden, its perfume weaving through the air, while the noblewomen lingered over tea. The walk had been Fyrn's idea, her attempt to pacify court murmurs about my nonconformity to Tallon's hand-picked attire.

"My goats?" She wrinkled her nose. "Surely you don't mean the Kuh'lir?"

"Tallon plans to take me to your father's manor in a week. He breeds them, doesn't he? It seems proper to learn more about them." I brushed my thumb along the crimson petal and let the rose fall from my grasp.

Goats were safer ground. Anything was safer than Tallon.

"Nienna, are you well?"

Her question snapped my gaze to hers, sharp and searching, as though my secrets might spill across my face.

"I'm fine."

"You've been distant all day." Her hand clasped mine, firm but gentle, and her brows knit with concern. "If something else weighs on you, or if you'd prefer to rest—"

"No."

Rest meant returning to my rooms, a gilded cage masquerading as a sanctuary. The entire palace suffocated me. Every hallway echoed with the fear of meeting the king or Tallon.

"What is it?" She lowered her voice, leading me past the colorful tea tables, away from the women exchanging pleasantries. Beneath a low-hanging tree, its leaves gilded with the first touch of autumn, she stopped.

"I see it in your eyes," she pressed, her mask slipping to reveal unguarded worry. "Something troubles you. It's about Tallon, isn't it?"

Him and his *father*.

"Let me help you," she added.

No one could fix this. My prison stretched far beyond stone walls and duty-bound corridors.

My resistance crumbled. I sank onto the bench beneath the tree's shade and dropped my head into my hands. "I'm a princess—I'll never marry for love."

Her shoulders softened, and she sat beside me, eyes distant. "No one expects high ladies to," she murmured, her words weighted by something more personal.

The wistfulness in her tone made me glance up. She wasn't looking at me but at some unseen thing, beyond the flowers swaying in the breeze.

Her lips twisted into a fragile smile that never touched her eyes. "It's not in the cards for me, either," she added.

"You've accepted no betrothal," I said, forming my words with care.

"Not yet. But the one I love—he won't have me." Her voice wavered, and unshed tears glimmered in her gaze. "I'm bound for a loveless union, to bear heirs and nothing more, while my heart belongs to another." She scoffed. "And they say men have it hard."

Her bitterness mirrored my own.

"I'd hoped I might grow to care for my match," I admitted, the crack in my tone betraying my composure. My focus fell to my slippers, the grass brushing their edges. "At least enough to be his friend. To prove my worth."

"He'll never see mine." Fyrn's jaw clenched, her words sharp and brittle. "I'll play the part, smile when required, but his heart will never belong to me."

"You can't imagine how much I understand that." A grimace pulled at my lips. "I know you're close to Tallon–"

"Acquaintances. Nothing more." Her dry chuckle carried a hint of pain, as if she didn't want to be attached to the man I loathed.

"When I'm forced to marry him, the stress alone might render me barren and send one of us to an early grave."

Her brows knitted, her worry deepening. "Then leave. Break the betrothal."

"No." The weight of duty settled on my shoulders, heavy and suffocating. "For the sake of both kingdoms, I'll endure. But could it even be called a marriage?"

Fyrn slipped her arms around me, her embrace warm against the coolness of the breeze. "At least you'll have me. You can always claim you need mountain air, and I shall escape my brood of children to join you."

"You'd better bring sticky buns," I murmured into her shoulder, a faint laugh breaking through the ache in my chest.

"Only if you bring the wine," she teased, nudging me as her giggle mingled with the rustling leaves.

For the first time that day, the cage felt less suffocating. At least someone sympathized, even if they didn't have all the information.

The afternoon unfolded more smoothly than expected. Sharing burdens with Fyrn—her secret and mine—was like balancing the scales. With that silent understanding between us, the pretense eased. We slipped our masks back on, even if the smiles weren't genuine.

My return to the noblewomen for tea brought the inevitable talk of the wedding. Murmurs churned like a gathering storm, and I braced for the onslaught. Fyrn must have noticed the tension in my posture because she steered the conversation away from Tallon, redirecting it toward subjects she knew I could tolerate.

"Who should paint the ceremony?" she asked, her bright tone lifting the mood like sunlight breaking through clouds.

Chatter turned to palace artists and their most beloved works, and Fyrn lamented the loss of one particular painter whose masterpiece immortalized a ceremony following the Great Hunt. The mention drew giggles from the younger women, but an older noblewoman from the north silenced them with a sharp look.

"The celebration of life is sanctified by Verdis," she admonished, her milky-blue eyes locking onto me as though searching for weakness.

I straightened my spine and let my expression settle into practiced reverence.

"Life demands death, and death precedes life," she intoned, raising her tea cup with a deliberate motion. Her scrutiny burned like a brand on my skin. "Radaan should lose the blessing of the gods if its royals scorn their will. Do not mock the sacred—such irreverence borders on blasphemy."

"We meant no disrespect, Madam Elain'gog," one of the younger women murmured, her voice honeyed with deference. "We only recall the... modesty of the painting."

Elain's glare could have frozen the tea in her cup. "There is no shame in what the gods have blessed."

"But imagine the painter asking Princess Nienna and Prince Tallon to disrobe–"

"Enough," Fyrn cut in, her words slicing like a sword.

The offender flushed crimson, shrinking into her seat, mumbling an apology to her tea.

Elain turned her withering gaze back to me. "A word of wisdom, Princess. You are in Radaan now, where we rise and fall with the gods' favor. Earn their hand, and your future will be secure."

Her meaning struck with all the subtlety of a dagger. Radaan's people demanded devotion from their rulers, their faith woven into their loyalties. A monarch without the divine might rule, but they'd find their throne cold and their allies scarce.

I swallowed hard, the tea bitter on my tongue. Kallias worshiped Elohios, the god of justice and truth. My chest tightened at the thought, guilt gnawing at the edges of my conscience. His devotion to honesty felt like a cruel irony in light of what happened in the library.

Choosing a deity wasn't a matter of faith—it was survival. If I hoped to save these people, I had to become one of them, even if it meant pledging myself to a god I didn't believe in.

My gaze drifted to the garden gate, the path beyond it calling to me like a promise of freedom I couldn't claim. It was a reminder that my life was not my own.

Fyrn suggested I skip the council meeting. I admitted I wanted nothing more—not just to avoid Tallon, but his father, too.

Still, we went. Together, hand in hand, we entered the chamber as a war general took his seat—Darius. I avoided the king's piercing gaze, offering only a polite bow. Fyrn dipped into a deep curtsy, her grip on my hand tightening as we straightened.

My chest constricted, each heartbeat a hammer's blow. I stood caught between the man my heart ached for, who wanted nothing of me, and the boy who openly despised me.

I lifted my chin. A future queen wouldn't cower before discomfort. Steeling myself, I stepped toward the row where Tallon sat, his conversation halting as he glared at me. His gaze crawled down my deep blue dress, his lip curling in disdain.

Egath's sharp smile greeted me, his jagged teeth a cruel taunt. I braced myself, but the sight of him sent a chill down my spine. Prepared for Tallon's hatred, I hadn't accounted for the Velli ambassador's unsettling presence. My hand tightened around Fyrn's, seeking her steadiness.

"Greetings, Princess." Egath rose, his bow shallow and mocking. The prince remained sprawled in his seat, eyes sharp with scrutiny, as though he could peel away my secrets.

"Ambassador," I replied, the smile on my lips brittle. My teeth clenched as I lowered into my chair.

Tallon shifted, moving his leg further from me with an exaggerated gesture. I forced a sweet grin, but the memory of pressing a blade to his throat simmered beneath it. He underestimated me before. He was foolish enough to do it again.

Egath's low chuckle slithered like some slick creature as he resumed his seat. I lifted my chin against the unease gnawing at me.

"Welcome, counselors."

Kallias' voice shattered my composure. My pulse stuttered as I met his gaze, the crowded room fading to a blur. At least twenty men separated us, yet his eyes made the distance feel like a whisper. His jaw tightened, his expression composed but strained as he dipped his head slightly.

"Welcome, Ambassador. Prince Tallon. Princess Nienna," Kallias said evenly, though his son let out a thoughtful hum when my name was spoken, drawing attention, "and Lady Fyrn'sol."

The king turned to the slim, pale man across the table. "Sai'glon, begin with the tensions in the foothills."

Sai straightened, his dark hair brushing his shoulders as he shifted, his discomfort obvious. "Yes, Your Majesty. In the Glon district, there have been multiple reports of threats and theft."

My heart sank. A week ago, I'd written to my father about the mounting unrest, but the whirlstorms would delay any response for weeks.

"Do we have any information about the culprits?" Kallias asked, his tone calm but probing.

Sai hesitated, his lips curling before he masked it with a wince. "The threats originate from Velli traders who approach the boundary. Our people refuse to trade with them."

"And the thefts?"

"Tracks lead east, through the Pass of Thousands."

Kallias turned toward Egath, his brow dipping into a controlled frown. "Ambassador, are you aware of these events?"

The Velli rose with deliberate slowness, his lanky frame unfolding as he addressed the room. "I've heard no such *accusations*." He drew that last word out with venom. "I will investigate, but perhaps if the Radaanians were open to trade, such *claims* would not arise."

Sai's glare burned into the wood, his hands hidden. "He admits it!"

"Peace, Sai'glon," Kallias said, firm but calm. His hand pressed flat against the table. "My people are free to choose their commerce partners."

Tallon leaned forward. "The Velli are starving."

The declaration made me frown—defending their enemy here, before his own council?

"We have more than enough," he continued. "Send a portion of our tax."

Gasps and murmurs rippled through the room.

"The tax belongs to Radaan," Kallias said, his voice sharp as steel, his hand curling into a white-knuckled fist.

Sai'glon's fury blazed in his eyes, though not for Egath—it burned for Tallon. "You expect us to give our crops to those monsters?" he growled, tone edged with disgust.

Generals leaned back, their faces unreadable but for the glint of curiosity or approval. Noblemen exchanged quiet glances, basking in the anticipation of a fight. Beside me, Tallon's lips curved into a smirk.

"They are blood crops, *boy!*" Sai'glon thundered. "A thousand fell in that pass–"

"*Prince!*" Tallon spat, rising from his seat.

Kallias rose, his fist slamming into the table, silencing the room. "Enough! This council will maintain order." His glare swept from Sai to his son. "Choose your words with care—or remain silent."

"Perhaps wisdom would honor the treaty," Tallon said, chest puffed with defiance.

Fyrn sucked in a breath, her gaze flickering between them. Egath stood to the side, his sharp eyes dissecting the scene with a precision I found unsettling.

"Radaan upholds the agreement, as does Vellos," Kallias spoke, each word clipped and deliberate. "As the foreign advisor, you might want to acquaint yourself with *your* people's grievances."

Before Tallon could utter something that could damn him further, I rose, placing a steady hand on his shoulder. "The dragons–"

He recoiled, jerking his arm free as his hand shot toward me. I flinched at the sudden motion, the sound of wood groaning under pressure punctuating the moment. With chin raised, I caught his hateful green gaze and refused to look away. His palm froze mid-air, trembling as rage rippled through him.

The room plunged into silence, the kind so heavy it pressed against the skin. The prince shook with fury, every taut muscle betraying his wrath. I forced a smile, though it felt more like baring my teeth. If he struck me, he'd doom his people—my dragons were their last chance.

Footsteps echoed across the chamber, but I didn't break from Tallon's stare. He would yield first. I'd been raised among dragons, not cowards.

A rough hand clamped onto his arm, yanking it down.

"Dare to raise a hand to her again," Kallias hissed, his voice low and razor-sharp, "and you'll lose it."

Tallon struggled against his grip, but he held firm, dragging him closer.

"See yourself out before you start a war," he growled.

"You're blinded by her–"

The crack of the king's hand across Tallon's face was so swift I staggered, colliding with Fyrn behind me. She caught my arm, steadying me as the room pulsed with unspoken fury. The prince froze, his cheek burning red with the imprint of Kallias' strike.

"Leave. Now," the king commanded.

Tallon spat a curse, his glare searing into me before he stormed out. Guards trailed after him, their boots thudding in obedient rhythm.

The others remained rigid, their hands clenched and expressions caught between disbelief and indignation. Shame crawled up my neck, hot and suffocating. This wasn't my fault, yet Kallias had to intervene—had to restore order in a way that left my position exposed.

His gaze softened as it found mine, though his voice stayed cold. "Radaan meant no insult, Princess Nienna. Forgive us for Tallon's actions."

His apology wasn't owed, but I knew why he offered it. As long as I stayed, my dragons were his. Still, I'd sooner die than let someone like Tallon wield their power.

"Words are slippery things when tensions rise," I replied, my voice steady despite the chaos in my mind.

The king turned, pinning Egath with a glare sharp enough to cut. "I trust we can *all* proceed with civility?"

Egath's mouth twitched, amusement tugging at the corners, but he inclined his head in agreement.

"My apologies, Your Majesty." Sai'glon's tone cooled, but the fire in his eyes still smoldered. His people bore scars too raw to endure more disrespect, especially from a bratty prince.

"Princess." Kallias gestured toward the council table, positioning himself between me and Egath. "I believe you had something to say." His blue eyes, bright as cornflowers but edged with caution, held mine. "Perhaps it would be better heard there."

Pleasure and unease wrestled in my chest. The lone vacant seat belonged to Tallon, a place I hadn't earned and likely never would when he sat upon the throne. Yet Kallias recognized my worth.

I swallowed hard, nodding as he led me forward. My hands trembled, skirts brushing against my legs as our steps rang out in the room's heavy silence. The weight of countless stares pressed on my back, but I straightened my shoulders, forcing my chin high.

Kallias paused to pull out the chair, his presence grounding me. I sank into the seat, smoothing my skirts as the nobles' murmurs ebbed. When he settled beside me, his knee brushed mine. My cheeks warmed, but I locked eyes with the assembly, deflecting their scrutiny with my own steady gaze.

"Your dragons," a grizzled general prompted, leaning forward.

I caught Egath's glare, sharp as a dagger, from across the table.

"*My* dragons..."

When the meeting ended, I spotted Kallias storming down the hall, each stride heavy with fury. I rushed to my rooms, throwing the door open behind me.

Scythe sat on the couch, four ribbons tangled between her toes. She struggled to weave them into an intricate braid, her foot yanking the threads tight. At the sound of my entrance, she jumped, a startled squeal escaping as she tumbled off the sofa.

"Oi! What happened to being a subtle princess?" she called, untangling her legs from the mess of skirts.

"Hurry!" I hissed, tugging at my overdress.

She tossed her ribbons aside, scrambling to help peel the dress off me. "Where to?"

I dashed to the dresser that blocked the old passageway. It felt heavier than I remembered and refused to budge under my weight.

"Oh! Adventures!" She squealed, grinning. She put her shoulder into it, and together we shoved the dresser aside with a groan of protest from the wood.

A narrow door emerged from the dust behind it. Just big enough for us to crawl through. If these passages led to the royal rooms, I hoped to catch a fragment of Kallias and Tallon's conversation again.

"What happened?" Scythe asked, her lamp casting a dim light on my face as she wedged herself beside me.

I opened the door and crept through. "I think your spare time would be better spent cleaning this than braiding ribbons," I muttered, brushing something soft and gooey.

"Creepy tunnels aren't on my to-do list," she snorted, following me inside. "It's below my pay."

The light confirmed my worst fear—rat droppings smeared across my hand. I wiped it on my leggings with a grimace. We crawled deeper into the pitch-black tunnel, halting at every creak above us.

The Spire was unlike other palaces. There was only so much stone to hollow out before reaching its limits. Older places like the Golden Palace had been built layer after layer, sections stacked over tunnels, halls over passages. I had no idea where we were, but I remembered where I'd last heard Kallias' voice.

As we rounded the corner, muffled sounds reached us. Scythe met my gaze, her eyes bright with mischief. She scrambled toward the small door ahead, marked by a trail less dusty than the rest of the crawlspace. With a quick flick, she dimmed the lamp to a faint glow and pressed her ear against the wood. I joined her.

"I am the *king!*" Kallias roared. "He pushes back on everything I say or do, taunts my nobles, and allies with the *Velli*. Elohios knows why he's been spending so much time with the eastern nobles."

"Kal."

A voice, too familiar. Someone close enough to call him by a nickname. Greaves.

"I would have killed him—wanted to," the king growled, the words muffled as if he were turned away.

"He mingles with eastern nobles, but doesn't like Sai'glon. Why?"

"I have no idea. You know him as well as I do," Kallias bit out.

"He's your son."

"Is he?" The question was chased with a scoff.

Scythe raised an eyebrow at me.

"If he wasn't, you wouldn't put him on the throne."

A thump sounded, followed by a muffled noise—something hit or thrown. "I've no choice. Tallon is the only option, regardless of whether he's mine. I'm not leaving Radaan anytime soon; I'll have time."

"Time for what, Kal? To teach him? Eldeiade had him for seventeen years. He learned all he would from her. You're not getting younger–"

"As you keep reminding me."

"Without another heir—the throne will be left to him. He's too open with his rebellion. If you don't do something drastic, he'll tear this kingdom apart and take Nienna with him."

"Do *not* bring her into this."

Scythe's brows shot up, and I frowned, pressing closer to the door.

Greaves' voice came again, darker. "Send her back."

"Enough," Kallias snapped, his tone icy, dismissing his guard without hesitation.

"You won't, because you can't, but it's what's best. You'll ruin her."

A loud slam echoed through the room, followed by heavy footsteps storming off.

Greaves groaned from the other side. "Gods, where are we off to with all that pent-up rage?"

"To do something drastic."

A door slammed.

Scythe turned the lamp up, her eyes wide. "What happened today?!"

"We need to find Tallon's room!" I hedged, searching the darkness in the direction the footsteps had faded.

"Nienna! What's going on?" She grabbed my arm as I tried to crawl past her.

"I hate Tallon," I hissed, struggling against her grip.

Her nails dug into my skin like claws. "I know!"

"And he hates me!"

"I *know!*"

"And I lo—like–" I faltered, my words strangling me. I glared down at her hand, desperate to pull free.

"Nienna, I know! But why is the king so riled up about you?"

"Because he kissed me!"

Scythe's jaw dropped. She snapped it shut, blinking as she digested that. Her grip loosened, and I sank against the wall, clutching my arm to my chest. My heart pounded, and I hated how wrong it felt to say it aloud, even though I trusted her.

"Is he a good kisser?"

Her mischievous grin pulled a reluctant laugh from me as she pressed against my shoulder.

"Gods, does Edith know?"

"She was sleeping like the dead when I snuck out. She's as clueless as the staff." I sighed, rubbing my face.

"Well, someone else knows."

"Greaves was the one who... well, he found us," I muttered, wiping away the spiderweb clinging to my leggings.

"Lucky man."

"Scythe!" I laughed, giving her a playful shove.

"What else happened between you and Tallon, then? His royal brattiness growing?"

"Worse," I groaned. "He's bitter and lashing out. He doesn't want this union, and the more time we spend together, the worse it gets. We're at each other's throats now. Last night, he attacked me–"

"And you didn't kill him?!" She twisted in the cramped tunnel, eyes scanning my body as if she might find a wound I'd hidden.

"Kill him?" My laugh was bitter. "With what? I have no dragons here. No magic. I stole his dagger and fended him off, but not before he accused me of seducing his father."

"That's not a bad idea. Do you think if–"

"Scythe." I cut her off with a sharp glare. "There is no me and Kallias."

She leaned against the wall, lips pressed together, studying me with quiet intensity. She lifted the lantern, holding it higher, like she could peer into the depths of my thoughts, my unspoken desire for the king.

"The contract says I'm to marry the prince. Think of the scandal if Kallias tried for my hand. Father would ride Argos here and lay waste to the palace." The blood oath could only be purged in dragonfire. "I'm marrying Tallon."

Scythe grimaced, wrinkling her nose, but she didn't push further. I was grateful. I didn't need her to fuel any foolish hope. Neither Radaan nor Draconia could survive that.

"Right then, Future Queen. We're missing *something drastic*."

Chapter Twenty-One

KALLIAS

Bloodlust coiled hot in my veins as I stalked through the corridors, every step an exercise in control. Decades of war tempered me, channeled the fury into a weapon. I wasn't some young buck prone to losing composure. I had a task, and I would see it through.

Perhaps there would be satisfaction in it, but that was secondary.

My heartbeat stayed steady, a drumbeat forged in countless battles with the Velli. This confrontation wasn't with an enemy, though—it was with family. My son.

Greaves was right. Tallon was my heir. Estranged or not, he bore my legacy. When Eldeiade died, I had hoped—foolishly, perhaps—that we could bridge the chasm between us. But the late queen's venom lingered, years of whispers poisoning him against me.

Every title I bestowed, and olive branch offered, he tossed back with disdain. In time, I returned his coldness in kind. He played his games, and I focused on securing Radaan, preparing it to withstand the storm Tallon's reign would bring.

But raising a hand to Nienna? That crossed a line—one impossible to ignore.

I shoved the door to his chambers open without hesitation. The sound echoed through the receiving room. Greaves hesitated behind me, but when he saw who lingered inside, he stepped in.

Egath flinched where he lounged on the sofa, his posture stiffening. I ignored him and strode toward Tallon, who leaned over a table, his palms pressed hard against its surface. A shattered vase lay in pieces on the floor, wine staining the rug like a fresh wound.

"See the ambassador out," I ordered without sparing the Velli a glance.

Footsteps shuffled behind me, and the door clicked shut as Greaves escorted Egath away. My attention remained fixed on Tallon. Hatred radiated from him like heat from a forge. His disheveled hair framed a face twisted with scorn, and his wild eyes darted to the wine bottles scattered across another table.

The room stank of stale drink and arrogance.

It could have been his mother's chambers—the same suffocating black-and-red decor, curtains drawn tight as though to block out reason itself. A sliver of light leaked through the edges, casting the chaos in an eerie glow.

"You've disgraced yourself," I said.

Tallon barked a laugh, walking with a swagger that failed to mask his unease. "I'm a disgrace? That wench you expect me to bed–"

I launched, closing the distance in two strides. My fist snared a handful of his tunic, then slammed him into the table. His head jerked back, eyes wide with shock as he grabbed at me.

For a moment, the silence held. I had never laid a hand on him before—not once.

The disbelief in his face twisted into a sneer. "You already slept with her, didn't you?"

Act. Don't react.

My fist connected with his jaw before I had time to reconsider.

"You are a boy!" I snarled, my knuckles burning as they hovered near his nose.

He gasped beneath me, head lolled, chest heaving as he tried to mask his fear with defiance.

"She is a princess," I hissed, my lip curling. "Not a tavern wench. Treat her with respect. Control your tongue, or I'll curb it for you."

"How exactly?" he spat. His green eyes burned with fury, but he didn't look away. "You can't make me do anything. I'm the prince!"

I leaned closer, letting him see the beast that stirred beneath my surface—the part of me forged in blood and fire. He recoiled, his boots scraping against the floor as he tried to push me off.

"Boy," I said, my voice dropping to a deadly whisper, "I have removed countless tongues for less. What is one more?"

"You wouldn't," he stammered, his bravado cracking. "You hate bloodshed!"

A laugh rumbled from deep in my chest. "Your mother taught you that, didn't she? But for Radaan, I would wade through rivers of blood." Nienna's face flashed in my mind, and I yanked Tallon upright, shaking him once for good measure. "I have turned a blind eye for too long. Start acting like a prince, or I will remove you from my line."

The words fell from my lips with a weight that chilled me to my core. They rang through my mind, daring me to find a lie in them, one that might earn Elohios' judgment, but none appeared.

What unsettled me most wasn't the truth in my threat—it was that I'd said it aloud.

"You mean to replace me."

His words carried no question, just cold certainty. He gripped my forearm where I still held his tunic in a crushing grip. Accusation hardened his features, his nostrils flaring as a thin streak of blood dripped from his nose.

"Don't make me." I loosened my hold and waited, unmoving. If he wanted space, he would have to create it himself.

His eyebrows, raised in momentary shock, knitted into a dark scowl. A sneer tugged at his lip as he stepped back, the distance a shallow pretense of defiance.

"I'll have your throne one day." Poison laced every word, a slow drip of venom meant to linger.

"Perhaps."

Let him simmer in the illusion of his own importance. Let him believe I would cast him aside. Not that I intended to wed again or risk bringing another heir into this cursed line.

Nienna's image seared through me—head tilted back, lips parted in a moan as I pressed between her legs. The vision burned, a vivid memory, a cruel fantasy. I blinked it away, burying it with all the other impossible futures. She had to marry him, this festering wound of a man. She would suffer as I had, trapped in a farce of duty. But would he humiliate her, as his mother had me? Would he hurt her?

Rage coiled tight. I could still see the snap of his hand as it rose to strike her. A gesture too quick, too practiced. How many before her had suffered the heat of his ire?

He reached for a bottle of wine and hurled it at me as I lunged. It bounced off my shoulder before shattering on the floor, splinters of glass catching the dim light. I grabbed his overcoat, dragging him close until his nose nearly brushed mine. He clawed for my sword, but I held fast to the hilt, my laugh a low, bitter sound.

"You think you're fit to rule because you wear silk and sit in comfort while others bleed for your peace?" My voice dropped to a dangerous hush. "Before you touch Princess Nienna again, ask Darius how many hands I've severed."

Memories surged, unbidden—blades hacking through Velli limbs, screams swallowed by the clash of steel, and blood-soaked fields that reeked of death. I let him see it, all of it, the burden of my title, Golden Warrior of Elohios, earned in bone and gore.

"A king can rule without hands, after all." I smiled, a sharp curve of teeth meant to cut, and shoved him back.

He staggered, trembling, his breath ragged as fury and fear warred in his expression.

Part of me dared him to lash out, to test the boyish bravado he'd only ever used on the weak. Let him face the warrior who carved victory from slaughter. But his courage faltered, and he stepped further away.

Disappointment pricked at me, but I nodded as if approving his retreat. Turning, I strode toward the door. The faint rustle of his breath followed me, but no bottle came flying this time.

Greaves met me in the corridor, his sharp eyes narrowing as he stepped closer. He adjusted the chains of my mantle with a practiced ease, his voice low enough to remain private. "There's blood on your hand."

I glanced down. A smear of red stained my knuckles, likely from the nose I had bloodied. Something twisted inside me—satisfaction, dark and unwelcome. I wiped the streak across my trousers, forcing the feeling back into the shadows.

It worried me, the ease with which I'd shed blood in the name of a certain princess.

My visit to the temple seethed with unwelcome thoughts of Nienna. Her voice curled through my mind like smoke, soft yet suffocating. I could almost feel her skin beneath my palm, remember the way she leaned into me—not with hesitation, but with a hunger that mirrored my own.

The cold bite of stone pressed into my knees, and I clenched my jaw, trying to wrestle my thoughts into submission. I was the king of Radaan, not some infatuated fool. If I let my desires take hold, I would be no better than Tallon, lashing out at the world with reckless emotion.

The image of his hand raised against her burned in my memory. My fists tightened, trembling with remnants of fury. She carried herself with strength and poise, even when faced with his disdain. Her defiance, the quiet fire in her eyes as she stood against him, marked her as a queen in every sense. Yet to him, she was a mere obstacle, an inconvenience.

He would never see her as I did—the way her compassion blended with her wits. He dismissed her beauty as if she were not a jewel among rubble. Her sea-blue eyes—deep, shadowed, endless—threatened to pull me under each time I thought of them. Frustration surged, and I tipped my head toward the heavens.

Elohios, take this temptation from me. Grant me the strength to endure.

But my pleas fell into silence. My thoughts spun back to her, ensnaring me again. She was a distraction I couldn't afford. My duty to Radaan demanded my focus, and yet, I let my guard crumble in the library. Her demeanor had wavered between boldness and vulnerability, a plea that shattered my restraint. She asked me to kiss her, and I obeyed without hesitation.

The memory burned through me, an intoxicating mix of shame and longing. I looked at my son's betrothed as no father should. Worse, I touched her. Kissed her. Shame coiled in my gut. With a growl, I slammed my fist against the floor. The jagged surface bit into my knuckles, the rough stone tearing at already raw knuckles. The pain was a hollow echo, unable to drown out the ache inside me.

Guide me. Show me what to do.

But no divine clarity came. Only the torment of images I couldn't banish. The idea of her bound to Tallon by duty and vow *I* gave, made my chest tighten. I imagined his hand clasping hers in ceremony, joining her in ways I could only dream of. It set my blood aflame. The thought of him claiming her, Nienna spread out beneath him, head turned and gaze distant to shield herself from the moment...

A snarl ripped from my throat as I surged to my feet, unable to endure the torrent any longer. My breath came shallow and uneven.

Forgive me.

Greaves entered without a sound, his movements precise as he draped the gold mantel across my shoulders. He steadied the weight while I secured the upper clasps. The metal pressed down with the familiar heaviness of duty—a reminder that Radaan's kings wore no crowns. The throne wasn't a trophy to display; it was a yoke of labor, a mantle of honor forged in sweat and sacrifice.

My gaze drifted past him to the stone depiction of Elohios above the altar. The god's sword rose high, his unyielding stare carved to pierce the soul. Those eyes seemed to strip away my defenses, laying bare the fractures I worked so hard to conceal.

Greaves finished the last clasp with practiced efficiency, then stepped back. His expression remained composed, but the faint crease between his brows betrayed his unease.

"We need to spar." The words came out rough, edged with desperation I failed to suppress.

He inclined his head, understanding etched into the lines of his face, but he said nothing. He knew as well as I did that prayer alone couldn't quiet today's storm.

Sweat clung to my skin and soaked my tunic as I entered my chambers before dinner. There was nothing as irritating as placing a clean overcoat over a soiled tunic. Yet, appearances mattered. Even with my hair plastered to my forehead and exhaustion weighing down every step, I had to present myself as a king whose life appeared ordered, even when it was anything but.

Sparring offered the briefest reprieve. The rhythm of battle—the snap of a parry, the satisfying clash of metal—quieted my thoughts in a way nothing else could. Years of combat ingrained the movements into muscle memory, freeing me to focus on the fight. Greaves' sudden feints and unpredictable strikes forced precision, leaving no room for distraction. Still, a welt burned across my forearm, a reminder of the moment my attention faltered. Nienna's image had slipped into my mind unbidden, and Greaves made me pay for it.

"Your right parry is slow," he said, his tone laced with amusement as he helped me remove my mantel.

I shot him a sharp glare over my shoulder, then walked toward the bedchamber. "You favor your left knee. You getting old, or clumsy?"

"At least I know my age," he retorted with a low chuckle, settling the mantle onto its display stand.

I peeled off my overcoat with a grimace at the sweat stains marring the fabric. "Maybe I should find a younger guard."

"Younger guards don't hit as hard," he scoffed, stripping his weapons with meticulous care. "They'd be too green, too nervous to land a proper blow."

"Respectful."

"Terrified," he corrected, a smirk tugging at his lips as he removed a set of throwing knives from his boot.

"As they should be. I'm the king."

"No," he said, shaking his head, "scared they'll break the frail old man."

I hurled my damp tunic at him. He ducked, moving with a swiftness that belied his age.

A year older than I, he bore the scars of a life spent in service. His dark hair held fewer streaks of silver than mine, and he carried himself with a vigor I envied. Despite the battles he endured—many of them at my side—his movements remained fluid, almost youthful.

"Why harp on my age today?" I asked, watching him unfasten the buckles that strapped thin daggers to his shins. "Not long ago, you were assuring me I had time to see Radaan settled before Tallon takes the throne."

His hands paused mid-motion, and he met my gaze, his expression sobering. "I think the way you look at a certain girl warrants a reminder."

Tension stiffened my spine. My jaw clenched, and I turned away, wrestling with the stubborn clasp of my belt as I strode toward the bathing chamber. The buckle resisted until I yanked it free with a curse.

Unlike the rest of the palace, my bathing chamber bore the marks of my paranoia. Nobles and dignitaries preferred grand tubs for soaking, but I couldn't forget the lesson of a knife slicing through the river's current toward my heart—pinned beneath the surface. That memory drove me to commission an engineer to design the room.

Water fell from hidden spouts, cascading in a controlled rush through tiny holes that slowed the flow, creating a private waterfall. It pooled before draining, leaving no stagnant depths.

Sunlight spilled across the space, illuminating walls paneled in rich oak and adorned with thriving vines that stretched toward the glass wall overlooking Radaan. The view never failed to calm me. No one could see in from below, but standing under the rush of steaming water, staring out at the fields, eased my torment.

The soothing cascade above muffled the world outside. My gaze lingered on the glass, tracing the outlines of the distant horizon. Radaan stretched vast and golden before me, yet it seemed as though the magnitude of it rested solely on my shoulders.

Greaves leaned against the doorframe, bare-chested, his arms folded and his lips drawn tight. He didn't speak. Instead, he picked up my discarded trousers, tossed them into a washbasin, and moved toward the wide window. His eyes scanned the view as though the answer to my troubles might be written in the horizon.

"I haven't seen you lose control like that since Eldeiade," he said.

I shut my eyes and reached for the soap. Peace wouldn't come easily tonight. "I didn't lose control."

"You drew blood."

"He needed to learn his place."

"There's a Velli in the palace."

The soap slipped from my grasp, and my core clenched like someone struck me. My gaze drifted to my knuckles, still raw.

The enormity of my mistake surged forward like a wave. Blood spilled within the palace walls—my palace—while a Vellos ambassador lurked nearby. Not just nearby. In the prince's chambers.

Horror clawed at the edges of my mind. I fought wars to keep blood magic from tainting this kingdom, yet my recklessness might have handed Egath a foothold on the throne.

"Send word to Tallon's staff–"

"It's done, Kal," Greaves interrupted. "You were too caught up in your own rage to hear me give the orders."

His rebuke stung, but I swallowed my retort. He stood by the window, his reflection hard and unyielding, a soldier who knew my flaws better than I cared to admit.

"They'll burn any cloth his blood touched." His eyes shifted, catching mine in the faint light. "But your actions—they're a greater concern."

If anyone else dared to chastise me like that, I would have reminded them of their place. But this was Greaves. He fought beside me, had seen me at my worst. He spoke truths others feared to voice. And he knew me better than anyone—my strengths and weaknesses.

"It won't happen again," I muttered, scrubbing at my skin with a cloth as though I could strip away the shame along with the grime.

"It will." His sigh carried the weight of years. He dropped into a chair, positioning himself to watch both the door and the window. "As long as she's here, you'll be distracted. You need space, Kal. You're too hot-blooded right now."

"What are you suggesting?" I growled, scrubbing faster. The sooner this bath ended, the sooner his lecture would, too.

"Send her away."

My hands stilled. The suggestion hit just as hard as earlier. The thought of Nienna absent from council meetings or the dinner table carved a hollow ache in my chest. Those fleeting moments in the corridors—the ones I pretended didn't matter—would vanish.

"Careful, Greaves. What you're suggesting borders on treason." My tone turned icy as I shut off the water and snatched a towel.

"I'm not saying void the contract or deliver her back to Draconia." He leaned forward, resting his elbows on his knees. "Send her and Tallon to another district. Give yourself time to clear your head."

I wrapped the towel around my hips, glaring at him as he stood. "You forget your place."

To send Nienna away would crush her. She longed to see more of Radaan, but she would know the truth behind such a command. She'd think she was the problem. The blame for the library incident already rested on my shoulders. I wouldn't let her carry it.

"Do I?" His voice softened, but his gaze pierced me. "My place is to protect you. That's what I'm doing."

"Your job is to protect my body." I straightened, letting the weight of my title settle into my expression. "My heart is mine to protect."

Leaving the room felt like pulling at the final frayed threads that held my life together—unraveling what little control I still had. He was right to worry. His words weren't out of line. Yet they forced me to confront the truths I couldn't escape.

I could handle Nienna.
But could I handle myself?

Chapter Twenty-Two

NIENNA

Tallon was missing. His seat to my left remained empty, yet Kallias led the dinner as though nothing was amiss. I couldn't decide which unsettled me more—the absence of my betrothed or the cold indifference radiating from the king after the council debacle. Alone beside Egath, the tension gnawed at me.

The Velli ambassador behaved impeccably, his manners and etiquette intact. For once, his arm hadn't strayed to my chair, nor had he invaded my space with insincere closeness. His polished demeanor made his presence tolerable, though no less unsettling.

"I hear it will be a spring wedding." He cut into his thin-sliced beef, his tone casual yet probing.

When I met his clear green gaze, I struggled to mask my unease. Egath was handsome, the kind of man whose charm cloaked a venomous bite. I'd seen the predator beneath his affable façade, glimpsed his smile sharpened into a weapon. Tonight, his eyes danced with feigned curiosity, tempting me to let my guard slip.

"You heard correctly." I pushed the potatoes around my plate, too nervous to eat. My voice came out steady, though my nerves frayed under Kallias' silence and Egath's chatter. "New life comes with spring—flora, fauna, and, of course, the royal house."

The implication struck me like ice water. New life. I would have to consummate my marriage. My hand trembled as I set down my fork and dabbed at my lips, hoping the motion would disguise my disgust. How could I endure that duty while Kallias still dominated my thoughts?

Egath's voice broke my spiral. "I've heard dragons will arrive before then. Though I'm sure they won't be used until the union?" He carved another piece of beef, his tone almost careless. "After all, Radaan wouldn't own them until afterwards."

My spine stiffened as I turned to him, forcing my expression into a mask of polite confusion. "Radaan? Own dragons?"

With a condescending smile, he replied, "The beasts would belong to the kingdom. They'd answer to the king, would they not?"

"They will answer to me." The steel in my voice surprised even me. "The Dragon Riders serve Draconia—a Draconis queen and no one else."

"Ah," he murmured, his nod slow and calculating. "That explains why you couldn't negotiate for them."

"There is no negotiating for dragons," I snapped, though I tried to temper the sharpness in my tone. "They aren't commodities, but the lifeblood of *my* people, as sacred as the land itself. They belong to Draconia, now and forever."

The mere thought that he believed a Dragon Rider would obey a foreign king was laughable.

Draconis were born of pride. Our island was the cradle of our existence; the Spire loomed over us, its jagged silhouette etched into the soul of every newborn. It was as intrinsic as breath itself. The roar of dragons resonated in our blood, their calls echoing in our hearts. Even my father, with all his power, could not command the riders to bend to a foreign throne. They answered only to the Dragon King or the Dragon's Heart.

He paused, humming a low, thoughtful sound, but I noticed the subtle twitch of his cheek. Was that annoyance I glimpsed in his forest-green eyes? He was calculating something, and when he leaned back and dropped his chin, I knew he had reached his decision.

"I meant no insult, Princess," he said. "Vellos knows little of the Draconis—rumors, legends, nothing more."

"Likewise," I replied, taking a sip of my wine. "Perhaps I'll visit the library." Memories intruded, unbidden: rough hands on my waist, strong thighs nestled between mine.

Egath's voice yanked me back. "You'd have to imagine any books Radaan holds would be tainted by their hatred for my people."

I steadied my breathing, suppressing the heat that rose to my cheeks. "And where would you suggest I learn of Vellos?"

His grin widened, flashing his sharpened teeth. "I'd be happy to educate you."

Kallias' voice rumbled like distant thunder. "Ambassador, diplomacy requires tact. If you're suggesting you *educate* a princess, you have much to learn."

Egath nodded. "Of course, Your Majesty. Due to Prince Tallon's state, I only meant to–"

"You know nothing of the prince's state," Kallias cut in, his jaw tightening. He rose from his seat, shoving his chair with his knees, his glacial gaze locking onto mine.

I leaned back on instinct, suspecting that glare was directed for Egath. I glanced his way as the rest of us pushed to stand, joining the king.

"Your Majesty?" My voice cracked, betraying my nerves. I had been raised for court, taught to control my every word, but this man—this moment—shattered all my composure. "What is Tallon's condition?"

If it was possible, he stood a little straighter. "He is unwell," he said.

Without saying more, he turned on his heel and strode from the dining hall, his hand resting on the pommel of his sword.

I watched him go, noting the rigid set of his shoulders, the tension coiled in every step. He didn't pause to speak to the nobles; he moved like a storm, barely contained.

"Unwell," Egath muttered under his breath.

I snapped toward him, catching the smirk curling his lips. "Is it a plague?"

He chuckled, shaking his head. "Not quite. Though I'll leave that for the king to elaborate."

The untouched food on my plate mocked me. Four courses remained, each one promising more forced smiles and veiled barbs. I couldn't endure it.

Rising from my seat, I followed Kallias down the dais, the guards trailing close behind. At the main corridor, I hesitated, my gaze drawn to the path I knew led to the roof. He would be there, taking refuge from the suffocating pretense of court.

I exhaled, letting the tension drain from my shoulders, and turned the opposite way.

"The shoulder looks lopsided."

"It's supposed to be."

"What, is he standing with his hand on his hip like some sassy wench?" Scythe's words came muffled, her mouth full of pastry.

I snorted. She choked, spraying powdered sugar across the bed. I yelped and fanned at the sugary cloud, shoving the sheet higher over our heads. Her laughter turned into a cackle as she struggled to swallow, flinging her book aside.

"I can just see him!" She gasped, pressing a hand to her chest. "'Now, Nienna, don't look at me that way, or we'll do something improper.'"

"He doesn't talk like that!" I whacked her arm with my sketch pad and she giggled.

Earlier, when I retreated to my room, Scythe left to forage for food and returned with two bowls of stew and a plate piled high with pastries. We ate by the fire until the shadows stretched long, then set up a makeshift tent of thin linen over my bed. Moonlight filtered through, faint and silvery, making the space seem private and safe.

She read while I sketched, the cool glow illuminating my work. I shifted on the pillows, tracing lines across his chest with my pencil, smudging edges with the side of my finger. I focused on his scars from the foothills.

"How does a king talk before he kisses you?" she teased, peeking over her book with a smirk.

"I'm not telling you," I said, laughing as I worked faster, lines dancing under my fingers.

"Better than, 'Kiss me or I'll dump milk on you,' I hope."

I cast her a sideways glare. "Aye. Who told you such nonsense?"

"Gregor." She sighed, snapping her book shut and staring at the swaying sheet. "The milkman's boy doesn't know how to woo a Draconis woman."

"And how did he react to your refusal?"

"I kneed him in the balls."

I threw my head back, laughing until my ribs ached. Edith would scrub her mouth with soap for a week if she overheard that.

"He'll walk like a reformed man for days," I said, grinning as the last sweet bread disappeared into her hands. "Don't let Edith catch wind of it. She'll put you on chamber pot duty."

"She already has." With a groan, she shook her finger at me. "You'd best avoid the blasted bean soup these people serve every other night."

"I'll avoid the soup when you keep your hands off the pastries. I swear you've doubled in size since we arrived."

Her mouth fell open. A pillow flew at my head, and I squealed, returning fire with one of my own.

A clatter stopped us. We froze mid-motion, clutching pillows, our gazes locking.

Holding our breath, we waited. And waited.

Edith wouldn't intrude—not during Scythe's shift—unless something serious had happened. Rumors about Kallias or, gods forbid, Tallon hadn't reached her, had they?

Scythe peered down at the plate. It tipped and tapped the bedframe. She grabbed it with a quiet laugh, then set it on the floor.

"Thought we were done for," she whispered, curling beside me with her book. "If Edith catches me 'being a rascal' again, she'll send me back to Draconia."

"She doesn't have that power," I said, shifting to hold the sheet aloft with my knees. "But I could."

"Aye, but she could write to your mother. If the Dragon Queen demands my return, I'm as good as gone."

"Mother wouldn't. You're my only friend here."

"Besides Fyrn."

"She's different." I sighed, shading the curve of his thigh. "I need noble friends in court. You? You've been at my side since we were babes. No noblewoman could replace that."

"I'm irreplaceable." She grinned and flipped her page with a flourish.

"Oh, hush and read." I smoothed bold strokes across his legs, scowling. Kallias and his blasted thighs—they'd haunt me for eternity. Couldn't he find larger trousers? They were enough to drive a woman mad.

The quiet filled with soft scratching and the rustle of pages until her voice returned, low and uncertain. "Do you think he loves you?"

My pencil paused mid-stroke, hovering over his hand. Did Kallias love me? The thought sent my pulse stumbling. I drew short, sharp lines for his fingers, my words subdued. "He loves the idea of me. He needs someone who can secure Radaan's future. Brains for the lack of Tallon's."

"But now you're more to him than that."

"They don't know me. Not him, not Tallon. They knew Ronan in passing. What they wanted and what they got are different things."

The plate rattled again.

We both stilled, staring at the shadowed outline beyond the sheet. A figure loomed—too gaunt for Edith.

A knife ripped through the linen.

Scythe screamed as I dove off the bed, hitting the floor hard and rolling to my feet. I ran for the door, but froze. Light from the corridor spilled in, revealing guards crumpled in crimson pools.

Scythe's shriek snapped me back. She kicked, tangling the attacker in the sheet. I spun to help her, but halted in horror. A sword pierced her chest, its tip shining wet with blood.

"No!"

She clutched the figure's neck, fingers digging into flesh as they locked together in a violent tangle. A guttural grunt escaped the attacker as my pencil jutted from their throat, Scythe's trembling hand gripping it tight.

"Go!" she gasped, choking on blood as she held them fast.

Instead, I charged. My hands found the pencil, and I yanked it free, warmth spurting across my knuckles. I plunged it back into their neck. Again. Again. My arm jerked with frantic, brutal motions, my only thought a primal demand to end this monster. Crimson spattered my face, hot and metallic, the reek of iron choking me as the figure buckled beneath the assault, his body falling limp against the floorboards with a sickening thud.

Scythe wasn't moving.

I dropped to her side, pressing shaking hands against her crimson-soaked nightdress. Too much blood. Too fast.

"No, no, no!"

Not her. Not Scythe.

Her unseeing eyes stared past me, their light extinguished. My breath hitched, my chest heaving as the world blurred.

Behind me, a crash tore through the suffocating silence. My head snapped up. Another assassin loomed, closing the distance with terrifying speed.

I stumbled to my feet and bolted for the hidden passage. The dresser, still shoved aside, offered my only escape. My heart hammered as I clawed at the narrow door, yanking it open, then throwing myself into the pitch-black tunnel.

It slammed shut behind me, but a gloved hand wedged into the gap. I kicked, my heel connecting with the wood in desperate, jarring blows. I hurled the latch down, and a sharp cry followed the brittle snap of bones. Dust coated my bloodied fingers, filling my nostrils with the scent of must and old timber.

The door shuddered as if something heavy rammed against it.

Fear choked me as I scrambled on hands and knees into the suffocating darkness. My palms slid over uneven planks, splinters biting into my skin. My breaths came fast and shallow, each one laced with the coppery taste of blood and panic.

I had no light. Only memory guided me through the twisting black void.

A sudden stab of pain lanced through my palm. I cried out, pitching forward as my head struck the wall with a hollow thud. Stars burst behind my eyes, but I shoved off the ground, feeling along the rough wooden walls.

Panic gripped me, tightening its hold as I edged toward what I prayed was the right turn.

The door crashed open.

I bit my tongue, muffling a whimper as I clawed forward. *Please, please, please.* My nails caught on the small splintered frame. I shoved it, my mind racing, my body quaking.

"Gods!" I hissed, thrusting my shoulder into it.

It didn't move.

I rammed it harder, but it stayed in place.

A scuffle of footsteps sounded behind me.

"Please—just—*help!*" I screamed, pounding my fist against the wood. "Help me!"

When it jerked free, a firm hand grabbed mine, yanking me through. The ragged doorframe scraped my nightgown, tearing it with a sickening rip. I spun, scrambling back on my rear, eyes glued to the opening.

"Greaves, now!" came a sharp order.

A muscular man, wearing only underbreeches, clutching a sword, darted into the darkened passage. My breaths rushed in desperate gasps, but I stumbled forward to follow. He had no light. He didn't know the way.

Rough hands seized my waist, lifting me off the ground. A half-naked stranger dragged me through a maze of shadowed rooms. I clawed at his arm, my body thrashing to break free.

"Let me go!" I screamed, twisting, thrashing.

He grunted at my resistance, then kicked open a door. "Assassin! Lock Reem down! Guards!"

Chaos exploded. Metal clanked as men poured in, fanning out through the rooms. Lanterns flared to life, casting harsh beams over the earth-toned walls.

The man stepped back, and recognition slammed into me. Kallias stood there, his large hand settling on my shoulder. His eyes, sharp as steel, followed every movement of the soldiers.

I made it to his rooms.

My knees buckled. The world tilted, and I stumbled. Shouts echoed down the corridors.

He caught my arm, his gaze scanning me in a cold, quick sweep. "Fetch a healer!"

"I'm fine," I snapped, pulling away. I wasn't hurt.

Not physically.

But my heart pounded, too loud, too fast, threatening to burst. I looked down at my nightgown, stained dark with blood, threads of web and debris clinging to the lace. A ragged tear split the fabric from my hip to the hem, and I tugged at it, trying to hold it together.

"Rooms are cleared, Your Majesty!" A guard called, jogging over to us. "We'll station two in each room while we search the palace."

Kallias' gaze locked on me. "How many were there?"

I stared at my toes, blood splattered across the fair skin. Was it Scythe's? Or the assassin's?

"Nienna, how many?"

The panic in my chest made my breath catch. I crossed my arms over myself, fighting the tremors. "At least two. One we killed. The other was in the passages. I don't know if there were others."

"I want a report of the palace in fifteen minutes, and Reem within the hour." His command cracked the air, and the guard saluted before darting out.

I shivered, my vision swimming with tears. My knee buckled again. I reached for something—anything to steady myself—but found nothing.

Kallias grabbed my arm, steadying me, but I pulled away with a whimper. He couldn't touch me. Not now. Not with the guards here.

A cold surge of instinct swept over, screaming that I had to create distance between us. I was in a shredded nightgown, thin as a spider's web. He stood beside the door, only linen trousers clinging to his hips, exposing too much of his skin.

Scythe was dead. But I couldn't face it. As a princess, I was meant to accept these threats to my life.

I forced down a sob, lifting my chin, standing taller. His jaw clenched, his hand curling into a fist as his eyes swept over me. They lingered, cataloging every drop of blood.

Scythe was gone.

My shoulders shook. My arms tightened around me, nails digging into flesh. I could feel the pain. This wasn't a dream—it was a waking nightmare.

She was dead.

I collapsed in on myself, crumbling into the grief, my breath hitching. Guards charged through the palace, hunting the assassins, oblivious to the fact that I lost my best friend.

"Nienna, tell me what you need." Kallias' voice cracked, worn thin by the late hour.

"Nothing." The word burned as I forced it out.

My back stiffened, but the effort to straighten crumbled beneath the pressure of another sob. My teeth sank into the flesh of my cheek. Nails bit into my arms, leaving crescents in tender skin. I was a princess. I was trained for this. It didn't matter that I wanted to crumble, that I was desperate to be anything but the strong one.

Tallon wouldn't be here when the next attempt came.

I had to do this alone.

"Tell me how to help you!"

"You can't!" I shrieked, my gaze snapping to his. Though my vision blurred with tears, I saw his body tense. "You can't," I repeated, hissing through my teeth.

I longed for my brother and Gyrak, for my father and Argos. The Nest, the smell of sunshine and sea, was a thousand times better than this palace. The stench of rot lingered here, choking every breath.

Kallias closed the distance between us, his grip seizing my chin, forcing me to hold his gaze. "I am the king of Radaan. You do not get to tell me what I cannot do."

My body chose that moment to collapse. The world spun as my legs gave way. Then—I wasn't falling anymore.

Kallias lifted me. His arm cradled me beneath the knees, the other holding me tight against his chest. Then he strode through his rooms until we reached his bedchambers.

"No one comes in except Greaves." He ordered, and the guards bowed, retreating with quick steps.

The two beds made the space feel even smaller than mine. Both were mussed as though they had only just roused. A desk sat in the corner, a washbasin nearby. Several small dressers and trunks rounded out the sparse furnishings.

He set me on my feet near the bed furthest from the door. I shuddered, clinging to his arms for balance, the wave of helplessness crashing over me.

Scythe was killed. An assassin tried to kill me. And now, here I was, in the king's rooms, drenched in blood.

He stood half-dressed, his expression hardening as if he wanted to murder someone. "Your handmaiden?"

"Dead." I choked on the word, dropping my gaze. I couldn't meet the fire in his stare.

I tracked the scars crisscrossing his body, a map of battles etched in pale white and angry pink against his skin. Thin lines and jagged edges streaked his chest and stomach, but one scar stood out—thick and gnarled, carving through the dark hair over his heart like a cruel brand.

A wave of shame surged through me, sharp and suffocating. It pressed against my ribs, stealing air as my thoughts spiraled. This shouldn't have happened. None of it. She wasn't meant to die. He wasn't supposed to be the one holding me.

"Sit." The word was a command, low and quiet, but unrelenting.

My legs moved before I could think, folding beneath me as I sank onto the bed. My eyes stayed rooted to the floor, the worn grain of the wood blurring under my focus. I refused to look at him—not now. Regret already coiled in my stomach, cold and heavy. This was a mistake, a reckless misstep we'd both carry.

My breath faltered, a shallow hitch I couldn't smother. The questions would come. They always did. He'd demand to know how I found the passages, what secrets I stumbled on, what truths I overheard. And I had no answers—none I was ready to give.

"The escape routes connect to the royals' chambers and a few dignitaries' quarters. They're sealed." The slosh of water punctuated his words, rippling through the tense air. "Greaves will find them."

"What about you?" My chest tightened as my gaze flicked to the open door leading to the passages. Shadows pooled there, an endless void. "What if they double back?"

Kallias drew a sharp breath, stepping between me and the doorway, his frame blocking my view. A scabbard and belt dangled from one hand, the other clutching a damp cloth that dripped along the floor.

"I wish they would." His voice was a low growl, thick with menace.

I watched a bead of water fall onto my lap, staining the delicate lace in an inky bloom.

"I am the king of Radaan," he said, his rage palpable. His gaze locked with mine, cold, fierce. "I fought at the front for eighteen years. Faced countless attempts on my life."

He knelt, leveling himself before me, his glacier-hued eyes aflame with conviction. "Let them come. Let them try to reach you."

He pressed the chilled cloth into my hand. The coolness seeped into my skin, grounding me as my fingers curled around it, trembling against its rough weave.

"Now," his tone hardened, controlled but barely, "do me a favor and assure me that isn't your blood before I lose what little sanity I have left."

I dragged in a ragged breath, the air catching in my chest. He didn't flinch. His gaze burned with a brutal intensity, sharp and unrelenting, demanding my truth.

"It's not mine," I managed, my voice breaking.

No, it was Scythe's. The assassin's. My palms, still stained with the evidence, trembled as guilt and horror clashed inside me.

"Prove it," he growled, the calm veneer shattering, exposing the fury simmering beneath. "Or I shall have to take matters into my own hands."

Frantic, I scrubbed at my skin with jerky strokes. Red streaks mixed with water, smearing the story of my survival. His gaze bore into me, no longer cold but searing, the assassin's attack leaving cracks in the mask of indifference he had worn so well.

The cloth dragged over the cut on my palm, and pain flared. I flinched. Kallias' fingers closed over mine. His thumb grazed the edge of the wound, rough yet steady, anchoring me to the moment. A shiver ran through me at the contact. When his grip on his sword tightened, I yanked my hand back, but his focus never wavered from the door, every muscle poised for an attack.

I resumed scrubbing the grime from my hands, each stroke harsh. Kallias stood unmoving, a dark silhouette framed by the dim corridor beyond. He was a barrier of steel and resolve, planted between me and whatever threat lurked in the shadows.

The cloth, once pristine, now carried the night's horrors—its white fibers streaked with ash-gray smudges and dull red stains. The scent of iron clung to it, bitter and metallic. Scythe's lifeless face burst into my mind: her gaze empty, her body crumpled. The sensation of the pencil driving into flesh resurfaced, the primal terror of survival clawing at my chest.

Grief coiled around me, crushing, suffocating. Tears stung the corners of my eyes, but I refused to let them fall. Her vacant stare wouldn't leave me. A ghost scorched into memory.

We weren't in Draconia. There would be no burial at sea, no dragonfire to carry her soul skyward. Here, her body would be buried or burned on a pyre—both choices felt like a desecration.

The decision rested on me. A princess was supposed to have answers, a spine unbent by grief. But as her friend, neither path was enough.

Worm food or funeral pyre. Dragonfire left no trace behind, its heat erasing everything. I wasn't sure I could watch her soul drift in a haze of ashes and smoke.

Silent sobs tore through me, ripping at the fragile barriers I'd tried to build. My teeth sank into my lip until the metallic tang of blood spread over my tongue. The air around me felt hollow, stripped of her laughter and the sly edge of her teasing. I could almost hear her sharp wit, the echo of her voice under the stars during stolen moments of rebellion. All of it was gone.

She was *gone*.

Kallias dropped onto the bed beside me, his weight tilting me toward him. I buried my face in his shoulder, the tears breaking free in an uncontrolled torrent. His arm wrapped around me, anchoring me as my body quaked with grief.

"This is your first," he murmured.

I couldn't answer. My throat constricted, blocking my attempts to speak. "Assassins don't–" My voice broke. "Draconis don't get attacked."

I wanted him to pull me closer, to shield me from the reality crushing down on me. But I clung to myself instead, keeping some fragile barrier between us, even as my sobs consumed me.

His hand pressed to my waist, his grip firm, fingers digging in as if to keep me grounded. "Because of the dragons," he said.

"Because of our magic," I spat, the bitterness sharp on my tongue.

Magic defined Draconis—ours to wield for weeks, months, even years. My father held it like an unyielding fortress. I couldn't hold it for a day.

"And yours?" His tone softened, curiosity threading through his words, void of judgment.

"Gone," I whispered. "I gave it to you."

Kallias turned, his face unreadable, but I didn't meet his gaze. My focus stayed on the tears streaking his skin, slipping down to stain his clothes.

"When I bestowed the Dragon's Kiss, that was all I had left."

I couldn't tell him how hollow I felt, how unworthy. Let him believe I gave him all I could and held nothing back—that if I'd kept my power, Scythe might still be alive. That it wasn't my fault.

But it was.

He shifted, his hand moving to cradle my head. The steady pressure broke what little resolve I had left. My arms encircled him, clinging as my cries burst free, muffled against his chest. His fingers tangled in my hair, the motion gentle, the only movement in his unyielding frame.

This wouldn't have happened in Draconia. Not if my father or brother were here. Not if I'd been stronger.

It shouldn't have happened.

But it had.

And it wouldn't be the last attempt.

Chapter Twenty-Three

KALLIAS

She was drenched in blood. Not hers, thankfully—Reem owed the stars for that. She escaped with only a small cut on her palm.

If something had happened to her... I would have torn the city apart.

Even now, with her pressed close, skin feverish against mine—a blazing proof of life—my fury churned beneath the surface. I would have answers. Who dared to orchestrate an assassination within my palace walls? How did they breach its defenses? Why hadn't an alarm been raised? Why had I received no warning?

Nienna trembled against my shoulder, tears falling in a steady, soundless stream. Her first taste of danger came in the form of a brutal trial of fight or flight—a desperate struggle, a narrow escape, her life hanging by a thread.

And it happened under my roof.

Her nails dug into my arm, tiny crescents of pain as she fought to contain her sobs. My hand tightened around my sword hilt, the metal biting into my palm. Somewhere in the palace, Greaves hunted the intruder. They had better be alive when he found them. I had questions, and someone would answer them.

Instinct pointed to Egath, but I forced those thoughts down. What motive could he have for targeting Nienna? Vellos was desperate, yes—drought choked their fields, and famine hollowed their people. I'd seen their gaunt faces myself: starving women, skeletal children, infants too frail to cry. But they couldn't risk provoking another war. They didn't have the strength to survive one.

Not yet

No, Egath wasn't the hand behind this. But I would still keep him close. Darius would see to that, assigning a Thresher of Nyryn to shadow his every step. The elite soldiers blessed by Nyryn were ruthless, a force of precision and carnage.

The war general likely deployed them already, sweeping the palace in disciplined silence.

Nienna's sobs softened. She sniffed, swiping at her nose as she straightened. My hand slid from her waist to her back, reluctant to let her go. Her blond hair fell forward like a curtain, hiding her face as her fingers fumbled with her nightgown, tugging at the torn fabric that bared her skin from hip to hem.

The impulse to have her strip the ruined gown and offer a tunic of mine struck hard and fast. I would see for myself that she wasn't hurt. No one would get close to her tucked away in my rooms. She would be safe.

A sharp knock shattered my foolish haze. My hand fell away as Greaves slipped inside, his face grim. His eyes danced between us, frown deepening as if he could see where my thoughts had been.

Blood streaked his bare chest, smearing across the lines of muscle. He'd found trousers, though they hung loose and unfastened at his waist. His disheveled state mirrored my own, and I clenched my jaw, rising to grab tunics for us both.

"I—I should go," Nienna whispered, rising to stand.

"Stay." My voice was firm as I tossed a tunic at Greaves and pulled one over my head. I gripped my sword, heart thrashing at the idea of putting it down while she might still be in danger. "You're safest here."

Her gaze darted to me, cheeks flushing crimson as she skimmed my torso. Her scrutiny burned into my skin. For a split second, I saw myself through her eyes—bare, disheveled, dangerous. Her lips pressed into a firm line as her focus settled on the bed, where I tossed my sword.

It felt as though she was committing the scene to memory, stealing a final glance, as if she might not get another.

"Where is he?" I demanded, fastening my belt and re-sheathing my weapon.

"Dead."

I sucked in a breath through my teeth, biting down on choice curses. "How?" Surely not by his hand.

"I chased them to the wall," he said, his tone measured.

His gaze flicked to Nienna, who stood motionless, her head bowed, the edge of a grimy cloth slipping through her fingers. He hesitated, a silent question if she should stay for his report.

"The princess remains at my side until Reem is cleared," I said.

His expression tightened, though he gave a curt nod. We both knew she should have been secured in another room. Too many lines had been blurred tonight—by the assassin, by me. There was no undoing it.

"What happened, Greaves?" I shifted, rolling my shoulders to loosen the tension creeping into my stance. Nienna had to see him as more than a guard. She needed to understand that if I faltered, he could be trusted to protect her.

His jaw worked before he moved to his bed. The wary set of his eyes didn't waver as he retrieved blades scattered under the mattress and pillow, securing them with practiced efficiency.

"They fell from the wall," he said, fastening a strap around his arm. "Broke their back against a wagon's side. Dead by the time I got there."

"I want to see the body." My words cut through the stillness, leaving no room for discussion.

"In the medical wing, untouched for your inspection."

"And the palace?"

"All clear, save for the ambassadors' quarters," he replied, adjusting a belt of throwing knives strapped across his chest.

"Egath?"

"Already searched. His rooms were dismantled. He's furious, but servants are making repairs."

"I don't care about how he feels," I snapped, shoving my feet into boots. "When the palace is secured, call the council. I want everyone accounted for."

Greaves nodded, but I barely noticed. My focus lingered on Nienna, her fingers curled against her sides, her nightgown so sheer I could see the pink of her skin beneath it. The night's events had shaken her, and her quiet presence cut through my fury like a jagged edge. She had no one—no kin, no safety beyond what I could provide.

Her gaze stayed fixed on the floor, a tear slipping from the tip of her nose. Shoulders hunched, she looked adrift, her vulnerability stark against the chaos of the night. She stood in a room with me half-dressed and Greaves fastening an arsenal of blades to his chest, both of us hardened by battles she had only just begun to glimpse. She faced death tonight, crawled through ancient passages like some animal, and was now alone.

"Shall I call for Fyrn'sol?" I asked, tightening the straps of my boots.

Her head dipped in a silent no.

"I'll summon your maids," I offered.

Her control snapped, a sob ripping free as she collapsed onto the bed, trembling hands hiding her face. The sound clawed at me, hollowing out my resolve. I turned my glare to Greaves, and he froze mid-motion, boots in hand, sorrow carved into his features. He raised one finger, shaking his head in warning.

The realization hit like a hammer. Not only had Nienna endured an attack, she witnessed her maid fall. Grief knotted in my chest. I watched countless men die, but imagining Greaves' end was a weight I couldn't bear. For her, that loss had already come.

I raised a finger in a silent query, my brow arched.

He shrugged, the answer clear.

How many maids had she arrived with? Three? No—two handmaids. And now one was gone, leaving just a single thread tying her to her people.

I rose, the movement deliberate. Greaves shadowed me, his frustration simmering. He was but a man, caught between two tasks: keeping her alive and ensuring my safety.

He moved first, rapping on the door before opening it to address the guards outside. His body blocked mine as I leaned to see past him.

"Summon an emergency council," I commanded, my voice sharp as a whip. "Tell Fallione to gather who we need. And find Princess Nienna's remaining handmaiden."

They moved, shouts echoing down the corridor as Greaves slammed the door, his jaw clenched. "She needs her own guard," he growled.

"Right now, she has you."

A snarl curled his lip as he kicked the passageway shut, wrestling the latch into place. "I am *yours*," he hissed.

Nienna's sobs softened, but the iron in her stature hadn't returned. She folded inward, shrinking into herself. The sight gnawed at me, and I bit back the urge to tell Greaves to leave so I could offer her the solace she deserved.

But she didn't need coddling. She needed to stand, to face this, and I had to lead her through it—not walk beside her like a crutch.

Greaves leveled her with a glare. I felt his anger, though it wasn't aimed at her. It was the situation—the chaos, the helplessness—that stoked his frustration.

Yet it stoked mine too.

Fury simmered beneath my skin—not at her, but at the night that had stolen her resolve.

Greaves was mine, but right now, so was she. And I wouldn't fail either of them.

Edith was exactly what Nienna needed, despite the silent rebuke etched into the older woman's gaze as she dipped into a curtsy. The sharpness in her eyes cut through me. Was it because I refused to let the princess leave my chambers, or because the attack occurred under my roof?

Both were my fault, and her wordless condemnation only deepened my guilt.

I sat in the chair by the hearth, tipping back a mug of kahve. Wine tempted me, but war taught me the folly of drinking while danger prowled nearby.

The flicker of the fire played across the walls as I waited, restless, while Nienna finished changing her clothes behind the closed door of my dressing room. I wouldn't let her out of my sight until Reem was cleared. Even then, the thought made my stomach tighten.

The queen's quarters crossed my mind—more secure, more fitting. And only a few steps from my own.

I rubbed my brow, shame burning hot. Across the hall, she might be safe from assassins, but not from me—a man who had already failed to keep his distance.

That temptation would be more than I could bear.

The door to my receiving room creaked open, pulling me from my thoughts. Darius entered, his broad shoulders filling the frame, followed by a massive figure who seemed more stone than flesh. The tattoo curling above his collar marked him as a Thresher, vengeance sworn into his blood.

"You need a Thresher." His voice was as blunt as his entrance, his gaze sweeping the room with military precision.

I grunted, the mug warming my palm as I took another drink. "I have Greaves."

The general's sharp eyes flicked to my body guard, lingering with unspoken skepticism. His sigh echoed with the burden of a battlefield veteran watching a fledgling soldier. "Fallione has gathered the council."

"I'll join you shortly."

He frowned, his jaw tightening. Even at this late hour, with exhaustion shadowing his face, he stood as if carved from the same unyielding stone as his companion.

"Why delay?"

"Princess Nienna will accompany me."

His reaction was immediate. His brow shot up, disbelief painting his features. "The princess?"

As king, I rarely waited on anyone, much less a princess who might not have the composure to face a council after such a harrowing night.

But I knew her. She was made of dragonfire and sunshine.

"We can take her guards' accounts," he argued.

"They're dead."

"And those posted in the hall?"

"Enough, Darius." I stood, my tone brooking no further debate. "I won't repeat myself. You'll hear the full report in the council chamber."

His jaw clenched, and his glare dropped to the floor. "Yes, Your Majesty."

Though he didn't say it, his posture spoke volumes—he despised being kept in the dark, especially when it hindered his duty to protect Reem.

The dressing room door opened before I could respond. Nienna stepped out, her presence commanding the space like a gale sweeping through a still meadow.

For a moment, I forgot myself.

Men like Darius would assume she'd retreat behind locked doors, trembling at every flicker of a shadow. She had all the reasons to do so, to surrender to fear.

But it was not a frightened girl who emerged. It was the Princess of Draconia. Her chin lifted, her steps steady, and the weight of the moment transformed into unyielding resolve. Though her cheeks still bore faint traces of tears, her eyes burned with a fierce determination that ignited something primal in me. It wasn't just courage—it was her defiance that sent my blood roaring in my veins.

A long black gown flowed over her form, hugging her throat and waist before cascading to the floor. Slits revealed breeches beneath, tucked into polished boots.

She'd turned her grief into a shield, her fear into armor.

Greaves shifted behind me and I frowned, wondering if I had made some noise of approval.

A crown of golden braids circled her head, the handiwork of Edith's deft fingers. The speed and precision left me marveling, though the effect wasn't lost on me.

Nienna was no princess tonight. She was a queen forged in fire, prepared to wield her sorrow like a blade.

Beside me, Darius bowed as she halted before us. Worry pulled her lips into a frown, and she picked at the bandage wrapped around her injured hand before she caught herself and dropped her arms to her sides. The nervous gesture revealed more than her composed expression intended.

I itched to give her a blade. Even untrained, it was better than nothing.

"Princess," I murmured, though the warmth in my tone betrayed more than I meant to.

Her ocean-deep eyes caught mine, revealing pain she tried to mask with a tight, deliberate smile. "Your Majesty. General," she greeted, her voice steady, her demeanor poised.

"The council awaits." I offered my arm, feigning propriety to excuse my need to keep her near.

Her fingers curled over my elbow, betraying her tension. It was only appropriate, I assured myself, though her touch sent a thrum of pleasure through my heart.

Behind us, the Thresher shadowed our steps, and Darius stationed himself at Nienna's side as we entered the corridor.

Guards flanked the doors, their eyes alert, while staff darted like shadows in the periphery. Chaos hummed in the air, yet protocol kept everyone moving.

"Prince Tallon has requested to remain in his quarters," the general announced with a bite of disapproval.

Refused to attend was more likely, but I wasn't about to push for answers—not when his disdain for the prince was written in every taut muscle of his frame. It was better this way. I didn't need him near Nienna in her fragile state. He'd only fan the flames of an already tense situation.

Let him skulk in the shadows.

My hand settled on the hilt of my sword, the leather grip grounding me. "His presence isn't required."

"As the foreign advisor–"

"He's relieved of that role." My words cut through the air, sharp and final. Nienna's fingers twitched against my arm, her unease palpable. I drew my elbow closer, brushing her hand with a firm yet subtle squeeze meant to steady her. "Malarnath will assume the position."

Unlike Tallon, he wanted the position and had the diplomacy to handle it.

Darius let out a low hum, the sound thoughtful but guarded. Whatever musings played in his mind stayed locked behind his stern expression as we navigated toward the heart of the palace.

Nienna's posture remained poised, her chin high, though the subtle flicker of her eyes betrayed her wariness. Her hand clung to my arm—not in fear, but with a resolute grip that mirrored her determination. As we entered a nondescript room and headed down a spiraling stairwell, the air cooled, thick with the faint tang of stone and damp.

The lanterns, suspended at measured intervals, cast their uneven glow on sandstone walls, their light trembling with each movement. The spiral staircase wound downward until it emptied into a narrow hall. Greaves pushed ahead, taking the lead in the confined space, while Darius slipped to the rear, flanked by a Thresher.

The passage was devoid of grandeur, built for necessity, not splendor. Bare walls whispered of function over form, their starkness a reminder of their siege-born purpose. Greaves passed shadowed corridors, black pits that yawned into nothingness.

Nienna's gaze flicked toward one, curiosity pulling her head as she glanced into the abyss.

My jaw tightened. I wanted to reassure her, to explain that these were storerooms and siege shelters—not dungeons. She would know soon enough. But curse it all, Darius didn't need the satisfaction of seeing how attuned I was to her every worry.

Greaves slowed his pace, rounding the corner to hold open the door to the underground council room. Nienna's grip on my arm loosened, but I pressed her hand back into place, unwilling to let her stray. She had to remain by my side. It wasn't just for her safety—it was a statement, a clear sign that she was under my protection.

The chamber mirrored its purpose: sparse, functional, stripped of luxury. A modest bar stood in one corner, stocked with wine and mead, while an oval oak table dominated the center, ten chairs tucked around its edges. As the door clicked shut, sealing us in, the men already present rose to their feet.

"Your Majesty," they greeted in unison, their voices blending into a formal chorus. One by one, their gazes shifted to Nienna. "Princess."

"Councilmen. Advisor." My tone carried a low rumble as I guided her to the seat at the head of the table, the one Tallon should have occupied. "Gentlemen."

Their faces were familiar but I couldn't place them. I pulled out Nienna's chair, letting her settle before I claimed the seat beside her. Greaves positioned himself to my right, a silent sentinel, while Darius slid into a spot flanked by two unknown men.

One bore the marks of age, his graying hair and sagging jowls giving him a hound's weary demeanor. The other, younger by decades, sat with immovable posture, his shoulders rigid, and despite the damp chill, a glint of sweat traced his temple.

I leaned back in my chair, fingers drumming the table once before stilling. The soft sound echoed in the quiet chamber, and every gaze fixed on me, expectant. The weight of their attention settled across my shoulders.

Darius gestured toward the older man, his tone clipped. "Your Majesty, this is Glendor, master of the city guard," he said before motioning to the younger figure beside him, "and Lukas, captain of the palace guard."

Lukas dipped into a bow, his head almost brushing the table's edge. A tense swallow betrayed his unease. "Your Majesty," he began, his voice tight, "I offer my deepest apologies."

I let the silence hang, heavy and deliberate. My palm brushed the polished oak, the faint gleam of my signet ring catching the lantern's flicker. "I do not accept apologies," I said, my words weighted and deliberate. "What I demand are answers. How does an assassin bypass three layers of guards and find their way into Princess Nienna's chambers?"

Glendor flushed a deep crimson and licked his lips. "They entered through the southern gate."

"They were identified?"

I resisted the itch to go straight to the body, but with Nienna at my side, I didn't want to take her to search and dissect a corpse.

"Recognized," Glendor admitted, nodding. "They were seen yesterday at the Singing Oak Inn."

"And how did they bypass palace guards?" My gaze locked on Lukas, unrelenting. My scrutiny bore down on him until his shoulders hunched, his resolve cracking under my frown. This man wasn't fit to lead, and I made a mental note to question Darius on his appointment.

"They killed their way through, my king," he stammered. "Seven dead. The guards at the princess' door among them."

A snarl twisted my lips. "Perhaps your men need more than training."

Nienna's knee bumped mine. My jaw clenched as I fought the pull to look at her. Was she trying to calm me? Or warn me of something I hadn't noticed?

Darius leaned forward. "Even if the assassins were skilled, how did no one notice? Bodies should have been found during the rounds."

Lukas winced, his face pale. "Our numbers... are thin. Too many were pulled for the northern harvests. Those on duty had been awake all night and were expected to stand the next evening. I had to lighten the shifts to ensure fresh guards."

Could I not even protect my own palace? The thought twisted my gut. How dare he imply I lacked men?

"Then you make the rounds, Captain," I spat. "Do I not pay you well enough? Is your bed too comfortable to rouse you?"

The man faltered. "Your Majesty, you ordered the draft–"

"Hold your tongue," Fallione cut him short. "Guards can be reinforced. What matters now is discovering where the assassins came from."

I inched back from the table, staring at Lukas. A bead of sweat traced his cheek, and he seemed to find every corner of the room more appealing than meeting my eyes. Good. He should be afraid.

Darius' fingers tapped a slow rhythm against the wood. "They had nothing to identify them. Dressed in black Radaanian garb. No scars or tattoos."

"Their teeth?" I already knew what he would say.

"Flat. Like ours," Fallione said with a resigned sigh. "They weren't Velli."

He turned to Nienna. "Princess, may I be so blunt?"

"Ask, Advisor," she replied, her voice clear and strong.

"Who would have reason to see you dead? Who stands to gain the most from such an act?"

His shrewd gaze dissected her, testing her. I didn't like it. She wasn't here for his prying questions.

"There are many who would benefit, as you're aware."

I bit the inside of my cheek to stifle the smirk threatening to form. She had claws.

"The Velli would prefer no dragons at their border," she said. "Other nations might aim for Tallon's hand to secure an alliance with Radaan. However, neither Draconia nor I have enemies of note."

"They fought like northern Radaanians."

Greaves' words hit like a mountain storm, cold and unyielding, filling me with dread.

Darius' chair scraped against the stone as he sat forward, disbelief flickering in his voice. "They faced you? I heard they fled."

"I cornered them in the western hall. They used the passages to the queen's rooms, then slipped into the servant corridors and an empty noble suite to reach the main corridor."

"Pity you didn't keep them alive," Glendor muttered, barely audible.

"Pity you didn't keep them out," I snapped, my tone as cold as the frost on the highest peaks.

"If they were Radaanian..." Darius trailed off, casting a wary glance at the captain seated beside him. He didn't dare voice his thoughts.

But I knew. If the assassins were Radaanian, then treachery ran deep within my own borders. There was a Harvester among us—a traitor hidden in plain sight.

The revelation clamped against my chest like an iron vise. It would be a long night.

Chapter Twenty–Four

NIENNA

I recall the captain and master of the guards leaving, Darius following with his Thresher. I remember Kallias' hand on my knee beneath the table as he spoke to Fallione.

What I don't remember is how I fell asleep.

Strong arms roused me, pulling me against something warm, solid. Cold metal bit into my skin. For a fleeting moment, panic seized me—someone held me. A corded arm slid under my knees, another along my back.

Then his scent reached me.

I relaxed, curling into his embrace, the familiar essence of cinnamon and cloves grounding me. Kallias. I blinked, taking in the shadowed contours of the underground chamber.

"Easy," he murmured, his voice a steady hum against my cheek.

We were alone—save for Greaves. He cast a sardonic frown before turning to lead the way out.

"I can walk," I whispered, but I hesitated. Part of me longed for this, for someone to hold me and promise everything would be fine. I knew I'd manage on my own, but that didn't erase the desire to be cared for. To be protected.

And Kallias would do that.

"I can carry you," he murmured as I leaned my head against his gold mantle. The hard, cold surface was nothing like the softness of his shoulder when I had cried in his rooms.

I sighed, trying to memorize the feel of his hands around me. "Fallione must think little of me."

"I assure you, he's quite understanding."

"He's had many attempts on his life?"

He grunted as he turned up the stairs. "More than one."

He didn't set me down, and I allowed a fraction of a smile to form. Just a little longer. It was only me and Kallias the man, not the king of Radaan.

"And you?" I slid my hand between his neck and mantle, my thumb brushing his throat.

He stiffened, swallowing hard, his pulse thumping beneath my touch. "Too many."

My chest tightened at the idea of someone trying to kill him. That terror—the helplessness of knowing I was outmatched—flared again. At least he knew how to wield a blade. I never thought I'd need that kind of skill—and neither had Scythe.

I rested my cheek against the chilled gold on his shoulder, tracing the sensitive skin on his neck. His warmth seeped through the layers of clothing. He was alive. He was here. And he would keep me safe.

At the top of the stairs, he paused. Shadows clung to the walls, and only a single lantern cast flickering light. His hands tightened around me as his attention shifted to Greaves.

"Go."

"Kal–"

When the king said nothing more, his bodyguard loosed a breath, his shoulders sagging with resignation. He hesitated, then stepped out, closing the door behind him.

The silence stretched, broken by the flickering light against the bare walls. Kallias stood still, his breaths even and measured. I forced myself not to hold my own breath, waiting for something—anything—from him. His bright gaze gleamed, fixed on the door as if it held all the answers.

I reached up, my hand cupping his jaw, feeling the coarse scruff beneath my palm.

"Gods, Nienna," he groaned, his eyes drifting shut. "I'm trying to do the right thing."

The night's oppressive toll settled over me, dragging down every guard I'd built. With him, I couldn't pretend. Scythe's death shattered that illusion—it showed me that life could end in an instant. Tomorrow was never promised, not to him, not to me.

"Don't take me to my rooms." The thought of returning—no matter how many times it had been cleaned, how thoroughly the reek of death had been erased—was unbearable.

"I want to bring you to my bedchamber."

Heat flared inside, shame and desire coiling together. My heart raced as my thumb brushed over his lips. In his arms, with his scent surrounding me, I would forfeit my crown. I would sacrifice everything for him to turn his head and kiss me senseless.

"I'd give you the queen's rooms," he murmured, then snatched my finger between his teeth, running his tongue along it.

My breath quickened, my body trembling. Butterflies stirred low in my belly, and sanity abandoned me with a quiet whimper.

With a tortured groan, he set me on my feet. One hand pressed against my back, pulling me closer, while the other tangled in my hair. I gasped, meeting the fire in his gaze, my body responding to the heat of his proximity as he leaned down.

"You did beautifully," he whispered, voice thick with longing. "Gods, you're already a queen." His fingers curled into the fabric of my dress, as if fighting to keep his composure.

I didn't want his control.

"Kiss me."

The words barely escaped in a whisper, but they shattered his restraint. In an instant, he was on me, his body pinning me with urgency.

The embrace in the library was a distant memory, a mere shadow of this. No hesitation. No seduction. This was raw, a desperate reminder that we were alive. His mouth slammed into mine, and I moaned, ravenous, opening to him without thought.

His tongue plunged between my lips, stroking, teasing. The faint taste of kahve mixed with the warmth of him. I whimpered, fingers clutching his shoulders as I matched him, stroke for stroke. Our tongues met with a fierceness that our bodies never could—his taking, demanding. And mine—pleading, *encouraging.*

His hands tore from my waist and gripped my thighs, lifting me. I gasped, wrapping my legs around him as he spun, slamming me against the rough wall. His lips burned a trail down my throat, biting through the delicate fabric grazing my collarbone.

"You dress like you can conquer kingdoms."

I threaded my fingers into the short hair at the nape of his neck, tugging him closer. "And all I want to conquer is you." I hissed, pulling him back to me.

He growled, taking control with a fierceness that made my breathless laugh slip against his lips. His hands slid higher, gripping me tighter.

With a curse, his fingers dug into me before ripping away, slamming his palms against the wall. His hips held me in place as his gaze locked on mine. "Nienna, we can't."

"Don't stop." I snarled, scoring my nails down his neck.

He shuddered beneath me, his eyes fluttering closed. "Elohios, help me."

A powerful grin lifted my lips as I leaned in, kissing the red welts I'd left on his skin. "Praying for aid?" I whispered in his ear, nipping at it.

"For sense. It has abandoned me." His voice cracked, tremors running through his body, veins standing out in his neck as he struggled for control.

I refused to admit that my sanity already fled, left behind in that council room. My fingers slipped down the chains of his mantle, moving toward his trousers.

He grabbed my wrist, pinning it against the wall. "There's a point of no return, Nienna," he warned, his eyes flashing.

"Then I'll find it." I promised, pulling him back into the kiss.

He slammed into me, his mouth claiming with a force that stole my breath. His hips ground against me, sending a moan spilling from my lips. His tongue slid over mine in slow, deliberate strokes, and I twisted against him, matching his rhythm.

A sharp rap on the door broke the moment, pulling us apart.

I gasped for air, the heat of him still pulsing beneath my skin. My body hummed with need, aching for him, more desperate than I'd ever been. I wanted him—needed him more than breath itself.

His gaze bore into me, not with regret, but with a silent promise—this wasn't over. His teeth clenched, breaths rough and uneven. "I can't move you to my hall."

Desperation tightened its hold as I searched his eyes, willing him to retract the words. The prospect of returning to my quarters was unbearable.

"I wouldn't stay away," he said. "I'd ruin you."

"Then ruin me," I whispered, clutching at him as he lowered my legs, his hands firm on my waist. "Ruin me, Kallias."

His eyes closed as he drew in a long breath, a tremor passing through him. When he looked at me again, his gaze was heavy with something darker. I smiled, a quiet challenge.

He stepped back. "I just might."

I blushed, stealing a glance at his trousers, then bit my lip, smoothing my skirts in a vain effort to compose myself.

He adjusted his belt, and ran a hand through his hair, the slight tug he gave it made my insides melt. As he patted down his chains, he glanced up at me before a pained groan escaped him. He closed the distance between us, his thumb skimming the collar of my dress. "It's torn."

A wicked grin spread over my face. I traced the claw marks I'd left on his neck, feeling the muscle in his jaw flutter at my touch. He swallowed hard, pulling away, his gaze flickering with restraint.

"I can make up something," I assured him.

His brows dipped in a disapproving frown, and he shook his head, as if my attempt to lie would be offensive. Then he offered his arm and nodded toward the door. "I'll see you to your quarters for the night."

"Not my rooms," I reminded him, taking the crook of his elbow.

"No. The guest suite in the southern hall, near Fyrn. Just for tonight." He reassured, opening the door to the small room.

In the corridor, the light from a thousand mirrored lanterns stung my eyes. I flinched and lowered my head, trying to shield myself from its sharp glare.

"Oh, there he is."

My heart plunged at the sound of Tallon's voice. I peered up, recoiling at the sight. Dark bruises marred the skin beneath his eye, and his nose was swollen, bruised, and angry. Had he crossed paths with an assassin, too?

"Tallon," Kallias rumbled, his tone as controlled as ever.

A wave of guilt surged within me—nearly caught with the king, and worse, by his son.

By my betrothed.

The prince didn't speak. Tension thickened, suffocating the air. Greaves stood aside, eyes darting between us. His gaze flicked over our necks, then scanned our bodies.

"What is it?" Kallias bit out.

"I was looking for you."

"You've found me." The creak of his grip on his sword was unmistakable. His irritation was palpable. "Now, what is it?"

"You're removing me as foreign advisor."

Tallon's gaze trailed downward, fixing on my belly before drifting lower.

I shifted my weight, wishing to hide behind Kallias, but that wasn't who I was. I didn't cower. "It's rude to ogle a woman's body, Prince."

His eyes snapped back to mine, disgust boiling beneath the surface. His lip curled into a sneer before he masked it with a scowl.

"Princess Nienna survived an assassination attempt while you slept." Kallias dismissed him with a gesture, taking a step to lead me away. "Maybe you should have addressed your concerns at the council meeting you missed. I'd think my heir would care more about what happens during an emergency."

Tallon's hand brushed the dagger at his hip, and Greaves moved between us, a quiet but firm presence. Kallias turned and led me down the hall, his silence heavy.

"He hates me," I whispered.

He sighed. "You're not the only one."

The moment I sat down, everything came crashing back.

Scythe's scream. The sickening squelch of the blade sinking into her flesh. The strangled catch of her breath.

At the time, those details seemed small, fleeting. Now, they were seared into my memory, impossible to erase.

Blood had poured over my hands, hot and sticky. The assassin's neck had been difficult to puncture with the pencil, resisting even the sharpest point. Again and again, I stabbed. Were they dead before they hit the floor?

I glanced at the small cut on my hand, no larger than a finger.

That was all I had to show for surviving the assassination attempt.

But Scythe was gone.

The morning was waning, blending into midday, but rest eluded me. My mind took a break during the council meeting, and now it refused to let me relax.

"Sleep, Princess." Edith hadn't asked questions, nor had she pushed for answers.

She sat in the thin slant of light fighting through the heavy curtains. These new rooms were cramped—just a bed chamber and a small dressing room that doubled as a washing area—but they felt safer than my own.

I watched her hands move, steady and practiced as she knitted. Each stitch a quiet rhythm. Would she be next? Or would they succeed and kill me instead?

Edith set her knitting in her lap and the light caught the wet trail down her cheek. "Princess."

I wasn't the only one lost without Scythe. She had been her friend too, a bright spark in our small circle. Her laughter, her energy—she was the joy of our little group.

"Regrets won't bring her back, Nienna." Edith's blue eyes met mine, cloudy with age, steady as they had been countless times before. "She would want you to sleep."

No. Scythe would have climbed into bed with me, holding me until I drifted off. Or she'd have insisted on crawling through tunnels, dragging me along with her.

I sank into the mattress, drawing the thin sheet over my body. The fabric clung to me as I kept it taut, careful not to obscure the view of the room.

Scythe's discovery of those passages saved me. If we hadn't explored them—I'd be dead.

Grief clawed at my heart, and tears fell. It was just me and Edith now.

Waking to a world without Scythe was so much harder than slipping into sleep. Reality pressed down as I surfaced from restless dreams, the palace's quiet bustle threading through thin walls. The scrape of a hearth being cleaned reached my ears, followed by muffled voices filtering through cracks in the stone. Life went on, indifferent to the void she'd left behind.

I had taken the silence of my old rooms for granted. Or perhaps the world simply roared louder in her absence.

A shuddering breath rattled through my chest. I pressed the heels of my hands to my eyes, stifling the sting. A sharp jab in my palm made me hiss.

The bed dipped under Edith's weight as she settled beside me. Without a word, she reached for my hand, unwrapping the bandage with a practiced touch.

"It's nearly time for dinner," she murmured, peeling away the crimson-streaked cloth. "Shall I send for a meal?"

My stomach grumbled. A full day had passed since I'd last eaten. I dreaded facing Egath or Tallon, but staying hidden wouldn't do. Whoever sent the assassin needed to see I was still here—stronger than them. Defiant.

They couldn't get rid of me so easily.

Edith prodded the wound, and pain lanced, forcing a grimace. The gash was deeper than I realized.

"I should fetch a healer," she said. Her thin lips pressed together, her wrinkles deep with worry.

"I need to dress." After pulling my hand from hers, I sat up, bracing against the ache in my muscles. To skip dinner seemed unthinkable, and I straightened my back, determined. "I won't miss it."

"It's expected." She searched my face. The bloodstained bandage dangled in her hands as she added, "No one would blame you for retreating. A few days would be understandable."

That was the difference between Scythe and Edith. She embodied propriety, a reflection of her upbringing as a nursemaid and later as a lady's maid. Etiquette clung to her like a second skin.

Scythe, on the other hand, was Draconis through and through. A handmaiden only in title, she would have leapt at the chance to help me prepare for dinner. She would've slipped a dagger into my bodice without a second thought.

"I'll wear red."

My legs protested as I pushed off the bed, muscles still stiff from the previous night's events.

Edith, ever composed, said nothing as she retreated to the dressing room. I headed to relieve myself, moving with the sluggish determination of someone dragging their grief behind them.

At the washbasin, tears blurred my vision as I splashed cool water on my face. Crying had to wait. I wouldn't show up to dinner with swollen, red-rimmed eyes. I braced against the vanity, studying the reflection staring back at me.

The woman in the mirror was fractured. Her features were youthful, almost soft, yet her midnight-blue gaze held the burden of someone aged by grief. Her jaw tightened, struggling to keep the burning wave of emotion at bay.

Kallias would protect me—I believed that much—but I couldn't rely solely on him. I required more than promises; I needed a blade, and to know how to use it. No false sense of security would lull me again.

Next time, I would be ready.

Why hadn't I thought of this before my father signed the marriage contract? I was marrying into a kingdom fresh out of war. I'd been naïve, a fool clinging to fantasies. Now, my best friend was gone, and all I'd done was cry.

Straightening, I raised my chin, determination hardening my gaze. The woman in the mirror was a princess—one who would become a queen. No others could face this for me. No one else could bear the crown. Life would never be fair, but I had to take it as it came.

My lips curled into a sneer as I spun from the vanity, my steps sharp as I stalked toward the dressing room. Fury boiled my blood, and I wrapped it around myself like armor. Anger at my naivety. Rage at the assassin. Shame for failing to protect her.

I would carry it all, and I would not break.

Edith selected a modest deep red gown, simple and unassuming. Its practicality grated against the sharp edge of my mood. With a shake of my head, I brushed past her and made my way to the small rack of garments delivered to my room, then reached for the one Scythe would've picked.

"I'll dress, but I need you to fetch something first." As I laid the gown across the bed, the crimson hem trailed behind me, and I smoothed the fabric with deliberate care.

"Yes, Princess?"

"My blade from my old room," I said, shrugging out of my nightgown. The cool air prickled my skin as I stood bare. "The one with the green gem in the hilt."

She hesitated, clearing her throat. Her fingers twisted the fabric of her apron before she met my gaze. "As you wish," she murmured at last, dipping her head.

"Thank you," I said, waving her off.

She left without another word, leaving me to dress in solitude. The silence that followed stung. Scythe would have been the one lacing my gown and fussing over details.

I wasn't ready to replace her.

After some rummaging, I found black breeches and tugged them on. The gown's blood-red fabric draped in soft, elegant waves, the slit climbing high along my thigh. Scythe had always loved this style—bold enough to scandalize Radaanian women, though the legs remained covered.

The dress left my arms bare, the neckline dipping low before curving around my shoulders. Without Edith to lace the back, the fit hung loose. I tugged on tall, black-heeled boots—impractical for a fight but perfect for staring down anyone complicit in last night's chaos.

At the jewelry case, I chose rubies and onyx. The scarlet necklace fastened at my throat like a bloody slash, the gemstones catching the light with every breath. I wanted everyone to see what was attempted. Let them choke on their failure.

I combed through my hair, each stroke unraveling a thought I couldn't ignore. At some point, I'd need to write to my father, to tell him what happened. Kallias would send his own missive. Still, Father's reaction loomed over me like a gathering storm.

My hand froze mid-air, brush caught between locks. His rage would come swift and unrelenting. His love burned, protective to the point of destruction when someone harmed his own. He wasn't always rational in anger, though Mother often tempered him.

His wrath turning toward the king made me uneasy. They had never met, and I cared little about Father's opinion of Tallon—unless he decided to break the blood oath. But Kallias? I wanted him to earn my father's favor.

The message would take weeks to reach Draconia, assuming the whirlstorms broke long enough for safe passage. Until then, I could only wait, bracing for what might come.

Edith's return snapped through my thoughts. In her hands, she held a cloth-wrapped object. "Princess, there's no sheath."

"I know."

I rose, unwrapping the white linen to reveal the dagger's gleaming blade. From the chest at the foot of my bed, I pulled a black scarf, knotting it around my thigh. The weapon settled against my leg, concealed beneath my skirts. Crude, perhaps, but sufficient.

Edith made a strangled noise of protest, the kind that might have once earned my attention. Now, I didn't even glance her way.

"Lace the dress, please," I ordered, tugging the scarf tighter. The edge in my tone left no room for argument.

She stepped behind me, her fingers quick and practiced as she pulled the laces taut. The gown molded to my frame, cinching my waist and draping in crimson waves. Though red wasn't my favorite, tonight it suited me. The color held its own kind of power, one I intended to wield.

With the bodice secured, Edith turned her attention to my hair, arranging it in intricate, loose curls that framed my face. She crowned the style with a pearl-studded tiara, the soft shimmer of its surface at odds with the fire rising beneath my skin.

As I made to leave, Edith's quiet voice halted me at the threshold. "Princess," she whispered, her plea carrying a weight she dared not speak aloud. "Please be safe."

I nodded, then took my leave. When I pulled the door open, I barely had time to react before a gasp choked off my breath. I snapped my mouth shut with a click.

The man before me filled the doorway, a towering figure draped in dark leather armor. Only his pale skin was visible at his neck and face, even his hands covered by gloves. A jagged swirl of black ink curled from his hairline, skimming the corner of his eye, and winding beneath his jaw.

Brown eyes, cold as tempered steel, locked onto mine. Despite the anxiety rippling through me, the calm demeanor of the guards flanking the doorway stayed my hand. This man wasn't here to harm me—not right now, at least.

Metal glinted across his armor, an array of blades strapped to every surface. Some weapons I recognized, others baffled me with their odd shapes. Two short swords rested against his back, their hilts jutting over his shoulders, adding to the impression of sheer, unrelenting size.

A Thresher. Just like last night.

"You're here to escort me?" I asked, my voice catching before I cleared my throat. Even with the added height of my boots, I hated how far I had to tilt my chin to meet his gaze.

He didn't reply. He inclined his head and stepped aside.

Silent and deadly—just what I needed tonight.

The halls stretched long as we headed toward the dining hall. To my surprise, the six guards clad in plate armor remained behind. Only the Thresher stayed at my side.

By the time we arrived, the first course had already been served, and every gaze snapped my way as I crossed the threshold. With my chin raised and my stride unbroken, I walked toward the dais, ignoring the whispers that faded into silence behind me.

The Thresher followed, his imposing shadow drawing more attention than I cared for. Kallias sat at the head of the table, Darius beside him. Egath and Tallon were absent.

My steps faltered for the briefest moment. I would sit alone.

Loneliness dug at my chest. Fyrn and her endless questions would have been preferable to the isolation awaiting me.

When I reached the dais, Kallias' gaze swept over my dress, approval sparking in his expression, warming the cold knot in my stomach. It was a small consolation, knowing I hadn't chosen poorly.

I dropped into a shallow curtsy, the motion fluid despite my unease. He inclined his head in response, a faint smile playing at his lips, and gestured to his right.

After a steadying breath, I climbed the final steps. The crowd's scrutiny weighed heavy, as though I stood alone against an encroaching storm. Each step felt deliberate, the muted rustle of my gown the only sound I allowed myself to hear.

The Thresher moved to stand beside Greaves, his presence a solid wall of tension at my back as I approached my chair.

"Princess," Kallias said. His rise prompted the entire hall to follow suit, their movements a ripple of deference. "In light of recent events, and Tallon's absence, I ask that you sit beside me."

I froze, my pulse thrumming in my ears. A polite smile formed on my lips, practiced and unshakable, as I fought to steady my thoughts. That seat wasn't mine. It belonged to Tallon—the prince.

The place of a future queen.

Horror and exhilaration clashed, twisting into a chaotic storm that left me breathless. Every eye in the hall burned into me as his offer loomed. I needed to tread with care, to find the perfect words. But how could I respond when Radaan's king offered me his right hand?

"Thank you." Hollow—but I said it, anyway.

A servant darted forward to pull out my chair, the scrape of wood on stone louder than I expected in the hush of the hall.

Kallias and I sat together, his presence steadying the frayed edges of my nerves. Even so, I remained quiet throughout the meal, prodding at the food on my plate. Hunger gnawed at me, but every bite turned to ash under the pressure of so many watchful stares. The thought of eating while they scrutinized me made my stomach churn.

Nobles approached one by one, their voices low and measured as they addressed the king. They avoided mention of the attack, skirting the subject as if it would contaminate the delicate civility of dinner. I forced polite smiles, though the muscles in my face ached with the effort.

When the final course arrived, a tiny apple pie glistening with golden syrup, I felt Kallias' gaze shift to me. His scrutiny lingered as I nudged the dessert with my fork, breaking the crust but not eating. A crumb made its way to my lips, more out of habit than appetite, and his stare burned hotter.

I kept my back straight, my posture flawless—a porcelain doll playing the part of the perfect princess.

But inside, I shattered.

Everything felt wrong. Scythe was gone, a hollow ache where her presence used to be. Tallon despised me, and I couldn't stand to draw breath in the same room as him. My betrothed's insults echoed in my mind, layered over the memory of my near-murder. My dragons were oceans away, and my family safely tucked within the Spire.

And here I was, seated beside a man I could never have.

Each rumble of Kallias' deep voice sent a shiver through me, an ache to edge closer, to brush against him, to feel the solid warmth of his arm beneath my touch. My hands stayed in my lap, fingers clenched to resist the pull.

The stares of the court weighed heavy on my shoulders, suffocating. I longed for his hand to rest on my thigh, grounding me in the storm of their scrutiny. More than anything, I craved his call—a whispered invitation to his chambers, where I could find sanctuary in his embrace.

But the distance between us remained, an invisible chasm that could never be crossed. A breath apart, yet untouchable. I yearned for the stolen moments we'd shared: the quiet on the balcony, the intimacy of the library, the secrecy of the underground stairwell.

Those fleeting seconds, just him and me, felt impossibly distant—another life entirely.

Doubt twisted through me, knotting every thought. How could I endure this? A palace gilded in lies, bound to a man I despised, while *he* prowled these same halls? How could I remain faithful to a brute like Tallon when his father, the *king*—intoxicating, untouchable—pierced me with a gaze that burned with desire? And if there was another attempt on my life, would the next blade find my heart, or would it be too shattered to matter?

"The hour is late."

Kallias' voice broke my spiral. I jolted, almost losing my grip on the fork. The pie remained untouched, mocking me with its sticky sweetness. I pasted on a smile and faced him.

His brow furrowed, his jaw tense as his gaze roamed my face. "I retire and advise the same to you."

No request lingered in his tone. It was a command.

"Yes, Your Majesty," I replied, my voice steadier than I felt. The uneaten dessert blurred in my vision as Kallias rose, his movement signaling the hall to follow suit.

"I shall see you to your rooms." He extended his arm.

His offer sank deep into my chest, its weight unmistakable, yet I accepted, threading my hand along the crook of his elbow. My lips pressed into a thin line. How far could he push before someone dared to question his intentions?

"She has Vyre," Darius interjected, his voice a calculated drawl. He leaned forward, dark eyes narrowing on me. "Surely, a Thresher can offer a secure escort, Your Majesty."

Kallias stilled, his piercing gaze locking onto mine. "I am the king. If I wish to see Princess Nienna to her rooms, I shall."

My fingers tightened on his arm. His muscles flexed beneath my grip, steel wrapped in velvet.

"Get me answers, Darius," he ordered, his voice sharp enough to cut.

Without waiting for a reply, he led me from the table. Every eye followed us as we descended the stairs. My stomach churned, the intensity of their frowns more suffocating than the air in the hall.

Whispers would come. One rumor could topple everything. A single word could tear the trust of his people to shreds. With a kiss, the oath binding our kingdoms could shatter, leaving the promise of dragonfire looming. An embrace could strip Radaan of the protection only dragons could provide.

But I didn't let go.

I couldn't. He wasn't just the king. He was Kallias. The man who stood beside me when no one else dared, who held me as tears came unchecked, judgment absent from his eyes. The one who valued me in ways my betrothed never could.

So I remained, my grip firm, even while my resolve wavered, fragile but unbroken. For him, I stayed.

The corridor stretched ahead as Kallias guided me from the dining hall. My fingers brushed the coarse fabric of his sleeve, holding on as though it could tether me to something solid amidst the chaos of the evening. When we reached a modest kitchen tucked behind a carved archway, Igor awaited with two steaming mugs of cider. His kind eyes, weighed with understanding, flicked between us, the faint tilt of his head speaking to a silent awareness of the night's horrors.

The mugs warmed my palms as we continued toward the balcony. At the top of the stairs, Kallias broke his silence. "Vyre, secure Princess Nienna's rooms."

The command released some of the weight pressing on my chest. Without hesitation, the towering guard turned and strode back down the hall, his movements as fluid as a predator's.

"Wait here," Kallias called to his bodyguard, stepping out onto the balcony.

A muffled curse reached my ears, drawing the faintest twitch from my lips.

As the entry closed behind us, the quiet night enveloped me. My shoulders sank, and a rush of breath left my lungs, one I hadn't realized I'd been holding.

As I let go of Kallias, I swept damp strands from my forehead, the spiced aroma of cider blending with the crisp evening air.

"You didn't need to come." His hand pressed against the small of my back as he guided me to the sandstone railing.

"Yes, I did." My voice wavered as tears burned at the edges of my resolve. The unfairness of it all roared in my chest. "Whoever orchestrated last night must understand they cannot break me."

Kallias took a measured sip from his mug, the flickering torchlight carving shadows across his features. He leaned on his elbows against the railing, gaze distant yet calculating. "They thought you'd hide. Darius said you'd stay locked in your chambers—"

I scoffed, the sound bitter.

"—I told him otherwise."

Heart pounding, I searched his face, the sharp planes illuminated by the starlight. His eyes, cold, though softened by something unspoken, reflected the night sky. A faint smile ghosted his lips, a rare crack in his regal armor.

"I am in awe of you, Princess Nienna, the Dragon's Heart." His voice dropped, resonant and deliberate. "Any other woman—queen or peasant—would have crumbled after what you've been through. But you stood before the council with steel in your spine, and tonight, you walked into that hall like a warrior claiming victory."

The words settled between us, heavier than the night itself. His praise wrapped around me, a balm against the relentless burden I carried. For a moment, his belief in me outweighed the doubts clawing at my heart.

"I am Draconis," I said, lips lifting in a small smile.

"No." He shifted his weight, leaning closer, one hand braced on the wall, his other cradling the mug. His gaze pierced mine over the rim as he sipped. "You are not just Draconis," he said. "You are you, and that's what makes you strong."

My smile faltered, and my eyes dropped to his golden chains, their delicate clink a faint reproach. "Sometimes, I don't want to be strong."

The confession spilled out, a fragile thread of honesty breaking the silence. Strength had been my shield, tempered by years of knowing this path awaited me. Yet now that it stood before me, I craved something else entirely. Simplicity. A world where Kallias ruled nothing, and I bore no title—where we could choose each other without the crushing weight of kingdoms dictating every choice.

His hand, rough and warm, tilted my chin until his gaze held mine. A tear escaped, trailing along my cheek, and he brushed it away with his thumb. "Here, you don't have to be strong," he murmured. "I will carry your burdens."

My jaw tightened, a futile attempt to dam the flood.

"Gods," he hissed, setting his drink aside before yanking me against his chest.

The cool bite of the chains pressed into my skin, a stark contrast to the solid warmth of his embrace. He pried the mug from my hands, and I clung to his overcoat as though the fabric could anchor me.

He was steadfast, unshaken, and yet I hated how easily I crumbled in the sanctuary of his arms. In public, I stood alone, a pillar of composure. In private, I dissolved. A queen would not falter like this. She wouldn't weep for a servant lost or doubt herself at every turn.

His broad hand settled between my shoulders, grounding me. The other slid to the nape of my neck, fingers working into the tension coiled there.

A shudder rippled through me, my cries muffled against his chest.

Draconia called to me, but I refused to go back. My people and his depended on me staying. Scythe's steady presence, my mother's touch—those were the things I longed for. I wanted my brother's laugh, the comfort of familiar faces. The man holding me? I didn't want to love him.

The word pierced me.

Love.

A sob tore through my defenses, splintering the fragile walls I'd built. I loved him—not Tallon, my betrothed, but Kallias, the king of Radaan.

With a grunt, he lifted me, settling me on the wall as though I weighed nothing. My arms wrapped around his neck, desperate, while his scent enveloped me. Spices, the tang of cider, the warmth of baked goods.

He didn't speak, nor did he press. He held me as my tears fell, tracing paths over the gold of his mantle, pooling on the sandstone below.

Above, the stars shimmered, their light fractured and mournful, as if they mourned with me.

Chapter Twenty-Five

' Kallias

Black leather armor gleamed on the Threshers at every turn, their presence an unshakable force. It was an irritation I couldn't ignore—an itch out of reach. Though I wasn't surprised, the sight still set my teeth on edge.

More often than not, they lingered in the shadows, barely a whisper—rumors of dark men, lurking like monsters that only came out after dusk. Since the assassination attempt on Nienna, they swarmed in numbers I never expected. Darius had far more of them under his command than I realized.

Apparently, the war was a perfect time for vows of vengeance to be traded for strength.

Threshers gave themselves to Radaan, to Nyryn, God of Vengeance. If they were chosen, the priests would mark them, branding their devotion in exchange for whatever their hearts desired. In return, they served the kingdom as lifelong soldiers, bound by the oath they swore.

Much like the Harvesters.

The thought of those assassins sent a cold shiver through me. Fallione handled their guild master, and I trusted his word that they had no part in Nienna's attack. As king, I learned to keep my distance from them.

Too many eyes would watch if we so much as exchanged words. If people started turning up with blades in their backs, fingers would point in my direction. Radaan's assassins had to remain a secret.

The walk to the temple was doing nothing to ease my irritation.

We still had no answers. I'd seen the bodies. The wounds. Radaanian, all of them. Field workers with tan lines etched across their knees and shoulders. Farmers. But their skill—too refined for simple laborers.

Sources confirmed their weapons came from a blacksmith in Reem. They arrived with a shipment of wheat, disguised as commoners.

Deception clung to me, heavy as stone, pressing down on my chest. I had every right to demand the truth. Nienna's attack was a personal insult, having happened within my walls. I frothed at the mouth, desperate for resolution.

But this couldn't be rushed. I had to trust my people to do their jobs. To drop everything and march north demanding results wasn't an option.

Nienna's broken form wreaked havoc on my thoughts—how she shattered in my arms like a wave crashing against the shore. Her body trembled, as though I were the only thing keeping her grounded in the chaos of her own emotions.

She didn't deserve this.

If I knew who orchestrated the attack, I would have made some reckless decisions that night. Ignorance, in its bitter way, kept me grounded.

I had guided her to her chambers, cursing the distance between us. The thought that she couldn't be in my rooms ate at me. Despite the Thresher guarding her door, she was still too far—too unreachable. Even within my halls, if she needed me, I wouldn't reach her in time.

I was the king—the father of her betrothed.

Gods, I was a mess. No matter how often I reminded myself of my role, reason slipped away whenever she was near.

When she set fire to her maid's body, much to the chagrin of the staff, all I could do was stand at a distance—caught between chasing Darius and Fallione for answers, and struggling not to race to her side like a fool.

Somehow, I kept the mask of a king, watching her tears mingle with the rising smoke.

Radaan would need to adjust to their way of burial. We returned our dead to the earth, nourishing the soil for the next generation. Draconis, however, burned their bodies or sent them to the sea—sky or abyss.

I stepped into the cool shadows of Elohios' temple, knowing Radaan's people would struggle with the idea that Nienna didn't worship their gods. Greaves followed me, his presence a silent weight as he helped remove the heavy mantle from my shoulders. His gaze flicked to mine, a furrow between his brows. Then, without a word, he placed it on the altar and retreated.

Nienna didn't worship Radaan's gods, but she respected them. That thought tugged at the corner of my mouth, and I allowed myself a small, fleeting smile as I retrieved a rug, kneeling upon it. She was willing to embrace our traditions, to make them her own.

She would be a fine queen.

A chilled breeze swept over my shoulders. I closed my eyes, seeking the quiet place between myself and my god.

Elohios. Father of Justice and Truth.

The tightness in my chest loosened, and I exhaled. He was listening today.

Forgive me.

Nienna's face came to my mind. I shoved the thought away, focusing instead on my prayer. *Give me strength to resist temptation.*

My heart twisted painfully. I winced, eyes snapping open to focus on the crimson cloth beneath my knees.

Was that his disapproval? A rebuke for lusting after my son's future wife?

Guide me. I tried again, but silence stretched. The wind died, leaving the space still. Had he abandoned me once more?

Elohios, deliverer of answers, grant me wisdom. The breeze returned, this time carrying the faint scent of lavender. He was answering me today—our connection restored.

I straightened, bracing myself. *Help me. Show me who would so brazenly attack your servant.* I devoted my life to the god, serving with honesty and justice. I never faltered—except when it came to Eldeiade and now to Nienna.

The bridge of my nose cracked. I recoiled, pressing against the sharp sting. A trickle of liquid ran down my nostril.

Blood.

I wiped it away, watching as it stained my fingers. The crimson spread, dripping over my lips. Was this an answer? Or another rebuke? Had I asked too much, pushing Elohios to remind me of my place?

Had he grown so angry with me that he could no longer ignore me? Or was this a sign—my own blood?

Tallon.

I frowned, and Greaves' heavy footsteps grew closer, his unease palpable.

The prince didn't have the capacity to hire assassins in the palace without me knowing. He would have used the Harvesters, who would've reported his request to me.

"Your Majesty?" Greaves rumbled from behind.

I wiped my mouth with the back of my hand, scowling at the crimson still dripping down my face. I wasn't ready to move, not yet—not if this was a sign from my god.

"The answer is blood," I muttered, focusing on the mantle above the altar.

Did it mean mine was to be spilled? Was I the intended target, or was it a consequence of another war with the Velli?

Egath.

Horror gripped my chest. I clenched my teeth, forcing myself to remain calm. The urge to blame Vellos was strong, but I had to be cautious. To accuse them without proof would make me seem paranoid, eager to plunge my kingdom into war.

Greaves shifted, his leather armor creaking—a subtle signal that he needed an explanation.

Thank you.

I bowed before the statue of Elohios and stood, meeting Greaves' questioning gaze as he helped replace the mantle. My mouth was dry, and I wasn't about to share my thoughts with him here, not now.

A drift of feminine voices reached me on the wind. The cadence almost sounded like Nienna.

She hadn't shied away from her duty or Radaan's people, but court was wearing her thin. I saw it in the furrow of her brow, the way her gaze often drifted, distant and tired. The loss of her maid only added to her burden.

The thought of Claydon's mountain manor gnawed at me. Perhaps an escape from the palace would offer her respite, but there was also risk. She didn't know Clay as I did, and around him, she would feel the need to wear her mask. She might not relax. And if Egath was there...

I couldn't let him go. Not if there was a chance he was tied to the attempt on her life. I'd keep him confined to his rooms and the gardens.

Greaves stepped back, grimacing at my bloodied face. Another drop fell onto the mantle's chain. "Priest," he barked, jaw clenched.

A man emerged from the shadows, ready to assist. The public temples were just beyond the palace walls, their offices tucked inside the thick barrier.

His red robes whispered as he darted into the alcove, returning with a basin of water and a white cloth. His young features twisted with a mix of horror and fear.

I cleaned my face, pressing the damp fabric to my nose. The flow stopped, and I exhaled in relief. It wasn't an ailment—it was a sign.

"My thanks, priest," I murmured, dipping the cloth into the bowl of pink-tinged water. "Dilute it further, then dispose of it in the sewers."

I wouldn't take any chances with blood on palace grounds.

My frown deepened as my lips formed a tight line. Surely, the staff were handling Nienna's cycle with care. I forbid women on the battlefield for a reason. But with Egath within our walls, I had to ensure her cloths were burned, not discarded.

The bright sun made me squint as I looked down the path. Black armor absorbed the sunlight, reflecting none as a Thresher stood sentinel before the temple of Veridis.

Curiosity tugged at me. Instead of returning to the palace, I headed toward him. Threshers had been assigned to the most vital nobles since the failed attack on Nienna. I didn't know this one personally, but I needed to see if she was among them.

I passed the temple of life, casting a brief glance inside.

The princess knelt on the stone floor, her deep blue dress spread over a white fur. Her golden hair tumbled in waves, obscuring her face. Fyrn knelt beside her, hands clasped, head lowered in prayer.

A quiet relief settled in my chest. Perhaps she was seeking solace from the goddess, hoping to heal her grief. A Draconis princess, bowing in a Radaanian temple... The two priestesses watching from the alcove would be quick to spread the word. Nienna had chosen a god.

I ran a hand through my hair, thoughts churning as I walked. She was winning the hearts of my people, one moment at a time. Her presence at the council, her resilience after the attack, and now this—Radaan would be eating from her hands.

She was cunning. I expected a bride from Draconia—a princess—who would know her place and duty. But she'd never before left Draconis' shores. I thought she would take time to learn our culture, the ways of my people. I anticipated mistakes, moments where I'd have to cover for her, guide her.

Instead, I found myself picking up the pieces from Tallon, while she proved she was more than worthy of being Radaan's queen.

An image of her sitting on the throne, draped in the queen's mantle, burned through my thoughts. Her chin held high with pride, yet her grin would soften, warm, for her people. She would rule with fairness, blending kindness with justice. Elohios would smile upon her reign.

Gods, she would be a stunning queen—fierce. Beautiful.

A wave of heat swept through me, and I gripped my sword's pommel, fists clenched. She would be the envy of every nation.

But she would rule at Tallon's side.

Fury flared deep within. Life's unfairness still baffled me. How had I been so oblivious to Eldeiade? My youth had blinded me then—my naïve belief that she sought what was best for Radaan. Then she went and spawned a twin soul in Tallon.

I could only hope Nienna had more courage than I did, that she would face him head-on. I had been a coward with the late queen, avoiding her, letting her live her life separate from mine. All she craved was to be admired and served. She wanted nothing to do with the mantle, and I refused to let her out of the palace without it. It was too important to the realm—to us. The throne was no glory; it was a duty. A weight.

Nienna would shoulder that burden willingly, serving the people with both protection and provision.

Tallon, however, would not.

I drew in a shaky breath, aching to meet the princess after her prayer.

But I was the king, not the prince. Her future father-in-law, not her betrothed.

So, I kept walking.

Days passed, and Nienna grew too close. She was always at my side. At council meetings, she took Tallon's place when he was absent, sitting at my right hand. The initial wary glances turned into a quiet acceptance. Nobles weren't accustomed to a woman at the table, but she earned their respect with each meeting, offering sharp insights and clear thoughts.

She sat beside me at dinner, close enough that I detected the faint fragrance of water lilies in her hair. I caught the sparkle in her eyes whenever she understood a joke, that twinkle of wit and ease.

Yet, she was too far. Her chair sat just out of reach. I couldn't touch her, nor could I whisper reassurances when confusion flickered across her face, her brow furrowing at a nobleman's remark.

Her focus on learning the land's patterns—the crops, the livestock, the importance of each district—stirred a reckless urge in me. I longed to reach for her, to act on the temptation she kindled.

I kept my distance, avoiding the balcony in case she sought me there. My heart ached for her—I burned in her presence. I couldn't trust myself.

It had been mere moments after her maid's death, when I pressed her against the wall, taking her mouth like I wanted to take her body.

I shifted in the saddle, riding through the city. My thighs felt tight in my breeches, and I pasted on a practiced smile as I greeted the people of Reem.

If Greaves hadn't halted us at the library, if Tallon had not interrupted in the stairwell... I wanted to believe I was above it—above taking her like some careless youth. But clearly, I wasn't.

Her softness lingered in my memory, the feel of her hair slipping through my fingers. Her quiet moans as she yielded to me. And her persistence when I pulled away—how she reached for me again.

Reins in hand, I rested my palm on the front of my saddle, cursing my wandering thoughts. This wasn't the moment for recalling the sounds she made or how her legs felt wrapped around me.

We pushed deeper into Reem, stopping to speak with citizens along the way. They needed to see I was still capable of defending them. That I was steady and assured after the assassination attempt, one that surely already spread through the rumor mill.

I was discussing the rising cost of iron with a blacksmith's son when Greaves nudged his horse closer, his boot brushing against mine.

"No more melting down nails every day!" The boy went on with enthusiasm.

"Resources will grow each week now that the war's over," I replied, offering a smile, though my gaze shifted to Greaves.

His eyes stayed fixed on the road ahead, brows drawn in a sharp frown. The reins were taut in his hands, and his gelding stamped at the dirt.

I studied the path, searching for whatever unsettled him. Commoners weaved in and out around us, a familiar dance. They greeted me with smiles and waves, but knew I wouldn't be gone long. Some lingered, cautious but curious, staying just beyond the reach of Greaves' watchful glare—and, at times, his shouted warnings.

Among the crowd, my gaze snagged on the unmistakable gleam of black armor.

A Thresher.

"I've taken up too much of your time, Your Majesty," the boy said, embarrassed.

I returned my focus to him with a nod. "Next week, I expect to see those new nails!" I chuckled, straightening in my saddle.

As I spurred my horse forward, the crowd parted, scattering as they sensed the shift in pace. We kept a safe distance behind the Thresher, careful not to draw attention. It wasn't unusual to spot one within the city; it only meant a high-ranking noble ventured into Reem.

But Greaves' expression—his glower confirmed my suspicions. Without further comment, he urged his horse into a faster gait, taking a slight lead.

Nienna wasn't confined to the palace. She was allowed to roam whenever she pleased, yet by the gods, I wished she would have warned me. Whoever sought her life was still out there, and while the Threshers were elite, they could be overwhelmed.

A cloaked figure whirled on the Thresher, and a flash of blonde hair slipped free from her hood. She hissed, waving her hand at the guard, but he ignored her and pressed on. I could almost feel her frustration as she turned away, plunging into the crowd.

That was enough to snap me into motion.

We veered off the main road, guiding our horses alongside a rickety wagon. The side street was narrow, out of sight, and our mounts were shielded from view. A man, whose weathered face and bloodshot eyes suggested he'd spent too many nights in his cart, squinted at us.

"Your cloak, good sir," I said, dismounting.

The stallion snorted as I tethered him to the wagon, scanning the area. A few passersby noticed the gleam of my mantle, their faces scrunching in confusion before they bowed.

The man gave a low whistle. "Radaan's king? Asking for me cloak?"

Greaves cast a skeptical glance my way before dismounting. He extended a hand, his expression unreadable as he waited for the worn garment.

"You'll be repaid," I assured him, voice steady.

His posture shifted, eagerness replacing hesitation as Greaves approached the wagon. He looked ready to climb aboard, prepared to take the tattered cloak by force if needed.

"Oh, anythin' for Yer Majesty!" he said, shrugging it off.

Greaves retrieved the brown cloth and tossed it to me. I wrapped it around my shoulders, thankful for its size. It draped over my mantle and concealed most of my fine attire.

"My thanks," I called over my shoulder.

Nienna craved freedom, like a bird fluttering against the bars of its gilded cage. The palace, with its high walls and endless corridors, smothered her. If I had the freedom, I'd have taken her to the cities beyond. But that task belonged to Tallon—and he would avoid it at any cost.

My thoughts drifted back to the first time I caught her in Reem without a guard. Her maid had been with her then—the same one who'd been killed.

Was this rebellion born of grief?

No matter the cause, trying to dismiss the Thresher was a mistake. I meant to make her see that.

Greaves shuffled behind me, tugging a gray cloak over his armor. He bumped my shoulder, matching my pace through the crowd.

"What are you doing?" he hissed, his eyes darting beneath the edge of his hood.

I grunted, scanning the sea of faces for the familiar glint of black leather. "Finding Nienna."

"She'd be easier to spot on horseback."

"Running her down and tossing her across my saddle would be frowned upon." I caught a glimpse of her Thresher, and we plunged back into the throng.

"I frown upon this," he muttered, staying close. "Kal, of all the ridiculous things you've done for that woman, this tops them all."

"The library's outdone now, is it?" I chuckled, too amused.

Maybe this was why Nienna wanted to escape her guard, to lose herself in the city. Here, it was easy to pretend to be anyone. I wasn't the king of Radaan, just a man chasing down the woman my foolish heart was set on.

Greaves muttered another curse, weaving through the crowd to stay with me. People barely noticed us, and I was thankful Radaan's royalty wore no crowns. A mantle was far easier to conceal.

We caught up to the Thresher trailing Nienna as she barreled along.

Worry coiled up my spine when Greaves stepped in front of him. Was she fleeing from something?

The warrior spun, locking eyes with me. His gaze burned with the intensity of a storm. Nyryn's chosen warriors could intimidate even an army of Velli. Yet, here she was, trying to brush him aside.

"Dismissed, soldier," I grunted, brushing past. He hesitated, then fell behind. I spared no thoughts for what he might have been thinking.

Nienna dodged two children squabbling over an apple. A gust of wind tugged her hood free, and she yanked it into place. She didn't glance back once.

A wild urge surged within me, a predator's instinct to chase. She could navigate a room of nobles, but in the streets, she was oblivious. My heart thudded, steady, as I scouted the alleys ahead.

One—two—*there*, between the tavern and the potion shop. It was quiet.

"Second," I muttered.

Greaves groaned, understanding what I had in mind.

Nienna stumbled, her eyes darting over her shoulder, and I ducked, peeking from beneath my hood. Her gaze slid right past me. A small, triumphant smile tugged at her lips. She relaxed, her shoulders dropping just enough to show she was pleased at the notion of losing the Thresher. Her quick pace relaxed.

The street beyond thrummed with noise—laughter spilling from doorways, boots scuffing against cobblestones, and shouts rising above the din.

At the tavern ahead, a drunk staggered into view, weaving on the top step. He squinted at the world as if struggling to place it. She walked past, her gaze fixed forward, blind to any surrounding threats.

I surged, my hand cutting off her scream as I dragged her into the darkness between two buildings. The air turned cold and heavy, reeking of beer-soaked stone and decay. Behind, Greaves tripped the drunk, sending him sprawling. The man roared in pain, his shout stifled by the crash of another body falling into him. A scuffle broke out, voices snarling like feral dogs.

Nienna screamed again, the sound muffled against my palm. Her nails dug into my skin as she struggled. I pulled her further, a dark satisfaction curling within me for catching her off guard. She fought, twisting and kicking with all her strength.

When she sank her teeth into my finger, I hissed, and we turned the corner into a dead-end. I released her and threw back my hood.

"You son of a—" Her insult cut short. Her eyes widened in shock before narrowing in fury. She stood tall, enough to glare at me, though I still towered over her. "—of a swine," she finished with a scowl.

"Such filthy words, Princess," I chuckled. "You speak to your king with that mouth?"

Fire blazed in her deep blue eyes, an intensity that burned away the chill. I closed the distance, backing her against the wall, my palm braced beside her head. Her chest rose with quickened breaths, and tension crackled in the narrow space that separated us. Her lips parted, the faintest tremor betraying her fury even as she tilted her chin in defiance. The faint scent of her skin—something sweet. No, dangerous...

Her teeth clicked together, the sharp sound breaking the silence. For a moment, the fire in her stare faltered, as though she forgot what fueled her anger. Her voice was low, edged with steel, as she said, "I've kissed him with these lips."

Gods, the things that did to me.

Blood roared in my ears. My gaze traveled down her face, grazing her throat and the rise and fall of her chest, before snapping back to safer territory. Her hands clutched my cloak, fingers digging into the fabric. She wasn't as angry as she pretended to be.

"Had you dismissed your Thresher, you might have met another's lips in this alley." My words lingered, heavy with accusation, as I watched her eyes flash with indignation.

"You attacked me!" Her nostrils flared, betraying a fury that rippled just beneath her composed exterior.

"Better me than another man." My voice dipped, low and mocking.

I leaned closer, the rough stone of the alley wall grazing my arm. Her breath hitched as I brushed my lips close to her ear, the warmth of her skin taunting. "What would you have done if it wasn't me?"

I waited for her reply, letting the silence stretch between us. Her throat worked, tension radiating from her as she straightened. The sharp line of her jaw betrayed her struggle for control, her pulse visible where it throbbed at her neck.

"I can protect myself."

"Oh?" I pulled back, sliding my hands down her arms.

Her gaze locked onto mine, yet when I lifted her hands above her head, there was no resistance. Her wrists met the rough surface of the wall as I pinned them there, firm but unhurried. And as her tongue flicked out, tracing her lips, the gesture almost undid me.

"What *was* your plan?" I stepped closer, my body pressing her against the cold, uneven stone, trapping the last of her composure between us. The alley's grime clung to the surface, but I didn't care.

Her breathing faltered, her grip on control slipping like frost melting beneath the sun's heat.

Something hard jabbed at my hip. I drew back, my eyes dropping to the source. A breathless chuckle rippled from her chest, low and teasing, stoking the flames that already burned inside me.

"I told you," she said. "I can protect myself."

"And yet, you didn't."

My smirk deepened as her expression shifted, the fire in her gaze cooling to ice. The contrast was sharp, cutting. I almost laughed at how easily she masked her fury. "What do you think can protect you from me, Nienna?"

Pushing her felt too easy. Every line of her body was taut, like a bowstring drawn to its limit, but still, I pressed. Restraint had long since burned away, leaving only the gnawing hunger that demanded more. More of her. More of us. A force pulling me closer, sharper, darker, until something broke.

"Why don't you find out, Kallias?"

Her voice shattered my control. My name on her lips sent a jolt through me. She was already arching into me, her mouth upturned as I dipped to kiss her.

I tried to go slow—sun above, how I tried. But with us, there were only frantic, stolen moments. Her tongue brushed mine hesitantly, almost as if to test her bravery, and I groaned as I opened to her. Her hands tugged at my grip, but I held her firm. With my free hand, I hiked her skirts, desperate to find what she kept hidden beneath them.

I wanted far more than the blade I knew was there.

She whimpered, raising a leg against my hip, a silent plea to be lifted. I smiled against her lips. Demanding, as always. But I wasn't ready to give in.

My hand brushed against cold steel, and I broke the kiss, smirking down at her.

"This?" I tugged the blade free from the fabric she had wrapped it in, lifting it to her face.

Tallon's dagger gleamed in the faint light, dousing me with icy clarity. Her mouth snapped shut as I recoiled, stepping back, gaze locked on the familiar weapon. The emerald hilt glittered, the wolves chasing a stag etched into the steel, clear as the day I gave it to him.

The morning after his mother's burial.

"Why do you have this?"

"Give it to me," she snapped, reaching for it.

The blade stayed just out of her grasp as I tossed it in my palm. The weight was familiar—one I knew well, having picked it out myself.

"Did he give you this?"

Jealousy twisted my gut. Had they been closer than they let on? After the assassination, did he offer it as a sign of protection? Did she care for him, while I kissed her like some common wench in an alleyway?

"It belongs to me!"

"It was Tallon's. Early wedding gift?"

She snarled, grabbing my neck and hauling me down to her. Fury scorched her kiss, and I lowered the dagger. She jumped, wrapping her legs around my waist before I could lift her. Her hips collided with mine, and I hissed at the searing torture.

"Don't you dare—" she growled, sparks dancing in her wild eyes, "—mention my wedding again. Unless you'd like the reminder of me laying with another man, thinking of you."

The dagger clattered to the cobblestone. I threaded my hands through her golden hair, slamming her back into the wall. With a sharp tug, I exposed her pale neck and nipped at the soft skin. She squirmed against me, clearly pleased she'd riled me.

I didn't want to think about her in another man's bed, least of all my withering son's.

She let out a strangled moan as I brushed the sensitive flesh beneath her ear. Her fingers threaded through my hair, nails scraping down my nape, sending a jolt of exquisite agony through me. Her legs tightened around me, grinding deeper, and I bowed my head against her shoulder.

Not here.

Not now.

My breath caught, a wild hunger rising inside me. Blood burned in my veins. I needed her in every way—by my side, at my table, in my bed.

But I couldn't.

I wouldn't.

Somehow, I pulled away, a tortured groan slipping from my throat as she found her feet. Turning my back on her, the weight of my position settled heavily on my shoulders. King of Radaan, I reminded myself. I didn't take women in alleys.

No, I would bring them to my rooms, splay them across my bed like a feast.

"Did Tallon give it to you?" My voice thickened with longing, but I fought it back. I stooped to pick up the discarded blade.

"No." She choked out the word, clearing her throat.

When I turned, she was smoothing her skirts and fixing her disheveled hair. A blush stained her cheeks. Her lips were swollen from our embrace. Gods, if I didn't get out of this alley, I would do far more than kiss her.

"That's all I needed to know." I hummed, tucking the dagger into my belt.

"I want a blade." Her voice edged with concern.

I paused, studying her face as the hunger within me ebbed. Shadows marked the skin above her cheekbones, and she bit her lip, gaze falling to the ground. I understood that need—the desire for a weapon to feel safe, to believe she could defend herself.

"I can do better, Princess."

Her attention snapped to me, a mischievous smile curling her lips. Elohios above, the things I would do for this woman.

Chapter Twenty-Six

KALLIAS

The impact of my blade sent Greaves pivoting to the side. I gritted my teeth and charged forward, refusing to let him escape. Sweat slicked my skin, the damp tunic chafing with each movement. I parried his lunge, and in the same motion, drove my sword beneath his guard. He staggered back with a sharp grunt.

I pressed the attack, fury blinding my judgment. Tomorrow, we were meant to leave for the Sol district, but Tallon claimed to be sick. I'd been foolish enough to check on him—only to find him not ill, but violently drunk.

Too much wine would do that.

Healers already did what they could, administering charcoal to purge the alcohol from his system, but he would be in no condition to travel.

It was his duty to escort her, yet now he lay incapacitated.

Egath remained locked away in his rooms and garden, his movements restricted, until we could identify the mastermind behind the attack.

That left just two of us to make the journey to the mountain manor—me and the princess.

Frustration exploded through my strike, landing against Greaves' block. He staggered under the force, panting as he struggled to keep up. Determination flared in his dark eyes, and he shifted his approach, allowing me to hammer down on him.

Nienna needed to leave Reem. Though she excelled in court, a wild restlessness flickered in her gaze—something the palace walls couldn't contain. She was a creature of open air, suffocating in that gilded cage.

She deserved better.

Greaves found the gap in my guard, his fingers snatching my wrist. I jerked away, slashing a wide arc. He snarled and let go, his gaze flicking to my feet, calculating his next move.

No, she *needed* this escape, but I wasn't the only one who should be escorting her. The ride would take two days—all of which would be spent in her company. Sharing meals. Sleeping in the same house.

When we arrived, I would find sanctuary in the mountain manor. It was one of the few places I could lower my guard. Claydon had seen me at my worst on the battlefield. A healer, not a warrior, he disregarded his noble status to fight in the war, his hands stained with blood more than once. He'd patched me up countless times.

It would be too easy to slip into old habits. Too familiar. Clay was too trusting, and sneaking through the hall to another room would be effortless.

The temptation would be unbearable.

But this was what Nienna needed. What she craved. And I would give it to her.

And if she asked for more?

Could I say no?

Greaves slipped past my guard, driving his weight into my shoulder. The blow landed with a grunt, sending me stumbling back. Blood throbbed in my temples, and my sword tip dipped toward the ground. Frustration bubbled up as I ran a hand through my hair, tugging at it.

"I'm taking her," I hissed, wiping the sweat from my brow.

"And here I thought you took her in the alley," he shot back, grunting as he sheathed his blade.

My sword thudded into its sheath, and I tugged at my tunic, pulling it away from my damp skin. "To the manor, Greaves."

"I figured," he hummed, shrugging. "Will we be taking the Threshers?"

"I don't want them in the house."

"Too many eyes?"

I paused, letting my glare settle on him. "To give her space."

She needed a break from her guards, and the manor was the one place I could offer her that. If only for a few days.

We retreated to a cramped room beneath the stands, rinsing off the grime before heading to my quarters for a proper bath.

He settled beside the basin, his eyes fixed on me, lips pressed tight. "It's dangerous," he said.

It wasn't a question, but something about the way he spoke made me feel compelled to answer.

"Nothing will happen." I splashed cold water across my face, the chill biting into my skin.

Please, don't let me yield to her.

It was the truth. This had to remain a dead end. Stolen kisses were one thing—shameful, disgraceful—but the thought of going further with her? That was a line I dared not cross.

But it would be so easy. She wanted me. The way she kissed me, her hands drifting over me when I held her close. The soft gasps as I traced her skin.

Yet it couldn't go further. It shouldn't have even come this far. If I lost control and took her, the consequences would be worse than war. If I claimed her, we risked a child. The contract would be void. My name—tarnished. My god—forsaking me.

And there would be no hiding it. Tallon would know on their wedding night.

The thought of the healers inspecting the sheets made my stomach turn. They would announce she wasn't a virgin, and she would be sent back to Draconia—shamed, discarded, her worth diminished.

What would her father do? Even if he didn't know the truth, he would blame Radaan. And then I'd find myself at war on two fronts.

I couldn't afford to lose control around her. Too much was at stake, and it was too easy to forget that.

"Do you want me to step in?" Greaves asked, his voice flat. There was no teasing, no challenge in his tone. He wasn't probing; he was offering a lifeline. If I faltered, he was asking if he should risk his position—his duty as a bodyguard—to protect my reputation and hers.

I rubbed my face with a towel, my frustration rising. "Greaves, if I cannot be trusted to keep my trousers on, how can the people trust me to rule a kingdom?" I shook my head with a grimace. "No, it will be fine."

He sighed, stepping up to the basin. "It's supposed to be a vacation." He splashed his face with water. "Somehow, I think I'll get even less sleep."

Darius watched me too closely. His sharp gaze dissected each movement, every shift in my posture. I kept my distance from Nienna as she sat beside me, her presence too close for comfort.

I hoped he hadn't seen the flash of desire or recognition in my eyes when she walked down the aisle. Her skirt, split into panels, parted at the waist to reveal gold breeches beneath her deep green dress.

And the dagger strapped to her thigh.

My blade. Pressed flush against her skin, yet displayed for all to see. It was her silent challenge to the court: I won't cower. I have teeth. I have claws.

A dark pulse of satisfaction stirred within me, as if I had marked her, claimed her, for all to witness. Though no one knew—and she was *not* mine.

She belonged to the disgraceful sot who lay in his bed, a drunken mess.

I treated her with the respect her title demanded, cautious with every word and gesture. I had to remind myself—she was the princess of Draconia, nothing more.

The lie gnawed at my resolve, each breath a little heavier. How long before Elohios would strike, or worse, abandon me? I needed to shift Darius' focus, quell the growing storm in my chest, and avoid the twitch that threatened my eye all night. I gestured to a servant, ordering Fyrn'sol to the dais.

Nienna's gaze shifted, a smile threatening the corner of my mouth. She was intrigued. Never before had I called her friend to my table.

Fyrn descended the stairs, her wine-colored gown rustling with each step. She glanced at Nienna before dipping into a curtsy at the bottom. I nodded, and she gathered the fabric of her skirts, climbing toward us with careful steps.

"Good evening, Your Majesty," she said, her voice steady despite the slight furrow in her brow. Her eyes were sharp, assessing, betraying a trace of nerves.

I tucked that observation away.

"Evening, Fyrn'sol. How is your mother?" I asked, aware of Darius chewing next to me. He would catch anything I didn't.

Her hand clutched her dress, fingers twitching with uncertainty, as she glanced at Nienna. "Gayle'sol is well... as far as I know, my king. Do you have news?"

"I don't. But if it's been so long since you've heard from her—we're heading to your family manor in two days' time. I'd like you to come along."

A flicker of something foreign tugged at the corners of her mouth before she masked it. My smile remained steady, but unease coiled in my gut. Claydon was as fair as any man. Why would she distance herself from her own family?

"We'll stay a week, then return to Reem as planned. I'm sure the princess would enjoy your company."

I would appreciate the added witness, a shield to keep me from indulging any foolish fantasies.

"Of course, Your Majesty." She nodded and flashed a quick smile at Nienna, who I assumed would be pleased. The two were constant companions—when the princess wasn't slipping away unnoticed.

With Fyrn'sol at the manor, my temptation would be eased. The pull of desire, always lurking, would be lessened.

I could rest easy now.

There would be no resting. My hand settled against my thigh, a forced gesture of ease. Tension knotted in my shoulders beneath the mantle, but I kept my hips loose, moving in rhythm with my stallion.

Nienna rode beside me, in Greaves' usual place. As princess, she should have been behind me, alongside Fyrn, as we left Reem.

Unfortunately, the woman fell ill this morning. I inquired after her, hoping to delay our trip for her. The healers were uncertain whether it was something she ate or some minor plague, but unless I wanted Nienna trapped with someone vomiting their every meal, we had to leave without her.

When the princess arrived in the courtyard, reaffirming her choice to ride astride, a weight lifted from my chest. Riding horseback was grueling, but pulling a carriage up the mountainside was nearly impossible.

She hesitated before the white gelding, biting her lip in a rare show of nerves. Swallowing my pride, I offered her a hand up. She trembled under my touch as I slid her boot into the stirrup, my fingers brushing her calf before I let go.

A rush of memories flooded in—the library...

Her dress parted around her breeches, her skirts fanning over the gelding's rump. Black-clad legs emerged, the tight fabric outlining her form.

The sight of her brought an uncomfortable reminder of my own constricting trousers.

Despite the discomfort, a smile tugged at my lips. The people of Radaan had heard of our journey, tossing flowers beneath our horses' hooves. Citizens cheered, calling me by my titles—King Kallias, King of the Plentiful Plains. Golden Warrior of Elohios. Warrior of Sun and Spear.

But what warmed me most was the way they greeted Nienna.

"Blessed be Princess Nienna, The Dragon's Heart!"

"Long live Nienna of Draconia, loved of Veridis!"

Either the priestesses or Fyrn had spread word of her multiple visits to the temple. Had she claimed Veridis as her goddess? It would be unexpected for a Draconis, but it would win the people's favor.

And mine.

A warmth spread through me at the thought. To choose a Radaanian god would be an act of faith—one that a Draconis, who had never witnessed such gods in action, would find hard to make. For her to embrace Veridis would be a step beyond belief; it would be an affirmation of something deep and real.

She would be a queen to remember.

Tallon's queen, I reminded myself, teeth clenched as we passed through Reem's outer walls.

She was not mine, and never would be.

The thought soured my stomach. I shifted in my seat, trying to ignore the unease gnawing at me.

Nienna's gelding snorted, stepping forward in a sudden prance that pulled my attention back to her.

Her grip on the reins tightened, her knuckles pale. The smile she'd worn was long gone, replaced by a hard, neutral expression. A small crease appeared between her brows, only to vanish again. Her gaze flicked to mine, and I saw a streak of unease buried there.

Open fields stretched ahead, the crowd parting to let us through. Though fewer commoners lined the streets, the press of bodies still made it difficult to ask what bothered her.

The gelding's ears twitched. Another step, a restless prance, and Nienna pulled in a sharp breath.

"Easy," I murmured, guiding my stallion closer.

Her horse, a palace steed, was steady—one I'd sit a child on with confidence. Yet, it sensed her tension, its movements uncertain.

"It won't bolt." I glanced at the guards ahead, acknowledging the citizens who bowed as we passed.

Nienna's gaze lingered on the horizon, a shadow crossing her face. She would remember the last time she'd ridden a green steed—Tallon's foolishness still fresh in her mind.

"Yes, Your Majesty."

Her formality struck a sour chord. Here I was—King of Radaan, not Kallias. In front of my people, we were two royals, nothing more.

I swallowed the bitterness rising in my throat, keeping my stallion close as we left the palace behind.

When the sun reached its zenith, it began its slow descent toward the horizon. We continued to ride, the world stretching wide before us. Nienna seemed to relax with each passing mile, her mount growing steadier beneath her.

The hours slipped by, the sun casting a soft amber glow on the land.

Phares appeared in the distance—the city of sunshine, where the earth was cleared for miles around. Golden fields of wheat stretched out, glowing orange in the fading light. The harvest had begun, leaving patches of bare land where crops had been cut. No trees marked the horizon—just open, unnerving emptiness.

The sight unsettled me, but the dread that rattled my bones had nothing to do with the vista itself—but the people within those walls.

I wished I could prepare Nienna for what awaited her. She had already faced Tallon's cruelty, and I had no doubt she could handle whatever the Phares threw at her.

But Bac'phares—he was another matter. A stubborn man who resisted my efforts in the war, having to be ordered for every tax collection. He was a thorn in my side, tight-fisted and greedy, a brute whose selfishness knew no bounds. His wife was as thin as he was stocky and was known for her words that cut as deep and often as her whip.

Fallione had been tasked with finding a way to remove them. They had no heir, and I could place anyone I wished in their stead. If only I could find evidence to condemn them.

"Garett, let Phares know we're arriving." My voice rasped, thick with disuse. The bitter weight of being unable to speak freely with Nienna gnawed at me.

The guard nodded and gave a small bow. "Yes, Your Majesty!" He spurred his horse into a swift gallop, heading toward the city.

Bac would have watchers posted along the walls, so they should've been ready for us. But I never took anything for granted with the man.

"We are staying with the noble family tonight?" Nienna asked.

"Yes, the Phares." I turned toward her. "Only for the night. We'll share their table, then leave at dawn."

She narrowed her eyes, studying my face with intent. "And you chose them because they lie in our path?"

A small thrill stirred beneath my skin at her sharpness. Smart woman.

"In part," I admitted, choosing my words with care. "Their taxes have fallen behind. I intend to discuss the quality of his fields."

Her brow furrowed deeper, but she said nothing more. The truth was, Bac's taxes had been revoked. I'd ordered him to pay in gold instead of crops after the third shipment of spoiled straw. His goods weren't worth the trouble. His coin, however, would be.

The man was far from pleased.

We reached the city gates without ceremony. Garett returned, informing us that he'd sent a runner ahead to the estate.

The structure was impossible to miss. Dominating the skyline, the black tower rose at the city's heart, its dark silhouette stark against the setting sun. Nienna gasped, shielding her eyes from the last, blinding rays peeking over the city walls.

"The Phares prefer to be in full view of their people," I said as we threaded through the narrow streets.

Greaves edged his horse closer, and the guards ahead of us cleared a path.

"It looks like the Spire."

The sorrow in her voice caught my attention. I turned to find her eyes glossed with unshed tears, glittering in the golden light. She bit her lip, dropped her gaze, and swallowed hard. When she peeked up again, she offered a smile meant to reassure, but it twisted into a grimace.

"Your palace?" I asked, already knowing the answer.

I had seen paintings of the Spire—its grim, towering presence reaching the clouds, crowned by the dragon Nest. Compared to that, Phares' tower was a mere imitation, a pale shadow of something greater.

"My home."

Her words struck me like a blow. The longing in her voice ripped through me, exposing the weight of all she had endured—and all she still would.

It was a bitter reminder. Radaan was not her home. She belonged to Draconia. Her heart was with her dragons, not with me. Not with my people. What could golden fields and blossoming orchards offer to a woman raised amidst whirlstorms and the largest predators of the known world?

I saw the dark, oppressive estate as a looming, cold structure. She viewed it through soft, nostalgic eyes. Perhaps that would change once she met the nobles who resided within.

Bracing myself, I urged my stallion forward.

The city's people were distant, their smiles veiled with reserve. They bowed low, acknowledging us regardless of rank. I had demanded the same recruits of Bac'phares as any district. They'd seen me in battle. I earned their respect, at least.

That, I realized, might be all I had earned.

We arrived at the estate without ceremony, entering the courtyard with no formal greeting.

Nienna surveyed the barren space, her eyes tracing the bare earth. No shrubs, no trees—just sparse, low grass, as though they feared nature itself might challenge their fearsome fortress.

"Were we expected?" she whispered, scanning the empty courtyard for any sign of staff—bustling servants, attentive butlers, anyone charged with offering a greeting.

Any other day, I wouldn't care. The lack of welcome was nothing new, and I'd grown accustomed to it. But with Nienna? It wasn't just an insult to me as king. It was a slight to her as princess.

The thought made my blood surge, a flash of rage itching at my skin. I wanted to throw open the doors, drag Bac'phares from his chambers, and demand he grovel at my feet.

"Leon," I snapped, my voice low and cold. "Inform the Phares that their failure to offer a proper welcome to Princess Nienna has severely displeased their king."

The guard glanced between us, no doubt wondering why my anger seemed more on her behalf than my own. Without a word, he dismounted and sprinted toward the door.

I took a slow breath, steadying my pulse as he disappeared into the bowels of the tower. Dismounting, I braced myself against the saddle, shaking out my stiff legs. Long rides were comforting to my mind, but my body hated them. My spine popped as I stretched, trying to loosen the tightness in my joints.

When I trusted my feet to carry me, I turned toward Nienna. Her gaze was fixed downward, her mouth tight with discomfort.

"I can't feel my legs," she murmured, her lips barely moving.

I shifted, stifling a smirk, careful not to let Garett see. "My apologies. I should have made more stops."

I pushed her too hard. Long rides were second nature to me, but Nienna, a proper lady, wasn't accustomed to horses or their demands. It had been foolish to not consider her needs.

Not that I minded helping her down.

"I've got you." My voice was low, just for her ears.

She relaxed a fraction, her breath hitching as she gripped the saddle and swung her leg over. Her knee buckled as her weight shifted, and she tumbled. I caught her with a grunt, steadying her until her feet found solid ground.

"Abyss beneath," she hissed, her fingers clenched white around the stirrup.

"The numbness will fade soon."

"Before the nobles arrive?"

"Probably." I chuckled, my irritation at Bac for his negligence fading into a quiet relief. At least no one else had witnessed her stumble.

And yet, my hands still rested on her waist, unwilling to let go.

It would be so easy—so effortless—to pull her flush against me. Her unsteady form would melt into mine, soft curves pressing against my chest. I'd brush my lips along her neck, nipping at the tender skin, coaxing out those small moans that drove me mad.

"Pins and needles, but I think I can stand now," she said.

I dropped my hands, cursing the treacherous thoughts that clouded my mind. One touch, and all my restraint vanished.

Greaves caught my eye, his expression hardening. He looked more disappointed in my lapse of judgment than in the Phares' lack of courtesy.

Frustration simmered beneath my skin. I moved to the front of our group, my back stiff with tension. It wouldn't take long to find someone who deserved my ire.

The massive doors creaked open, revealing a lavish entryway. A chandelier, larger than a wagon, hung overhead, its light scattering across the mirrors that dotted the walls. The grandness of the space made me feel smaller, more distant.

A pair of staff members followed the Phares into view. Both were draped in purple and gold, an elegance unmistakable on the woman, but Bac? The colors clashed against his bloated frame, making him appear even more vulgar. He had the audacity to roll his eyes at me, his smile condescending, while his wife pinched her non-existent lips, gaze narrowed on Nienna in a portrait of disdain.

They approached us and leaned forward a breath—their cheap imitation of a bow.

"King Kallias–" Bac began.

I silenced him with a glare. "A missive was sent a fortnight ago, informing you of our arrival."

"Well, yes–"

"I did not give you leave to speak." The courtyard stilled. Not even a bird dared to chirp. I lifted my chin, raising my voice. "You received the message. You knew of our visit. Yet you offer no welcome, no greeting for your king. You insult Radaan with your negligence."

I extended my arm, and without hesitation, Nienna's delicate hand settled against my elbow. She followed my lead with little effort.

"You've been honored to host Princess Nienna of Draconia," I said. "The Dragon's Heart. Your offense to her is unforgivable."

Bac's face drained of color with each word, while his wife flushed a deep crimson. Her eyes stretched wide, threatening to burst from their sockets, her outrage contorting her features. Despite being no older than her husband, she looked like an ancient crone cloaked in jewels and painted in thick cosmetics. In contrast, his bloated frame gave him a semblance of youth.

"You may pay obeisance."

The command was flat, unyielding. Not a question. Not a suggestion. An order.

Bac hesitated, glancing at his wife for reassurance.

"Now." My voice dropped to a growl, impatience breaking through my icy calm. I was King of Radaan, not her—he needed his affirmation from me.

He crumpled into a bow, bending as low as his girth allowed. His wife followed with a shallow curtsy, her eyes flicking up at Nienna with barely contained malice. The fury in her gaze made my pulse race, blood pounding in my ears.

"Your king is satisfied," I said as they began to rise. "But the offense to Draconia still stands." They hesitated, sinking lower. "Ask her forgiveness. And mercy."

Was this too much for Nienna? Too sudden? She was only a princess, after all. Had she been taught how to respond when a noble was out of line?

Her hand remained steady on my arm, a quiet strength that reassured me more than any words could.

"We meant no ill will, Your Highness." Bac's voice was muffled from his bowed position, his cheeks now a curious shade of scarlet.

Still, his slight made me seethe. "I did not ask what you *meant*."

"Forgive us, Your Highness." Takal's high-pitched, nasally tone quivered as she faced the ground, her limbs shaking with the effort of holding the curtsy.

She wasn't accustomed to submitting to authority.

"Draconia is a land ruled by Dragon King Nereus." Nienna slipped her hand from my arm, approaching the couple with power in her stature.

Either she concealed her numbness well, or she recovered faster than most.

"Were you to disrespect the royal family there," she halted before Takal, bending low to meet her gaze, "you would be eaten by a dragon."

A surge of pride swelled within, but I fought to keep my expression neutral. I was the king. I was impassive. She was just a princess—but gods, she acted like a queen.

"I hear your plea, and grant your forgiveness," she continued, brushing imaginary dust from her sleeve. "Rise. We are hungry and weary from our travels."

The Phares straightened, their eyes flickering between the princess—who tossed her golden hair over her shoulder—and me.

The Nienna I knew held my heart in ways I could never express, but Princess Nienna claimed my very soul.

Chapter Twenty-Seven

NIENNA

The noblewoman's voice carried through the room, invasive and unwelcome. "Late Queen Eldeiade would have appreciated the roast pig, would she not, Your Majesty?"

My patience frayed beneath her words—the fifth time the dead queen's name intruded on the evening. Could Takal'phares speak of nothing else? Years had passed since Eldeiade's death, yet her fixation clung like a shadow, teetering on obsession. A glance toward Kallias confirmed my growing irritation was shared. His jaw tightened, the only crack in his otherwise rigid expression, as stoic as the estate's carved stone pillars.

Though I had never met Eldeiade, the king's bitter recounting painted a vivid picture—one that Lady Phares would not care to hear.

"Yes." He leaned back in his chair, his focus sharp and unwavering as he fixed Takal with a gaze that could cleave iron. He chewed with deliberate precision, his scrutiny impossible to miss.

The animosity between the king and the Phares was palpable. Their history lurked in the shadows of every pointed remark. I longed to ask him about it, but no opportunity would come. Not here. Not in this grand estate where privacy was a myth, and each move was scrutinized under the guise of propriety.

"Do *you* enjoy it, Princess?" Takal's sharp eyes found me, her tone deceptively pleasant.

My spine straightened as I forced my features into a calm, unbothered mask. "It is delicious, thank you." My voice was steady, but my focus lingered on her face, reading every flicker of expression like a map.

Her lips curved into a polite smile that didn't reach her eyes. "Will you be following in her footsteps, then?"

"When the time comes," I replied, "I will bear the mantle of Radaan."

Kallias shifted, the movement subtle yet loaded. His silence pressed against me like a weight. It was improper to discuss a future reign while the current king still lived. The thought churned in my stomach. One day, I would ascend—but only when he was gone. The image of shouldering the mantle alongside Tallon turned the taste in my mouth to ash.

"Ah, so you'll break tradition," Bac'phares interjected, his smirk a dagger aimed at the king. "Queen Eldeiade moved away from it, after all."

My gaze darted toward Kallias despite myself. Custom dictated that the mantle was borne by both ruler and mate—a shared symbol of power and responsibility. My studies made that clear. If Bac meant to rattle me, he would fail.

I wouldn't shy away from my duty.

I sipped my wine, letting the moment stretch. Careful consideration, not ignorance, would carry me through this exchange. Yet unease coiled deep in my stomach. Kallias remained silent, and I couldn't help but wonder why.

"I may not choose the same as the late queen," I said.

Takal leaned back, a scoff escaping her lips like the hiss of a serpent. "So you'll cast aside precedent? My, my, what changes you have in store for Radaan!" Her condescension was sharp enough to cut.

My jaw tightened. The wrong words had slipped past my guard.

"Tradition states both king and queen wear the mantle," Kallias broke in. He tipped his wine glass back and drained it in one long pull. Irritation flickered across his face, vanishing as quickly as it appeared, replaced by the icy glare he aimed at Takal. "Radaan would be honored if Princess Nienna chooses to uphold that practice."

Bac'phares chuckled, his tone dripping with mockery as he swirled his wine. "Curious, though. Why didn't you press Eldeiade to wear it? Or perhaps you did, and she refused?"

My grip on the fork tightened, the cool metal digging into my palm. Kallias' neck flushed, a subtle betrayal of the storm brewing beneath his composed exterior. His face remained unreadable, but his eyes burned with barely contained fury. The jab was a calculated blow, one aimed to wound.

If he admitted he hadn't pushed Eldeiade, they'd question his devotion to tradition. If he confessed she defied him, it would tarnish his authority. The man had him cornered.

"Be careful dredging up the past, Bac'phares," Kallias said, his tone a blade honed to perfection. "Some things are better left in shadow." He rose from his seat, adjusting his tunic with deliberate ease. "Now, come. We have matters of tax to discuss."

The smirk melted from the man's face. With a grunt, he shoved back his chair and trudged after Kallias and Greaves as they exited the dining room.

The door clicked shut, and the air shifted. Takal's gaze turned toward me, fierce and ruthless, her focus a hunter's fix on cornered prey.

Were I a dragon, my hackles would have risen in warning. Instead, I straightened my back, meeting her challenge with a cool smile. My lips curved in defiance, and I lifted a brow. Let her try.

"Tallon didn't know what he was getting into with you, did he?" Her words were blunt, an arrow fired without pretense.

Blunt, I could handle.

"I'm not sure what he expected," I said, setting my glass down with deliberate care. "But I *am* Radaan's future."

Her sneer deepened, contempt curling her lip as she leaned across the table. "Your choice of words amuses me, Princess. Tonight, we've spoken of the late queen, of her son, and yet you've barely uttered his name. Betrothed as you are, with a wedding mere months away, one might think you'd be eager to speak of him."

I dabbed my lips with the napkin, letting the moment stretch. Each second tightened tension's cord. "May I be honest, Takal?"

A wicked gleam flared in her dark eyes. "Elohios would demand it."

"It's none of your blasted business."

Her laughter erupted like a thunderclap, echoing through the chamber as she threw her head back and slammed into her chair. The sound clawed at my nerves, vile and grating. I held her gaze, forcing patience to temper the heat simmering beneath my skin.

Along the wall, the two servants stood motionless, their blank faces betraying neither surprise nor discomfort. This wasn't the first time they'd seen such insolence.

"Ah, I do love a blunt woman," she said, wiping at her eyes as her laughter subsided. Then, rising without permission, she smoothed her skirts with a deliberate flourish.

My fists tightened beneath the table. Princess or not, she reveled in her belief that she stood above me.

"I will see you to your rooms now," she said, her smile as bright and false as a polished coin. She stepped around the chair, already dismissing me.

"I am not finished."

Her steps halted. She turned, her mirth draining like wine spilled on stone. "You're done."

The words struck like a slap, igniting fire in my veins. "You *dare* tell me I'm done?"

Her lip curled in disdain. "The king of Radaan is not here, and these are my people." She gestured toward the servants, her arrogance suffocating. "I am High Lady of this house, and you'll find you have little power here, *Princess*. Now. To your rooms."

"You forget your place." Heat flushed my cheeks, but I refused to waver. "You are a noble, nothing more. An insect beneath the might of a dragon. I am Draconis. Have you forgotten our magic?"

A bluff, but her pale face betrayed her doubt.

"A single word." I let the threat drip like poison. "Just one, and your fields will wither. No wheat, no barley, not even grass for your sheep."

Her tone faltered. "You are loyal to Radaan–"

"I am bound to Radaan, but my loyalty is mine alone." With my head tilted, I steeled my expression into iron. "I am a dragon, and you are an ant. Remember your place."

Deliberation marked every movement as I raised a piece of pork to my mouth. The sharp tang of spice and rich fat coated my tongue as I chewed, my gaze fixed on her rigid form. Fury radiated off her in waves. Her knuckles whitened against the back of her chair, gripping it as though it might anchor her. She neither sat nor fled, unwilling to test the unspoken threats that lingered.

She wouldn't dare.

I took my time eating, dragging the meal out long past my hunger. Each bite was a reminder of her place, a punishment for her insolence. The silence in the room grew thick and oppressive, broken only by the faint clink of my utensils. My thoughts strayed to Kallias and how he endured similar affronts. Bac'phares' smugness earlier suggested his punishments had been far less subtle.

At last, I wiped my hands on the linen napkin and rose, the chair scraping against the floor. "I will retire now. Please, show me to my rooms."

Her jaw tightened, but she nodded, turning without a word.

The trek through the tower stretched in brutal silence. Shadows pooled in the narrow halls, the black stone walls blending with the darkness outside. The air carried the stale chill of a dungeon, and I longed for a window, for even a glimpse of the stars or the cooling brush of the night's breeze. Asking about balconies, though, would betray any semblance of authority I claimed to hold.

Lanterns flickered, illuminating little before it seemed to dissolve into the gloom. The corridors, devoid of windows, swallowed sound and light alike. Takal moved through them as if born to the shadows, her stride long and brisk. She walked, head high, every step deliberate. Though taller than me by a margin, her imposing posture made the difference feel greater.

I hurried to match her pace, trying to memorize turns and landmarks in the labyrinthine estate. No staff appeared to offer guidance. No guards patrolled the halls. The emptiness unsettled me, each step echoing against the walls, amplifying the eerie quiet. Perhaps privacy was a virtue in this place—or a shield for something darker.

At a bend in the corridor, Garett came into view, stationed near a heavy door. Across the hall, Leon lingered by another. My chest tightened. Could that be where Kallias would stay? The thought grounded me for a fleeting moment—so close, yet just out of reach.

Takal's sudden turn snapped me from my thoughts. Her sharp eyes pinned me as a knowing smile curled her lips. She gestured me ahead. "Your room, Princess."

I spared her no gratitude. My attention shifted to Garett, who paused for a moment before pushing the entrance open.

Once inside, despair hit like a battering ram. My feet moved of their own accord, bringing me deeper into the space as the door thudded shut. The chamber swallowed me in its stillness. My gaze darted to the dim lanterns casting muted light across the stone walls. It wasn't a guest suite. It was a cell dressed as one.

A cramped sitting area opened into a modest bedchamber. There were no grand windows, no dressing room. My wardrobe, shipped ahead of our journey, should have been here. Yet no sign of it greeted me. Unease twisted my stomach.

My feet dragged me to the bed, exhaustion like a heavy cloak pulling me into its embrace. Edith would have brought order to this chaos, but I'd insisted she stay behind. The journey would have been too taxing on her, though part of me admitted I didn't want her prying eyes fixed on Kallias and me.

Fyrn had been my other option, but illness kept her from traveling. I hated the relief that realization brought. Without either of them, I felt stripped bare, vulnerable in this hostile estate. The disdain from the Phares family during dinner rattled me more than I cared to admit. Their venomous remarks still lingered, as did the burden of my deceit—lies about magic I didn't wield, about power I did not hold.

I let myself fall against the mattress, grateful at least for the feel of feathers beneath me instead of straw. My body ached from hours of riding; muscles in my thighs throbbed, and my lower back pulsed with soreness. When I rolled onto my stomach, I cradled my head in my arms, debating whether I could endure another day on horseback or if I'd risk humiliation by requesting a carriage.

The Sol family would host us next. Their reputation at court painted them as kind, but estates often revealed truer natures. If they mirrored the Phares in cruelty, the week ahead would stretch unbearably long.

My thoughts spiraled, each worry tangling in knots. Pressing my palms into my eyes, I groaned at the sheer weight of decisions yet to be made.

A knock shattered my restless haze. I bolted upright, heart lurching, muscles screaming in protest. Another set of heavy pounding came before I could stand.

Who would dare bang on my door so insolently?

I scrambled to it, smoothing the wrinkles from my dress as I went. When I pulled it open, I froze.

Kallias stood before me, dark brows slashed low over eyes the color of storm-tossed seas. The muscle in his jaw jumped with tension, his lips compressed into a razor-thin line. His gaze flicked down to my boots, then back to my face.

My pulse hammered. Whatever brought him here, it wasn't good.

"Come with me."

Kallias spun on his heel, his cloak flaring in an arc behind him. I cast a quick glance at Greaves, searching for a clue to the king's temper—or if his ire rested on me. The man gave only a curt nod, offering no explanation. I swallowed a lump of unease, then hurried after the king of Radaan.

The echo of boots accompanied us as Garett and Leon followed behind. Kallias led with a certainty that spoke of intimate familiarity with the tower, ascending staircases and rounding corners without hesitation. I lifted the hem of my dress, struggling to match his pace, the fabric whispering against my legs. The burn in my calves stung, but I swallowed any plea for him to slow. I fought the urge to ask what had riled him so much that he'd forgotten to walk beside me, leaving me to trail him like a lower noble.

But I *was* less than him.

We were equals only behind closed doors.

Another staircase loomed, and my breath came in shallow bursts by the time we emerged onto a bustling floor. Servants moved in streams, converging in chaos, arms laden with blankets, lanterns, and buckets. They darted through the halls with shallow bows, too frantic to pause for the king's presence.

Kallias waded into the torrent without breaking stride, scattering workers like startled birds. I lingered for half a heartbeat, catching the startled look of a young maid who nearly collided with him. Her wide eyes found mine, and I offered a fleeting smile before plunging after him.

The new chambers glowed with warmth, walls painted in ivory and every sconce ablaze with light. Servants bustled in and out, arranging furniture, stacking firewood, and filling basins with steaming water. These rooms spoke of royalty, a stark difference from the cell I had been shown earlier.

Cool night air whipped into me as we rounded another corner, tugging strands of hair loose and chilling my skin. Kallias slowed his pace, but I couldn't stop. As a moth to the flame, my feet carried me to the sad excuse of a balcony—drawn by some unseen force.

Beyond the sturdy railing, Phares sprawled like a constellation brought to earth, its lights winking as if sharing a secret. My breath caught at the sight, and the wind billowed my skirts, teasing my sleeves.

The height sent a thrill through me, and I twisted, trying to glimpse the peak above. The gale seemed alive, plucking at my hair and pressing against my arms as if urging me closer to the edge. It reminded me of the Nest, high atop the Spire, where clouds would shroud the island, making the cities below feel as distant as the stars. The wind here had the same playful spirit, as familiar as an old friend, though it lacked the echo of dragon roars.

"You should have never been placed in that room." Kallias' tone was edged with simmering anger. A heavy cloak settled along my shoulders, carrying his scent—spiced cedar with an undercurrent of something sharper.

"It wasn't a mistake," I said, pulling the warm fabric tighter.

The last of the staff retreated, leaving Greaves leaning against the far wall. He caught my eye and the corner of his mouth lifted a fraction in response to my grin.

"The Phares have always been difficult, but this?" Kallias gestured toward the room behind. "This is an insult to Radaan itself. An entire floor is ours, and they try to quarter us among minor nobles."

"Have they done this before?" I asked, leaning forward over the railing. The city below blurred as the wind swept past my face, carrying me back to memories of flying on Argos.

"They've disrespected me, but you–"

I laughed, the sound bursting free before he could finish. Turning to him, I pressed a chilled hand to his warmer one. His scowl faltered, the lines softening as I smiled up at him. Rage was written all over his face and I tried to quell it in our stolen moment.

"I can handle myself. Takal might curse me if the crops fail next year, but don't uproot a district for my sake." The words were light, but warmth curled in my chest at his indignation on my behalf.

He raised an eyebrow, his gaze flicking to my lips. "You threatened her?"

"I reminded Takal of her place."

"And with my tripling of their taxes, I'm sure they'll rest peacefully tonight," he said, a wry note creeping into his voice.

The tension eased from his shoulders as the storm clouds in his eyes cleared. His gaze lingered on my face, his lips curving at my grin. In this moment, the titles that defined us dissolved, leaving only him and me beneath the open sky.

"You belong up here," Kallias murmured.

"This is nothing compared to the Spire." I stretched out my arm, letting the wind push and pull against my palm. The gusts streamed through my spread fingers like threads of silk, then surged upward as I cupped my hand. "And riding a dragon is far worse. If they dive or drop their head, you'd better be strapped in."

"You've flown on the beasts, then?"

"Since I was a babe." I gripped the railing, memories pressing down on me like an unseen weight. "My father took me up on Argos as soon as the queen released me. I wasn't even a year old."

"Your mother had to release you?" He chuckled, arching a brow.

"No, the queen dragon—Kalepsi." A mischievous smile tugged at my lips. "Didn't you know I was raised among dragons, dear Kallias?"

"Forgive my ignorance, precious Nienna," he drawled, a flicker of humor dancing in his eyes. "I did not learn every secret of your childhood."

I laughed, throwing my head back. The wind caught my hair, tossing it into a wild spiral. His flinch, subtle but there, only made the moment sweeter.

"I was born in the Nest at the Spire's peak. My mother risked everything. The scent of blood can drive dragons into a frenzy, but Kalepsi claimed me as her own. It's the highest honor in Draconia, to be chosen without being a rider."

The words stung, though I hid it. Dragons choose their riders, it cannot be forced. And despite Kalepsi's blessing, none chose me.

"When the bulls were drawn to the blood, Kalepsi drove them out herself," I continued, filling the silence. "For months, she refused to let my mother take me away. It's a dangerous thing, exposing a newborn to the elements, but the reward was worth the risk."

"Why would Queen Nyxaria take such a chance?" His tone, low and sharp, betrayed his disapproval.

"To be blessed by dragons is to stand above all others," I said, meeting his gaze without flinching. "Draconis aren't religious, like Radaanians. Among us, a dragon's blessing is sacred. For every daughter of Draconia, the risk is part of the legacy. Had I been a better Vessel, my power would rival even my father's."

Greaves lingered near the doorway, his attention fixed on a painting, feigning disinterest. I caught the faint curve of his lips as if he followed our words, nonetheless.

"It wasn't just for me," I continued. "Kalepsi's mark is protection. No one can harm what the dragons claim."

"They are fearsome creatures," Kallias admitted, his voice thoughtful. "Prince Ronan's black mount alone would strike fear in any army."

"There's a reason no kingdom has dared wage war on Draconia," I replied. "Kings have tried to claim the Wild Shores, to tame the dragons, but their will is not ours to command. No force rivals their might."

Kallias leaned a hip against the railing, crossing his arms over his chest. The faint lines on his face deepened as he stared into the sky, his expression unreadable.

I bit the inside of my cheek. How soon would my rooms be ready?

"When do you believe King Nereus might answer your request for dragons?" he asked after a moment.

"The whirlstorms are unpredictable this season," I said, sighing. "He'll send them when the skies clear. I've requested five. Once they fly, they won't stop."

His focus remained on the stars, his profile cast in silver by the moonlight, though a shadow of worry darkened his features.

I touched his arm, drawing his gaze to me. "Radaan will have my dragons. They'll guard your mountain passes. Nothing shall cross without your command."

His brows drew together, and a muscle in his jaw tightened. The moon caught the salt and pepper stubble on his face, highlighting the faint tremor in his mouth as if he warred with words he didn't dare speak.

"Radaan will have your dragons," he said at last, his voice strained. "But at the cost of your marriage."

The wind whipped around us, sharp and cold. I pulled his cloak tighter, the chill sinking deeper than my skin.

"Kallias–"

The door swung open, breaking the moment. Greaves moved with practiced precision, a knife flashing in his hand before the intruder even spoke.

"Begging your pardon, Your Majesty," the servant stammered, his wide eyes darting between us. "The floor is ready."

Kallias straightened, the warmth in his expression gone. "Send a maid to Princess Nienna's chamber," he ordered, his tone hard. "I need no assistance."

And just like that, we reverted to the roles of king and princess. I lifted my chin and slid into my mask once more, ignoring the way the hole in my heart tore a little wider.

Chapter Twenty-Eight

NIENNA

I rose before first light. The servant assigned to me worked by lantern glow, guiding me through washing and dressing with the detached efficiency of someone performing a chore. Her indifference contrasted with Edith's warm touch—the careful braids, the subtle gestures meant to make me feel beautiful. This woman saw me as nothing more than a duty.

I donned the same style as the day before: split skirts for riding astride. Tall boots gripped my calves, and I bit back a wince as I tugged on the dark brown breeches. The soreness from hours in the saddle throbbed in protest, but I told myself my backside could handle one more day. The white horse was steady and composed—a stark difference from the wild-tempered beast Tallon had insisted I ride.

Breakfast passed in tense silence. A messenger interrupted with news of an emergency that demanded the Phares' attention, excusing their absence. Kallias barely acknowledged the boy, too focused on the sharp strokes of his pen as he composed a letter. I nibbled on a few bites of egg and fruit, watching as he sealed the missive with the heavy gold signet ring on his finger.

"This goes to Advisor Fallione in Reem," he ordered. His glare promised dire consequences if the letter went astray.

"Yes, Your Majesty." The boy bowed and darted away down the hall, his footsteps fading into the distance.

Kallias exhaled through his nose, his jaw tightening as he stared down at his untouched plate. I itched to know what the missive contained. Hiding my grin behind another bite of egg, I wagered it carried a biting reprimand for the missing Phares.

We departed soon after. Kallias helped me into the saddle, his touch firm but fleeting. He squeezed my calf, and butterflies swarmed low in my belly. Then he swung into his own saddle with an ease that bordered on arrogance.

The way his trousers stretched over his thick thighs as he mounted left my throat dry. Shifting in my seat did little to chase away the heat blooming in my chest. Sunlight kissed his skin, tracing the sharp lines of his features. He glanced back and caught me looking. His piercing blue eyes flicked down, snagging on my exposed leg before rising to meet my gaze again.

Dragonfire—but the want in those eyes! They quickly shuttered as he turned away from me. Without a word, he turned and set the pace.

Our guards, Leon and Garett, rode ahead, with Greaves trailing close behind. As we moved through Phares, its beauty struck me—a city rich with gilded façades and opulent displays. Yet beneath the shimmer lay cracks. Poverty lingered at the edges, subtle but undeniable. Tattered garments hung on children darting through the crowds. Their wide eyes followed us with a hunger that went beyond food.

The townsfolk bowed as we passed, offering gestures of respect, but their faces lacked warmth. In Reem, the people brimmed with joy. Here, they seemed resigned. Content, perhaps, but far from pleased. Hollow cheeks and watchful stares told a story I couldn't yet decipher.

I wondered if the scars of war deepened as we approached the mountains. Would the desolation grow, or was this quiet desperation unique to Phares?

Once we cleared the city, Kallias guided his horse to fall in beside mine.

"Should I expect the same warm greeting at Sol" I asked.

"Not at all." He sighed, the motion rolling through his shoulders. "Claydon is an old friend. He served on the front as a healer and holds a great deal more respect for people."

Relief eased the tension in my back, and I sank a little deeper into the saddle. "He seemed kind enough when we spoke at the palace."

"The Sols are... enthusiastic," he admitted, a faint grin tugging at his mouth. "Sometimes overly familiar, but always generous in their kindness. Be warned, though—you'll hear plenty about his goats."

I groaned, drawing a laugh from him. "He *was* rather passionate about them."

"They're a peculiar breed, I'll admit. I'm certain he'll insist on showing them off."

"I can hardly wait." My tone dripped with mock enthusiasm, making it clear the creatures hadn't won me over.

His chuckle deepened. "Didn't you once suggest feeding them to your dragons when they arrive? Let's hope that little rumor hasn't reached his ears."

Heat crept up my neck as the memory resurfaced. It had been my first council meeting, and Fyrn had warned me afterward that her father wouldn't find my remark amusing. "I'll offer my sincerest apologies, should the need arise."

He scoffed, shaking his head, and we rode on in companionable silence. The mountains loomed ahead, their jagged peaks carving sharp lines into the horizon. Natural fortresses stood as both a border and a barrier—low enough for a dragon to soar over, yet far too treacherous for an army to climb. I imagined the battles fought in their shadow, wars funneled into narrow passes where the terrain itself decided the victor.

We bypassed towns and cities. I couldn't tell if Kallias wanted to save time or craved privacy. This journey had begun as a tour with Egath and Tallon, meant to acquaint me with the mountains, but illness and obligations had turned it into something else entirely. A secret part of me was glad. Without Tallon's barbs or Egath's brooding presence, the quiet felt easier. Even Fyrn's absence was a relief. She may have distracted me from my delusional attractions, but with her gone, I could unwind. Too many unspoken truths hung between us.

Perhaps that was it—there were no pretenses left with Kallias. We carried enough shared secrets to ruin each other if we chose.

As we neared the mountains, the midday sun revealed a city carved into the stone. I slackened the reins, letting my horse find its own way, my attention fixed on the sight. It shimmered with life despite its rugged construction, its walls blending into the rock. Yet Kallias led us around it, steering toward steep trails that hugged the mountainside.

When the path narrowed to a single line, he gestured for my horse to move ahead. I twisted in my saddle, arching a brow at him. "How exactly did you plan to get a carriage up here?"

His eyes snapped up from my backside and I smothered my surprise, smirking. He blinked, reaching up to rub the back of his neck. "We'd have taken the longer route, but even then... it would've been an ordeal."

His excuse earned a hum from me, though I swallowed the temptation to call him out on just where his gaze had lingered. Instead, I forced myself to focus on keeping my balance as my horse scrambled upward, muscles straining beneath me with each lurching step.

As we climbed higher, my heart was pounding. Sweat trickled down my temples, and my hands throbbed from clutching the saddle. Leon's mount slipped once, skittering on loose gravel, while Greaves' gelding stumbled over an uneven patch, recovering with an unnerving jerk.

The trail stretched upward still, daunting and unrelenting. I exhaled a shaky breath, gripping the reins with damp fingers, and steeled myself for the climb ahead.

We reached a plateau, and my attention caught on the line of soldiers barring the way. Their formation spread from one rocky edge to the other, immovable as the mountain itself. Beyond them, the path disappeared into a cavernous mouth hewn from stone, jagged and foreboding.

The sight of the cave sent a chill down my spine— its interior darker than the depths of any ocean. I halted my horse, gripping the reins as my heart thudded against my ribs. The path ahead vanished into shadow, a void so absolute it felt alive.

There wasn't a speck of light.

Not a glimmer.

"Onward, Nienna," Kallias commanded, his voice low but resolute as he rode past me without hesitation.

My hands shook as I nudged my horse along. The line of soldiers stood in green and gold, their stoic faces set and alert. Garett and Leon dismounted, leading their mounts aside as a man stepped forward, breaking ranks.

"You've been expected, Your Majesty," he announced, his tone brisk but respectful. Another slipped into the cave, returning moments later with a flickering lantern.

"Claydon'sol awaits your arrival," the first soldier continued.

Kallias leaned forward in his saddle. "I'm pleased to hear it. The mountain—has it been quiet?" he asked.

"No skirmishes in our district, Your Majesty," the man replied, his words laced with unspoken tension.

The absence of conflict here implied unrest elsewhere.

"And the mines?"

"Blessed by Dagden himself," he said with a reverent nod. "They're producing enough ore to supply the kingdom."

"Good. That ore will be used for tools, not swords," Kallias' tone lightened, and he straightened as they passed the lantern to Greaves.

One light? For that abyssal blackness? The small flame sputtered against the oppressive dark, its reach barely extending a few paces.

The soldier bowed before stepping into formation. "Thanks to your wisdom, Blessed King!"

Greaves rode ahead, and Kallias waited until I drew even with him.

I tucked a strand of hair behind my ear, trying to steady myself. I was raised among dragons. I didn't fear the dark.

The peak of the mountain loomed high above us, a shadow against the sunlit sky. My throat tightened. It wasn't the darkness I dreaded, but the weight of stone overhead—a tomb carved from earth.

I knew the wind and sea. Sun and sand. A shiver ran through me at the thought of riding through that tunnel.

I nudged my heels into my horse's sides, forcing him onward. His ears flicked, but he stepped into the cavern without hesitation. Hooves clattered, the sound reverberating through the still air. The ceiling soared above, unseen but vast. Shadows pressed in like a suffocating mist, thick and impenetrable.

My chest tightened as the light of the plateau faded behind us, shrinking to a distant pinprick. The horse remained steady, his confidence at odds with the crawling dread that crept along my skin. I twisted to glance over my shoulder, yearning for the open sky.

Kallias' stallion drew alongside mine, but my attention fixed on the lantern swaying ahead, its feeble glow a lifeline in the smothering black. He seemed unshaken, though my breaths grew shallow and ragged, no matter how hard I tried to suppress them. Panic coiled in my chest like a serpent, tightening its grip with every passing second.

How far did this tunnel go? How much longer until we emerged? Would the ceiling hold, or was it doomed to crumble without warning? What if the mountain caved in under its own weight? Even worse, what if the earth itself shifted, sealing us in?

The thoughts struck me like a blow: we would die here. Buried. Forgotten.

My limbs trembled, and I clenched my muscles, fighting to still the shaking. My horse huffed, its bit jangling as it tossed its head in irritation.

"Nienna?" Kallias' voice cut through the oppressive silence, his tone calm but edged with concern. "What's wrong?"

My teeth sank into my cheek, the sharp tang of blood searing my tongue. The pain grounded me, if only for a moment. Greaves angled the lantern toward me, casting Kallias' face in a dim, flickering glow.

"Gods, are you well?" he asked. His brows drew together as he seized my reins, slowing my horse.

"Don't stop." My voice broke as the words tumbled out, strangled by the iron grip of dread coiled around my throat. "Please, just keep going."

His stallion sidestepped, brushing close. The press of his leg against mine sent an anchor of warmth through the storm of fear.

"Is it the dark?" he asked.

"No." The denial came fast, too raw. "Please—we need to move." Every heartbeat spent in here stretched my terror thin, threatening to snap it into full-blown panic.

"It's the mountain," Greaves muttered.

Kallias moved without hesitation. His hands gripped my waist, firm but careful. Before I could protest, he lifted me.

I gasped, clutching at his shoulders. "What are you doing?" I hissed, though I made no effort to resist.

My legs shifted, accommodating his pull, and I found myself seated in front of him on his stallion. The saddle, built for one, forced me flush against him. No space to retreat.

I leaned forward, trying to create distance, but the attempt was futile. His thighs bracketed mine, solid and immovable.

His breath brushed along the nape of my neck as he adjusted his seat, pulling me against him. "Be still," he murmured.

Heat flooded my face as I straightened, every nerve heightened by the unnerving closeness.

Greaves took my horse's reins with a glance, his expression flat but knowing as he led us forward once more.

Shame warred with the warmth spreading through me. This was wrong. All of it. The need curling in my stomach, the burn of desire ignited by his touch, the way my body reacted to his presence—it defied reason.

And yet, I didn't lean away.

"Relax," he murmured, his voice a low rumble near my ear, each word brushing my skin like a spark.

But how could I? How I fit between his legs, molded against his chest, felt so... *right*. His strength steadied me even as my mind whispered how wrong it all was. Somehow, it was wickedly, achingly perfect.

"What if someone sees?" I whispered.

The darkness was absolute, thick as velvet, but the idea set my nerves on edge. My ears strained for sounds beyond the rhythmic clatter of hooves against stone.

"Claydon would understand. Anyone else?" His chuckle rolled through his chest, a deep vibration that tangled with the erratic pulse hammering in my veins. "I'm the king, Nienna. Have you forgotten?"

The corner of my mouth twitched, but when I glanced up, the oppressive ceiling loomed, heavy and unforgiving. How far would it have to fall to crush us? The question dissolved as his lips brushed my neck, soft and searing all at once. A shiver broke over me, and my gaze darted ahead to Greaves' broad back.

He knew. He had to. But the thought of him turning, seeing—why did that send a thrill through me?

"Don't think about it," Kallias murmured, his breath warm against my ear.

"There's an entire mountain above us, and you tell me not to *think* about it?" My voice sharpened, brittle with unease. "I was raised in the sky, dear *King*. Do not–"

The sharp nip of his teeth silenced me, a gasp spilling from my lips. He guided the reins while his free hand settled on my thigh, firm and warm. Heat radiated from his palm, burning through the thin barrier of my leggings.

And gods, how I wanted his touch to wander.

My heart thundered, each beat echoing through me as his presence consumed all corners of my awareness. The steady weight of him against my back made it impossible to think, every nerve alive to the closeness, the tension coiling between us.

Greaves rode just ahead, his figure unwavering. The tunnel stretched on, its length unknown, its shadows swallowing any sense of time. What we were doing was already reckless. To give in to more would be ruinous.

Still, the ride passed in a haze. The scent of cinnamon curled in the air, wrapping around me as I leaned back against his solid chest. His heartbeat thudded slow and even against me, grounding me as if I were tethered to him alone.

His hand flexed, fingers tightening against my thigh in a fleeting squeeze. My breath hitched, eyes darting to the faint gray smear that emerged ahead—the stairwell.

Relief warred with reluctance as he murmured, "The stairs are near. Can you manage on your horse?"

I tipped my head, a subtle smirk breaking free. "What happened to 'I'm the king'?"

He grunted, pulling me against him. His arm banded around me, his thumb brushing the edge of my ribs, so close it drew heat to my cheeks. "Do you want to test that theory?"

Yes. A thousand times, yes. My pulse betrayed me, pounding an answer I couldn't speak aloud.

Instead, I forced out, "I can ride. If you promise the mountain won't fall."

His laughter was soft, but his words carried a steady weight. "A promise? No. But this tunnel has served the Sols for a thousand years. If it's meant to collapse, it won't be today."

I swallowed hard and nodded. "Greaves?"

The guard halted, his dark eyes flicking to mine with an unspoken question etched into the lift of his brow.

"I can ride now," I said.

He scoffed, his smile teasing at the corners of his lips as he led the white horse toward us. With an easy grace, he held the beast steady while Kallias hoisted me into the saddle. The gesture seemed childish, being lifted like a doll, but I couldn't help marveling at his strength—earned not from youthful exertion but from years of seasoned endurance.

"Thank you," I murmured as he passed me the reins. "Greaves?"

"Hmm?" A low hum answered as the man resumed his place at the lead.

"Can I trust you?" The question gnawed at me, an itch I couldn't ignore.

The king trusted him, but I didn't know the full history they shared. Had they stood shoulder to shoulder in battle? How recent was he posted at his station? And who chose him—Kallias, Darius, or someone else? Who did he answer to?

He held the secret that could bring down Radaan and Draconia—and I was blindly trusting him.

Greaves met my gaze, his dark eyes steady and unflinching. Something in his expression turned my palms clammy.

"Princess Nienna," he said, his voice hoarse, "you can trust me with your life." His chin lifted toward Kallias. "And his. My loyalty belongs to him." Without waiting for a reply, he urged his horse ahead, tossing a parting jab over his shoulder. "And I'm sure he wouldn't appreciate my commentary on the library."

My jaw went slack with disbelief. The king grinned, rubbing his neck with a sheepish shrug. Clearly the two were closer than I thought.

The pale gray glow ahead grew brighter, stirring the air with anticipation. My pulse quickened as the hazy light resolved into muddled sunlight.

When Greaves veered toward the wall, Kallias nudged his leg against mine, his voice low and knowing. "Watch."

He pulled a rope embedded in the stone, and a metallic clang reverberated above. I snapped my head upward, squinting as shards of sunlight pierced the darkness. Mirrors descended in a measured sequence. Each new reflection amplified the light until it bathed the cavern floor in brilliance.

A ramp emerged from the shadows, a spiraling path climbing the immense shaft. Dust drifted in sparkling wisps, catching the newfound glow. My gaze snagged on the carvings that adorned the walls—intricate battle scenes etched in stone, hidden until now. I laughed, unable to mask my wonder.

"Welcome to the Manor in the Mountain, Princess," Kallias murmured.

He guided me toward the incline, and my fingers brushed the carvings. They felt smooth, polished from care rather than time's wear. The engravings stretched upward, a story spiraling as far as my eyes could follow.

"It tells the history of our gods and the rise of House Sol," he explained, his words filled with quiet pride. "A lengthy tale, but if you're curious, we can return later."

"I'd like that," I said, marveling at the details. My attention shifted to the dim shapes cast by our figures. "Tell me of Elohios."

"Why him?"

The cut on my cheek stung as I ran my tongue along it. "I want to understand the god Radaan's king serves."

"Tallon hasn't sworn allegiance to any."

"I didn't say Radaan's *future* king," I countered, my tone pointed.

Silence fell, the rhythmic clatter of hooves filling the void. A quick glance revealed Kallias, deep in thought, one brow furrowed while a ghost of a grin lingered.

He was a devout man, as were his people. Curiosity stirred, tugging at me to learn more about the god he served—and how I might earn that deity's favor.

A tiny voice in my mind said it was only because I wanted to make Kallias smile... and it wasn't wrong.

"Elohios has no birth, no origin," Kallias began. "He has always been. The Father, alongside Veridis, the Mother. From truth and life, all things came to be. It's tradition for Radaan's king to seek his blessing before his reign begins."

"Did you claim him before your coronation?" My gaze wandered, tracing the intricate carvings of battles and changing seasons that stretched along the wall.

"I did," he said. "I was seventeen when I pledged myself to Elohios."

"And when you ascended the throne, did he choose you?"

"Through his priests, he gave his blessing. They are his voice."

"You had no rivals?"

"None." His laugh came low and brief. "I was the only heir."

"There weren't many options, then," I teased, earning a slight grin.

"True, but the choice didn't matter. I serve Elohios with all I am. He demands truth from my tongue and justice from my sword."

"And Veridis? Where does she fit?" I tilted my head, frustration stirring as our horses' strides carried us past details I wished to study closer.

"She is the chaos to his order," he explained. "She creates life, and Elohios protects it. Without her, there would be no citizens to serve, no lives to honor with truth. She is the lifeblood of my people."

A faint smirk curled my lips. "Once, I saw a painting in the palace—The Great Hunt. A mammoth, I think."

"It's the king's duty to slay them, to protect his realm." His tone shifted, softer, as though the memory brushed against something distant. "It depicts King Galivard the Second. It hangs in the southern halls."

"There was someone with him."

Greaves coughed behind us, or perhaps it was a choke.

"After the slaying?" I pressed, casting him a sly glance.

His jaw tightened, and his nostrils flared as he stared straight ahead. "The hunt belongs to the king," he said, voice strained. "What comes *after* is the queen's charge. Veridis blesses her by opening her womb, ensuring life flourishes after death. It is balance."

"They seemed *very* balanced." My tone carried a teasing edge, but it faded when Kallias turned to me, pain stark in his gaze.

"Nienna." He spoke my name like a plea. "It's important. The king takes life, yes—but the queen cleanses him of death, reminding him of the lives he safeguarded with the sacrifice. She must bring life into the world. That's her duty."

I faltered, the weight of his words settling over me. Fyrn had mentioned Eldeiade never fulfilled her role, abandoning the rituals for reasons unknown.

The pain etched into Kallias' face told me it had cut him deep. Not just the act of the hunt, but her refusal to share in his belief, in his need for balance. It seemed such a simple thing—to wash away blood and share intimacy—but to him, it was sacred. And she had denied him.

The realization struck like a blow. How much destruction had he endured? Years of war with Vellos, leaving behind a trail of bodies. Hundreds, maybe thousands. Yet here he was, inquiring about crops, discussing mines, admiring gardens. He cherished life with the same hands that wielded devastation.

My chest ached for him, for the man who bore that burden in silence.

"Death is necessary, but life? Life must be treasured, Nienna."

Words hovered on the tip of my tongue. Kallias wasn't only violence and destruction. He guarded Radaan, kept her safe, gave her another chance at peace. Without him, could she have survived the war? Would she have endured?

I glanced away, swallowing unspoken thoughts. No words could ease his pain. I couldn't reach for him or soothe the weight he carried, no matter how I wished I could.

Instead, I focused on the engravings. Scenes of battle became sparse, yielding to stretches of farming and mining. The shift felt intentional, a quiet celebration of life's smaller victories. I traced a carving of a babe cradled in a woodland home, marveling at the artist's skill. Did they live still, or had their hands carved other wonders in this manor long before?

The staircase spiraled upward until we reached the summit. At its end, a pair of immense doors loomed, adorned with twisting vine carvings that seemed to pulse with life. Sunlight spilled through narrow windows, catching the mirrors and scattering its warmth down the cold, shadowed corridor.

Two guards snapped to attention as Kallias dismounted. He turned to help me down, his touch steady at my waist. I hid a smile as my feet touched the stone floor.

"Remember, Nienna," he said, brushing a loose strand of hair from my face. "You're safe here."

I nodded, his words sinking into my chest like an anchor in calm waters. Safe or not, the blade strapped to my thigh would remain within reach. Safety didn't mean letting my guard slip.

With my hand on his arm, we approached the entrance. Greaves trailed behind, silent and watchful. The guards turned in unison, hauling the great doors open.

The sight beyond stopped me in my tracks.

Claydon, hair a wild puff of white, stood braiding his wife's silken gray locks with meticulous care. His nimble fingers worked, though the effort pulled a grumble or two from him.

"King Kallias! Princess Nienna!" he called, his voice warm with familiarity. "I do beg your pardon, but this has been a great undertaking, I beg just one more moment!"

Behind them stretched an immense receiving hall. Vibrant tapestries of greens, pinks, reds, and blues adorned the walls, their summer hues banishing the gray monotony of the tunnel. A plush brown carpet sprawled across the floor, burgundy runes stitched in its weave. The dark wooden furniture clustered in welcoming nooks, paired with soft blankets and stacks of books, created an inviting, lived-in warmth. The room rivaled the palace in grandeur, yet felt homier.

"Good evening, my king, my princess."

Gayle's kind face lit with a smile. She wore a simple blue gown, elegant without pretension. Her husband, in sapphire overcoat and trousers, tied the braid with a flourish before leaning into a bow. She followed with a graceful curtsy, deeper than expected for her age and standing.

"Rise, Claydon," Kallias said, his voice free of the frosty formality he reserved for nobles. "I've told you for years to light that tunnel."

"And waste good oil?" he scoffed, one hand landing on his hip as his eyes crinkled with humor. "Pah!"

"Oh, were you frightened?" Gayle asked, stepping forward with concern, her outstretched arms a gesture of comfort.

"Not in the slightest," I replied, grinning as I clasped her hands.

Greaves cleared his throat.

"I had the king of Radaan at my side. What are a few shadows?" I laughed.

Gayle shook her head, her grin brightening as she studied my dress. "Andeluith herself would think twice before coming down on Kallias."

Claydon chuckled, drawing my gaze. My lips tightened into a thin smile. Could the tunnel collapse, then? The possibility gnawed at me, unspoken but heavy.

"You must be weary from your travels," Gayle said, pulling my attention to her. "Clay, take the men to the library for a drink. I'll escort the princess to her rooms so she can freshen up before dinner."

The older woman looped her arm through mine, her grip firm but kind, then guided me away. Twisting to glance back, I caught Kallias' amused grin. His nod urged me forward.

He was right. The Sols were a different breed—welcoming where the Phares were cold.

"I hope our reception wasn't too humble," Gayle said. "We've been waiting for so long. Claydon saw a plait design in the city and couldn't resist trying it. First on the goats, of course, but didn't have enough time."

Her words conjured a picture that made me stifle a laugh. "It's a beautiful braid," I managed, glancing at the intricate weave.

Her silver hair shimmered under the warm light of the lanterns lining the hall. The strands caught and twisted into an elaborate design that reminded me of quilted patterns.

"He's always brimming with new ideas," she said with a fond smile, steering us down another corridor.

Thick carpets muffled our steps, and the vibrant tapestries draped along the walls lent a surprising warmth to the otherwise cold stone. It felt familiar, welcoming.

"I've sent Poppy to fetch water for your bath. She's one of the two maids we house here, though I can arrange for more if you require."

"Only two?" I blinked, unable to hide my surprise. For a manor this size, the staff seemed small.

"Claydon values his privacy," Gayle explained, patting my hand. "We keep the staff we need. We're a close-knit household. Dinner is usually in the kitchen with the cook rather than in the dining hall."

Their humility caught me off guard, stark against the grandeur of the manor. They didn't wield their wealth like a weapon, as the Phares did. Instead, they shared their table with their people.

"Would the king normally dine in the hall proper?" I asked, curious.

"Oh, no," she said, her laugh soft but genuine. "Kallias—*King* Kallias—has been a guest here for many years. He knows how Clay is. He often joins us in the kitchen."

I hesitated, then tugged her to a stop. "I hope this isn't too forward, but would it be possible to eat with you as you normally do? Formal dining halls and endless rows of servants... I've had my fill of them."

Her brows arched before her expression softened, and a gleam of approval lit her eyes. "You're just like Kallias." She squeezed my hand. "Of course. You are welcome at our table. I'll fetch you when dinner is ready, but until then, feel free to explore the manor. Guards are stationed near the entrances if you need directions."

"Thank you." I nodded, though uncertainty stirred beneath my calm. Would Kallias mind if I wandered alone?

We continued, passing halls that grew increasingly grand. The stone walls reflected the warm light of mirrored lanterns, creating a golden haze. Despite Claydon's earlier protest about oil waste, the corridor glowed as though the sun itself dwelled within.

"And here we are," Gayle said, pausing before a heavy wooden door. It swung open on silent hinges, and she peeked inside. "Poppy isn't here yet, but I'm sure she'll arrive soon."

I stepped over the threshold, my breath catching. Tiny fragments of mirror adorned the ceiling, scattering the lantern light in a delicate dance across the walls. The room felt like a treasure trove of warmth and elegance. White and beige dominated, but muted green accents in tapestries and paintings provided a soothing contrast.

"It's beautiful," I murmured, venturing further.

The receiving area flowed into a dressing room, its chairs draped in furs, the decor plush and inviting. Beyond that, a massive canopy bed awaited, sheer curtains cascading around it like waterfalls of silk. A double door led to the bathing chamber, where more mirrored fragments turned the space into a sanctuary of light.

"How have I not heard of this place?" I asked, marveling.

Gayle's soft chuckle drifted from the doorway. "As I said, Clay values his privacy, and Kallias respects it in gratitude for his service during the war."

"The king told me he served as a healer."

"One of the best." Pride laced her tone. "He saved the king's life more than once. But those are tales for another time. Rest now, Princess."

She took her leave, her steps fading down the hall. I wandered into the bathing chamber, loosening the pins in my hair. The question of dinner lingered. How did one dress for an evening with friends? My wardrobe was tailored for courtly events, not intimate gatherings.

I sucked in a deep breath hoping Poppy had some ideas.

Chapter Twenty-Nine

KALLIAS

C lay had that look about him. The kind that said he was up to no good.

"I have bred moon-spotted Kuh'lir," he announced, his tone as proud as if he'd discovered a treasure.

Lounging in a deep chair, ankle resting on my knee, I felt a rare sense of peace settle over me. It had been too long since I last visited Clay's manor. This sanctuary, with its stillness and the faint scent of aged wood and books, was a reprieve from the world outside.

I swirled the spiked cider in my mug, watching the liquid catch the light. "You have spotted goats," I said, each word deliberate, as if speaking them aloud might make them sound less ridiculous.

Clay was particular about who he allowed in his home. He'd sooner house Tallon and Egath in the city than let their chaos touch his manor. Years spent tending wounded soldiers left him polite yet stubborn. He couldn't be bothered with dramatics or being forced around people he didn't care for.

And we were friends, so when he leaned forward, a boyish grin tugging at his lips, I scoffed but gestured for him to continue.

"*Moon* spots," he said, emphasizing the words like they were sacred. "They've only been seen in wild herds. Remember Stormcloud, the buck we caught last spring? He's already sired his first batch of kids. Those marvelous speckles are a unique hair variation—"

He launched into an enthusiastic monologue about goat genetics. I let his words wash over me as I tipped my head back against the cushion, my eyes drifting shut.

What room would they give Nienna? Not that I intended to visit her chambers, aside from escorting her if needed. Clay's minimal staff would handle such tasks, and the Sols were more than capable of attending her.

She would want a balcony. I cursed myself for not mentioning it earlier. Nienna belonged to the sky. She thrived in open spaces, where the wind kissed her skin and freedom called to her. My stomach twisted at the thought of her leaning too far over the edge. She'd been raised atop the Spire, where heights were second nature, but this wasn't home. No dragons waited below to catch her should she fall.

Still, this manor could offer her its own kind of comfort. The stone walls held a quiet warmth, their surface worn smooth by time and care. It was a place that embraced its visitors, offering peace to those willing to let it in. She would find solace here. I was sure of it.

If they placed her in a western-facing room, she'd have a view of the sunset. I could picture the warm glow casting her in gold, setting her hair aflame. The light would wrap around her, softening every dip and curve. Her lips would glisten, tempting me—

My eyes snapped open. Clay stood by the towering bookcases, rifling through a shelf until he pulled a leather-bound volume free.

"Wouldn't it be harder to dye the hair of spotted goats?" I asked, grasping at the thread of his earlier ramblings. "The colors wouldn't take evenly."

Clay whirled around, clutching the book to his chest with theatrical flair. "Kallias, you wound me!" He staggered toward a chair and collapsed into it with mock despair. "Wool is for dyeing. The hair of the Kuh'lir is for weaving. The natural patterns are prized art! Not something to tamper with!"

I sipped my cider, relishing the fiery warmth as it slid down my throat. "No dyeing then?"

He glared at me.

A low chuckle escaped me. I waved at his book. "Fine. Go on."

Clay perked up, flipping through the pages with zeal. "Now, long-haired Kuh'lir come from the northern herds, but I've heard whispers of a herd with *curls!* Can you imagine it?"

I lifted the mug again, hiding my grin behind the rim. Clay's passion was contagious, even when it was about goats.

"You look ready to face an army alone," I said, scoffing as Greaves shrugged into yet another belt of throwing knives. He slung it across his chest like a bandolier, the leather taut against his frame. My arms folded as I studied his absurd array of weaponry.

Blades peeked from every piece of clothing. How he managed to move without the clattering of a blacksmith's workshop was beyond me.

A hilt jutted from each boot, and the three curved knives strapped to his thigh gleamed in the firelight. At his waist hung a short sword, two daggers, and a throwing hatchet. Another pair rested at the small of his back, while ten more projectiles gleamed from the leather strap stretched across his chest. A longsword perched over his shoulder, its handle worn from use.

He adjusted the belt with practiced ease, revealing the glint of two blades at his wrists. I knew he had at least three more hidden beneath his clothing.

And that didn't even account for the poisons tucked among his garments.

"A man can never have too many weapons," he grunted, the words gruff but laced with satisfaction.

"Clay might disagree. Your arsenal's an insult to his security."

He smirked, the corners of his mouth lifting in a way that made him look younger. "I bet your girl will be wearing her blade tonight."

The shift of my feet betrayed my unease. My girl? Nienna wasn't mine. But I knew she'd wear my dagger tonight, and my thoughts wandered to where she might conceal it.

Unlike Greaves, my attire was understated—far removed from palace formality. The weight of my usual mantle was absent. I wore a simple tunic beneath a green overcoat, with black trousers tucked into worn riding boots. No jewelry adorned me besides my signet ring. My sole weapon, a dagger, rested at my hip. I wouldn't wear a sword in my friend's home.

"She needs to know how to use that blade," Greaves said, cutting into my thoughts. "Wearing it out is enough to deter some fools, but if anyone presses, they'll realize she only knows which end to point at people."

"And who should teach her?" I sighed, running a hand through my damp hair. The baths here left much to be desired, but I refused to show up to dinner reeking of horse.

"Jerek, of course," he said, referring to the palace blade master. "But let's not pretend you'll let him. You'll teach her yourself."

"If she wants to learn, Jerek can handle it. Why would I interfere?" Turning on my heel, I strode toward the exit, already dreading what I knew was coming.

"Because you can't seem to pass up an opportunity to touch her," Greaves said, his laugh following me like a taunt.

My teeth clenched, and I grabbed the handle, yanking it open before stepping into the hall, not bothering to wait for him.

The thick carpet muffled my footsteps as I stormed down the corridor, irritation flaring hotter with every step. His words stung because they were true.

Whenever she was near me, I had to fight the urge to touch her. When something was said, I wanted to look at her and gauge her interest, figure out what her mind was thinking behind those dark eyes. When a joke was told, I found myself turning to see if she found it amusing. It was maddening, this pull she had on me. And I hated how easily Greaves saw through it.

I kept my composure, masking the distraction she caused, but it was a tenuous hold. My interest in her was a dangerous indulgence. She was off-limits.

Anyone could claim it stemmed from my years of celibacy since Tallon's birth, but it went deeper than that. I encountered beautiful women before—stunning, graceful, magnetic—yet none of them were Nienna.

She saw the world through a lens few others shared. Duty didn't frighten her; it shaped her. Despite her hatred for Tallon, she would marry him—an act driven not by choice, but by necessity, to save her people. The weight of that sacrifice was evident in her eyes, yet she carried it with a quiet strength.

More than a mere figurehead, she was the lifeblood of her land, a living symbol of Veridis. Her passion surged when she demanded what she desired, even if it defied the rules. Still, beneath that fire, there was a tenderness—she cared enough to ask about my faith, her curiosity genuine, as though each question was a bridge between our worlds.

My blood sang at the way she looked at me when I told her about my god. And when she asked about the painting of the Celebration of Life? Elohios himself was testing my restraint. I knew in my bones if she were queen, she would take that role and embrace it.

I clenched my fists as I walked.

Those weren't safe thoughts.

The corridors of the Manor in the Mountains mirrored the grandeur of the palace, yet they carried a warmth the royal halls never could. I knew every turn and alcove as if they were etched into my memory. During the war, when rare moments of peace arose, Sol offered refuge. It lacked Eldeiade's venomous existence, and in many ways, it was more like home than Reem itself.

A sanctuary. A safe haven.

Nienna's presence here felt natural, as if this place had been waiting for her. After everything she'd endured, she deserved somewhere that offered both freedom and security. The manor's defenses were nearly impenetrable—though not for the Kuh'lir.

On several occasions, we'd found the goats roaming the manor. How they slipped past the barriers remained a mystery. Since Clay denied sneaking them inside, windows seemed the most likely culprit.

The savory scent of roasted meat, spiced pastries, and herbs pulled me toward the staff kitchen. The room's warmth embraced me as I entered, the crackle of a smoldering hearth mingling with the soft hum of activity. It was a cozy space, designed for function yet inviting with its worn oak table and the glow of brass lanterns.

"My king!" Will, the old cook, called out, his booming voice echoing over the clang of ladles against pots. His rotund frame shifted as he turned to bow, the aroma of gravy wafting from the platter he carried.

Clay sat nearby, a thick book spread open before him, his focus buried in diagrams. "Gayle's fetching the princess," he murmured, flipping a page.

I glanced at the table, noting an odd number of chairs. "You're one short."

"Bernard." Will's hands slowed as his face darkened with sorrow. "He didn't make it through the winter. Caught the yellow fever, he did, and couldn't shake it."

"I'm sorry to hear that—what of his family?"

Clay flipped a page and adjusted the lantern to peer at the book. "We're seeing to their needs. His wife receives his pay, and his sons are apprenticed. One's married now, with a child on the way."

"You honor them," I said, settling into a chair. Clay's dedication to his community was admirable, the kind of stewardship others could learn from. He didn't merely care in words—he ensured their well-being.

"My people are good to me," he replied, though his attention had already drifted back to the pages.

"Master Claydon'sol is mighty good to us," Will praised, setting out the food. "We would be blessed if his daughter returned to the manor and continued his kindness."

Clay slid a ribbon into his book, meeting my gaze. "About that–"

The door swung open, and a trio of figures entered. Gayle led them, her movements brisk, while Poppy trailed behind. But it was the woman in the middle that stole the breath from my lungs.

Nienna.

Golden hair, wrapped in a loose braid, framed her face in soft waves, wisps falling against bare shoulders. Her blue dress stretched across her chest to her arms, revealing a swath of creamy skin and a collarbone that flexed with tension. The dress was long, draping down her curves, but simple in structure.

There weren't any slits.

Where was her blade? Was it under all that fabric?

I straightened, warmth prickling at the back of my neck. The room felt hotter, the hearth's glow too intense. Clearing my throat, I gestured to the table. "Princess, Gayle'sol, Poppy."

The young woman giggled, darting behind Nienna, whose cheeks flushed a deeper shade of pink. Her gaze swept over me, lingering just long enough to tighten something in my chest. When her teeth caught her lip, I swallowed hard, tugging at the neck of my tunic.

"Tipo and Ken?" I asked, sliding the chair to my left out for Nienna.

"The lad will show up soon," Clay replied, pulling seats out for the other women. "Ken has dinner with his family now. They just had twins."

"Girls!" Gayle chimed in, her smile radiant. "They'll have their hands full if the babes take after their mother's looks."

"The climb's too much for them these days, so Ken takes their meal down the mountain," Will added, setting a platter of fresh bread in the center of the table.

Nienna eased into her seat, and I nudged the chair closer for her. The brief brush of her shoulder sent a current through me. My fingers itched to skim over her skin, but I locked them at my sides.

She twisted to grin up at me and I almost pulled her into my arms then. Her eyes sparkled with ease, her laughter weaving into Gayle and Poppy's chatter. They'd made her feel at home—safe, wanted, loved. Any doubts I'd harbored vanished.

Greaves claimed the chair on Nienna's other side, Will taking the one next to him. Only the spot beside Poppy remained unfilled, a plate resting in front of it, waiting.

The last time I'd seen Tipo, he'd been a wiry lad with wild hair, more interested in chasing the mountain hounds than learning to train them.

As I reached for the basket of bread, its scent—yeasty and rich—mingled with the steam curling from the loaves. "Are the rooms to your liking?" I asked, breaking one open to release the heat.

Nienna brightened. "They're beautiful! I love the ceiling! Who thought to add mirrors up there?"

"It makes the room seem bigger," Gayle answered as Will carved the roast. "The mirror makers toss out broken glass. Such a waste! We gathered the shards and used them here."

Across the table, Clay barely looked up from his book. "They sat in a heap for months," he muttered.

His wife elbowed him, sparking giggles from Nienna and Poppy.

Plates filled with roasted meat, warm bread, and spiced mead as conversation flowed, lively and unhurried. Between Gayle's cheer and Nienna's ease, the room pulsed with camaraderie.

"You were raised up there? So high?" Gayle asked, a hand to her chest as though steadying herself.

"I'd wager it's no taller than your mountain," Nienna teased, her eyes glinting. The casual tone—a reference to wagering like a commoner—hinted at her comfort. "And my mother stayed with me. My father took me on my first dragon flight when I was a few months old."

Poppy leaned over her plate. "What's it like?"

Nienna paused, as if searching for words. "Flying is... freedom. It steals your breath—you have to time it with the dragon's rhythm. But with them, you can go anywhere. They can fly for days straight, and nothing can defeat them, so there's no fear of being hurt. Besides, dragons don't let their riders fall."

"Have any ever fallen?" Will asked, stabbing a chunk of beef.

"They train for it—practice jumping off."

Clay's fork froze mid-air, a piece of meat dangling forgotten. "They *practice* jumping?"

"They can't fear falling. So they face it by jumping." Nienna laughed, leaning back. "For a Rider, trust is everything."

Will nodded, spearing a potato. "Same with a kingdom. We trust King Kallias, would give our lives for him, because he earned it."

"More than that, he's won our loyalty," Clay added. "Seventeen years of war, and he refused to surrender to treaty demands. No other monarch would have endured that."

"How many dragons does Draconia have?" I asked, steering the conversation back to Nienna.

"Sixteen," she answered. "Though one, Tsunami, remains wild. So, fifteen with riders."

The number hit harder than I expected. "And you've offered five for Radaan?" A third of their fleet—marriage alliance or not—was a staggering demand.

"Ten dragons can defend Draconia," she replied, her gaze steady. "What could possibly challenge even one dragon?"

I pressed my lips together. Fair point.

"Dragons?!" The kitchen door slammed open, rattling the room.

Gayle clutched her chest, Clay's book fumbled from his grasp, and Greaves had a blade drawn before I could blink.

The boy had gone through a growth spurt, all awkward limbs that tangled as he dropped into the chair beside Poppy. His knees banged against the table, and she hid a smile as she scooted closer.

Tipo's parents had perished in the war, their village consumed by the chaos of battle. Afterward, he was taken in at Sol, the nearest safe haven, and grew up under Clay's roof. Though still young, his skill with the hounds bordered on prodigious—a talent sharpened by years of instinct and an unyielding bond with the creatures.

With a sheepish shrug, he swept a messy mop of hair from his eyes and reached for the bread.

"Tipo!" Gayle's sharp cry rang out as Will whisked the basket out of reach.

"What?" He froze, yanking his hand away as though the loaf had scorched him. "Spot chased a fox again! That's why I'm late! Had to track him halfway down the mountain."

Greaves settled in his seat, the faintest smirk tugging at his lips, pulling the boy's gaze like a magnet. With growing alarm, Tipo's attention snapped from him to me.

His chair clattered to the floor as he shot to his feet, cursing under his breath. He stumbled into a hasty bow, but the movement was so rushed his forehead smacked against the table's edge.

"Sea beneath!" Nienna sprang to her feet, her voice sharp with concern. "Are you all right?"

"My king!" Tipo straightened, rubbing the rising welt on his forehead. "My apologies! And... who's this?" He squinted through unruly red curls, his gaze settling on Nienna.

"Nienna." She laughed, easing back into her seat, assured he wasn't injured.

"*Princess* Nienna of Draconia," I clarified.

His jaw dropped as though the floor disappeared beneath him. He fumbled to sit again, only to stumble when it wasn't there.

A swift kick to my shin pulled my focus to Nienna. Her lips pressed into a tight line to match her glare. Apparently, announcing her title had been the wrong move.

"A princess!" Tipo scrambled to right his chair, awe wiping the confusion from his face. "So... you're the one with dragons?"

"Aye," Will grumbled, shoving the basket of bread toward the boy. "We were discussing their numbers before you barged in."

"How many are there?" Tipo demanded, his attention bouncing back to me.

"Sixteen on the island, though only fifteen have riders."

"What's wrong with them?"

Nienna froze, her fingers tightening on the edge of her plate. Her brows pulled into a sharp *V*. "Nothing. Why would you ask that?"

"Ah, must be a predator thing," he offered, his words rushing to fill the silence. "You know, they have fewer babies to keep the balance. How many eggs do they lay?"

"Several," Nienna replied.

"And the matings?" He leaned forward, his curiosity sparking again. "Like eagles, right? Maybe the males aren't inside–"

Clay's book snapped shut with a resounding thud, startling the boy into silence. "Mind your speech, lad!"

"I was only trying to help!" Tipo grumbled, tearing into a piece of bread with his teeth, his voice muffled.

"To a Draconis, mating is as natural as breathing." Nienna dipped her chin. "And dragons certainly aren't subtle about it."

I rested the toe of my boot against her foot in a silent warning. Her gaze snapped to mine, and I held her stare, my expression stern. Some topics, no matter how common in Draconia, were improper at a Radaanian table.

Such as any discussion of mating.

A faint blush bloomed across her cheeks. My mouth twitched as I fought back a smile, sensing her urge to push further.

Her leg shifted, brushing against mine before looping around it in a quiet, deliberate motion. My jaw tightened as I forced my attention to the plate in front of me, pretending my leg wasn't tangled with a princess' underneath the dinner table.

Chapter Thirty

NIENNA

The crumbs on the platters had dwindled to almost nothing, and the pitcher of mead had been filled and drained three times before we decided it was time for bed.

Satisfaction thrummed through me. My shoulders felt unburdened, and laughter escaped without regard for propriety. Beneath the table, my right leg had engaged in a mock battle with Kallias, our playful jabs escalating as the evening deepened.

At some point, the skirmish ended, our feet entangling in a quiet truce. His teasing gaze darkened, pleasure lurking in those depths. The sight of him at ease—his mask of regal composure replaced by the warmth of shared companionship—stirred something restless in my chest. A flutter low in my belly, both unnerving and exhilarating.

"Mark my words, one day those four-legged carpets will be the salvation of Radaan!" Claydon declared, waving his book for emphasis before slipping a ribbon between its pages.

"If goats are your saviors, Radaan is in worse trouble than I thought," I shot back with a smirk.

"That's a job for your dragons, Draconis," Kallias murmured, his voice slipping through me like smoke, sending warmth straight to my core.

"Ah, you're right!" I sprang forward as if struck by revelation. "They will be the salvation because dragons need to eat!"

Claydon staggered back a step, one hand flying to his chest as if hit by an invisible blow. "The audacity!" he exclaimed, his voice dripping with exaggerated offense.

Kallias, unamused, shifted beside me and nudged my boot with his. The subtle gesture was firm enough to catch my attention but discreet enough to avoid notice. It carried an unspoken reprimand, yet the touch sent a sudden, searing warmth spiraling up my leg, settling somewhere beneath my ribs. My lips twitched in betrayal, fighting the urge to grin, but the trace of heat lingered, an uninvited thrill that tangled with the moment.

"Nienna, Clay's heart isn't as young as it used to be. Have mercy on the poor man," Gayle chided, mirth shaking her shoulders as she placed a hand on her husband's arm.

Claydon spun toward her, feigning insult. "Are you implying I'm old?"

"And aging like a fine wine, dear."

The table dissolved into laughter. I glanced around, soaking in the scene. Tipo and Poppy murmured in a world of their own, their foreheads nearly touching. Greaves chuckled beside me, his voice a low rumble. Will busied himself tidying the remnants of our meal, interjecting the occasional remark.

"Now, speaking of age—I'd hate to be a terrible host." Gayle rose, brushing imaginary crumbs from her lap. "As much as I'd love to linger, it's been a long day for all of us, and an even longer one for you three."

Claydon stood, offering her his hand as she said, "I'll take the princess to her room."

I glanced at Kallias who studied me with hooded eyes. My heart pounded, and my ears burned at the intensity of his gaze.

"Shall I assist you, Your Highness?" Poppy asked, perking up from her chair.

"Please no," I managed through a strained laugh. "I can manage tonight."

The prospect of quiet solitude had nothing to do with the hope that the king might find his way to my chambers later. Not at all.

"If you need anything, ring the bell, and I'll be there in a flash!" Poppy settled back into her seat, eyes sparkling with readiness.

Kallias stood, stretching his body, every movement deliberate, a display of controlled strength. My throat dried as his crooked smile held my gaze. He saw me watching, lusting after him, and reveled in it.

Behind me, he slid my chair back, his thumb grazing the bare skin of my shoulder. A shiver ran down my spine at the contact. Tilting my head, I caught his eye and smirked. His gaze lingered on my face, then dropped lower, tracing the curve of my chest.

"Thank you," I murmured, my voice silkier than intended. Did I arch slightly, offering him a better view? Maybe.

His throat bobbed. Satisfied, I lowered my head, letting my hair shield the grin tugging at my lips. There was power in being desired, and even more in knowing the desire came from a king.

Claydon's voice broke the moment. "Greaves, I've a few blades to show you in the morning. A blacksmith's been tinkering with a new ore. I'd like your opinion on the edges."

He rubbed Gayle's shoulder before stepping away, leaving the room to dissolve into goodbyes and the promise of stolen moments yet to come.

I drifted past Kallias, the heat from his body brushing my arm as I veered toward Gayle.

"With Kallias–"

"Permission," Kallias interrupted, dismissing his guard with a wave. His tone carried an easy authority that made me laugh. "Which I wholeheartedly give. Go, Greaves. I'll manage just fine."

"Kal, there was an assassination attempt," the man groaned, his chair scraping as he stood.

"You come to my table armed?" Claydon's voice was steeped in mock hurt. "Then insinuate I cannot protect my own guests!"

"Triple the guards," Greaves sighed, defeated. "And only the morning."

Gayle slipped her arm through mine, winking as she tugged me out of the room. "Success!" she whispered.

I glanced over my shoulder, catching Kallias watching me. His smoldering gaze and wicked smile promised things I could hardly name before the door clicked shut behind us.

"That was your plan?" I asked, raising a brow.

"Oh yes," she said, nodding. "Greaves deserves a break. He'll worry himself sick over the king, of course, but both men need their space."

"Kallias could order him away."

Gayle hesitated, then smirked knowingly. "And you know this how?"

"If he wanted to," I corrected, cursing the mead that loosened my tongue.

"Peace, child." She patted my hand with a chuckle. "He could, but he wouldn't. Greaves has been by his side since boyhood. He would never dismiss him."

Except when he desired stolen words. Or kisses.

"It's been nearly two years since they've had a reprieve," Gayle mused, leading me through the halls. "This will be good for both of them."

"Kallias takes his duty seriously," I agreed. "As does Greaves."

Her sidelong glance spoke volumes, but she let the comment hang. Silence settled between us, broken only by her quiet humming as we walked. Paintings of vibrant flowers and sweeping mountain sunsets lined the corridor. I paused at one that depicted a cluster of goats nestled in the hills, their shaggy forms almost hidden in the vibrant brushstrokes. Another painting. Another goat.

Laughter bubbled up as realization struck. "They're everywhere," I said, pointing.

Gayle joined in my mirth. "Yes, he truly loves the Kuh'lir."

We turned a corner into a familiar hall, and she opened the door to my chambers.

"It's been a lovely evening," I said. "Thank you for welcoming me into your kitchen."

"You're good for him."

Her quiet words stopped me in my tracks. My heart lurched to my throat, and I fought to paste a smile on my face.

"Come," she said, shutting the door before settling on a sofa. She patted the cushion beside her. "Sit."

Sun above, what had I let slip? Did she know about our feet? Had Greaves told her anything? I shoved my fear deep inside, pushing it away as I sat.

"I'm not sure what you mean," I began, unsure of where this was heading.

Her lips pressed together in a sad smile, her eyes heavy with sorrow. "It's been quite some time since I've seen him that relaxed. You should know something about him."

I opened my mouth to protest, but the words stuck. Whatever she was about to share felt too personal—too familiar, as if she already knew our secrets.

"I saw the way he looks at you. And how you look at him." Her hands, warm and steady, wrapped around my clammy ones. "He hasn't had an easy life. His path has always been hard, and I fear it always will be."

She paused, and the silence between us seemed to grow heavier.

"He was just a boy when his parents died. Barely a man, and the weight of Radaan was thrust upon him. He faced war, but instead of retreating, he rode to the front. He led our people against the Velli for years. A lesser king would have buckled beneath the pressure, but Kallias stood firm in negotiations. He wouldn't bow to Vellos' demands. Some still resent him for that, but he knew what was best for his kingdom."

She paused again, her expression darkening.

"And he did it all with Eldeiade at his back." She wrinkled her nose in disgust.

"You knew her?" I asked, my voice low.

"Unfortunately, yes. And I hid from that vile witch."

I blinked, confusion tightening my features. "What do you mean?"

"She was feared by the people, hated even. Her words were poison. The way she treated the king—it was shameful. We only went to court when Kallias returned, to show him our support. She called him back once a month—and we all understood why. She wanted one thing from him: an heir to use as a weapon against him."

She shook her head, her face tight with distaste.

"And still, he shouldered that burden without complaint. The poor man was broken inside, but he upheld his honor. Every time, he returned to her summons."

Her raw disdain cut through my discomfort. "Why are you telling me this?" I asked.

"Because," she said, tears glimmering in her eyes, "I've never seen him look at anyone the way he looks at you."

"I assure you–"

"Please, let an old woman ramble," she interrupted, her voice firm. "There have been no rumors, worry not. But if he has even the smallest chance at happiness with you, I'll do everything in my power to help."

"I am betrothed to his son." The words tumbled out, jagged and desperate. She couldn't say those things out loud. I couldn't hear them. My ears burned with treason.

She paused, her shoulders sinking under the weight of my denial. "Can it not be rewritten? There's no love between you and Tallon—*that* is no secret."

"No," I said, my voice cold. "The treaty was signed by Nereus, Dragon King of Draconia and King Kallias of the Plentiful Plains. His own blood sealed the oath, promising his son to me."

Her expression dimmed, sorrow etched into her features. Rising, she smoothed her skirts with trembling hands. "Then let me say this. Kallias deserves more than what life has given him. Here, you are free to act as you will—*choose* who you will—and in turn, I will remain silent."

My mouth fell open, but she didn't wait for a reply before sweeping across the room and out the door.

Chapter Thirty-One

KALLIAS

"I'm telling you, the tests show the milk from the Kuh'lir has far more fat than the sheep in the foothills. If you grant me a little more grain, I could make up for it next year in butter! Nienna's a lovely girl."

My eyes snapped open. I squinted at the ceiling of Clay's study. The rough wooden beams crisscrossed above me, contrasting sharply with the solid stone walls. The sight made my head throb a little harder.

"What was that last part?"

"I said I could make up for it in butter."

I raised an eyebrow. His sleeves were rolled up to his elbows, exposing pale, scarred arms inked with blotches. He smiled at me, that pleased, knowing grin of his, his halo of white hair catching the sunlight like a crown.

"No, the other part."

"Oh, I just meant Nienna is quite lovely." He shrugged, his gaze dropping back to the letter he was writing. "She's got her wits about her, that one."

"She's quick," I said, trying to keep my voice neutral.

He was fishing, and we both knew it.

He shifted, his chair creaking as he sighed. "I'm glad she can relax here. She is like you, bearing the burden of her kingdom even as it threatens to crush her. Pity she's bound to your son."

"Pity," I echoed, resting my head against the couch cushion. I drank far too much mead last night. "Pity will save Radaan."

"No, you saved us, Kallias." Clay clicked his tongue, shuffling the papers on his desk. "Her dragons may protect our borders, but you secured them."

I grunted, the familiar bitterness twisting in my chest at the reminder. "The marriage to Tallon secures them. That's all that matters."

Clay's lips pressed into a thin line as he gazed out the window, sunlight illuminating the hard lines of his face. "She'd make a magnificent queen," he murmured.

"Would?" My voice carried an edge, and I leaned forward. "She will."

His gaze grew distant, and he rested his chin on his hand. "She *is* a queen. The kind songs are written about. If only the king would accept her."

I stilled, the air between us heavy with unsaid truths. Clay couldn't be speaking of me. It was Tallon who needed to accept her. Not me. Never me.

"Gayle seems to enjoy her company," I said, the words edged with irritation.

His persistence grated on me. My thoughts already tormented me with images of her—alone in bed, the sheets tangled around her. No guards patrolled our halls. Greaves wasn't here to talk sense into me. That absence had led me here, to Clay's study, where a steaming cup of kahve sat untouched by my side. I needed a distraction, something to pull my mind from her.

"She does!" Clay snapped back to the conversation, swiveling in his chair to face me. His excitement spilled into the air. "In fact, she's organized a Sol dance!"

"Nienna will love that," I murmured, more to myself than him. The Sol dance wasn't just tradition—it was art, raw and untamed. Every movement spoke of passion, like wind bending the treetops or fire licking at dry wood. It had a wild beauty she would admire. She'd relish seeing the mountain folk, learning their culture.

"She's agreed to dance," he added with a sly grin.

I choked on my kahve, the heat burning my throat. "Nienna's *dancing?*" I managed, gripping the mug as if it could steady me.

"Oh, she is quite interested!" Clay said, his words spilling too fast. "Gayle told her you'd teach her the steps. She's never seen it performed–"

"You volunteered me," I accused, the bitterness sharp in my voice.

"Well, my wife and I are far too old to participate!" He waved a hand, dismissing my concerns as if this were the most natural solution in the world.

"Couldn't you have arranged for a proper teacher?"

"You're here. You know the moves."

"I'm the *king*, Clay."

"And what better way to show unity between Draconia and Radaan than having the king and princess share a dance? Tradition, culture, diplomacy—it's perfect!" His voice cracked slightly as he threw his argument down like a gauntlet. His raised eyebrows dared me to object.

"People think you are mad," I said. The kahve scalded as I downed the rest, the burn forcing my thoughts into sharper focus. "But I see through you."

His hand gestured for me to continue, his expression unreadable.

"I know exactly what you're doing."

I had let it slip. Some point either at the palace, or here, he had seen me be too familiar with Nienna. When two people like Gayle and Clay were in love, they could see it everywhere. Matchmakers and the worst of them.

True matchmakers. Not the logical kind that married for convenience or alliance. No, they had the burning, passionate love that was in the storybooks—and so they deemed everyone worthy of such affection.

No matter if they couldn't have it.

"You'll teach her?" His tone left no room for negotiation.

"Do you have a dance instructor hidden somewhere in this manor?" I groaned, pushing to my feet with deliberate slowness.

"Not a chance."

Rolling my shoulders, I winced as tension flared between my shoulder blades. If Nienna wanted this, I wouldn't refuse her. "Did you tell her *how* it's done here?"

"I doubt Gayle went into detail." He covered his mouth with one hand, though his mirth gleamed in his eyes. When his hand dropped, he beamed like a huntsman who just set the perfect trap.

I sighed, placing my empty mug on a side table. The gravity of the moment pressed down on me as I turned for the door. "Meddling old man," I muttered.

When Lady Sol brought Nienna to the ballroom that afternoon, I called on every ounce of composure I had left. Gayle, as always, looked the picture of nobility. Her long dress swept the floor, her silver hair twisted into an elegant braided crown. She moved with the kind of grace that declared her innocence, though I suspected her mischief.

But Nienna?

Restraint, I'd learned, was a muscle—strengthened with practice.

I had never been weaker.

Her golden hair, a shade that caught the light like the first sunlit morning of summer, had been braided with care. Soft tendrils framed her face, curling along her shoulders. A deep blue dress hugged her figure, its sleeveless cut scandalous by Radaanian standards. A sheer shawl draped over her, its fringe swaying with her movements. The hem skimmed the floor, but the front? A tied middle panel revealed breeches that clung to her legs, tucked snugly into black boots.

My wonders of how tight those breeches were answered with every step she took.

I forced my gaze higher as Gayle waved her forward. My jaw tightened, regret sinking like a stone in my stomach. She faced me, her lips curving in a shy, maddening smile, making me teeter between fight and flight.

Logic whispered for me to call her back, to send Nienna away. But I hadn't listened to sense where she was concerned for a long time.

"I hear there's a dance tomorrow night." Her voice, low and warm, curled around me like smoke, stoking heat beneath my skin. She hugged herself, her lashes brushing her cheeks as she peeked up at me. "But I don't know the steps."

"Clay told me you wanted to participate," I said, surprised by the steadiness in my voice. My feet stayed rooted as she inched closer, the distance between us evaporating.

"If I'm able, yes." Her tongue darted out, wetting her lips, which gleamed under the sunlight filtering through the windows. "The people of Sol deserve to see me embracing their culture. Don't you think?"

"They'd be honored simply by your presence." The words tumbled out before I could stop them. Elohios, why couldn't I shut my mouth?

"If you'd prefer not to teach me," she said with feigned innocence, "I could ask a guard–"

"I'll show you how, Nienna." My voice dropped into a growl as I dragged a hand through my hair. The thought of the guards anywhere near her sent a jolt through my chest.

She grinned and a thousand curses bounced around my head, realizing she goaded me into that reaction.

Her eyes wandered the ballroom, lingering on the raised stage, the carved pillars, and the empty rows of chairs, before finally returning to me.

"Shall we?" I extended my hand toward her, palm up, steady and waiting.

Her gaze lingered, brow furrowing as if she weighed the consequences of taking it.

"Sol's people are not formal," I said, my voice quiet but coaxing. "This won't be like the structured dances you're used to."

"Do you think I'll learn it in a single day?" Her laugh, light and nervous, escaped her as she slipped her hand into mine.

Warmth spread where our palms met, her fingers threading through mine with an ease that made me forget to breathe.

Together, we climbed to the stage.

"It's less about the steps and more about the flow of the music," I assured her.

Lifting her hand, I spun her once as she moved onto the platform. A delighted laugh bubbled from her lips as she twirled. I caught her at the waist, her frame aligning perfectly with my hands, a maddening reminder of how well she fit against me in every way.

"Am I following you, or the tune?" Her voice softened as I pulled her close, her smile playing at the edges of her lips. Her gaze drifted, skipping across my face and halting just shy of my mouth.

"Both."

"But there's no music."

"Then follow me."

"Are you going to command me, *King Kallias?*" she teased, her breath brushing my neck as she leaned closer.

"Do you want me to?"

Her lips parted, and sanity frayed at the edges of my control. I spun her away, her fingers still clasped in mine. She extended her arm in a dramatic flare, her movements precise yet fluid. A subtle tug drew her back to me, and I pressed a palm against her stomach.

"The dance... it's intimate," I cautioned, the words heavy with meaning.

Her head dipped in acknowledgment. "Most dances are."

The rhythm of my pulse thundered as I tugged her closer, angling my body. She bit her lip, surrendering to my pull.

"Tell me to stop." I whispered. It was a plea and a prayer, and one only she could answer.

"Never." She pressed her chest flush against me, her heart beating a frantic rhythm. Her legs slid around mine, cradling my thigh between hers. The warmth of her core seared at my skin like a damning brand. Guilt and lust throttled through me.

"Our chests never part," I murmured, the words more breath than sound. "Our hearts move as one."

She nodded, wide-eyed, as I guided her hand to rest on my shoulder, the other held firm in mine.

"It's the legs," I explained, my voice rasping. "That's where the dance lives. The only mistake is stepping on your partner's toes."

"Do you have steel on your boots this time?" she quipped, her smirk as sharp as a blade.

"You couldn't hurt me."

"No?"

Her breath fanned against my ear as she lifted her leg, her boot dragging a slow, deliberate line up my calf. Her knee hooked around my thigh, pulling us even closer until the pressure of her against me wrung a hiss from my throat.

"You sound pained," she murmured, tilting her head to expose her neck, all but begging for my lips.

"There are different kinds of torture—"

I pressed my thigh between hers, her gasp shattering the silence. She stumbled back a step, her body trembling with the tension between us.

"—Some are laced with pleasure."

Her gaze dropped to my feet as we moved through the next steps. I backed her two paces, then shifted the momentum, pulling her toward me. She didn't falter, sliding forward to straddle my thigh once more, her heat igniting a spark within me.

She wanted to be there—pressed against me, letting her body speak louder than words. The realization struck hard. Her desire mirrored mine, raw and unguarded, a sensation that left me dizzy.

I knew the hollow hunger of noblewomen, their eyes devouring power rather than the man behind it. They wanted Radaan's throne, the weight of its crown, not me. Nienna was different. She saw past the title. Without our titles, I would only have to ask and she would have me. Take me not as a burden or with distaste but with vigor.

She adapted quickly, catching my cues and testing boundaries with a confidence that stole my breath. Encouraged by her boldness, I quickened the tempo, leading her across the stage. Her hips dipped with deliberate intent, and I shifted, guiding her to the side. She took the lead for a heartbeat, brushing against me before weaving through my legs. A twirl spun her into position, her thigh pressing firmly against mine.

A grin tugged at my lips as her chest heaved, caught between the mental effort of matching my steps and the physical pull of our closeness. Her body told one story, her mind fought to tell another, and both unraveled beautifully before me.

The ballroom swallowed all other sounds. Only our labored breaths and the occasional scrape of boots on stone broke the stillness. Her foot snagged against mine, and I steadied her, but her other boot betrayed her, sending her sliding between my legs. Her weight threw me off balance, forcing me to stagger as I caught her. In a single movement, I lifted her against my chest. Her hands flew to my shoulders, her breath a shaky gasp against my ear.

"Too quick on your feet," I murmured, her gaze searing into mine. "Slow down. Relish it."

"What if I don't want to?" she shot back, her voice defiant as she pulled free. With a flick of her wrist, she discarded her shawl, tying it low on her hips in one fluid motion.

I flexed my fingers, unable to stop the smirk that crossed my face. "Some things are better when savored."

Her steps were deliberate as she moved toward me, the fringe swaying with each subtle shift. "I'll savor the memory," she whispered. "Let me be consumed."

A growl tore out of me, a low primal approval as I swept her back against my chest. She practically climbed my thigh, wrapping her leg around to tuck me against her. Her lips parted in a breathless gasp and I didn't allow her to catch her breath before I moved her.

Inside, a symphony played. Drums pounded a wild rhythm of need while violins screamed in crescendo, their urgency matched only by the pressure of her body against mine. Her gasps became part of the music, feeding the blaze beneath my skin.

When she spun away, my focus faltered, drawn to the sway of her hips. She matched my tempo as if hearing the same invisible melody, moving with a synchrony that defied reason.

As if we shared the same soul.

She came crashing close, and the music surged to its climax. My hand found her thigh, jerking it to my waist. Her whimper cut through the pounding in my ears as she arched against me. Her hair spilled toward the floor, her back bending with a grace that defied logic. Every part of her leaned into my strength, trusting me to hold her as her chest rose and fell, her hips grinding against my thigh. She offered me everything without hesitation.

I could have taken her—there on the stage, against the wall, anywhere. I wouldn't have needed words. Already, she belonged to me in every way that mattered. She stoked the fire in me, daring it to consume us both. Whatever I gave, she would take and demand more.

But she wasn't mine.

She. Wasn't. Mine.

I tugged her upright, and she wavered before finding her footing. When I let go, her body seemed to protest the loss. Sweat glimmered at her temples, and loose strands clung to her flushed cheeks—a portrait of effort and passion.

"You know the steps," I murmured, my fingers twitching at the loss of contact.

"You'll dance with me?" Her words came in ragged breaths, her chest rising and falling in rhythm with the question.

"If another man dared to try, I'd kill him." My voice dropped to a growl, raw with everything I couldn't express. Every fiber of me burned to pull her close, to let instinct take over, but I held back.

Her blush deepened, the red blooming across her cheeks betraying her attempt to stifle a grin. She knew. She basked in my jealousy, soaking it in like sunlight.

"We might burn Radaan to the ground in the process, but yes, Princess. I'll dance with you."

Dinner with the Sol family felt like stepping into another life. Here, I could almost forget my crown, my title. Nienna's leg curled around mine under the table as she chatted with Gayle about mountain folk fashions. The warmth of her touch made it easy to imagine we were ordinary.

Not a princess promised to another. Not a king who had signed away his own son to her hand. Just two people, ripped from the grip of reality, clinging to a fragile illusion.

But I was too far gone. Our hearts were too tangled.

Her laughter rang out, unguarded. Golden hair spilled over her shoulders, free of royal pretense. The simple dress she wore carried no embroidery, no jewels—just her. She looked as if she belonged to another world, one that didn't care for crowns or courts.

Our eyes caught—hers, gleaming with quiet joy. The subtle shift of her calf against mine made my heart lurch. Her touch was a silent plea, tugging me closer, tethering me to the moment. I eased my leg against hers, giving in.

We were a tangle of contradictions, our lives as entwined as our legs underneath the table. Our secrets lay hidden there too, just beneath the surface, waiting to rise and destroy us.

This couldn't last.

But for now, I would savor every second.

The following morning, the Sols led the way to the manor's only other entrance. Nienna's fingers tightened around my arm as Greaves trailed behind, a new blade strapped to his chest. He looked content, his usual restlessness replaced by the calm of his task.

He had returned by midday and, as we prepared for dinner, he rambled on about ore and blacksmiths. I listened with half an ear, more focused on him than the heat building inside me from the proximity to Nienna. It was difficult to keep my attention elsewhere.

Somewhere between his eager talk, I'd agreed to buy some of the ore for the palace blacksmith's use.

The massive doors to the manor groaned open. They were towering, thick as a man's chest, reaching from the vaulted ceiling to the stone floor. Four guards strained against their weight, pushing them apart. Sunshine flooded the courtyard, making Clay and his wife stand a little straighter.

Nienna stiffened beside me, her hand clutching my arm. I placed my own hand over hers, holding tight, feeling the tremble in her fingers. She was leaving the manor's safety behind. In public, she wore a mask—a role she played well.

"You're safe," I murmured, my eyes on the guards but my words for her alone.

"From the people, yes." Her breath hitched, her gaze fixed ahead on the bright courtyard. "It's you I'm worried about."

I gave a low scoff as the Sols moved along, hand in hand, into the sun's full embrace. "Scared of me?"

"I fear they will see far too much," she answered with a smile, the edges strained.

A smirk tugged at my lips. I lifted my chin, stepping forward as the sunlight bathed us both. It wrapped around me, warm and full of promise—a lover's touch. My body, starved for the sun, opened to it like a plant stretching toward the sky—a blessing from Elohios.

A brief tremor stirred deep inside me. Was I worthy of his blessing? Was I still his chosen? The lies, the deception—they weighed on me. When would I cross the line? Would he take it all back?

Nienna's fingers dug into my arm, grounding me, pulling me into the moment.

That was a problem for another time.

Guards flanked the staircase leading up to the manor. The entrance itself seemed carved from the mountainside, its doors a portal through rock. From the porch, it looked as if the stairwell dropped off into nothingness. Clay and Gayle led the way to the edge, where the narrow stairs curved to the side, too tight for any carriage. Only a stone barricade offered a flimsy guard against the long drop.

But a single misstep from the top and the fall would be fatal.

A gust swept across the mountainside, biting and strong. Nienna didn't falter. She leaned into it, her smile genuine, unshaken.

There it was—my Dragon's Heart.

My attention, however, was more focused on the Sols, making their way down. I feared they might slip, but this was their home. They moved with ease, every step confident. At the base of the stairs, five mules waited, patient and steady.

Their coats were dappled, spotted like stones in a stream, and their ears flicked toward Clay as he called out to them. More sure-footed than horses, they were bred in these mountains. Our own horses could make the journey to Sol, but the risk would be far greater.

"They have such long ears," Nienna murmured, awestruck.

I led her to the white beast. "Never seen a mule before?"

"It's not a horse?" she asked, reaching out to stroke the mule's nose. It snorted, soft and warm, against her palm.

"Crossbreed," I answered, a reminder of her unfamiliarity with this world. "Sired by a donkey, dam's a horse."

I reached down, my hand brushing along her knee before sliding up her calf as she gripped the saddle. She tensed, a sharp breath catching in her throat, but I didn't pull away. With a swift motion, I lifted her, guiding her boot into the stirrup. She steadied herself, the reins slipping through her fingers, her eyes focused on the creature's massive ears, swiveling to track every sound.

"Mules are known for their deft feet!" Clay's voice rang out from his mount beside his wife's.

"And their sour disposition," I added, swinging myself onto a brown-and-white mule. It stiffened under me, as if sensing my words, and I adjusted the reins. Being bucked off here would not end well.

"These were bottle-raised," Gayle said, urging her mount toward the winding pathway. "A mare kept throwing spotted foals, and Clay had to have them."

"It's a rare mutation!"

I chuckled, checking Nienna's seat, making sure she was steady before nudging my mule into motion. I stayed to the outside of the path, putting her safely between me and the mountain. Greaves, no doubt fuming behind me, couldn't understand why I wouldn't let Nienna near the cliff's edge. She was too inexperienced on horseback.

A single wrong move, and a buck would send her tumbling to her death.

The Manor in the Mountains was one of the safest places in Radaan for good reason. The only paths leading to it were through a secured tunnel or a narrow cliff-side trail.

Sol itself was carved into the mountainside, but between the manor and the settlement stretched broad swaths of semi-level ground where the people farmed and raised the Kuh'lir. The area was easily defensible—only approachable over the mountains or up from the foothills, while the Velli side was a sheer rock face.

There was no conquering Sol. Its inhabitants had fought and bled for their land, but their homes and children remained safe throughout the war.

As we neared the slopes, the view of the stronghold vanished. Nienna shifted, her attention torn between the mule beneath her and trying to peer past me toward the valley. The sure-footed mules navigated the steep descent with ease, their ears pricked forward.

When we rounded the outcropping, Nienna's gasp made me smile.

Seeing Sol from the ground was one thing; up close, it was a different world.

The city sprawled across thirteen levels, the lowest still a considerable ride from the base of the foothills. The highest level barely reached halfway to the mountain's peak, leaving room for generations to come.

But the real wonder?

Much of Sol was hidden from view. Built into the mountainside, it was a labyrinth of mining shafts now turned into streets and homes. As miners dug deeper, the city expanded, filling the empty tunnels with life.

The Andeluith, Sol's pride, rose above us. From the outside, it was a dull gray stone, but its inner levels gleamed with white marble, glowing like a pearl beneath the sun. Even from here, I could hear the faint laughter of children and the hum of daily life.

"Behold, the jewel of the mountains!" Clay spread his arm wide, pride shining in his eyes. I couldn't blame him. Sol was a sight to behold.

"It's beautiful!" Nienna's voice trembled with awe as she leaned forward. The mule beneath her balked at the sudden shift, and I snatched the reins, steadying her mount as she gasped, gripping the saddle.

"Remember where you are," I warned.

She shot me an unapologetic glance, but I didn't release my hold until she settled, her weight balanced once more.

"I've never heard of Sol."

"You don't know the districts?" I asked, surprised. She had seemed so prepared when she arrived in Radaan.

"Oh, I read the names," she said, "but how did the books miss the beauty of it?"

I chuckled.

Gayle turned to answer. "We're a private people. Few brave the climb."

"Self-sustaining, dear." Clay corrected with a knowing glance.

"You don't let many up the path through the mountains," I added, drawing out the words.

"It goes through my home—of course not." He scoffed. "They're free to try the passes if they want."

I shifted in my saddle, my eyes tracing the narrow bridges below, where they zigzagged across the gap between the cliffs and the sharp angles leading up the mountain. It wasn't for the faint of heart.

We rode on, Gayle pointing out the flowers growing in the cracks of the rock, while her husband narrated each layer of stone we passed. When we reached the first plateau of sloped grassland, she rode ahead to check on the city's preparations.

"You must see the Kuh'lir!" Clay urged.

It didn't take long before Nienna spotted one.

"By the sea beneath, is it flying?!" She shaded her eyes against the sun, squinting at the steep cliff.

He burst into laughter, his wild mane of frizz bouncing as he shook his head. "Oh no. That's just how good they are at climbing!"

Far up the rock face, a massive golden ram clung to the mountain, its hooves tucked into invisible footholds. It tore off a handful of flowers, swinging its horns our way. Unfazed by our presence, it chewed the plants with slow, deliberate movements.

"That's Er'oer," Clay said, pride lacing his voice. "The largest of our bucks. I'm breeding a line big enough to mount."

"You want to ride them?" I raised an eyebrow. That was a first.

"The Kuh'lir are known for their hair, but *these* could carry a rider into the mountains within a few generations. Imagine it, Kallias," the man twisted in his seat, his eyes gleaming. "A mountain force that could go straight through the peaks!"

"Dragons can fly over."

Clay blinked at Nienna, and I stifled a smile. She knew how to rattle him.

"Yes, well, it would still be an imposing force."

"The larger the goat, the more food for the dragons." She grinned, mischief lighting her eyes. "Please, don't assume I'm opposed to your breeding plan."

He sputtered, grappling for a response. "You think I would let those creatures eat Er'oer's kids?!"

"Onward, Clay." I chuckled, waving him forward. He grumbled under his breath but reluctantly led us on.

"Save your taunts for when we're safe in Sol," I warned Nienna.

She snickered but pressed her lips together, remaining silent.

The path widened as we reached a grassy ledge hemmed in by stone fences. The largest goats I had ever seen lay basking in the sun, some sleeping, others bounding off the steep rock walls. Small barns nestled against the mountainside, and the air was filled with the shrill bleats of the herds.

Commoners paused in their work, bowing as we passed, offering greetings to their lord and king—and eyeing the princess with astonishment, followed by wide smiles. We wound our way to a lower ledge, even larger than the first, thick with green sod.

"How do you grow grass out of rock?" Nienna asked, surveying the second pasture. Here, the goats were smaller, their fur longer and shimmering with health. A spotted buck, its horns as large as my mule's head, stood among a herd of does.

"It's all about the species," Clay said, slowing his mule to ride beside Nienna. "They favor the mountain pastures, but it won't grow in the valley. We redirect the snowmelt, carry the rocky silt up to the ledges." He dismounted and grabbed a handful of the sharp-bladed grass, handing it to her. "Then we seed it, and it grows just like it would in the wild, but in fields."

Nienna ran her finger along the narrow leaves, inspecting them. "Do you supplement their diet?"

"With grain and hay from the valleys, yes." Clay beamed, clearly pleased with her interest. "They stay here because they know they'll get a consistent supply of food, especially in winter."

A loud snort pierced the air, drawing our attention to the herd. The spotted buck, without hesitation, approached a doe. With a quick, assertive motion, he mounted her.

"There he goes!" The man practically cheered as he swung into the saddle.

Nienna tilted her head, studying the scene.

I let out a slow breath. "Clay, maybe it's time to show the princess the nursery?"

"Why? 'Tis nearly empty. The next breeding season's starting."

Nienna spun, eyebrows raised. "It is only natural."

I met her gaze, leaning over my saddle. "And when dragons mate in the skies of Draconia, do all the good folk stop and watch?"

"Yes, actually. It's an exciting day when a dragon takes a mate. Eyes are on the sky, from young to old."

That explained a lot. She'd been raised around creatures that claimed their desires openly. And now, she wanted something—yet couldn't have it.

I shook my head, nudging my mule forward. "Come on, Clay. Your buck can tend his herd another day."

The man sighed but took the lead again, guiding us down the mountain path toward the city. We traveled slowly, taking in the towering cliffs and sweeping views. I clenched my stomach whenever we neared the edges, but I kept my unease hidden. Nienna, however, said nothing.

The fields below, though small compared to the plains, were Sol's treasure. Every inch of land was nurtured—flowers, herbs, crops sprouting from the rock itself. They made the most of what space they could.

As we rounded the final outcropping, the gleaming city reappeared, blinding in the sunlight. White marble stretched as far as I could see. The hooves of our mules struck the cobblestones, catching the attention of the citizens.

Soft cheers rose as we entered, and I straightened. Sol, like Reem, was a place I knew well, where people recognized me. Nienna's sharp eyes darted over the bustling streets, slipping into the shadowed alcoves of shops carved into the mountainside.

Children laughed, darting around us, sketching small bows. Women threw flowers in our path, and men offered respectful salutes. I'd fought beside many of them. They quickly returned to their tasks, but all still wore their swords.

It would take years to undo the marks of war.

We traveled down the tenth main street, and soon Clay led us up a flight of stairs to the eleventh level. Sol was a work of art—every crevice adorned with carvings, ivy etched in sprawling designs, and statues of goats leaping from pillar to pillar.

We continued up, nearing the thirteenth. Workers lived there, but the heart of the city—markets, shops, the dance hall—was at the top.

By midday, the streets buzzed with activity, people finishing errands before the evening's festivities. It was clear Clay had announced my attendance; the air crackled with excitement. Several women curtsied to Nienna, whispering behind their hands. She was a novelty to them, a rare guest in their city. I couldn't predict when she'd come again. Tallon didn't care for the Sol, he favored the plains. Which made his sudden friendliness with the nobles along the Craggs interesting.

We stopped in front of the dance hall. Nienna tilted her head back, eyes wide as she took in the stone eagles perched above the entrance—attached only at their wing tips, a breathtaking feat of engineering. I didn't dare ask Clay about it, or he'd launch into an impassioned speech.

"Milord!" A young boy dashed up, eager to take the reins. "My king!" he called, ducking under the mule's head with a grin.

"Blessings," I greeted, sliding from my saddle. As I reached for Nienna, she dismounted with grace, and I steadied her waist as she found her balance.

"It's beautiful here," she murmured, turning to take in the city, her gaze sweeping over the marble streets.

"She's the pride of the Andeluith," I replied, reluctant to pull my hands from her.

"Sol is a marvel," she said in awe as she approached the doors.

Greaves moved close, and we followed Clay and Nienna inside.

The building was massive, the vast open floor made more impressive by its lack of furniture. A few benches lined the corners, and stone pillars wrapped in living vines supported the roof. Mirrors at the doors and windows bounced light inside, reflecting off crystal and glass chandeliers.

The room dazzled, casting a thousand reflections. It bathed Nienna's midnight blue dress in flickering spots that resembled the stars. She looked around, her lips parted in wonder, marveling at the marble that stretched deep into the mountain. Potted plants dotted the hall, and tapestries depicting lush hills and towering mountains softened the echoes while allowing the music to carry.

Gayle spoke with a musician in a corner while her husband led us to a long table laden with refreshments. The well-off citizens were already gathered, some bowing in my direction, waiting for the signal to approach.

We had barely raised our wineglasses when Clay gave the nod.

Once again, I donned my mask. I wasn't just Kallias now. I was the King of Radaan.

Chapter Thirty-Two

NIENNA

I sensed the shift when Claydon gave the cue. Kallias didn't stiffen, sigh, or draw a deliberate breath. No outward signal marked the change, yet I felt it. The man I knew was gone, replaced by Radaan's king.

A noblewoman brushed past, steering me a step away from him. I allowed it, though every instinct screamed to resist. Here, I was Princess Nienna of Draconia—not the woman who longed for him. For now, I could play the part—until the dance began, at least.

"Greetings, Your Highness. I am Avoth."

"Princess, it's an honor. I'm Luna."

Names and titles whirled around me, as countless faces blurred into a kaleidoscope of fine silks and pinned hair. Their practiced smiles came and went like waves on a shore. Then the commoners trickled in. Worn tunics and patched skirts replaced gilded fabrics, their tired faces a stark contrast to the nobles' polished veneers. Though they'd done their best to tidy up, they stood in the same line to greet us. For this moment, the divide between rich and poor had narrowed. Yet, the furtive glances exchanged across the hall suggested that equality lived only within these walls, and only for tonight.

I kept my composure, relying on years of training to navigate the endless parade of introductions. A noblewoman named Sherry stepped closer, her bright laughter grating on my nerves, but before I had to engage further, Greaves appeared at my side. His subtle gesture drew my attention over my shoulder.

Kallias stood across the room, speaking with a man dressed in fine-embroidered garb. Despite the conversation, his eyes found mine. A flicker of light sparked in their icy blue depths, and warmth bloomed beneath my ribs. My mask almost slipped as a smile tugged at my lips.

How had I let myself drift so far from him?

"The king has summoned me," I announced, inclining my chin toward the four young women circling me like inquisitive hawks. Their questions about Draconia faded into the background as I moved away, not waiting for permission.

Wineglass in hand, I crossed the room to Kallias, straightening my spine and steadying my breath. His gaze caught mine again, roving to my boots before snapping back to the nobleman. A reminder flickered in my mind—not too much wine tonight. The last thing I needed was to lose my balance during the dance.

The setting sun spilled molten gold through the windows, igniting the white walls and polished surfaces. Kallias stood at the center of it all, bathed in an amber glow that made him seem untouchable. Almost.

With a single word, he dismissed the nobleman and crossed the space between us, his hand finding the small of my back. His touch was firm, anchoring, and he turned me away from the throng.

"Are you ready?"

"Are you, dear Kallias?" I whispered, lifting my drink for a final sip, my gaze locking with his. His eyes burned, unrelenting.

"Enough." The word came out rough, nearly a groan. He plucked the cup from my hand and set it aside with a sharp clink. "We will open the dance."

"Do you remember our first?" I murmured as he turned me to face the waiting crowd. People had already parted, as though sensing what was to come.

"I was only a replacement," he said, guiding me to the center of the room. "Tallon should have been there."

The music faded, leaving a charged silence. Conversations dwindled. Even the musicians stood poised, waiting for our signal.

I resisted the urge to bite my lip and instead lifted the front panel of my dress, tying it with deliberate precision. Sol women tucked their dresses into their belts, Gayle had said, though mine wasn't cut for that style. My fingers brushed his chilled gold mantle as I steadied myself, resenting the barrier it placed between his warmth and my touch.

He caught my hand in his, his grip firm but careful, his gaze unwavering. His palm settled low on my hip, tugging me flush against him. The press of him stole my breath, and his thigh slipped between mine with effortless confidence.

His breathing stayed steady, unaffected by the eyes fixed on us. My pulse hammered, my mind racing with fears of missteps and imagined disasters. What if I tripped? Or stepped on his boot? Worse, what if everyone saw the truth etched across my face—that I loved him?

I loved him.

"Peace." His voice rumbled low, pulling my focus to his eyes. His palm slid up my back, spreading warmth through the fabric as he held me closer. "I feel your heart."

But did he hear what it whispered with every frantic beat?

The light caught on strands of silver at his temples, accentuating the weathered creases near his eyes. No longer did I wonder if those lines were carved by smiles—they were etched by sunlight and war. The same silver dusted his scruff, lending an edge to his otherwise polished appearance.

I nodded, unable to find my voice. With him, I was safe. I trusted him.

He drew in a breath, and the musicians responded, launching into a vibrant, pulsing rhythm. Relief coursed through me, loosening the tension in my shoulders. His lips quirked as though he knew, and I wet mine in response.

His thigh pressed between my legs, forcing my retreat. I dragged my boots against the polished floor, hips swaying to match his lead. He pulled me forward, then back again, asking me to follow with a steady rhythm.

A grin teased at my lips, but I refused to let it break through. Instead, I chased his movements with growing confidence.

The dance ignited between us, as fiery as our rehearsals. Heat seeped into the air, thickening with tension after every step. As the music quickened, it urged our pace into a frenzy. When he pivoted, I hooked my leg around his to anchor myself, refusing to lose the solidity of his body.

He hummed, a growl of approval, as he guided me through another set of steps. It felt like a game—a dangerous, intimate game. His movements asked; mine answered. When I spun into his arms, his hips pressed against my backside before he quickly ducked them away, a smirk curling my lips.

The tempo surged, my feet flying to keep up. A misstep faltered my rhythm, but he disguised it with ease, crushing my chest against his. I gasped for air, clinging to him as I regained my footing.

Heat flushed through me, both from exertion and the undeniable pull of desire simmering beneath my skin. How would I walk away from him? How could I possibly go about my night pretending I didn't burn with need? The hunger for him lurked just under the surface, threatening to tear its way out.

The music reached its crescendo, and he flung me out with practiced precision. When I returned, I crashed into his chest, his hand gripping my thigh. His fingers pressed hard enough to leave an impression, and a sharp gasp tore from my lips.

Arching against him as he bent me over, the music faded around us. His thumb brushed the dagger strapped to my leg, and I glanced at Greaves upside down, who arched a brow.

Kallias pulled me upright, slow and deliberate. My hand trailed up his chest, settling beneath the cold chains of his mantle.

When our gazes met, the hunger blazing in his nearly buckled my knees. His jaw flexed as he steadied me, eye twitching as his focus dropped to my mouth.

I turned my head, surveying the room. To my surprise, the crowd had joined us at some point, their dances drawing them into their own private worlds.

Kallias released my thigh with agonizing slowness, his fingers curling against me before falling away. My breath came in shallow, ragged bursts, his tension echoing mine.

Dragons above, how I reveled in the unrestrained lust in his gaze, a fire threatening to burn through his resistance.

"Well done!" Claydon called, his applause crisp and deliberate as he and his wife strode over. Their movements were unhurried but purposeful, hemming us in against the crowd. "I daresay you've set the bar quite high for the night!"

"And to think you didn't know the dance, Princess," Gayle added, her warm gaze gleaming with amusement.

"I had the best teacher," I replied, feeling the heat of Kallias' presence beside me.

His jaw stiffened, and his fingers twitched at his side. The king of Radaan, always stoic and collected, stood unsettled.

By me.

"Will we dance again?" I asked, tilting my head toward him.

"Yes!" Claydon blurted.

"No," Kallias countered in unison.

Gayle chuckled, mirroring my amusement as we studied the two men. The musicians struck up a new rhythm, and Kallias ran a hand through his hair, a rare slip in his composed demeanor.

"I don't have it in me," he admitted.

"Ah, yes. Your journey must have taken its toll," Claydon offered, eager to fill the silence. "Well, do stay to watch! Evett and Miram are here tonight, and they are magnificent—a true spectacle."

We retreated to the edges of the room, wine in hand. The drink offered no relief from the fire smoldering beneath my skin. Kallias and I stood in shared silence, an unspoken tension crackling between us as the evening unfolded.

The sun dipped below the horizon, and lanterns bloomed to life along the walls, casting warm light that scattered in fractured rays across the room. The once-bustling dance floor thinned, leaving only a few couples who moved with the grace of practiced performers. Their steps grew bolder, each motion a challenge, as if daring the others to falter.

The crowd hummed with energy. Some sat in a circle, cheering the last dancing couple. The woman's hair clung to her damp face, her cheeks flushed from exertion. Her partner's temples glistened with sweat, yet both wore triumphant smiles. They bowed to the applause, fingers interlocked, before the musicians teased them with a playful refrain, urging them into one final movement.

She leaned into him, her lips curving into a coy smile, and he sighed with a mirthful smirk, waving toward the players in surrender.

This moment was unlike the others. While Kallias and I had begun the night in a frenzied rush, this pair moved with deliberate intimacy. Each step was a seduction, every motion a silent promise. He skimmed his hand along her arm, withdrawing just before their bodies met. When she raised her leg for him to grasp, the act was languid, a slow drag that left the air charged.

My cheeks heated, and I swallowed a sip of wine, averting my gaze. Watching them seemed intrusive, as though I had stumbled into a private moment, where passion mingled with restraint.

It was a game of hot and cold. Give and take. Of secrets and truths.

Of Kallias and I.

I stole a glance at him. He stood rigid, his left hand resting on his belt, the other gripping his untouched wine. His eyes, shadowed and intent, never wavered from the couple. A muscle ticked in his jaw, and the faint scruff along his face glinted in the lantern glow.

Speckles of light danced over his mantle, and I caught my reflection in the brilliant gold. A princess who loved a king. A king bound by a blood oath. Two lovers tangled in a web. It was forbidden.

And I never wanted anything more.

Darkness wrapped everything in its embrace as we rode back to the manor. The hour hung between night and dawn, the world snared in an uneasy stillness. Crickets had fallen silent, and the birds had yet to stir. It was the quiet moment when even Radaan seemed to hold her breath, waiting to see if the sun would rise again.

When we arrived, the Sols slipped away, exhaustion evident in their brisk goodbyes. Gayle cast a sly smile in my direction, and Claydon raised his brows at the king, a silent exchange that left me smirking.

Enablers, the both of them.

"I've got her, Greaves," Kallias rasped, his voice rough with fatigue.

The guard snorted. "Who's got you?"

I caught the faintest flicker of amusement on his face. His raised brows, etched into his weathered forehead, spoke volumes.

Kallias' gaze softened before he straightened with a shrug. "I can manage."

Greaves gave a derisive huff, his palms lifted in mock surrender. "Just don't get yourself killed—or worse."

Kallias leveled a glare at him. I bit back a laugh, the tension between them lightened by familiarity. Shaking his head, the guard muttered under his breath as he disappeared into the shadows of the corridor.

The silence deepened once he was gone, leaving us alone. No servants bustled through the halls, no echoes betrayed prying ears. Only dim lanterns broke the gloom.

"Tired?" Kallias asked, his voice low.

A thrumming energy coursed through me, a restless spark I couldn't quite name. "Not at all."

His chuckle reverberated through the quiet. His elbow pressed my hand against his side, and he led me forward. "Then come with me."

The manor's darkened halls stretched ahead, their walls a blur as my focus narrowed to the warmth of his arm beneath my palm. Faint, flickering lanterns cast fleeting shadows across statues and paintings, their details lost in the gravity of his presence.

We passed my rooms, heading deeper into the estate. Questions stirred, each step tightening a knot of nerves. Was he leading me to his chambers? The thought sent a jolt through me, but before I could voice it, we rounded a corner—and my breath caught.

The corridor opened into an expanse alive with greenery. Stone tiles gave way to soft moss underfoot, its lush texture absorbing the sound of our steps. Shrubs and flowers spilled over pathways, and trees—some slender, others towering—reached toward a ceiling of glass.

Moonlight poured through the panes, painting the garden in a silvery glow. Shadows mingled with soft light, and the space seemed to stretch. Foliage obscured the far wall, creating the illusion of a boundless forest.

"The gardens," Kallias said, his deep voice reverent.

"One would think gardens belonged outside," I murmured, laughter slipping out as I moved forward, my hand sliding free of his.

"They wouldn't survive the Kuh'lir."

Trailing my fingers along a massive leaf, I marveled at its size—as broad as a dragon's claw. These plants seemed foreign, more suited to the southern lowlands than the cold heights of the mountains. Warmth lingered in the air, a product of sunlight trapped by the glass ceiling, nurturing the lush array of life within.

A blossom the size of my head drew me closer. Its pristine white petals—like silk beneath my touch. Its sweet fragrance mingled with the earthy scent of moss and stone. I could almost believe we stood in the heart of a wild forest, far from the confines of the manor.

"Moonstar. It blooms at night." His voice came from behind me, warm and close, though he didn't touch me.

"It's beautiful."

"It pales in comparison to you."

A shiver curled through me, and the sudden rush of butterflies in my stomach felt more like a storm than a flutter. My breath hitched, throat dry as my heart stumbled over itself.

The world outside the glass garden had vanished. No people, no noise, just moonlight and shadows. He and I stood cloaked in this hidden space, lost in the quiet companionship of flowers and stars.

His hand grazed my side, light as the whisper of wind. "Come," he murmured near my ear, his breath a soft tickle before he stepped away.

My chest tightened as I fought to reclaim my composure. Each step he took down the mossy path seemed to pull me with invisible threads, his silhouette commanding under the silver glow of the moon. How far would I go tonight? How far would he allow?

And what boundaries would I dare to test?

The soft rays of moonlight caught his mantle in brief gaps between the trees, reminding me he was not just Kallias. He still shouldered his nation, and yet he was sharing this moment with me.

My mouth went dry as I stared at his body. He moved with such power and grace. He carried himself unlike any other man I had met. Strength coiled with every step, his shoulders softly rocking with his strides.

The path opened to a clearing bathed in cool light. Glass panels arched overhead, framing the stars, while the ground, covered in moss, cradled a small pond. Purple spires of flowers swayed alongside delicate lilies, their petals glowing like fragile cups of light.

Kallias paused, sinking to the earth, his mantle shifting with the movement. One leg stretched out, the other bent, his arm draped across his knee. The moon's silver glow caught his face, softening the sharp lines and the tension he carried.

Exhilaration rushed through me. A king was at my knees.

I sank down beside him, my thigh brushing his. We turned to the stars that winked down at us. They seemed to laugh at how close we were, and yet so far. It clawed at my heart, tearing pieces from it. Wanton desire mixed with a sense of duty and loyalty.

"Do you ever dream of being a common man?" The words slipped out, softer than I'd intended.

He didn't answer at first. The stillness stretched, his gaze fixed on the stars as though they held the answers.

"I think it best not to dwell on what can't be." His voice carried a soft resignation. "I was born a prince, destined to be king. Just as you are a princess who will one day be queen."

"But not yours."

His breath caught.

"No."

The quiet honesty of the word gutted me, even though I'd expected it. A lump clogged my throat, and I blinked hard against the blur of stars overhead.

"Do you have regrets?" My voice wavered, but I couldn't bring myself to face him.

"Many," he said at last, his tone rough with something unspoken. "But you are not one of them."

I turned to him, searching his profile for the truth behind the words. His jaw tightened as though holding back more than he'd let escape.

"And you? Do you regret coming to Radaan?"

My lips twitched into a bitter smile. "My only regret is settling for the prince when I could have had the king."

His mantle caught my eye, glinting. My hand lifted, fingers brushing the intricate links. His gaze dropped, tracking the motion.

"I would not have taken another bride," he muttered, his voice laced with bitterness. "I've been down that road. It's a miserable affair."

"With the wrong person."

His eyes snapped to mine, piercing and unyielding. "Sometimes, we don't get the person we want."

A single link fell free beneath my fingers, the quiet sound like a challenge to the silence between us.

His breath came measured, deliberate, though his nostrils flared as I undid another link. Chain by chain, I peeled the weight from his shoulders, freeing him from his obligation piece by piece.

The mantle clanked against the moss as I set it down, ringing in accusation, calling out for him to put a stop to this. It was heavier than I'd expected. It wasn't just gold, but something far more profound—the yoke of his duty, the burden of a kingdom. My hands trembled as I turned back to him, my chest tight with emotion.

What I wanted, the king of Radaan couldn't give.

He let me struggle with it, either unable to relieve himself of the yoke, or needing to see me take it from him. My fingers twisted in my skirt as I fought to steady them, his quiet focus never leaving me.

"Kiss me."

His eyelids fell shut, his face screwed in anguish. The line of his jaw twinged, as though he were wrestling an internal battle.

When those cornflower blue eyes returned to mine, something broke in him. I knew I had won.

He reached for me, his hand warm as it tangled in the hair at the nape of my neck, drawing me closer. I melted into him, our lips brushing in a kiss so tender it ached. This was not the desperate, consuming heat we had shared before. This was sorrow incarnate—a language of everything unsaid and every promise we could never keep.

He pulled me down, the soft press of the earth at my back as he curled beside me, leaning over me like a shield. His lips hovered, warm and hesitant, brushing mine with a question and a plea. His breath, spiced with wine, fanned over my face as his mouth trailed over my cheek, pausing to capture a tear sliding free.

Anger burned, hot and wild. This wasn't fair. We weren't fair. My fingers trembled as they fumbled for the buttons of his overcoat. One by one, they gave way, releasing the tension beneath my touch. His lips found mine again, this time firmer, hungrier, as though answering the fury in my grasp.

I tugged the hem of his tunic free, and his breath hitched as I slid my palms underneath, pressing against bare, taut skin. His muscles tensed, his body betraying him even as his mind resisted. He froze, shivering when I moved my hands higher, tracing the ridges of his stomach.

Breaking the kiss, his head fell forward, forehead brushing mine as his breaths came in shallow bursts. He trembled above me, his restraint pressing down like an unspoken force.

His fear struck me harder than words ever could. The king of Radaan, a man forged in fire and battle, was terrified—of me. My heart shattered under the realization.

Eldeiade's cruelty ran deep. I hated her with every fiber of my being. How could I fix what she had broken? I couldn't be his queen, could never right her wrongs.

I pushed against his chest, and his startled gaze locked with mine. Pain flickered there, raw and unguarded, but he allowed me to strip away his tunic and overcoat.

Kallias kneeled before me, bare to the moonlight, his hands braced on his thighs. Shadows softened his form, but the power in his frame was unmistakable. Light hairs scattered across his chest, rising and falling with his uneven breaths. My eyes wandered lower, tracing the hard planes of his abdomen, the dip of strength along his sides, and the trail of dark hair that disappeared beneath his belt.

He tensed, and I looked up, meeting the vulnerability in his gaze. I despised the doubt I found there, the fear that I might push him away. Reaching out, I pressed a hand to his chest, urging him back until he lay under me. His hands clung to my waist, and when I tried to pry them off, he shook his head.

"Let me touch you." The plea was husky with need.

"I'm not going anywhere, Kallias," I murmured, leaning forward, settling my weight along his hips.

"Elohios, spare me."

He groaned, a low, guttural sound that stirred something primal within me. I kissed the edge of his jaw, trailing downward to his chest, tasting the salt of my own tears mingled with the faint musk of his skin.

"Grant me strength," he pleaded through clenched teeth.

I smirked. "Oh, he already did that."

Beneath me, his body quivered, every muscle wound tight, as though bracing against the pull of what he wanted but couldn't take. His fingers dug into my sides, as if he feared to move them.

When I reached for his belt, his hand caught my wrist in a grip that bordered on bruising. His breaths came in pants, and he arched into my touch, his body demanding I continue—but passion hadn't clouded all of his sense. His voice was hoarse, trembling on the edge of control. "No."

The word cut deeper than I expected, and when I glanced up, fear shadowed his features.

"I'm not her, Kallias," I whispered. "I would never hurt you. Not now. Not ever."

His eyes closed as if he were praying for strength, but when he looked at me again, his expression hardened. "That is why it cannot be."

I wasn't his queen.

I would belong to Tallon.

Fury surged through me, sharp and blistering, clearing the haze of desire clouding my mind. I could no longer stomach the thought of lying with him. Duty or not, there would be no bed shared with the prince. If I had to, I would fight him off with a knife or a dragon—but I would not let him defile me. A ceremony would bind our hands together, but my heart—and my body—would never be his.

"Take me."

"I cannot!" His voice broke, desperate, as he tried to pull away.

I grasped his belt, fingers digging into the leather. "I will have no other as my first, Kallias. You were my first kiss."

He pried my hand off, a twitch of pain flickering in his eyes. He shoved me with gentle force, rising to his knees, wincing as his body shifted. His mouth pressed to my forehead—tender, chaste—and a wave of sorrow swept through me.

"And you will be my last." His voice trembled as he lifted my chin, his lips meeting mine with a quiet finality. "But I cannot be that for you."

A dagger of anguish pierced through me. Why couldn't I have just one more stolen moment with him? His refusal twisted inside me, sharper than any wound. My chest hollowed as I struggled for breath, the weight of it suffocating. I wanted to scream, tear out my hair. This wasn't how my life was supposed to unfold.

"You would have me return to the palace," I spat, fury rising within, "and spread my legs for your son–"

"No!" His roar cracked through the night, making me flinch. "I would have you feed your people! Secure peace for Radaan!" His voice broke, his hands curling into fists. "Do you think this is easy for me? That I don't burn for you every moment, knowing I can never have you?"

"Then do not let him take me!" I choked out, the words trembling with desperation. "Write my father–"

"Yes, I'll write your *father*, Dragon King of Draconia, and tell him that after swearing my blood-oath to protect his daughter, after promising my son would marry her, I've changed my mind and want her in my bed instead."

"It would be the truth."

He choked out a bitter laugh, raking a hand through his hair in frustration. "You're not helping." With a quick, sharp movement, he shot to his feet and grabbed his tunic. "What do you think your father would do?"

I already knew the answer. That's why I'd never dared mention it. Kallias had given his word—sealed it with blood and his signet. His promise was a binding oath, one that tied his people to him. To go back now would break Draconia's trust, and it would bring dragonfire down on Radaan.

And if my father discovered our deceit—if he learned I had kissed and nearly lain with a man when I was promised to another? As both a parent and a king, he wouldn't rest until he shed blood.

"There's your answer, Nienna," Kallias said, pulling his tunic over his head. "That's why I cannot write him. No matter how badly I want you, I can't have you. You'll marry Tallon, bring your dragons, and provide for your people."

Tears blurred my vision "I don't love him."

"I know," he said, his voice tinged with something more than regret. "But you don't have to love someone to wed them."

Silence fell between us, heavy and suffocating. I wanted to scream, to claw at the injustice that had woven itself into the fabric of our lives. Instead, I whispered, "How can I marry someone when my heart belongs to another?"

He froze, his words brittle. "You don't love me, Nienna. You cannot."

The force of his denial crushed my chest, and tears seared icy paths down my cheeks. I clenched my fists, forcing myself to breathe through the ache.

"Tell that to my heart, Kallias!" My voice cracked as I hauled myself upright. He extended a hand, but I refused it, stepping back as though his touch might shatter me completely. "Tell that to my soul when you're the first thing I think of when I wake. When I look for you throughout the day just hoping for a glimpse of your mantle. Tell me that when I lie awake at night, consumed by a fire only you could quench."

The words tumbled out, raw and unforgiving, as I swiped furiously at my tears. I despised the way he stood there, fists tight at his sides, his restraint as unyielding as the chains of his duty.

"You don't get to tell me who I can love," I said, my voice trembling with defiance. "My heart is mine to give."

Turning away, I dragged each step down the moonlit path, the foliage dissolving into a blur around me.

Just before the darkness swallowed me, I whispered to the night, "And it's yours to break."

Chapter Thirty-Three

KALLIAS

My jaw throbbed from clenching too often. Every time Nienna crossed my path, I swallowed my emotions like bitter poison. The maddening urge to seize her, to tell her everything had been a mistake, clawed at me. I wanted to spirit her away, far from duty and consequence.

But there was no escape.

I was a widowed king. She, a princess, promised to my son. Her father was a man of ferocious love and boundless rage. To suggest a change to the alliance would do more than stain my honor. It was a direct act of war that would risk dragonfire.

Disgust coiled in my stomach. I dragged a hand down my face, my fingers digging into my eyes as though I could rub away the shame. What kind of man would allow his daughter to marry someone twice her age? Worse, she had been here for weeks—enough time for a predator to circle, exploiting her innocence and naivety.

That predator was me.

A monster.

Lusting after her.

Elohios must have turned his blessing from me long ago. Perhaps this was some cruel test from the gods, one I had already failed.

Guilt gnawed at me, unraveling what little remained of my sanity. Stolen moments weren't worth the damage they caused, and yet, when she passed me in the halls? The rejection in her eyes splintered what was left of my heart.

She treated me with deliberate indifference, cold as frost on glass. Even Clay and Gayle noticed it the next morning at breakfast.

Our legs stayed tucked beneath our chairs, the space between us never crossed. She angled herself just enough to avoid seeing me without effort.

And she succeeded.

The absence of her attention consumed me in ways I hadn't imagined possible. I thought I cherished her company before, but now her memory haunted me. Dreams of her depthless eyes, hair spun gold, and those rare, radiant smiles filled my nights.

My soul yearned for her gaze to meet mine again. One more smile. One more touch.

I needed it like I needed physical food.

A deep breath stretched the ache in my chest as I leaned forward, bracing my elbows on my knees, hands folded against my mouth. The library floor, scarred and worn, offered no answers.

She was in pain. I could see it in her face, raw and unshielded when she thought nobody watched. She played her role, crafting the polished smile of a princess, but it never touched her eyes. I wanted to punish whoever hurt her. I craved their blood on my hands.

But I was to blame.

When had I started to mislead her? At our first dance, when I downed a glass of wine for courage? Or earlier, when I let her kiss me instead of Tallon?

The memory of fire blazed to life—the heat of her magic searing the air. It burned, a miracle it hadn't set the palace aflame.

It was also a vivid reminder of my end if her father ever learned what passed between us.

"I don't think it warrants a sigh like that."

Clay's voice cut through the haze of my thoughts. My gaze drifted upward to find him at his desk, a faint frown creasing his brow. I did not respond, didn't even shift. Every nerve in me screamed to rage, to storm through the halls, to pull Nienna into my arms and beg her forgiveness—to take her to my bed and atone in ways that words never could.

Instead, I froze. My control felt thin, brittle. Trusting my voice or my body would lead to disaster.

"Really, the production of my milk goats hardly deserves such a dour expression."

His taunt swept past me, faint as a breeze against stone. My eyes dropped to the worn floorboards, though my thoughts turned inward, unspooling the chaos I made of my life. There was no salvaging it. The only path left led forward into a pit of my own making.

Forgiveness from her was a dream. I could only hope for absolution from the gods—and that my people never uncovered the truth.

There would be nothing more between us. No stolen moments. No hushed confessions on shadowed balconies. I ended it, told her I couldn't give her anything else.

What arrogance made me think she wouldn't want more?

I did. The longing gnawed at me. If it consumed me like this, how much worse must it burn for her? I fed her fire with secret kisses and touches, stringing her along for nothing more than my selfish desires.

Now she would despise me. Between her disdain and Tallon's wrath, the palace might as well become a battlefield.

Tallon. Gods, if he found out.

A sharp pang struck my chest. He opposed the alliance from the beginning, scorning Draconia and my plans for peace. Suspicion burned behind his narrowed gaze, his mind churning with doubt.

He'd accused me outright of bedding her, though he had no proof.

Clay and Gayle had their suspicions, but only Greaves saw the truth. The Sol dance—a tradition meant to symbolize unity—had been nothing more than an innocent cultural exchange. Or so I tried to tell myself.

The signs were obvious. Too obvious. Even Darius noticed something amiss. Tallon's accusations lingered, waiting for the slightest spark to ignite into fury.

Greaves remained loyal, but all it would take was one word from Nienna, intentional or not.

Frustration surged, hot and unwieldy. A guttural groan escaped as I shoved my hands into my hair, yanking at the roots in an attempt to drown out my spiraling thoughts.

"Wigs!" Clay exclaimed, his voice bright with sudden inspiration. He snapped his fingers. "The Kuh'lir's hair—it's perfect! The way you're pulling yours out, you could be the first customer! Start a new trend. Help a friend out."

"Stop." My tone dropped to a low warning.

"Is that what she said?"

My control shattered. "No more!" I lurched to my feet, fury uncoiling like a serpent. "You and your meddling have done enough damage. When I tell you to stop, I expect you to heed your king's command and close your withering mouth!"

The words flew out before I could pull them back. My anger spilled over, reckless and misdirected. It wasn't Clay who deserved my wrath. It was me.

He leaned in his chair, his expression unreadable. When he set his quill down with deliberate care, he folded his hands over his knee.

Silence stretched between us like a taut string before he spoke. "Apologies, Your Majesty. I meant no insult."

Liar.

The stiffness in Clay's apology stoked the fire already raging inside me. His lie mirrored my own. I lived as a fraud—pretending to be a noble king while slipping through shadows to meet Nienna. Feigning fatherly concern while my actions desecrated the honor of my son's betrothed.

I pivoted, teeth bared in a snarl—and locked eyes with Greaves. His glare struck with the force of a slap.

A growl escaped as I stormed past him. "Yes, I know. Such a disappointment."

"Kallias–"

Clay's protest was cut short by a bellow of a horn. The deep, mournful note swept over the mountainside, reverberating through stone and marrow. We froze, the breath stolen from the room.

Dread crept in, cold as a knife pressed to the skin. The echoes lingered, each one promising death.

Elohios.

The horn blared again. Clay shot to his feet, the room erupting into chaos.

"I didn't know!" His voice strained to rise above the relentless blast.

Greaves closed the space between us in an instant, gripping my arm. "Call for the Threshers!"

"They'll never make it in time." My words emerged steady, unnatural calm overtaking the storm within me.

"They're nothing but whispers now!" Clay's disbelief spilled out as he jogged over. "Scattered sightings in the Craggs—they haven't crossed the Andeluith in decades!"

The horn's cry faded, leaving a suffocating stillness in its wake.

"Ready what soldiers you can," I ordered, swallowing the bile that rose with my fear. "I ride within the hour."

Clay clasped my shoulder, its pressure both grounding and infuriating. "Elohios be with you, friend."

I shrugged his hand off and strode toward the door. "He forsook me long ago. We both know that."

The truth settled over me like a shroud. My sins ran too deep, my deceit too entrenched. Now the whole of Radaan would see the cost.

I shoved through the study doors, rounding the corner with determined steps.

Nienna appeared in the corridor, halting when she saw me. Her lips parted, but no words came. Confusion shimmered in her gaze before she blinked it away, locking her emotions behind an unreadable mask.

"What's happening?" she asked, her tone careful, her body pulling back.

"A mammoth has been sighted." I moved past her without pause, boots striking the floor with hard finality.

"He's going to kill it?" she asked.

Clay answered, his words steeped in resignation. "He has no choice. He is the king. The Protector of Radaan, blessed by Elohios."

If only I still held the gods' blessing.

A golden spear thrust toward the heavens, its polished shaft catching the sunlight. The gleaming surface mocked me, its reflection echoing the royal armor I wore.

As I stepped through the manor gates, my stride faltered. Nienna stood at the base of the stairs, her figure framed by the blazing sky. She turned as if sensing me, her hair catching the light and casting her face in a warm glow that made my chest tighten.

Shoving hesitation aside, I gripped the spear tighter, its weight digging into my palm.

Five horses pawed the ground nearby, their bridles jingling. Each mount bore a saddle, ready for its rider: the king of Radaan, Greaves, the lord and lady of the manor—and Nienna.

The thought of her witnessing my failure churned my stomach. It wasn't Radaan's citizens who worried me most. It was her. She would watch me either fight to the death, or be the shame of my people. Somehow that made it worse than my citizens seeing it.

Greaves lingered at my side, his quiet presence unshakable. He strapped the golden plate onto me earlier. It hadn't been worn since the last battle with Vellos. Its weight dragged at my shoulders, every motion chafing at my unworthy body.

"He's slain his share," I overheard Gayle whisper to Nienna as I passed them. "You'll see his blessing for yourself."

Blessing. The word rang hollow in my ears. She wouldn't detect light or divine favor. She would witness my end.

Clinging to what honor remained, I halted before Claydon'sol, standing tall despite the tremor in my spirit. My fist struck my chest with a metallic clang, the sound sharp in the still courtyard. With a low bow, I declared, "The call for aid has been heard. The King of Radaan answers."

"Elohios bless you," he replied, returning the bow.

I climbed into the saddle, resting the spear within reach. Greaves swung up onto his horse beside me, covered in black armor. Always my shadow, even in the midday light.

Before the others settled into their saddles, I guided my mount down the path, leaving them to catch up. My thoughts, unbidden and unwelcome, drifted to Nienna. She sat astride a horse–not a mule–on the narrow trail.

Enough. I shoved the image away, locking it in a mental vault. If I survived, I could worry about her safety then.

This wasn't my first encounter with a mammoth. Six of the beasts had fallen by my blade. The creatures towered above, their tusks as thick as a man's torso and twice as long, bearing a faint resemblance to boars. But their similarity ended with their shape. A mammoth's rage dwarfed any beast's fury.

They didn't just lash out when provoked. They sought life to snuff it out. Villages, forests, even herds of animals—nothing was spared. Once roused, they wouldn't stop until every living thing within reach lay lifeless. It wasn't madness; it was annihilation.

I flexed my hand, glancing down as if I could see the tanned and weathered skin under the gauntlet. Elohios showed his blessing with light. Soldiers had seen firsthand their king glow with the radiance of the sun, blinding the enemy. I fought by that light, used it to my advantage.

But not now.

There would be no radiance. Only a hollow truth. If I failed, it would confirm what I already knew: I was no longer blessed. To live as a king stripped of his god's favor would be a fate worse than death.

Even so, to wish for an end was to surrender Radaan to Tallon. His reckless ambitions would unravel everything. Nienna wasn't bound to him yet; his power had no anchor. Without me, the kingdom would fall into chaos.

Doom pressed in from all sides. There was no victory here, only choices that led to ruin.

The road to the foothills teemed with people. They lined the path, their cheers swelling like a tide that grated against my ears. I urged my horse forward, its hooves skidding on the steep descent. This wasn't the king they welcomed with revelry days ago. That man stayed behind. Now, I was the warrior that would protect them.

My horse's muscles bunched and stretched beneath me as I adjusted the reins, steadying its stride. Foam flecked its neck, streaking through sweat as the foothills drew closer. The sun slanted low, casting long shadows, but there would be no pause until the mammoth fell.

Clay took the lead once we crossed the precarious wooden bridges spanning the land's deep gorges. The structures groaned beneath our mounts, and the wind keened through the narrow ravines. I hated this place. Years ago, it nearly claimed my life during a battle with a Velli. Today, it might claim more than just me.

The mammoth waited somewhere to the south, between us and Reem. It needed to die before it reached the villages.

When the land leveled out, our horses surged into a gallop, hooves pounding the earth as we wove through shallow valleys and twisting roads. The townsfolk here moved with frantic energy, darting toward flimsy shelters. They weren't cradled in the safety of mountains but stranded in the open, vulnerable to the beast's wrath.

We skirted the Andeluith, racing for Lume. Its northern gates stood wide, a silent summons as we thundered through the opening in the oak walls. The streets lay empty, a sanctuary carved from fear.

Our horses heaved for breath by the time we reached the lord's estate. The guards Clay assembled waited outside, their weapons gleaming in the dimming light. As I reined my horse to a stop, the ornate double doors swung open. An elderly man in fine robes emerged, bowing low, with a fist pressed to his chest. I mirrored the gesture, though my thoughts churned with urgency.

"You've called for aid!" My voice cut through the huffing of the horses.

"Beyond the southern gates, Your Majesty!" the man shouted. "A mammoth is tearing through the outlying villages!"

Wasting no time, I spun my horse and signaled Greaves to follow. Hooves hammered the ground as we turned toward the southern road.

"Princess, no!" Gayle's shout broke through the clamor.

A quick glance back showed Nienna pulling hard on her reins, her face pale, her wide eyes betraying panic.

"I've seen dragons dismember–"

"You'll get in his way!" Clay's sharp voice cut her off as her horse shifted beneath her.

I didn't bother trying to dissuade her with reason. Nienna couldn't be scared into submission or cowed by tradition. Telling her the battle would be too bloody or improper would only strengthen her resolve. The only truth that could hold her back was that she might hinder me.

With a final glance, I turned away, leaning low over my horse's neck to spur it into a gallop. The estate vanished behind us, taking Nienna with it.

Greaves remained at my side, his silent loyalty unbroken, but a shadow of doubt followed me. It wasn't the fear of a king losing a princess. It was something deeper, more fragile—the terror of a man leaving the woman he loved behind, knowing he might not return.

Screams reached us before the devastation came into view.

A chorus of terrified cries rose over the treetops, mingling with the thunder of hooves. Two massive draft horses burst from the tree line, their coats lathered in sweat and their eyes wild with panic. They veered, their movements frantic, as if fleeing the shadow of death itself. My horse sidestepped, nostrils flaring at their scent.

Ahead, the village crouched at the forest's fringe, its rooftops quaking from the distant crashes. I whirled my mount around, steering toward the chaos. The edge of the woods loomed in the distance—a battleground I preferred. There, the trees would force the beast to fight not just me, but the forest itself.

The sharp squeal of splitting timbers rent the atmosphere. My horse surged forward at my command, hooves pounding into the earth. A woman stumbled from a side street clutching a crying infant. Two children ran after her, their small legs pumping to keep pace.

"My king!" she shouted, her eyes locking on the green-and-gold banner of Radaan.

I spurred my mount past her, unwilling to waste time. Smoke curled skyward, and the village's cries grew sharper, the clash of collapsing buildings echoing through narrow streets. Anger burned in my chest as I turned toward the destruction, cursing the beast for breaking through the village's heart.

The ground trembled as I rounded another corner, and then I saw it: the mammoth. A living mountain of muscle and rage. Its tusks, red with blood, swept through the ruins, crushing what little remained of the shops and homes. Bodies lay strewn in its wake, some half-buried beneath rubble, others painted in crimson. Flames licked at the skeletal remains of a building, their heat pressing against my face as I rode closer.

The mammoth's sheer size staggered me—a towering behemoth, four wagons wide, its legs thick as tree trunks. Its shadow swallowed the ground. For a fleeting moment, the crushing reality of my mortality shattered my resolve. What was my frail human body against such overwhelming might? But I was King Kallias of the Plentiful Plains. Protector of Radaan. Golden Warrior of Elohios. I would not bow to fear.

I roared, drawing my spear and leveling it beneath my arm.

The beast turned, hooves smashing through rubble as it barreled toward me. Behind me, soldiers fanned out, but none moved to engage. This was my fight. My duty. A boy darted from the debris ahead, his small form scrambling for shelter. The mammoth's head snapped his way, tusks lowering.

I kicked hard, driving my stallion into its path. The beast charged, and the earth quaked. My weapon gleamed in the sunlight as I swung its tip upward. My horse faltered, tripping over splintered wood, and the mammoth crashed into us.

I flew from the saddle, the air stolen from my lungs as I planted my spear in its chest. The beast's bellow shook the sky. My horse's scream ended, a massive hoof crushing its skull. I gripped the weapon, its shaft pressing into my palms as the mammoth charged forward, pulling me with brutal ease. My armor scraped against the ground, every jolt threatening to rip me free.

Pain flared through my body as rubble struck the rim of my pauldron, wrenching my shoulder. With my legs twisted around the spear's shaft, I drove it into the earth. The point sank deeper into the beast's hide, hitting muscle and bone.

The mammoth shrieked, rearing, its massive head swinging. I lost my grip and flew, crashing into a crumbling wall. Wood splintered against my back, and darkness swallowed my vision.

When the world returned, the mammoth's bloodied tusks loomed before me. Its breath came hot and rancid, filling the narrow space. I dove forward, sliding beneath its forelegs. The scent of dirt and sweat clung to its flesh, mingling with the metallic tang of fresh blood.

It wheeled, hooves scattering debris, but I grabbed my weapon. Heat poured over me as the mammoth's chest spilled crimson, hot and sticky, soaking my armor. I wrenched it free, stumbling as the creature recoiled.

I barely wiped my eyes before it lunged. Something stabbed into its shoulder, sending it spinning out of my path. I dropped, narrowly avoiding Greaves' spear shaft as it whizzed by. After I shoved myself upright, I sprinted for the stone well, desperate to get off the ground.

The ruins of a house crumbled beneath my feet as I charged toward the small structure. Grunting, I scrambled up the jagged stones and spun to face the mammoth.

It was already on me, its massive tusk swinging in my direction. I raised my arm, catching the ivory in my elbow. The force wrenched me, pulling me off my feet. I swung my spear into the soft flesh of its snout.

With a deafening roar, it jerked its head, tossing me aside. I slammed into a wooden beam, the impact knocking the air from my lungs. My plate armor dug into my back, sending waves of pain through every inch of me.

Agony ripped through me, my chest arched toward the sky. I gasped for breath, but my body refused to cooperate. Air wouldn't come. Gritting my teeth, I rolled to my stomach. Blood stung my eyes as I blinked, meeting the creature's frenzied gaze.

It pawed the dirt once.

Greaves shouted, charging the beast with swords flashing.

Arrows sank into the thick hide, little more than a nuisance.

The mammoth lowered its head and charged. Scarlet tusks swept aside bodies and rubble. It barreled toward me, and I couldn't move.

Tallon would rule. Radaan needed me. Nienna needed me. I wasn't ready to die.

Air finally rushed into my chest. I twisted and whipped my spear up. It caught in the beast's mouth, grinding against its teeth. The mammoth jerked its head to the side, flinging me.

I crashed into a wall of flesh. A horse backed away, snorting in fear, as I rolled to my back. A soldier's silhouette loomed above me. He raised his bow, terror etched across his face.

A Radaanian soldier who relied on my protection. I protected what was mine.

I struggled to my knees, then hefted my spear. Greaves was behind the mammoth, running toward it. The beast faced me, panting hard, crimson dribbling from its mouth and chest. Elohios had abandoned me. This was my punishment for my sins, and I'd face it.

It shook its head, blood splattering from its tusks.

I pushed to my feet.

We both breathed heavily, knowing one of us wouldn't survive the next clash.

Then, we charged.

The beast screamed as I lunged forward. A heap of smoldering ruin stood between us, and I launched myself up it, propelling into the air.

Light erupted from the cracks in my armor. The mammoth ducked, blinded by the radiance. That brief movement gave me my chance. I slammed my spear into the soft tissue at the base of its skull.

The weapon sank deep into the spine, jarring against the vertebrae. The beast twisted as the shaft drove deeper, past shifting bones. It convulsed, then crashed to the ground. I tightened my grip, refusing to let go.

Short legs buckled beneath its weight. With a groan, the mammoth collapsed. I gave the spear a brutal twist to ensure it was dead. It twitched once, then lay still.

My limbs trembled as I sank to my knees against the rough hide. Armor scraped against wiry hair.

Shaking, I loosened the buckle on my gauntlet, my throat tight as I yanked it off.

Weathered, calloused skin glowed with the light of the sun. Warm. Assuring. A shudder ran through me, and I slumped forward, eyes burning.

"Elohios be glorified," I whispered, tears carving trails through the blood on my face. He had not forsaken me.

Greaves reached me, his hands fumbling at my chestplate. "You did it, Kal. Radaan is safe."

The heavy plate slid off the beast, crashing into a pool of crimson.

Light erupted from my chest, seeping through the layers of padded clothing as if they weren't there.

"Rise, Golden Warrior, Chosen of Elohios." Greaves' words pulled me to my feet. I rose, bracing my boots upon the fallen mammoth, and cheers rose from the crowd.

Civilians and warriors stood side by side. Soldiers pressed their fists over their hearts in salute. Commoners cheered, their cries interspersed with sobs as families clung to each other.

The light beneath my skin flickered once, flaring with power before it blinked out. Just like before. As if nothing had changed. As if the only difference in this fight had been my doubt.

I turned my face to the sky, my soul stretching outward, searching for answers. Had I been forgiven without asking? Had I been shown mercy? The deception of my relationship with Nienna churned in my gut—so vile, so wrong. Yet Elohios had still granted his blessing.

I was the Protector of Radaan. King of the Plentiful Plains. Golden Warrior, chosen by Elohios.

A confused soul.

Chapter Thirty-Four

NIENNA

Watching Kallias ride away, death etched across his face, was unbearable. The day I left home had been easy compared to the raw ache that tore through me when he turned his back, spurred his horse, and vanished into the distance.

My chest burned with loss, shoulders weighed down by dread. Dageel's estate felt suffocating, a silence thick with worry as we waited—listened—for the blare of a horn. A signal that he had slain the beast—or fallen to it.

Gayle sat in the sitting room, the faint creak of the sofa barely audible as she shifted. I remained by the window, staring out at the sprawling green that had swallowed Kallias whole. The absence of my dragons gnawed at me. This was his duty, a trial of kingship, a blessing from a god—but with a dragon at my side, I could have kept him in view.

I could have known.

Whether he was hurt.

Whether he had died.

"He is blessed, Princess," Gayle murmured, her voice heavy with worry. "More than any ruler before him. Elohios will guide him."

"He's still just a man." I whispered. Radaanians had no dragons. No magic. I'd studied the paintings of the mammoths—towering behemoths that would dwarf any human. A king on horseback would barely reach their chest.

"You haven't seen him in battle."

"The soldiers will help him?" I asked, uneasy. Her words carried a gravity that implied everything rested on him.

"No."

I spun toward her, disbelief striking. "You can't be serious."

She stood and crossed over, joining me in the silence. "Princess, your land is far from here. You worship no gods, only dragons. Magic comes from creatures you can see. Here, we have faith in the unseen. Elohios has given Kallias a sign of his blessing—a rare gift. When he fights, he... glows with light that stretches across the Veil."

Her words sank into me like stones into a still pond, unsettling the quiet resolve I clung to. I thought of the countless battles fought without the aid of miracles—wars where strength and steel decided fate. This light, this sign of his god's favor, felt intangible. It was hard to grasp how belief alone could triumph against tooth, claw, and mammoth-sized savagery.

"He has magic?"

"He has faith."

"Does this glow protect him?" I demanded.

"It doesn't offer physical protection." Her eyes softened as she stared at the hills, peaceful on the surface. "But it gives him something greater. It lets him believe in himself."

My hopes crumbled again. How could light defend a warrior? How could it slay a monster?

"Princess, come. Pray with me." Gayle extended her hand. I hesitated, eyes flicking to her palm before turning back to the window. "You will do him no good by watching for his return. But if you seek the gods' favor, they might show mercy."

I clenched my jaw, tears threatening to spill. If Kallias fell, I would be shattered. The alliance rested on his shoulders, and if he faltered, everything would crumble. Tallon's loyalty hung in the balance—would he uphold the union? Would he even marry me and feed my people? Would Radaan survive the reign of a selfish prince?

My heart wouldn't survive Kallias' death.

Her hand, warm and steady, closed around mine. "I'll pray with you."

Her touch anchored me, and she pulled me close. She guided me down the hall, moving with purpose. The walls, sparsely adorned with paintings, seemed cold. This was no palace or mountain manor, but it still tried to appear cultured. I barely noticed the art as we passed.

We stepped into an open space, unguarded by doors. At the far end, an altar stood waiting, the worn path of a thick carpet leading to it. Small replicas of statues from Reem's temples rested beside candles that flickered.

The room was dim, the air heavy with the scent of burning wax. Clay and Dageel kneeled, their heads bowed in reverence. I swallowed my nerves as Gayle led me away from them. Her hand was warm in mine as she lowered herself, settling onto the rug.

I dropped to my knees beside her, my hands folding in my lap. What now? Should I speak? I craned my neck, trying to catch a glimpse of Claydon. His lips twitched, but he remained silent.

"Who do I pray to?" I whispered, my gaze scanning the small figures on the altar.

Gayle's fingers squeezed mine, her touch grounding. "Elohios is the Great Protector. But Veridis, his mate, is the Goddess of Life." Her eyes sparkled. "If you seek his favor, you may want to call upon her. She might soften his heart."

"But what should I say? I haven't memorized the prayers." Frustration soured my stomach. I longed to be with him, not stuck here, hoping unseen powers would heed my plea.

"Speak from within." She released my hand and bowed her head. "No prayer written by others will be as powerful as your own."

I fixed my gaze on the statue, letting the image fill the silence. The sculptor had captured Veridis as a pregnant woman, her rounded belly full with promise. One palm cradled the earth, a sprout breaking free into bloom, while the other seemed poised to bless the unseen. Her face held a serene smile, her eyes warm with an enduring kindness that felt almost foreign.

My breath trembled as I lowered my head.

Veridis, Goddess of Life. It was some sick jest. Talking to myself while Kallias risked his life. *You owe me no allegiance. I am Draconis—But my heart belongs to Radaan.*

I glanced at the statue again, searching its serene expression for meaning, for answers it could not provide. The candlelight flickered against the sculpted features, making them seem alive, though they remained as silent as ever.

A knot of emotion tightened, clogging my throat. Impossible to ignore.

It belongs to Kallias.

Warmth curled around me like an embrace, loosening my shoulders as tears pricked my eyes. I lost everything: my homeland, my people, even Scythe, cut down by hands meant to end me. Draconia starved while Tallon seethed with hatred, his promises a noose ensnaring my neck. Kallias had been my last refuge, and he had pushed me away.

The ache swelled, raw and consuming.

I wiped at the tears carving paths down my cheeks, frustration blooming with each pass of my hand.

Protect him. I cannot stand without him. He shields me, grounds me, keeps the shadows at bay. He... loves me.

The truth struck hard, unraveling in scattered memories: his piercing gaze, his warmth, the unspoken confessions lingering in every touch. Though he had never spoken the words, they clung to the spaces between us.

Veridis, hear my prayer. Protect his life. Don't let him die. Bring him back to m e.

Tears fell unchecked, staining the fabric of my dress.

A faint pressure brushed my shoulders, like the touch of unseen fingers. My eyes flew open, searching the chamber.

Gayle remained kneeling, her posture unbroken. Her husband and Dageel stayed motionless, their foreheads bowed in reverence. The room held no answers, yet the sensation lingered—soft, elusive, impossible to ignore.

Goddess? The faintest breeze brushed my cheek, cool and deliberate, like a whisper against my skin.

Could the gods of Radaan hear a prayer from Draconis lips? I didn't claim to understand their ways or believe they meddled in mortal affairs, but what harm lay in trying?

Veridis, I vow to honor you. As Radaan's queen, I shall proclaim you my goddess and devote my life to preserving yours. I swear to seek your priestesses, follow their wisdom, and guide your people back to your light. Return Kallias to me, and I will serve you as no other queen has.

A tremor of doubt rippled through me, twisting in my gut. What if no one listened? What if the gods were myths, and I whispered into emptiness? But if they were real...

I will complete the celebration of life.

The sacred ceremony Eldeiade left unfinished—the second rite of the Great Hunt. Veridis demanded its completion.

The air shifted. A sudden gust swept through the chamber, far too forceful for a mere draft. Gayle's breath caught as I lifted my gaze to the altar. The flame beside the statue leaped, blazing wild for an instant before softening to a steady glow.

My throat tightened as realization sank in. What had I done?

My words pressed against me, heavy and inescapable.

I had struck a bargain with a goddess.

A horn sounded, sharp and commanding, breaking through my thoughts.

My head snapped up.

A second blast followed, low and resonant. Gayle's face remained calm, though a faint frown tugged at her brow.

The third note rang out. Her lips curved into a quiet smile. "The mammoth has been slain."

"And Kal—the king?" I swallowed hard, forcing his name back down.

A weight settled in my chest as I searched their faces for any sign of hope, but their expressions gave nothing away.

Clay pushed to his feet, his movements slow, deliberate. He offered a hand to Dageel, helping him rise. "One summons the fighters. Two announce victory but warn of injury. Three mean the threat is gone, and the king stands unharmed."

Relief surged through me, leaving my limbs weak. My vision blurred, though no tears fell. I turned toward Veridis' altar and let a silent prayer escape me.

Thank you.

A strange warmth settled over me, as if unseen arms wrapped around my shoulders. The sensation startled me, but my lips lifted in a grin despite my unease. Imagined or not, I wouldn't dismiss Radaan's gods—not after this. Not when Kallias made it out alive.

Gayle struggled to stand. I extended my hand, steadying her as she rose. She accepted it with a motherly pat before linking her arm through mine. Her gaze sparkled with quiet pride. "We'll be there to welcome him."

As we approached the estate's entrance, the energy outside swelled. What had been still and silent now buzzed with life. Voices rose in excited waves, filling the streets with chatter. Children darted between patches of wildflowers, their laughter spilling into the air as they plucked blossoms. Families clung to one another, sharing embraces filled with joy and relief.

Gayle leaned closer, her words nearly drowned by the crowd. "It has been years since the last mammoth. This is more than a victory—it's a reminder. Our king is blessed by the gods."

I clasped my hands, drawing them tight against my chest. My gaze swept southward, pulled by the growing cheers that rippled through the town. My thumb traced restless circles across my palm. Every nerve in me urged me to push forward, to part the crowd and find him.

I needed to see him.

Gayle threaded her arm through mine, offering a firm squeeze. "He will rest here tonight. Tradition dictates the king stays where he slew the mammoth."

My throat tightened, an invisible hand wrapping around my heart crushing it. I struck a bargain with Veridis. There was no turning back. The celebration of life demanded the queen wash the king's blood away. Kallias had made it clear he wanted no more from me than duty, and I would honor that boundary.

Cheers erupted, their jubilance reverberating through the streets. Hooves pounded against cobblestone, the rhythmic clatter quickening the pulse in my veins. Then he appeared.

Kallias.

A sharp inhale escaped me as Gayle clutched my arm, grounding me where I stood.

He looked like a specter from a nightmare, drenched in gore. Blood streaked his face and matted his hair, turning its golden strands into deep mahogany. His tunic stuck to him, soaked and stiff with dried carnage. The gold of his armor caught glimmers of light through streaks of crimson, a haunting contrast. His spear hung at his side, still crusted with violence, ragged bits of flesh clinging to its edge.

Our eyes met.

Cornflower blue, piercing through the horror. My breath hitched. His bloodied brow furrowed, but the intensity softened as his gaze lingered.

"Give him space," Gayle murmured, pulling me toward the edge of the street.

"Why?" The question escaped, though I allowed her to guide me.

Even as he passed, his attention never wavered from mine.

She leaned closer, her voice low. "He's more than a king now—a warrior bound by vengeance and death. Until it's washed away, nothing else exists for him." Her gaze flicked to me, a hint of sympathy in her eyes. "The man you know will return, but not before the blood is gone."

Kallias dismounted with a warrior's grace, his movements deliberate and heavy. The crowd parted in hushed reverence as he ascended the stairs, leaving only the smell of iron and the memory of his unwavering gaze behind.

I bit down on my lip, my eyes locked on him as he ascended the steps. His gait faltered, uneven yet somehow commanding. Each stride carried a predatory grace, marred by exhaustion.

Gayle dipped into a curtsy, tugging me down with her. Across from us, Dageel and Clay bowed low, clearing a path to the estate.

Greaves trailed behind at a measured distance. Blood flecked his face, but his dark armor concealed further gore. His gaze flicked to mine, and his frown deepened.

Kallias reached the top of the stairs and stopped before the doors. Silence swept through the crowd. I peeked up at him, catching his bare hand curled into a tight fist, knuckles white, before relaxing, as if restraining himself from hitting someone... or reaching out.

"You have our eternal gratitude, Golden Warrior of Elohios," Dageel called out, chin still dipped in reverence.

Kallias gave a low grunt, pushing the doors open with a single, forceful motion. Their hinges groaned in protest, the sound loud enough to stir the quiet.

A heavy silence descended, like a thick blanket of fog, and every gaze turned toward the entrance in unison. When Greaves stepped inside, he pulled the doors shut with a firm motion.

"Is he angry?" I whispered, scanning the throng, now chattering with renewed fervor. Clay clapped Dageel on the shoulder, laughter rippling between them.

"Perhaps," Gayle murmured, her sharp eyes studying me. "But not with us—at the circumstances." She let out a shallow sigh, pressing her lips together. "Come. We'll stay in the library until dinner."

The estate entrance loomed ahead, plain and unassuming, yet it felt impenetrable. A pit formed in my stomach. I longed to be close to him but dreaded my possible failure to fulfill my end of the bargain—or worse, that he might mock my attempt.

Dageel swung the doors open, and Gayle led me through the dim corridors, her steps hesitant, her head low, as though treading near a volatile storm.

She paused at a doorway, her hand lingering on the frame. Her face darkened with sorrow, the corners of her mouth pulling taut. After a moment's hesitation, she turned and opened the opposite door.

Sunlight poured into the room, illuminating its cozy interior. A soft sofa rested in the sunbeam, surrounded by bookshelves that stretched along the walls. Dust floated in the golden light, shimmering. Beneath our feet, a thick rug muffled every sound, adding a fragile stillness to the air.

I moved to the window, clasping my hands at my back, the cool glass reflecting a distorted version of the room. Behind me, she lowered herself onto the sofa without a word. My teeth caught on my lip as unease prickled along my skin. She remained here, in the same space, while Greaves, who answered only to his king, stood guard, and Gayle had made it clear she wouldn't interfere.

But where was Kallias? Had he taken the room across the hall? The thought of slipping into his chamber churned in my mind, potential humiliation tightening my throat. Would he turn me away? Would servants whisper?

"Gayle–"

"Nienna–"

I spun, words dying on my tongue as her sharp tone cut through the silence. "Yes?"

She stood again, hands rubbing together in restless loops. Worry etched her face, her mouth tight as though struggling to shape her thoughts. "It's not my place—not at all—and I beg your forgiveness if I overstep." Her grimace deepened before she continued. "Something happened between you two. Anyone with half a brain can see it."

The air hung heavy between us as I pressed my lips together, waiting.

"But he needs you."

My breath hitched. He needed me. Not the court, not a servant—me.

"I would never ask you to do anything against your will," she said, her gaze steady but filled with urgency. "Veridis knows I'd never force you. But if you still care for him—if he'll allow it—Kallias needs you."

"And if he won't?" The question slipped out, sharp and trembling.

"Then he can take it up with his god."

Wrapping my arms around myself, I hugged tight, indecision pressing hard against my ribs. "If someone saw me..." The words faded, too dangerous to complete.

"His guard will keep silent," she assured me. "Greaves is closer to us than any outsider. Betrayal isn't in his nature. I'll make sure no one disturbs this hall tonight."

"But if–"

"I am Gayle'sol of the Andeluith." She dropped her hands, her posture straightening as if claiming an unseen crown. An air of nobility wrapped around her, almost regal, until she ruined the moment with a wink. "None here would dare cross me."

A slow breath escaped me as I steadied myself. "I claimed Veridis."

"I know."

A faint smile tugged at my lips. Tilting my head, I studied her with mock suspicion. "You are far too clever, Gayle'sol."

One brow arched, and she extended her hand. "Being married to Clay, I have to be."

Her fingers felt cool, a soft contrast to the damp heat of mine. She gave a reassuring squeeze before pulling me toward the entrance. My stomach twisted at the thought of sneaking across the corridor—of finding him drenched in blood.

Of washing it away.

Gayle eased the door open and peeked down the hall. A quick nod followed, and she nudged me forward with an impatient push.

"Go. He needs you."

My hand trembled as I raised it to knock.

"No! Inside!" She waved her hands, urging me on.

A glance down the dim corridor revealed nothing but shadows stretching along the walls. Doubt creeped in, but I shoved it down, gripped the handle, and stepped in.

—and immediately collided with Greaves.

I stumbled, gasping as he caught himself on the wood, then slammed the door behind him. His armored bulk loomed, a wall of dark steel and dried blood.

"Princess." His voice grated low, and he lifted a hand, more gesture than apology, as he slid a dagger into its sheath. Red streaks marred his trimmed beard and face.

I pressed myself against the door, trying to shrink beneath his towering presence. Up close, he was a fortress of muscle and steel, a figure I had only seen from a safe distance. The scent of iron and sweat adhered to every inch of him, sharp and suffocating.

His expression softened, the hard angles of his face easing as he dipped his head. Dark eyes, deep and unreadable, swept over me in a slow appraisal before rising to meet mine again. He stayed rooted in place, unmoving, as if deciding what to do with me.

"Please."

The word fell from my lips, stripped of authority. I was not a princess commanding a guard to step aside; it was a plea. I wasn't asking for access to a throne room or a strategic council—I was asking someone to let me at their friend when they were vulnerable.

I stood there, holding my breath, hoping for something—a sign, a shift in his stance. My pulse hammered in my ears, as if the air itself was charged with the depth of my request.

Greaves watched me, his dark eyes unreadable, his posture a wall of uncertainty. Whatever Kallias had shared with him, it must have been enough to make him hesitate. If he knew we had fought, that I might have been part of Kallias' pain, why would he trust me now?

I needed him to trust me.

A slow breath escaped Greaves before he shifted, his heavy boots scraping against the floor as he stepped aside.

My gaze landed on Kallias.

He sat behind a desk, his broad shoulders slumped, legs braced apart as though they anchored him to the earth. One bare hand cradled his bloodstained head, his fingers curling against his temple, nails caked with dried crimson.

His gaze lifted to mine, and something cold and sharp lanced through my chest. Accusation burned there, mingling with wariness. Yet the fatigue in those eyes lingered longer, heavy and haunting, like a storm that never cleared.

The exhaustion in his face carved him into a stranger. This wasn't just a man who had fought the Great Hunt. It was someone who had endured its aftermath, over and over. How many times had he sat here alone, waiting for a reprieve that never came? How often had he scrubbed death from his skin, knowing no one would share the burden?

My feet carried me forward, drawn by an invisible pull.

"I have claimed Veridis," I said, the words rasping through my dry throat. They lingered heavy in the air, unanswered. He didn't flinch, did not blink. His hollow stare followed me, trailing my movements with a numb detachment.

I glanced over my shoulder. Greaves inclined his head once before slipping from the room, the door closing behind him. My chest constricted with the hope he would stand guard, giving us privacy.

Wiping my damp palms against my dress, I took in the quiet of the study. At the room's center, a large tub sat undisturbed, its water still. Beside it, a cloth lay draped over the rim of a wooden bucket, forgotten for now. Sunlight spilled through tall stained glass windows, streaking the bookshelves with vibrant colors. The desk stood solid, its polished surface reflecting the soft light. Everything here felt suspended in time, untouched by the chaos beyond these walls.

I crossed to the tub, filled the bucket, and soaked the cloth. A trail of droplets marked my path as I carried it to Kallias. The quiet tap of water on the floor matched the rhythm of my thoughts. Stopping at his feet, I wrung the fabric, each motion slow and deliberate.

He didn't move. His head in his hand was so unlike him it unnerved me. He was distant.

Blood clung to him like a second skin, a macabre mask. It wasn't just the crimson streaks or the metallic scent of death that filled the room—it was the way he seemed hollow beneath it all.

Kallias, the man I loved, felt impossibly far away.

"How many have you slain?" The question left my lips in a low murmur, the words fragile. Approaching him was no different from stepping toward an angry dragon, every muscle tense with caution.

He didn't reply. My gaze drifted upward, searching his face for an answer that wouldn't come.

Uncertainty gnawed at me. Was his silence anger? Resignation? I hated not knowing and cursed myself for failing to press Fyrn for more details.

Wash the blood off. That was my role. The queen's duty.

My duty.

I shuffled closer, slipping between his legs with measured steps. My focus stayed locked on his face, hunting for any flicker of emotion, any warning that he might push me away. I reached out, the damp cloth trembling in my grasp, and brushed it against his forehead.

His eyes shut, and his brow furrowed into a deep line. Panic rippled through me. I must have done something wrong. I drew back, but his hand shot up, snatching my wrist with a bloody gauntlet. The metal bit into my skin, smearing crimson along my arm.

He didn't open his eyes. His mouth twisted into a grimace, the expression full of unspoken pain.

Then his thumb shifted, drawing slow circles, easing my tension.

Don't stop.

When I returned the cloth to his face, his fingers released me. They fell to his thigh with a muted clink of metal against leather.

It wasn't easy. Blood clung to his hair in matted clumps, dried to the point of near permanence. Mud filled the creases around his ears, blending into the edges of his beard. I worked slowly, each pass dissolving another layer of the grime. His face relaxed bit by bit, the harsh lines easing as the cloth moved across his skin.

A strange sensation settled within as I cleaned him. Watching him hold still, trusting me, filled an emptiness I hadn't realized was there. Stroke by stroke, the barrier between us thinned, as though with each sweep, I was uncovering not just his features but something I'd thought lost.

When his face and hair resembled the man I knew, I stepped back. My hands found my hips as I studied him, chest rising and falling with the effort.

He looked more like Kallias now. And for the first time in what felt like hours, so did I.

"I need your help to get the armor off," I said.

His eyes fluttered open, a twitch passing through his brow.

"Up, my king. I must attend to you—"

He blinked, his gaze heavy with disinterest.

"—It's my duty."

A deep shudder wracked his body, followed by a breath that hissed out through clenched teeth. The wince made my chest tighten, but he slowly rose to his feet.

"I swear, if you're injured under all this grime..." I muttered, fingers already working at the buckles on his pauldrons. My words lacked weight. What could I do? Call a healer and stutter through an explanation of how I knew Kallias was hurt?

The pauldron slid free. I paused, realizing I should've removed the vambraces first. Cursing under my breath, I adjusted my grip and tackled his gauntlet.

His armor was a chore I would gladly leave to Greaves next time. So many buckles, latches, pieces—each more stubborn than the last. Kallias would not assist, no matter how spiteful my complaints were.

Apparently, this was part of the ritual.

I set the pieces aside on the desk, clearing his arms and shoulders. Beneath the armor, the hard padding was soaked with dried blood, stiff against my touch.

"And I suppose you won't help with this, either?" I huffed.

His mouth curled in amusement, a small reward for my persistence.

I gripped the hem of his padded tunic, tugged it free of his belt, and rolled it up. The sight of his muscled abs made my stomach flutter. I squashed them, then pulled it higher. This would only be about washing.

He lifted his hands, wincing with a quiet hiss. Worry snagged at my chest as I stepped closer, ready to help. He doubled over with a low groan, and I seized the opportunity to pull the tunic off. It fell to the floor with a damp slap, blood from the beast still clinging to its fabric.

His face twisted in pain as he straightened. I slipped two fingers into his trousers, earning a startled grunt as I yanked him away from the desk. When he followed, I let go, circling around him with a deliberate step.

A streak of red marred his spine, thick as my hand. It wasn't a cut but a bruise, as though he'd been slammed into a tree. I traced the damaged skin with my finger, my eyes following the map of scars etched across his back and shoulders. He shivered, a small tremor under my touch, and I savored the way he remained still, vulnerable.

A double-edged sword for him.

Satisfied that he wasn't bleeding out and nothing seemed broken, I stepped around him and sank to my knees.

I noticed how his body stiffened, but didn't acknowledge it. Instead, I bent over, reaching for the armor protecting his boots. When my hands encircled his thigh to loosen the cuisses, the room was suffocating, the heat rising with each ripple of his muscles beneath my touch.

He shifted, flexing the muscles under my palms. I paused, my glare meeting his as his darkened gaze locked with mine, crossing the expanse of his muscled stomach.

My fingers slipped on the clasp, frustration tightening my chest. I forced a calm breath. This was my choice. He came back to me, and I would honor that.

The buckle gave way. I exhaled as I set it aside, retrieving the cloth from the bucket. I ignored his unrelenting stare as I rose. Hunger smoldered in his eyes, a reflection of a man starved for something I wouldn't give.

I couldn't. He didn't want that from me.

Water dripped from the scar across his chest, the same one that haunted the sketches I'd made of him. The innocence of those drawings seemed so distant, the contrast stark between then and now. Scythe had been taken. I wasn't the same woman anymore.

I washed the blood and death from him. Each sweep of my hand, every stroke across his skin, brought him closer to me. His back was filthy, and I stroked his broad shoulders, easing the dirt away. When I reached the wound, I was gentle, cautious. He stiffened, but said nothing.

I worked my way to his chest, dragging the cloth below his navel. His stomach clenched, and he held his breath as I lingered. My finger traced the space above his belt buckle, a soft caress that made his hand snap out, closing around my wrist. His grip didn't crush, just prevented me from going further.

The damp rag hung between us, cold against the heat of his skin. I tilted my head back to meet his gaze, inches away. My blood thrummed in my veins, pulsing with the proximity. His jaw flexed, and a smirk crept onto my lips.

There was power in taunting him. A wonderful, awful power.

His grip on my wrist pulled me closer. I stumbled, body pressing against his, hands trapped between us. His gaze never wavered, a storm of conflict swirling behind his eyes—just as fierce as the battle with the mammoth.

Fighting a beast was one thing. Confronting the monster inside was something else entirely.

His head dropped forward, inch by inch, each breath bringing him closer. My heart thundered, desperate and erratic. My breaths quickened, caught in the warmth of his, air brushing my cheek. This time, I wouldn't beg him to kiss me. I would not plead.

But I lacked the will to push him away.

His lips grazed mine, and my legs buckled beneath me.

"Prince Tallon!"

Chapter Thirty-Five

Kallias

Greaves' voice shattered the tense silence, and Nienna's head snapped toward the entrance. I grabbed her arm, yanking her beneath the desk. She stifled a yelp but obeyed, scooting back against the wood's solid support. I slid into the chair, bracketing her between my legs.

The door creaked open, and I fought to keep my rage in check as my son entered, a sneer curling his lip as he flicked a disdainful glance at Greaves. My friend's eyes swept the room over Tallon's shoulder, catching mine. With a subtle nod, he retreated into the hall. I didn't need his assistance to protect Nienna—not this time.

Her hand found my calf, fingers trembling with fear. The pressure of her grip anchored me to the moment, but the fear in her touch stoked the fury still boiling beneath my skin. The urge to shield her was visceral—raw and untamed. It wasn't the careful calculation of a ruler, but the savage instinct of a beast. After the Hunt, I was never in any shape to make logical decisions.

"You look terrible, Father." Tallon's smirk was razor sharp, his eyes flicking to the tub and bucket beside me, his gaze lingering for a beat too long.

Cold water trickled down my leg, pooling in my boot. My eye twitched and I slipped a hand under the desk, waving my fingers in a subtle gesture.

"Careful, Tallon," I warned, my voice low and clipped. "You've never known bloodlust. Choose your words with care."

Nienna shifted between my legs, her shoulder grazing my knee. A cool cloth pressed into my hand, and I lifted it to wipe the sweat from my brow.

Tallon's gaze sharpened on my movements, his smirk vanishing as he sank into a chair. We locked eyes, the air thick with tension. My anger simmered beneath the surface, building with each passing second.

"Why are you here?" I snapped.

He ruined the ceremony, cutting short what should have been a moment of peace. For once, I didn't have to face this alone. Nienna was here, honoring our gods and traditions—her hands steady as she wiped away the blood. With every swipe, she showed me the closeness between life and death, how bloodlust and desire often danced in the same shadows. And then he had to show up. I despised him for it.

If he found her, there would be no stopping him from telling the high court. Her reputation would be in tatters. My own standing would crumble. I'd be forced to send her back to Draconia, away from the mob that would surely come for her. Then the dragons would fly for Radaan, but not in peace—but to lay waste to Reem.

"Didn't miss me?" He chuckled. "I was feeling much better. Thought I'd show the princess around, but it seems I've lost track of her."

When did he arrive? If he already searched for her, he must have come shortly after me—which meant he heard the horns.

"You ask me where she is while I'm in this state?" I leaned over the desk, irritation twisting inside me. The movement pulled my hips further from her, a dark frustration flaring at the separation. "She'd be wise to stay away."

It wasn't a lie. It was foolish to approach me after the Great Hunt. Even the generals knew better than to speak with me after the bloodshed on the battlefield. Men either needed time to recover, or a woman to slate their hunger.

I never had the latter.

"Has she seen you since you arrived?" He scoffed. "I wasn't worried about her attending to you, Father. You look like you've rolled in blood."

"She knows her place. Do you, Tallon?" My voice dropped low. "Yours was at my side. The fact that you're here so soon after the slaying means you were close enough to hear the call for aid. Did you choose to ignore it?"

"I rode as fast as I could. Not all of us can claim glory."

"Perhaps you should aspire for greater things."

"Perhaps I do," he huffed, stubborn. "I've decided to visit Gog."

I leaned back, narrowing my glare. He slouched in the chair, dark hair falling across his forehead. His green eyes flicked away from mine, landing instead on the tub of water beside me. Nienna's grip tightened on my calf, and I scowled at him.

"Why?"

"Verard told me about a horse race. Thought it best to strengthen relations with the districts along the Craggs."

"You avoided the Maize road?" I asked, voice sharp.

It was a direct route. I left him bedridden with alcohol poisoning, the orders clear—no wine while I was gone. Tallon was foolish, immature, but this? Pretending he was on his way to Gog and avoiding a visit here? Even he wasn't that stupid.

No, this was intentional.

"You didn't take the most direct route either. Passing through Phares? Did you have to provoke them so? The letter they sent me was splattered with ink. They were enraged!"

"Tallon." My voice dropped, a low threat that simmered with growing frustration. His games were growing tiresome, and the fury beneath my skin was becoming harder to restrain. Nienna was too close for me to deal with him directly, but later—later there would be time to pry the information out of him or a Verard'gog.

A small hand crept up my thigh, pulling my focus away from Tallon. Nienna's fingers kneaded my leg. The mix of anger and the sudden rush of desire twisted together, a knot of impatience coiling tight.

"I thought you'd appreciate the company." his words dripped with mockery, and he grimaced, crossing his arms as if defensive.

"You come too late," I muttered, covering Nienna's hand with mine, holding it steady. "Mocking Radaan's gods, then telling me you're off to see a nobleman about a race? After your people were slaughtered not an hour's ride away? Tell me why I shouldn't send you through the Craggs to search for the mammoth's young."

"I've failed you yet again," he grumbled, avoiding my eye. "I was told by a servant the princess was down this hall. Thought she might welcome my company. Not many places to hide in a dump like this."

Nienna's nails dug into my leg, her panic palpable. I traced soothing circles over her hand, keeping my gaze fixed on Tallon. Nothing would happen to her—not while I still breathed.

"She won't welcome your company after you abandoned her for a horse race."

"It's not like she'd have a choice. As my future wife, she would have to entertain me."

A smirk tugged at the corner of his mouth, a look that made my stomach clench.

"Out."

"You will clean before dinner?" He sneered. "Can't imagine she finds the gore in your hair attractive." He stood, the chair scraping behind him.

I kept my posture stiff, my muscles coiling in readiness. If there had been a dagger within reach, or if Nienna weren't between us, I would've drawn blood.

"You go too far, boy," I snarled.

Tallon's gaze drifted over me, his lips curling in disdain. His sneer lingered, dragging a chill over my skin where I usually felt steel-plated confidence. The scars etched into my body, once emblems of resilience, were exposed and hollow. Nienna's presence rooted me in place, trapping me between lust and rage. To move would reveal her, but staying still made my anger fester.

A low chuckle escaped him, sharp and derisive, before he turned on his heel. He strode off without hurry, the arrogance in his posture igniting a deeper fury. Greaves pushed the door open, his eagerness to see him leave evident. Without a word, Tallon brushed past him, disappearing into the hallway's shadows.

Greaves glanced back at me, his expression laced with unspoken questions. I shook my head, gripping Nienna's hand as if it was the only thing tethering me to sanity. No one else could stay. No words would help. Only her presence kept my turmoil from splintering entirely. Her calming touch felt dangerous, soothing and agitating all at once, like an addictive venom.

When the door clicked shut, my glare lingered on the polished wood. The silence left me balancing a precarious anger I couldn't dispel. Small fingers traced up my thighs, forcing me to recline, shifting away from her reach. She propped up on her knees, poking her head from beneath the desk.

Her eyes were fierce. "Why do you let him say things like that?"

My teeth ground together as I fought to form an answer.

Tallon was my son. As much as he disrespected me, as deep as his actions cut, he was still my heir. Blood bound us, and that alone meant I owed him protection. A king's duty—despite the hatred that burned in my chest.

I loathed his existence, but the truth was, I needed him. As a father, I failed him in ways I had no dream of mending. After Eldeiade's death, the thought of remarrying—it disgusted me. To sire another heir, to risk replacing Tallon—the notion turned my stomach.

She shattered whatever desire I had left for a woman.

Then Nienna entered my life and reignited it, a blaze impossible to resist.

I cupped her chin, my thumb grazing her lips, lifting her gaze to meet mine. My eyes traced the delicate curve of her neck, stirring the hunger within me.

"I do not always trust my tongue."

Some things were better left unsaid. Tallon provoked me to the point where words spilled out before I could think. As king, I was calculated, careful. I couldn't afford to speak impulsively—not even to him.

"You should have told him off," she hissed. "He deserved to be put in his place. Why is he here? A race? I don't believe it."

"He's here." I slid my hand along the nape of her neck, fingers tangling in her hair. I pulled, tilting her head back, exposing her throat, feeding the primal beast inside me. "Because he knew the rumors of the mammoth. He guessed to find you here."

She swallowed, the movement bobbing, but didn't pull away. Fire spread through me, eroding whatever control I had left. Everything tightened, ignited. Every twitch of her fingers along my thighs stoked the heat inside me. My pulse stuttered when her gaze lingered, skimming over my body before it snapped back up, avoiding temptation.

"But you didn't know about the mammoth."

"He's not always childish. He wants the truth for his theory."

If I took a chance, I'd wager Tallon hoped to find her here, in this room, in this position—her head between my thighs, washing me clean of the past, completing this celebration of life.

He was dangerous. Though still a prince, he was becoming a man. A man whose power could rival mine one day. Immature, yes, but he was learning. If he discovered the truth of my relationship with his betrothed... if he had proof?

The throne would crumble beneath me, regardless of how well I bore the weight of Radaan.

"He thinks there's something between us," she murmured.

My fingers clenched in her hair, and my body went rigid. "What did he say to you?"

It was one thing for him to hurl accusations at me, but to approach her? To push her? He had no restraint. If he dared touch her, I'd make good on my promise.

Her eyes lowered, avoiding my gaze. She focused on my stomach, a defensive move. "He said he thinks we plan to replace him as heir."

A heavy sigh escaped me, and my grip loosened. "I have no such hopes."

Whether Tallon was truly mine, I couldn't say, but I claimed him—for Radaan's sake. For stability.

My kingdom had to lean on tradition. We were fortunate I survived the war, and the queen somehow conceived in the times I visited.

Bile surged in my throat, and I fought the impulse to pull away from Nienna as dark memories flooded my mind.

Greedy hands. Poisoned words. Scornful laughter. Ridicule. Demands and humiliation.

Nienna's hand brushed my knee, then stopped, as if the disgust was written on my face. She studied me, her cheek resting against my leg, eyes shimmering with concern. A furrow creased her brow, and color warmed her cheeks. Her lips pressed into a tight line, a silent struggle.

Another reason I refused to let anything happen between us. She would want a child one day, and I couldn't give that to her. Physically, there was no question—I could take her, but I would never father a bastard.

"You could still sire an heir." Her attempt at a smile faltered, slipping into a frown as her gaze lingered on the set of my jaw.

Shame twisted through me, killing the last of my desire. She didn't deserve my anger—rage that festered for years. I had no right to take out my frustration on her—a woman who gave and gave. Time after time, she offered me her warmth and passion, and I returned only bitterness. She was owed more than I could ever give.

"If you're worried about my skills in bed," I smirked, leaning over her—safely tucking my hips away from her, "I assure you, I could still father a child."

Her blush deepened, lips parting as she absorbed my words.

"But I've done that duty." I stood, forcing myself to part with her. A groan tore at my throat, pain echoing through me as our hands released. The distance between us was unbearable, a sharp ache that cut through my chest. "Now, I face different battles."

Like the one pulling me away from her.

She sank onto her heels, palms resting on her thighs, her lips parted in invitation. The raw need in her eyes drowned in the hurt I caused, and I despised myself for it. I couldn't give her more. I had no way to rewrite the oath that bound her and Tallon. There was no way to take back the moments we shared—how I fed her hopes, how I fed my own, knowing we would never have the satisfaction we craved.

"Princess Nienna of Draconia," I extended my hand to her.

She gripped it, allowing me to pull her to her feet.

"The Dragon's Heart." A smile tugged at my lips as I brushed a loose strand of hair off her cheek, then tilted her chin upward. "You've washed the blood from my body, and the stain of death from my soul."

Her expression softened at my words, and the itch to pull her close nearly undid me.

"Thank you," I whispered, pressing my lips to her forehead, fighting my restraint. "Elohios grant me strength to protect Radaan."

Veridis, grant me the passion to bring Radaan new life.

I resisted the impulse to tell her the words she was to speak in return. She had already given so much—too much—for me, for my kingdom. It troubled me that such a moment must remain a secret. A princess of Draconia risking everything for our traditions, laying it all on the line in the name of the gods.

"Now go, before Tallon finds you here."

She lowered her head, a smile playing at the corners of her lips. I grinned as she curtsied—a shallow dip. Whether out of respect for my new role or simple nerves, I couldn't say—and frankly, I didn't care. The beast within me roared with satisfaction, basking in the gesture.

I watched her move across the room, quick and graceful, pausing only to crack open the door. Then, Greaves, ever the loyal friend, swung it wide, using his body to shield her as she slipped back into the library.

My heart swelled with a triumphant thrill. We had not been caught. She respected my traditions. Putting herself in subjection to my perceived needs.

Sun above, why did it feed the monster inside me?

Greaves slipped into the study, leaning against the doorframe. His eyes traced the length of my body, and he lifted a brow. "Want me to finish?" he asked, a grin playing on his lips.

I shot him a sharp glare.

He chuckled, shaking his head, and crossed the room. "Didn't think she'd go through with it."

"She shouldn't have," I muttered, reaching for the latches on his armor. It wasn't the king's place, but after the Hunt, I owed my friend the courtesy of helping him out of his gear.

He paused, his gaze meeting mine, and the humor melted from his face. "Kal, after everything, this is the one thing you deserve."

I waved off his concern and jerked on the armor's belts and latches. "This? Coming from the man who can't stop reminding me of my age?"

"You did well for an old man today."

The buckle gave way, and I yanked the chestplate free, setting it down beside my own gilded armor. "You can handle the rest."

He chuckled when I turned to the tub full of cold water, doubling over to dunk my head under. I longed for my private bathing chambers, but this would have to suffice.

"And for that, you'll personally see to my armor," I said, scrubbing my scalp.

"That's the servants' job," he groaned.

I straightened, working at my belt. "It's your job to protect me." I smirked. "Wouldn't want them to miss oiling a strap or cleaning a buckle."

He deadpanned, lips pressed tight as he set about removing his armor.

Nienna had done more for me than she realized. She hadn't just honored our traditions; she lifted a weight from my chest. There was a humiliation that accompanied a slaying knowing my queen wouldn't do her part—knowing I didn't want her to. Eldeiade's death had opened a new door to guilt, to memories of the times she'd called me, demanding my service.

Nienna's choice to come of her own will—not bound by duty or tradition—and to take it on without hesitation eased something deep within me. It lightened my soul.

Our secret was like a candle's flame, flickering in the dark. The more I knew her, the brighter that flicker grew. It threatened to turn into a bonfire, one that might expose us, burning my world to the ground.

The world I had given everything for.

Chapter Thirty-Six

NIENNA

My stomach coiled into knots whenever Tallon drew near, the sensation more than just ire laced with disgust. He thrived on finding excuses to linger, wedging himself between Kallias and me, his mere presence chilling my blood.

The cold wasn't metaphorical.

That creeping, unnatural impression I once associated with Egath now clung to Tallon. It lacked the intensity of Egath's venomous grip, but it lingered. An echo—a faint prickling where there should have been warmth.

With Kallias, my blood pulsed with fiery longing, a symphony of passion luring me toward him like a siren's song. Tallon's presence warped that melody into something rancid. My veins churned and rebelled, twisting under the weight of a wrongness I couldn't shake.

When we returned to Reem, I forced myself to ride beside him. At dinner, nausea clawed at my stomach as his wicked smile landed on me, his expression too knowing. He seemed to relish my discomfort, feeding on it as predator devours prey.

Escape wasn't an option. Kallias had pulled away after the celebration of life, leaving our garden conversation to fester. Those confessions of what could never be hung in the air like a shadow. The ritual we'd shared was nothing more than a gesture to appease the gods, a cold transaction.

Once spoken, words could not be undone.

I had laid my heart bare, and he turned me away.

There would never be an '*us.*' There would only be the façade of Tallon and me, the prince and princess bound by title. A union devoid of love. The thought of our wedding night filled me with dread, the idea of bearing his heir more revolting than I could stomach.

Bile burned its way up my throat.

Tallon's appearance was everything one might desire. His raven-black hair gleamed, his emerald eyes glittered with a predatory sharpness. High cheekbones framed a chiseled jawline, blending boyish charm with the wiry strength of a man. Women everywhere would have fallen at his feet.

But whatever beauty nature had bestowed was undone by the vileness coursing through his heart.

His hair was as dark as his soul. His eyes gleamed with a vile, greedy hatred. Full lips were always mocking—leering at others. His straight nose was constantly lifted in a sneer.

When we arrived at the palace, I searched for Fyrn at once. I found her in the gardens, reclining on a bench with a book, the sunlight giving her cheeks a healthy flush.

"Nienna!" she exclaimed as I approached, her face lighting up. "How was the trip?"

Her warmth eased the tension swirling inside me. Smiling, I clasped her hand and gave her a quick once-over. "It went well. Are you feeling better?"

"Oh, yes." She laughed and tugged me onto the bench surrounded by fragrant rose bushes. "The servants must be relieved. I doubt they stopped scrubbing the floors for days."

Her eyes flicked to the Thresher lingering in the shadows, his watchful presence as constant as my own shadow.

"He refuses to leave," I said with a frustrated sigh, turning my body to block him from view. "But how did you manage to not tell me how amazing your home is?"

"You liked it?" Her lips quirked. "My parents at least invited a few lesser nobles to liven up that cave?"

"No. Just us."

Her brow furrowed, and she pressed a hand to her forehead. "But they must have used the receiving hall! And for the love of Veridis—please tell me they prepared the dining room?"

"They welcomed us to the kitchen." I tilted my head, fighting a laugh as her expression crumpled in dismay.

"The king too?"

"He didn't seem to mind." In truth, the informal setting soothed his usual severity.

Fyrn groaned and buried her face in her palms. "They can't do anything right!"

"It was nice." I pulled her hand from her cheek and leaned closer to catch her gaze. "I needed the escape. The high court, the nobles, the crown—"

Tallon.

"—It was exactly what I desired," I said, resting my fingers over hers. "I only wish you'd been there to share it."

Her lips twisted with amusement. "Did they at least show you the city, or did my father corner you in his study to prattle on about his precious goats?"

I leaned back against the bench, the roses nearby lending their fragrance to the soft hum of the garden. "We visited Sol." My words hesitated on the edge of more. How much could I reveal? Would mentioning the dance betray anything?

"Is the dance hall finished?" Her voice carried a flicker of nostalgia, tempered by wariness. "It was nearly done before I left, and Father wanted it completed before his return."

"It's magnificent. You have to see it yourself."

"Never would be too soon," she snapped, then softened, closing her book with a resigned sigh.

Her gaze turned distant. "You've seen the best Sol has to offer. I was never so fortunate. Trapped in cold, barren halls, with only servants and my mother for company. I endured the years when war brought waves of wounded to our door. My father opened his halls, but there aren't enough tapestries in the world to muffle the echoing screams of the dying."

Her words struck like a chilled wind, the raw pain in them unmistakable. "I'm sorry." My throat tightened. Her childhood had been swallowed by bloodshed, each memory marred by suffering.

"That's why I'll never go back." Her hands smoothed her dress as she drew a steadying breath, eyes settling on the flowers. "That place holds nothing for me but sorrow." Her tone shifted. "Tallon joined you?"

"After the king felled a mammoth."

She tilted her head, curiosity sharpening her features. "The Great Hunt? Is he well?"

I hesitated, the image of Kallias' pain flashing in my mind. His every movement spoke of discomfort—the grimace when he dismounted, the moment his hand braced against the saddle for balance. Scratches marred his skin, but his strength remained unbroken.

But I shouldn't know that.

"He's alive and appears well enough," I replied, keeping my voice even.

"It must have been his first time seeing a mammoth. Did he tell you about it?"

My frown deepened. "Oh, you mean the prince," I said, catching on. "No, he arrived after the slaying."

Relief softened her shoulders as she glanced down at the book in her lap. "Those beasts should have been hunted to extinction long ago. The king's chosen to face them, but Tallon is Radaan's future, and he's never even laid eyes on one. How can you prepare to kill what you've never confronted?"

He could have seen it—if he'd been with us. He likely avoided the creature, leaving the burden to his father.

"I don't mean to upset you." Her quiet words pulled my focus back. Worry flickered in her gaze. "I'm sure he could kill one if it came to it."

Could he? I doubted that.

Her eyes studied mine, her brows knitting with concern. "Did something happen between you two?"

I shifted, casting a glance toward the Thresher lurking too near. "No—we are still set to be wed," I said, each word chosen with care.

Everything happened. Yet nothing changed. My heart remained trapped beneath the weight of duty, my future a tether I could not sever.

She seemed to read the resignation in my tone, the bitter acceptance that colored it. Silence settled between us, broken only by the faint rustle of the garden. Flowers dipped and swayed in the breeze, their petals kissed by the sun. Insects darted through beams of light, their wings catching flashes of gold.

I could not escape him. Tallon was my future, no matter how much I wished otherwise.

Egath sat on my right, his presence looming like a storm cloud. I prodded a bean across my plate, nausea rising in waves I struggled to suppress. His words flowed past me to Tallon, their conversation a tempest with me as the lone, stranded island.

Fallione had secured Egath's release. No evidence tied him to the assassination attempt, and the ambassador's threats to return to Vellos forced the king's hand. Egath claimed his confinement was unjust, a mistreatment that would strain relations with the Velli king.

Kallias simmered at the far end of the table, his anger a silent flame. I kept my gaze fixed downward, reminding myself of the chasm between us. Future relatives—nothing more. Twin islands, each battered by different storms.

A ripple beneath my skin startled me. My pulse surged as something squirmed inside my forearm. Had I caught worms? Turning my arm, I traced the spot with trembling fingers.

"Everything all right, Princess?" Egath asked, his fork poised over a chunk of beef.

"Just an itch," I replied, forcing a thin smile. I noted the flicker in his gaze—a quick glance at Tallon before his attention dropped to his plate.

"I hope you avoided the mountain plants," he said. "Some will have you scratching for weeks." His knife sliced through the meat with deliberate precision.

The shift in his demeanor unsettled me. Politeness had replaced his usual barbs, as if I passed some unspoken test.

"You didn't wander anywhere you shouldn't, right?" Tallon jeered.

My stomach churned at his tone, too smug to be innocent. His smirk, paired with the rise of his brows, dared me to react.

"I was with Gayle'sol almost the entire time," I answered.

"Almost?" Egath mused, his knife scraping against the plate. "Surely they didn't leave you alone. The Craggs are dangerous."

"I can handle myself," I shot back, anger simmering beneath my calm exterior. Caught between them, their words closed in, each more pointed than the last. With the prince, I could hold my ground. With Egath, every move felt like stepping onto thin ice.

"The assassination attempt a few weeks ago suggests otherwise."

That remark shattered my fragile veneer of civility.

I spun toward Tallon, the dinner knife firm in my grip. "I took my first life that night, dear prince." My voice barely carried beyond him, each word a venomous whisper. "His blood covered my hands. My only weapon was a pencil. Let's see how you'd manage in my place."

His eyes lit with that insufferable, predatory thrill, his face far too close to mine. "If you hadn't taken a servant to bed, perhaps you would be better off."

Heat surged through my chest, sharp and suffocating. Scythe. That word—cutting, biting—sent a painful crackle of rage along my nerves.

"I would be dead."

His smile sharpened, a blade in itself, and still, he said nothing. Our faces hovered a breath apart, the air thick with loathing. The knife trembled in my hand, my fingers aching from the strain of restraint. Every fiber of my being craved to plunge it into him, but I held back. That would be giving him exactly what he wanted.

He sought my end—not merely my departure, but my death.

Tallon might be my future, but it would not be a long one.

"The king requests your presence in the battle hall."

My chest tightened, but I steadied my breath and nodded. "I'll be there shortly."

The servant dipped into a curtsy before retreating down the corridor. My Thresher shut the door behind her with a soft click.

"He calls you for a viewing?" Edith asked, putting her knitting aside to rise to her feet.

"There haven't been any duels or sparring matches since I arrived." I trailed her to the dressing room, the thought twisting uneasily in my mind.

"He sparred with the prince once," she replied, her tone carrying a hint of disdain.

That wasn't sparring. It was discipline—deliberate. A memory of Kallias putting his son in his place surfaced, stirring a mix of nerves and satisfaction in my stomach. If only he'd do it again. Tallon deserved far worse.

But the thought soured. Days had passed without a word from him. At dinner, his gaze barely grazed mine, the cold distance growing like a chasm. Whatever had once bound us together had vanished, leaving only emptiness. He wouldn't stand with me against his son.

"I believe that was an isolated incident," I muttered, glancing at my dress. The long fabric concealed the blade strapped to my thigh, but the lack of slits made access cumbersome.

Edith motioned for me to sit, her hands steady as she wove a tiara braid into my hair, leaving a few loose strands to brush my shoulders. Her hum filled the silence, soft and contemplative.

Once she deemed me presentable, I followed the Thresher through the palace corridors. Each turn came to mind moments before we took it, my memory of the layout sharpening. Only one mistake slowed my stride—I'd know the way soon enough.

The battle hall's open doorway revealed the sandy arena beyond. Greaves stood by Kallias, removing his mantle and setting it on a nearby rack. Tallon lingered off to the side, arms crossed, his glare fixed on his father. Another man, older with snow-white hair and a neatly trimmed beard, watched the scene from a distance. His intense gaze shifted to me as I descended the stairs.

Eyes, shadowed with age but fierce, scanned me from my dress to my face before sliding back to his king.

Why had I been summoned?

"Come, Princess," Kallias called. The deep timbre of his voice pulled at something in me, even as he avoided my gaze. Rolling up the sleeves of his tunic, he revealed forearms corded with muscle, veins ridged like paths carved into stone. Heat crept into my cheeks, and I looked away, stepping into the soft sand.

"I told him this wasn't necessary," Tallon muttered, shifting his weight.

The older man dressed in a loose tan tunic and brown pants scrutinized the prince's stance with a frown. He held the composure of someone who'd seen countless soldiers come and go. His fingers twitched, as if preparing to adjust his stance, but he remained silent.

"It's important," Kallias replied, his tone final.

"She doesn't need to!" Tallon snapped, a scowl twisting his features. "That's what the Threshers are for, aren't they?"

I glanced at the giant in black leathers towering behind me. "How can I be of service, Your Majesty?" My voice wavered, betraying the silent plea for him to meet my gaze.

"Your training is insufficient," Kallias growled, his words sharp as the turn of his back. A flare of indignation straightened my spine.

"He wants you to wield a blade," Tallon sneered, his tone laced with scorn. "You have the right to refuse."

Shock prickled through me. My eyes darted to Greaves, the only one who hadn't turned away.

A frown tugged at his brow, and he held my gaze, steady and unreadable, before passing a sword to the king.

"Do you refuse?" Kallias asked over his shoulder. The pause in his movement betrayed something deeper, but he still wouldn't look at me.

My focus shifted back to Greaves, seeking an anchor. His small nod was a quiet reassurance, the only permission I needed.

"My father never taught me swordplay," I said, my voice even. "I was never expected to carry one into battle."

"There. She refuses," Tallon sighed, his arms dropping with exaggerated relief.

"However," I added, my tone sharper, baiting him. "As pointed out, I cannot always rely on my guards. I would welcome instruction with a dagger."

The Thresher shifted, his weight pressing into the floorboards. I resisted the impulse to turn, to reassure him *his* efforts had never fallen short.

Tallon groaned. "Fine! Then you'll train with me!"

"She trains with Jerek," Kallias cut in, his words cold enough to frost the air. "You need the practice, Prince."

His eyes narrowed. "Practice? For what? To fight in a war you ended?"

Jerek, silent until now, studied me from head to toe. His gaze lingered on my arms before he shifted and murmured, "Your Majesty, I've never trained a woman."

"She is more than capable," Kallias snapped, his voice steeled with irritation.

"She's delicate. What weapon could she possibly–"

The king whirled on him, the blade master recoiling as his fury radiated like the sun. The measured mask he wore cracked, revealing the raw temper beneath. "She was raised among *dragons*. Fragile is the last thing she is. She carries a blade of her own—make her use it."

The arena stretched into silence. Greaves' face tightened, his mouth pressed in disapproval. Tallon's eyes flicked from me to his father, his shock evident in the part of his lips, his shrewd gaze calculating.

Kallias' sword hung low, his grip tight, knuckles stark white against the hilt. Tension radiated from his shoulders, the anger pouring off him like heat.

"Your king gave you an order." His voice dropped to a dangerous growl. "Maybe I should find another blade master."

Jerek's eyes widened, shifting to me.

This was all wrong. Kallias was Radaan's king, but his actions didn't reflect the man who'd always been in control. The question was, would people end up looking to me for the answers for his change in disposition—or would they come up with some other reasoning?

Jerek stepped back, bowing low, conceding to his authority. "I will train her."

Kallias snarled, then spun away. As he turned, his eyes met mine. The fury in them cut deep, his sky blue gaze devoid of warmth. Only pain flickered there.

A dull ache spread through me. I wasn't the only one suffering. I could cry over my own struggles—tied to Tallon when I longed for Kallias—but the truth was, his heart was breaking, too.

It was my father who signed my name to the marriage contract, but it was Kallias himself who bound his son to me. He destroyed any chance of happiness with me when he swore on his honor as a king, and gave the promise of his nation that his heir would marry me.

Whereas I was just a casualty of the agreement, Kallias had fired the arrow that pierced both our hearts.

He stormed past me. I caught Tallon's gaze.

A cold knot of dread twisted in my stomach. His green eyes gleamed with recognition. His brow furrowed as his suspicions were validated. He knew there was something between us.

There *had been* something between us.

He followed his father, and the blade master crossed his arms, head tilted. "Do you have a blade, Princess?"

"Yes."

"Let's see it."

I froze. "It's... in a discreet location." My heart sank. The one time I chose to wear a Radaanian dress—it concealed everything I needed under it.

"If I'm to train you, I need to know what you're fighting with." His gaze flicked to my skirts, his neck flushing with a sudden heat.

I bit my cheek, shrugging with a raised shoulder as I tugged at the edge of my dress. I wore breeches, but Jerek's sharp intake of breath and the shuffle of the Thresher behind me told me the sight was still improper.

My palm slid beneath the fabric, pulling free Kallias' dagger. As I stood, the hem of my skirts kissed the sand, and I handed the weapon hilt-first to Jerek.

Small, the blade was just a touch longer than my hand. Simple gold made up the hilt, ivy winding around it with no jewels or ornamentation. It was crafted for one thing: protection.

"Where did you get that?" Tallon froze, his gaze snapping to mine, his expression hard.

I glanced at Kallias. His jaw clenched as he swung his sword with a fluid rhythm. His movements were sharp, powerful, muscles flexing beneath his tunic with each strike as he purposefully ignored the exchange.

The prince whipped toward his father, eyes burning.

"Disappointed it isn't yours?" The words slipped out before I could stop them, and both men faced me.

Kallias faltered. A quick glance shot my way before he turned his back, resuming his movements.

Tallon's lip curled in a sneer, but he said nothing.

Relief washed over me. I wasn't just keeping Kallias' secrets—I was safeguarding Tallon's, too.

I remembered the hunger in his eyes when he found the prince's dagger on me, the bloodlust when I admitted that his son suspected something. What would he do if he knew Tallon attacked me beneath the balcony? His mask was already cracking; he didn't need more weight to carry.

"It's a fine blade." Jerek's voice, rough and raspy, drew me back. "But with this, there's little I can teach you. If someone gets close enough for you to use it, it'll be a mad scramble for survival."

He flipped the dagger, the steel clinking. Behind me, Tallon and Kallias' swords clanged together, and I fought the urge to flinch. Greaves' gaze was fixed on their movements, eyes tracking every strike.

"I should start with self-defense, but..." Jerek hesitated, eyeing me. "It's wiser to use your Thresher. He knows better than I."

I turned to the giant in black leather armor. His arms were crossed, his chest broad, and he didn't shy from my gaze. Instead, his eyes narrowed, a sharp glare meeting mine.

The only warriors I had seen with tattoos were Threshers, the dark ink of his mark peeked from the collar of his tunic.

"We'll use your fists in place of your dagger." Jerek set my weapon on a table and moved closer. "An attacker will always try to sneak up on you. Thresher, what's your name?"

Gray eyes flicked to the man, an eyebrow lifting in silent response. That icy gaze returned to me, sending a shiver down my spine. He could snap me in half without effort. Lucky for me, he was charged with protecting me, not hunting me.

"It's only polite to know the name of my sparring partner." I smiled, tilting my head, trying to sound lighthearted—but it wasn't the playful gesture I intended. It felt more like offering my throat to a dragon.

He inhaled, his chest expanding with the effort. "Lynx."

"Nienna," I replied, dipping into the slightest curtsy. A silent thank you.

He didn't react, but his lips formed a line, his massive arms lowering to his sides.

"You understand he'll lay hands on you, Your Highness?" Jerek asked.

"Yes, I imagine that comes with the training."

"Right then, Lynx, if you would–"

A wall of muscle wrapped around my neck. The pressure of a solid arm dug into my shoulders. I gasped, fingers grasping at the black tunic beneath my chin as he leaned in, his body heavy against mine.

"The first lesson is to stay calm," Jerek's voice cut through the roaring in my ears.

"Gods!" Tallon cursed, but my focus was on the scent of leather and man that engulfed me, thick and suffocating.

Lynx's arm remained firm, not crushing, but holding. No real danger—but still, fear crawled along my skin, racing through my veins.

"I want you to move slowly," Jerek continued. "Think about what you'd do. No mistakes now. Forget what's right—just slow down."

My heart hammered against my ribs, a frantic rhythm clashing with Jerek's calm instructions.

"I would grab my dagger?" My voice was muffled, my chin bouncing off the hard muscle of Lynx's chest.

"If your dress would allow it."

A sharp reminder of Draconis fashion. How did Radaanian noblewomen defend themselves? Judging by the men's reactions, most likely none of them dared try.

I yanked at the hem of my skirts, imagining my dagger still tucked there. My left hand clenched into a fist and swung back, but the giant was too tall. He shifted his body, avoiding my strike and jostling me in the process. I squealed, stumbling over my feet.

"Always stay on your feet," Jerek said, circling us.

I fought the urge to slap him, wishing he'd try wrestling this beast.

"Go for his shoulder."

My fist hit the spot where Lynx held me. Harder than necessary? Probably. But he deserved it for yanking me around like a rag doll. He grunted, releasing his grip on my neck. I gasped for air, a grin tugging at my lips.

Then his hand shot out, fingers curling around my throat. A scream clawed for release, but the burn of his hold tightened my chest, choking the sound.

"Stand down!" Kallias' roar sliced through my panic.

I stifled the scream, jerking away from Lynx's grasp. My hands flew to my neck, rubbing the skin, fighting the sting.

The king stormed between us. His tunic sleeve was torn, stained with crimson. My shock deepened when I realized Tallon had struck him.

"Thresher, you are dismissed."

Lynx didn't flinch at the king's order. Unbothered, he left the arena, his steps echoing with quiet authority.

"I'm fine, Your Majesty." I forced the words out. "He just surprised me."

"And she will be surprised, my king." Jerek's frown deepened. He raised his hands in a placating gesture. "I can't teach her to fight without first teaching her to defend herself."

"Never use a Thresher with her." A command, firm and final. "That is not their duty."

"My apologies, Your Majesty."

"Perhaps I should train with her," Tallon said, smooth and mocking. He strolled toward us, his eyes gleaming. "She'll be my wife, after all. If anyone should have their hands on her, it should be me."

Heat rushed to my face at the thought—his arm around my throat. Lynx's towering presence seemed far less threatening.

"You'll save those touches for after your wedding." Kallias' jaw tightened as he faced me. "My apologies, Princess."

He had tried to teach me. To show me how to defend myself, how to use my dagger beyond the basic knowledge that the pointy end went in first. But I messed up. And now, there was nothing more he could offer. We were tethered by our titles.

Desire ached in me at the thought of him teaching me. To feel his arms around me, to have him pull me close. I wanted the heat of his breath against my ear, but none of that would come.

His mask faltered. Anger flared in his gaze, followed by something softer—pain, resignation.

"No insult was taken." I forced a smile, tight and brittle. "Thank you for the offer, but I think I'll rely on my own wits."

"Until I can train you," Tallon added. His voice twisted in my gut. I knew his idea of training. He would try to kill me—this much was certain. "Stay. Watch me and my father. Maybe you'll learn something."

"If the king would permit it," I murmured, meeting Kallias' gaze. His expression shuttered again.

"Jerek, you're dismissed. Princess, if you'd like to remain, stand by Greaves." Kallias' voice was low as he turned to face the arena.

Jerek offered a bow and made his way toward the stairs, exiting the hall.

Tallon's gaze tracked me as I approached Greaves. The guard adjusted his stance, positioning himself between us. A small move, yet it spoke volumes in his protective role.

"Tallon," Kallias called, summoning him to the ring. The prince obeyed, a wicked grin curling his lips.

Soon, I understood why.

A tightness in my wrist flickered first, followed by a slow, creeping sensation that felt like something was prodding my insides. It was him. Somehow, he had found a way to do what Egath had done—but with far less control.

A cold wave of dread washed over me. Could Tallon be part Velli? Was he a true bastard, sired by a Velli noble?

His gaze locked with mine over Kallias' shoulder. Those green irises glittered with dark amusement.

My stomach churned. I pressed my hand to it, eyes wide with growing horror. "Princess?"

Greaves' voice rasped with concern, but it was cut short by a vicious hiss from Kallias. He staggered back, wiping at his arm. Crimson soaked through his tunic. Greaves let out a strangled sound, stepping closer.

"Still fit to rule a kingdom, Father?"

Kallias' gaze flicked to me for a breath before he raised a hand to stop his guard. "You know nothing of ruling."

"Court the nobles, gather advisors, form alliances." A leer twisted his lips as his glare slid to me. "Fill a queen with heirs."

Kallias exploded.

He lunged, knocking the leer from his face. Tallon yelped, the sound swallowed by the harsh rhythm of blows his father rained down. I couldn't tear my eyes away from Kallias at full strength. His boots kicked up sand, shoulders straining with the power of his strikes in spite of his wounds from the Hunt.

Greaves' hands remained empty, clenched into tight fists, his helplessness palpable.

Tallon backed up, throwing frantic blocks. His foot caught, and Kallias charged. He slammed into the prince, knocking him to the ground with a thud. Greaves relaxed, stepping back to stand at my side while the king loomed over his son, sword hovering at his throat.

His chest rose and fell with heavy breaths, his growl too low for me to hear. The weapon's tip pressed against Tallon's skin.

One breath.

Two.

Finally, Kallias stepped back, shaking his head. He stormed toward me, sheathing his sword with a sharp motion, his fury now turned on me.

"I will escort you to your rooms."

Just like that, the fight ended. The king had put the prince in his place. I had failed in my training.

Tallon rolled onto his side, his raven hair matted with sand. I expected rage, accusation—but what I saw instead sent a chill through me.

Thrill.

Chapter Thirty-Seven

NIENNA

Days blurred into one another, each sunrise a dull repetition. The only constant was Fyrn. She arranged social calls, took me to tea with noblewomen, and guided me through the gardens, pointing out hidden pieces of art.

My soul was torn between Kallias' icy presence and the constant pressure of Tallon.

I missed Scythe—her sharp wit, her comfort.

Edith sat nearby, knitting with quiet focus, her eyes flickering to me every so often, laden with concern. The ache behind my ribs deepened. Alone. In love with a king who could never return it. Given to a prince who loathed me. And now I wondered if Tallon's blood was tainted by the same darkness that clouded his soul.

Endless questions remained unanswered, and Kallias' cold distance made them even harder to reach.

I buried myself in books, devouring every scrap of information on the Velli—though there was little to be found. Perhaps I was searching in the wrong places. Radaan's palace wasn't likely to hold various texts about their enemies, especially after so many years of conflict.

Tallon's birth didn't concern me as much as how to survive our wedding night. I knew he would savor my pain. I needed leverage to keep him at bay, something to protect the fragile remnants of my spirit. If he forced himself on me, it would destroy what little was left.

Fyrn remained my one true friend, the only source of any comfort. When she sent a message summoning me to the stables, a flicker of hope sparked within me. It was unusual for her to send a message instead of coming for me herself—perhaps a surprise. It had been too long since I'd set foot outside the suffocating confines of the palace walls. I longed to see more of Radaan, but for now, Reem would do.

I dressed in a simple riding dress—a blue garment with pale breeches beneath. After I secured my dagger to my thigh, a sharp ache ran through me, a reminder of who'd given it to me.

But that was over.

Whatever we had was done.

Lynx, unaffected by the sparring incident, trailed behind me, a silent shadow. Thanks to Fyrn's help during those long, tedious days, I knew the halls well now.

The guards opened the courtyard doors, and the sun's heat hit me as I crossed the western garden toward the stables.

They were built into the stone wall separating Reem from the palace, much like the temples. Eager horses and busy stablehands filled the air with a lively, comforting din. As I stepped into the shade of the first stable, I slowed my pace, scanning for any sign of Fyrn.

A white horse thrust its head from a stall, letting out a soft wicker, its ears pricked forward. I smiled, reaching out to stroke its velvety nose. I wasn't afraid of horses, even though I feared riding them.

"Have you seen my friend?" I asked the creature, my gaze drifting down the aisle.

The horse huffed, sniffing my dress as if it expected treats. I chuckled, patting its mane before continuing.

The stablehands made themselves scarce; the work here had already finished. Clean aisles stretched before me, free of hay, while the horses were content in their stalls, preoccupied with their breakfast.

A sense of calm settled over the barn, the only sound the quiet munching of oats. I hummed, enjoying the stillness. In the palace, there was no peace. My rooms were the only place that offered an escape from the endless noise, the whispers, and the expectations surrounding my impending wedding. The day loomed over me like a storm cloud.

The air was growing colder. Draconia savored the chill, as it signaled the end of the whirlstorm season, a cause for celebration. Here, it only marked the approach of my doom.

A sudden cry shattered my thoughts. I stiffened, scanning the aisle.

Another muffled scream followed, cutting through the stillness.

I froze, skimming the rows of wooden stalls. Then Lynx's imposing figure loomed into my space, his presence suffocating.

The sound wasn't one of a threat—it was pain. Someone was hurt. I crept forward, Lynx at my side, moving with caution. The horses ignored me, their heads bent to their grain as I peered into each empty stall, searching for the source of the cries.

"Come on!" The hiss was sharp, followed by the sickening crack of a hand striking flesh.

My spine stiffened, a cold breath catching in my lungs.

Kallias would never tolerate violence within his walls. Neither would I.

I lifted my chin, my resolve hardening, and prowled toward the end of the passage, following the sharp, ragged breaths.

Lynx grunted, stepping forward as I neared the source. I shot him a glare—his height gave him a better view—but he grimaced and stepped aside, allowing me to round the corner.

Tallon's trousers hung low on his hips, clinging to his thighs, his tunic falling to cover his lower back. Fyrn stood pressed against the stall, her breath hitching, her hands pinned high above her head. Her skirts twisted around her waist, the fabric bunched, revealing pale skin.

My world tilted, each detail searing into my mind like a brand. Fyrn's parted lips trembled. Tallon's shoulders heaved as if he had run a mile. A shudder ran through me, clawing up my spine, my fists tightening as though they could crush the scene before me into nothingness. Vision red-tinged, I froze, the betrayal striking deeper than any blade could.

Tallon's head jerked in my direction, a damp lock of hair stuck to his sweaty forehead.

Bile surged up my throat. My feet wouldn't move. I couldn't look away. His grin spread, savage, malicious.

Rage boiled through me, the heat burning my veins.

"How dare you!"

Fyrn, my only friend, twisted toward me. Her wide eyes locked with mine for an instant, but whatever she meant to say came out as a choked moan, silenced by Tallon's hand pressing firmly against her spine. He shoved her back into place with a callousness that turned my stomach.

"You stay," he growled, his tone as sharp and cruel as a whip.

Disgust surged through me, a cold wave that left me trembling. This was Tallon, my betrothed, the person who made my life in Radaan a quiet torment. Now he stood here, brazen and unrepentant, bedding someone I had trusted above all others. Fyrn wasn't just a friend—she was supposed to be my anchor, the one person who had always been safe.

But here she was, exposed and vulnerable, her skirts tangled and her dignity stolen, in the shadow of a filthy stable. A fissure of betrayal cracked through my chest, cutting deeper than I thought possible.

"Care to join us, future wife?" His voice slithered, thick with venom, coiling around my heart like a poison.

I staggered back, my limbs heavy. He was monstrous. The prince was vile—but this? This was too much.

Lynx stepped in front of me, his body a solid wall between me and the nightmare unfolding.

I sucked in a shaky breath, stumbling from the stall. Away from the sad excuse of a man who wanted me broken—and Fyrn, the traitor I had once trusted.

There was no escape. How had I been so blind? How had I missed the signs?

My feet carried me farther, moving without thought, pulling me from the sounds of their shameful tryst. I didn't know where I was going, only that I needed distance from the wretched scene.

Tallon would never leave me in peace. Marrying him would bind me, mind and body. My people were starving—what was the worth of my soul in the face of their suffering? I could break the blood oath, claim I wanted to return to my father, and he would let me. Kallias would let me.

Kallias.

I slammed into a stone wall, my vision spinning. I collapsed onto a crate in a shadowed alcove, my body heavy with grief. Lynx moved to shield me from sight, his back a silent barrier between me and the world.

Still, running blind wasn't the answer. I needed a plan. The only light in this dark was the thought of being close to Kallias, but that light would burn my soul to ash. We could never be together.

But he would understand. He would anchor me in this storm, steady when I faltered.

I drew in a long, deliberate breath, letting the cool air fill my lungs, each second stretching to calm my pounding heart. The rhythm slowed, though my chest still felt tight, like it might split apart if I moved too quickly. No one would see me running through the palace—a fragile, broken girl. I wouldn't shatter so openly. So I straightened, smoothing the trembling in my limbs with sheer force of will.

I was not just a girl—I was a princess. One day I would be queen. I would act like one.

A queen did not crumble. Composure was her shield; control was her weapon. She stood tall in the face of storms, never letting them see her bleed.

She shaped the world to her will.

And she got what she wanted.

My boots thudded against the stone, and Lynx's steady pace matched mine as I pushed past a stablehand and into the harsh sunlight. It no longer felt warm, only cold and distant. I stormed through the gardens, forcing myself to slow, unwilling to run back into the palace.

How long had she been with him, tangled in secrets and shadows while I remained blind? The thought lodged in my chest like a splinter, raw and aching. Tallon's betrayal stung, but the pain was dull, a distant echo of what I might have expected. It was the truth about Fyrn that cut deeper, jagged and unforgiving.

She wasn't just a friend—she had been my anchor, the steady hand that had guided me when my world tilted. She had always been there, her presence soothing the unspoken battles between me and Tallon, her quiet words tempering our sharpest edges.

The breath I took caught in my throat, jagged and sharp, as the realization hit with the force of a blade. She hadn't been mending the rift or pulling me closer to him. She'd been standing at his side, her loyalty already spoken for.

Always close, a shadow at his heels, smoothing over his flaws, making them seem smaller than they were. Her smiles had never been meant for me; they'd been his to claim, each one a quiet offering. He was her storm, her sun, her center.

And all this time, I had been nothing more than a blind fool, circling the edges of a life that had never truly belonged to me.

The realization twisted my gut, bile rising as the image of them together seared itself into my mind. My breaths came shallow and quick, my grip tightening on my skirts as I hurried through the halls, desperate to outrun the sickening thoughts clawing at my sanity.

Behind me, Lynx let out a soft grunt, his long strides nearly breaking into a jog to match my frantic pace. Each hurried step seemed to draw more attention, servants and nobles pausing in their tasks to watch as we rushed by.

I didn't care.

I spun down another corridor, barely catching myself on the wall, before charging past two guards and into Kallias' study.

His cornflower blue eyes snapped up to meet mine, his dark brows furrowing in surprise. Greaves stiffened, but made no move, realizing I was no threat.

I strode into the room, chin lifted high, despite the sting of a tear that threatened to fall and the sharpness in my chest.

"Out." Kallias' voice was sharp, and Lynx withdrew without a word.

He pushed himself to his feet, his gaze narrowing as he studied me, as if trying to peel back the layers of my distress.

My body trembled. My heart pounded, urging me to close the distance, but my mind warned me I shouldn't be here.

"Gods, Nienna—what happened?" His fist clenched, his eyes scanning me, seeking the cause of my pain.

"Tallon," I choked, struggling to hold back the flood of emotions, "in the stables."

The words barely left my throat before a tear slipped down my cheek. I refused to carry this anymore. Each passing day, I felt myself withering inside, suffocating under my duty. Born a princess, with the heart of a commoner. I was expected to do a duty that would kill me.

"Greaves."

Kallias crossed the room in a single stride, wrapping me in his arms. The cold bite of gold chains pressed against my cheek as he pulled me against his chest.

"Kal–"

"Go!" The command rang out with the authority of a king—not a friend.

The door slammed shut behind him.

"Did he hurt you?" Raw emotion drenched every word—concern, anger, a promise of vengeance.

"Fyrn..." The name tasted like ash on my tongue. My lips twisted into a bitter smile, and I laughed—a hollow, jagged sound that scraped my throat. "I'm so stupid."

The weight of my own words pressed against me. I should have seen it. The stolen glances, the way her smile softened when he was near, the moments they disappeared together. I'd been too blind, too desperate for someone to trust, for a friend.

"She never cared about me," I muttered, my voice trembling. "She only ever wanted him."

Kallias stiffened, his hands faltering on my arms. "Tallon and Fyrn?" His tone was quiet, measured, but something sharp lurked beneath the surface. He eased back, his grip loosening enough to meet my gaze, his expression carefully unreadable. His eyes searched mine, as if trying to piece together the tangled web of betrayal I just revealed.

I scoffed, swiping at the fresh tear tracks on my cheeks. What she had done was unforgivable, but in this moment, I almost felt she wasn't worth my sorrow. "Rutting like animals in the stables."

Kallias sucked in a sharp breath, his gaze flickering between mine. The muscle under his left eye twitched in irritation, his lips formed a tight line.

"Men and their mistresses." I tried to laugh, but the sound broke, raw and bitter.

His arms remained steady around me, though I felt his focus shift, as if he were dissecting my pain. The heat of his anger pressed against the edges of his concern. We both understood what Tallon's disdain for me meant—that he wouldn't think twice about taking someone else to his bed.

Kallias' jaw tensed, his eyes flicking upward as if the words he needed hung out of reach. "It is... unseemly to take a mistress in public."

"Only in public?" My scoff came sharp and cold.

Just because it was common practice didn't make it any less vile. My hand moved, trembling, tracing the green brocade of his coat. Fury and despair warred inside me, leaving a heady, disorienting ache in their wake.

"And a private study?" I asked.

If Tallon thought he could take whatever he wanted, then so could I. There'd never be love between us—only ink and signatures. An empty union.

His eyes snapped back to mine and he tried to retreat, but I tightened my grip in the thick green brocade of his overcoat.

"If it is acceptable for him to take Fyrn," I whispered, "it's good enough for me."

"A mistress?" He spat the word as if it were poison, recoiling as much as I would allow him. He jerked back, but my hold anchored him in place. His hands clamped around my waist, firm but hesitant, as if warring with himself. "You would have me treat you as less than what you are? Sharing the bed with my son at night, and bed me in closets and in secret? Is that what you want? To live with lies on your lips and deceit in your heart?"

His words sliced through me, cutting deep. This was the best I'd have, the only happiness allowed to me. And I would take it.

"We already live a lie," I hissed through my clenched teeth. "This game we play, the secret glances, the long, empty nights... We lie to ourselves, to everyone! We wear our masks and pretend there's nothing between us."

I laid myself bare before him, my soul a raw, aching wound. I was dying inside, holding on to the one thing that might make me feel alive. "Take me, Kallias. I want to be your mistress."

His frustration flared, and before I took another breath, he stepped forward, shoving me against the wall. His hard body trapped mine, and he raised a hand to grip my chin, forcing me to meet his stormy gaze, his eyes burning with wrath—and something darker.

"You are worth more than that. You–"

"I can't have more than that, Kallias!" My voice cracked.

"You deserve–"

"What? What am I allowed to have?" I snapped, swallowing the scream that threatened to tear free. My fingers dug into his coat. "Tell me what part of you I can claim—what role might I play in your life besides a hidden secret? Will you ever make me your queen–"

"The blood oath–"

"Is for Tallon and me. Yes. But if you wrote–"

"If I wrote your father, the sun-scorched king of Draconia," he interrupted, slapping a palm over my mouth, silencing my protest. "To tell him I have lied, forsaken the promise of my blood and decided to bed his daughter rather than give her to my age appropriate son—he would send a fleet to Radaan, but instead of aiding me—they would raze the fields!"

I bit at his hand, frustration searing my flesh. He cursed, yanking it back and bracing against the wall, towering over me.

"Then not as your queen. My title might belong to Tallon, but let me give you myself. *That* is mine to offer." I tugged at him, desperate, feeling him fight against the pull, but his resistance only added fuel to my fire.

"Your body is sacred." His voice was a growl, his grip tightening at my waist as he lifted me, his strength forcing me into the wall. "It deserves to be worshiped. Do not throw it away."

"I'm throwing it at you, fool!" I locked my legs around him, pulling him closer, desperate for the contact. He thrust against me, driving his hips into my core and I gasped arching my back as a painting above us teetered.

"You would have me treat you like a common wench." His words were filled with rage, his gaze searing through me as it trailed from my face down to my chest.

"I would be yours." My breath hitched, and I pressed myself closer. "Take me as yours."

Something wild snapped in him. His mouth crashed onto mine, fiery and demanding. A moan escaped me, both relief and pleasure flooding my senses. I parted my lips, surrendering, and his tongue swept in, relentless and ravenous. One hand held me up, while the other brushed the front of my gown, grazing my breast with a heat that ignited every nerve.

I scrambled at his overcoat. Buttons flew as I tore at the fabric, desperate to strip it away.

So many more layers to go.

He broke the kiss with a growl, his gaze burning with need. "Easy, Nienna."

I snarled, threading my fingers through his hair and yanking him back to me. His groan filled the space between us as I took control, demanding his mouth with a flurry of tongue and lips—needy, hungry.

He spun me, stumbling toward the desk. His hands swiped at papers, sending them scattering across the floor. He dropped me onto the surface, my backside jolting against the hard wood, the ink from scattered reports smudging against my skin.

I tugged at the hem of his tunic, freeing it from his trousers. My hand traced the ridges of his abs, then moved up the dusting of hair on his chest. He made a strangled sound, pulling back against my fingers tangled in his locks. With a swift, decisive motion, he seized my wrists, pinning them to the desk.

"Wait," he gasped, his breaths ragged, his eyes frantic as he searched my face, trying to clear the passion clouding his mind.

"No." The word came out low, a growl.

He couldn't stop—I refused to let him think of all the reasons this shouldn't happen. I had memorized them during those long, lonely nights. Hooking my legs around his waist, I pressed my hips to his. I arched, grinding against him, desperate for more. So much more.

A string of curses spilled from him as he bucked against me, his control slipping. He released my wrists, and I immediately reached for his belt. When he attempted to shove my hand away, he leaned down for another kiss, but I hissed and smacked his arm, tugging at the buckle with impatient force.

With a grunt of surprise, his eyes flashed with something darker. A spark of wariness crossed his face, but vanished as quickly as it came. With a single motion, he gripped my sleeve and tore the fabric, the seam giving way to reveal my shoulder and the top of my breast, sending a chill of air over my exposed skin.

I froze, breath catching, shocked—but thrilled. His chest heaved as he paused, meeting my gaze, asking for permission. Waiting for me to pull away, to be the voice of reason.

My only answer was to unfasten his belt.

He crashed into me, pinning me beneath him, my hands struggling to push his trousers down. His lips blazed a fiery trail across my jaw, down my neck, along my chest, each kiss a mark that left me gasping. With a rough yank, he pulled at my dress, exposing my breast to the cool air, groaning as his hips ground into mine. I arched against the desk, the impact sending glass, ink, and paperweights clattering.

Pulling back for a quick breath, he fumbled with the panel of my skirt, pushing it up to my thighs. "Cursed breeches!" he muttered, reaching under my dress to grip my waist. My laughter was breathless as I lifted my hips to help him, letting him yank the fabric down to my ankles.

I kicked at the constraints, struggling against him, but he tackled me again. Our legs tangled as we fought to break free, only to pull closer in the process.

His lips burned a trail of fire across my chest, large hands searing my backside. "I need you!" I hissed. "Now!"

His low chuckle vibrated through his chest as I kicked one foot loose, wrapping my legs back around him, trousers hanging from my ankle. I purred in pleasure, simply having him so close, my core aching with desire.

He gripped my backside, pulling me flush against him, the cool chains of his mantle brushing over my bare skin. I sat up, reaching between us, trying to yank his trousers down, cursing as they caught on his hips.

He grunted, shoving me onto the desk, his palm pushing my skirts higher, the other unfastening his trousers. I panted, eyes locked on his movements, my tongue darting over my lip.

Two buttons undone, I slipped my hand between us, sliding inside. His head fell back, a guttural groan tearing from his chest as his grip tightened painfully on my bare hip.

"Gods! Ni–"

The door to the study slammed open.

Kallias spun, throwing me off the desk with a force that sent a lantern crashing, its light flickering out in a burst of glass. My heart pounded as he twisted, placing his body between mine and the intruders. Panic surged through me, my breath shallow as my mind scrambled to catch up.

I clutched the sides of his tunic, searching his face for the calm, the control that always defined him—the man who had faced flesh-eating wizards and walked away victorious. The self-assured king who never wavered.

"Well, well. Father, you really should learn to take your whores to your bed."

Tallon's voice, thick with ridicule, hit me like a slap. Kallias' left eye twitched, his facade cracking for just a moment. Then it was gone, replaced by the cold mask he wore so well. He tugged at the torn pieces of my dress, a futile effort to cover me, as if that could undo everything.

"Sea beneath, Tallon."

Horror flooded my veins, icy and biting. The crease between Kallias' brows deepened, his face draining of color. His pupils constricted to tiny pinpricks, nostrils flaring, his breath ragged as his grip on my shoulders tightened.

"We'll come back, Your Majesty." Ronan's words thickened with disdain.

My brother—he was here. Why was he here?!

Egath's voice cut through the tension, sneering. "Oh! Isn't that the princess' signet ring?"

I yanked my hand from his side like it had been seared by fire, clutching the damning ring close as if it might shield me.

Kallias' eyes fluttered shut. His breathing slowed, deepened. He braced himself for the storm to come.

But I wasn't ready.

None of us were.

"Your Majesty?" Ronan's voice had dropped an octave, dangerous now. "May I see the lady's face?"

"We didn't get a good look when she was splayed over your desk," Tallon added, his words dripping with malice.

Silence.

Kallias was so still. So quiet. Assessing. Judging. His mind raced, calculating the best course of action. He just needed a moment to think of a way out of this mess.

A mess I had put us in.

"Give us privacy," he commanded, his voice low, cold, and laden with authority. It was his last bluff. We both knew it.

The room spun. My breaths were shallow, frantic—this was all wrong. If Ronan found out like this, if he saw me, he would drag me back to Draconia.

As if on cue, Gyrak's roar shook the palace walls—loud enough to rattle the floor. A response to his rider's distress.

"I'm going to have to ask to see her face. Just a glimpse." Gone was the respect, the 'Your Majesty'—Ronan was demanding now.

Kallias' blue eyes—once the serene color of a midsummer sky—opened, but the pain was unmistakable. Wrinkles deepened at the corners, and his jaw clenched with frustration. His mask of calm cracked, revealing the regret he couldn't hide. His eye twitched again, his face a portrait of tortured decision.

We were trapped. There was no way out. Kallias stood between me and my brother, with Tallon and Egath at his side. The path was blocked, and there was no escaping the mess I had created.

Gritting my teeth, I mouthed, *I love you.*

Then, I stepped from behind the king who owned my heart.

A breath of silence. A fraction of a second was all I had before Tallon's brow arched in amused surprise, realizing his father had been seconds from bedding me.

Gyrak's scream rattled the paintings on the wall, and Egath recoiled, eyes wide with shock.

My brother's face drained of color, then flushed deep and blotchy. His gaze swept over my torn clothes and disarray, before landing on the king.

Kallias remained unshaken, standing tall as he met Ronan's furious glare.

"You rutting bas–"

"Ronan!" I snapped, stealing a glance at Greaves.

His tortured expression betrayed his internal struggle. The palace guards stood behind him, their helms concealing their faces, though I knew they'd witnessed every second.

"Nienna!"

My brother lunged at me, his grip vicious as he wrenched my arm, pulling me farther from Kallias. I tripped over the breeches still tangled around one ankle, fumbling with the scraps of my torn dress. I barely managed to keep them from falling.

"You sick bastard!" Ronan roared, Gyrak's fury echoing his.

"Your dragon!" I shouted, my shriek desperate in the chaos.

"He'll tear this palace apart!" He seethed.

"Tallon, Egath, remove yourselves." Kallias demanded, as the dragon's scream above us caused dust to fall from the ceiling. "Nienna–"

"Don't you dare say her name!" Ronan stepped in front of me, cutting me off from him.

The Velli ambassador watched in stunned silence, but Tallon's leer was the worst. His eyes, filled with mockery, danced over my exposed form, savoring my discomfort.

I fought with my breeches tangled around my boot while clutching onto my torn dress. My glare fixed on the prince—my enemy. I had misjudged him. He wasn't the fool I'd imagined. No, he had more of Kallias in him than I ever wanted to admit, evaluating my every move.

"Princess Nienna shall be escorted to her rooms–"

"I swear by the stars, if you say her name one more time—"

A thrum of power pulsed through the room. I shot up as a ball of flame swirled in Ronan's hand.

"—I will *kill* you!"

Kallias' lips pressed together, his jaw tight. His gaze locked with mine over my brother's shoulder, heavy with both warning and an unspoken pain.

"You don't get to look at her!" Ronan snapped, his temper flaring.

I grabbed the back of his leathers. "Ronan!" I hissed, tugging at him. "Don't be stupid!"

"Me?" He whirled, fury burning in his eyes. His gaze dropped to my chest, the shredded remnants of my garment barely covering me. Hatred twisted his features as he seized my arm.

"Let's go." I tugged on him, trying to pull him toward my rooms, hoping I might calm him—and Gyrak—before they both destroyed everything.

"Yes, let's!" He snarled. "I'm taking you home. Where men don't steal their sons' wives and treat them like common whores!"

He spun, dragging me along. I stumbled but bit my tongue, swallowing every retort.

Kallias stormed around his desk. The look of pure devastation on his face made my heart lurch. My vision blurred as Ronan dragged me away.

"Pray, King Kallias." His voice was cold, controlled, dangerous. "Pray to your gods that dragons don't fly for Radaan."

Then he hauled me out of the room.

The hall loomed, filled with nobles drawn to the commotion. Humiliation threatened to swallow me whole as gasps echoed through the onlookers. My dress tangled around my feet, and I stumbled. Lynx rushed to catch me.

Ronan whipped, pulling me to his side. Fire crackled in his palm, his voice low and venomous. "Careful, warrior. You've never faced a Dragon Rider."

The man hesitated, his expression unreadable, eyes darting, seeking a way to pry me from my brother's grip.

"Go back, Lynx," I whispered, tears now streaming down my face.

Ronan's arm tightened around me, pulling me closer. No matter how much I hated him in that moment, it was him I clung to. His presence, a strange comfort against the accusing, disgusted stares of the court. He was the only one who could shield me now.

"The oath between Radaan and Draconia has been torn asunder," my brother called out. "Our trust has been shattered—"

"Ronan, stop!"

"—and to impede us or come after us is an act of war!"

His words slammed into the room, and a ripple of shock spread through the crowd. Servants peered around corners, eyes wide with disbelief.

When he turned to leave, I didn't resist. I rushed to keep up, his grip unyielding as Gyrak's screech rattled the windows. The sound of dragonfire followed. I needed to get them out of here—before the destruction became irreversible.

But dragging me through the palace like this would leave an impression no one would forget.

We burst into the courtyard, and chaos erupted.

Gyrak landed with a deafening crash, his massive body obliterating part of the garden. Stone benches shattered beneath his weight. The dragon threw his head back and unleashed a torrent of flame that lit up the sky.

Ronan pulled me toward the beast's shoulder, but I yanked, digging my heels into the ground.

"Stop it! Please!" My voice cracked.

"He should have stopped!" He jerked my arm again, his rage barely contained.

"Just stop for one blasted moment!" I hissed, my hands shaking from the fury that refused to quell. I cursed my lack of magic to make him stop and think about this.

"Ronan, let me get changed!"

"You're not setting another foot in that palace!"

"You don't decide what I do!"

Gyrak's enormous snout slammed into me, shoving me toward his saddle as soldiers flooded the courtyard, their boots pounding against stone. I whirled, pointing a trembling finger at the dragon's snout.

"No!"

Something cracked deep inside me, a surge of energy rippling across my skin. Gyrak recoiled from my touch, his pupils narrowing to slits.

"I am a Dragon Rider, Princess." Ronan's words were thick with authority. "I outrank you by position and birth."

Fury burned through me like wildfire, painting my vision crimson. A daughter. That's all I was. A tool to be traded for alliances.

A broken tool.

"Don't do this."

"I won't abandon you here." Ronan's voice softened, but his presence loomed, towering over me, forcing me to tilt my head to meet his gaze. "I won't leave you with him."

The weight of his words pressed down on me, a finality that shattered my resolve.

This was it. No turning back now. There was no convincing him or undoing the damage. Kallias couldn't follow me—not without sparking war. He'd lose everything.

The truth had spilled. Our secret was exposed, and nothing would ever be the same.

I had destroyed it all. Radaan, Draconia, my future—Kallias' peace. His hard-won stability was shattered by the recklessness of a single moment.

"Come with me, Nienna. There's no future for you here."

His grip tightened, pulling me toward Gyrak, and this time I didn't resist.

Ignoring the shredded remains of my gown, I climbed onto the black-scaled shoulder of the beast. A sob wracked through me, painful and raw. Cold leather bit into skin as I settled in. Ronan followed, his movements mechanical as he buckled my boots into the stirrups.

I caught his angry looks at my naked legs, diverting his gaze from my thighs.

There was something painfully exposing about being laid bare to so many. But more than that, the humiliation of it shattered what was left of my heart. My shoulders slumped as Ronan pressed his body tightly against mine, pulling his flight goggles over his face.

"Hold on. We're going home."

His strong arms encircled me, locking me in place as he gripped the ridge of the saddle. Gyrak roared beneath us, the force of his fury ripping a shrub from the earth. With a mighty beat of his wings, the dragon launched into the sky. Ronan's body was an ironclad wall, holding me steady as we ascended.

The thunderous clap of wings echoed like the final strike of a hammer on a coffin. We soared, Gyrak's enormous form cutting through the air with surprising speed. Below us, the palace shrank, its bustling life reduced to nothing more than ants scrambling over the ground. We climbed higher, toward Draconia, the land that should have been home.

But home was no longer a place—it had become a man. The invisible tether between me and Kallias stretched, taut and unyielding, urging me to turn back, to race into his arms. Nothing would ever be right without him. Life felt hollow without him.

But there was no life with him.

A low whimper escaped me before I could stop it, and Ronan's grip tightened, drawing me further into his embrace. My eyes squeezed shut as panic clawed at my chest, my fingers grasping at the broken thread that once connected me to Kallias.

Then it snapped.

Secret clubs

AND OTHER NONSENSE

If you want insider sneak peeks, and to be part of the team that chose Between Flames and Deceit as my next book, you can join the cool kids!

Top-Secret, Super-Secret, Not-So-Secret Club

The Codeword is "Daddy"

I take a bow!

THANK YOU

Between Flames and Deceit started with a muse running around my head. Some headstrong woman running around, demanding that she wanted more than the prince she was promised to. She wanted his father.

I wasn't ready to put the story together (or pantser my way along, as I do) but I offered my Fan Page the option of a fleshed out story idea, or this princess and king.

They chose Nienna and Kallias. So you have to thank those cool kids for this book.

I would like to thank my Alpha Readers, Millie and Jessie. You guys are amazing and helped me get through those rough humps when I know the end of the story, and want to give up on writing. If it weren't for you two, I would have never finished. Extra thanks to Millie who helped me choose the title!

We *all* owe a massive thanks to my husband. Without him, I wouldn't have had the confidence to write my first Dual POV book. He still doesn't like Kallias, but has the hub's seal of manly approval.

A huge thank-you to my beta readers: Kate, Brittany, Leann, Ashley and Jericha. You all helped polish up BFAD and flesh out Nienna and Kallias just a bit more.

And, if you've made it this far, I owe *you* a thank-you, dear reader. My books would be nothing without readers. Thank you for taking the time out of your busy days to consume my art. That means everything to me. Thank you.

M.A. Frick

M.A. Frick is a mere peasant.

Once upon a time, she read to escape the world. Now she writes to create worlds.

Not only the mother of worlds, but the mother of three children—she is joined by her husband who supports every adventure, no matter how absurd it may be.

www.ingramcontent.com/pod-product-compliance
Lightning Source LLC
Chambersburg PA
CBHW030738310726
48969CB00005B/1261